Praise from Readers

Fantastic Book!

Not since Stephen King's "It," can I remember a book that so well captured the potential terror faced by teenagers about to enter the "real world." But "It" involved an other-worldly monster drawn from King's rich imagination. There are monsters, too, in "Copperhead Road," but these monsters all have human faces. They interact freely with their neighbors in the community and conceal their depraved acts behind a facade of normalcy and friendliness. As his book makes crystal clear, Roger Canaff is all too familiar with this kind of all-consuming, penetrative, evil. But to his credit, his novel demonstrates that love is stronger than hate, and that friendship sometimes, not always, creates bonds stronger than those forged by trauma. This is by no means inevitable, but it is always possible. Roger Canaff teaches that this--the elevation of love over hate--must be the goal of all of us who have been affected, directly or indirectly, repeatedly or just once, by the insidious horror of childhood sexual abuse. It is far easier said than done. But it is well worth the effort.

-K. Mulhearn

Poignant, Moving Story

"A coming of age novel unlike any I've ever read. Just could not put it down, even when tears ran down my face. I'm so very sorry Roger Canaff had to endure things too horrible to want to ever remember, like the many children he helped. Like his Daddy said, the only real monsters are in the people around us. You just can't see them until it's often too late."
—T. Licia

Challenging Topic, Well Worth the Read

"Will be recommending this to my book club. Well written. Takes a very difficult subject and brings it to life with just the right amount of detail, angst and emotion to hold the reader's interest and bring light to the issue of sexual abuse in our society. Well done, Roger Canaff."
—B. Johnson

Don't Miss This Book!

"...I like books with many rich characters, and subplots woven masterfully throughout and tightly connected to the main story. If you decide to buy this book, set aside some uninterrupted time because you won't put it down for long."
—D. Jackson

A Book You Won't Soon Forget

"Tragic and horrifying, the sexual abuse at the heart of this remarkable first novel by Roger Canaff is the conduit for a heart-wrenching and memorable journey for the characters and the reader. This book has everything: edge-of-the-seat drama, compelling characters, beautifully

crafted imagery, and a story that will resonate in the mind of the reader for a long time."
—B. Henn

Tough Subject but a Great Read
"John has a secret that he can't share, but when young boys start dying, he looks for help. This novel was difficult to read because the subject is a hard one. However, I really liked how the author dealt with it. I found it hard to put it down, and read it quickly because of that. I recommend it highly."
—P. Sibley

I Could Not Put It Down
"I was hooked from the first page. Well written and thoroughly engrossing, Roger did a fantastic job of making me feel personally involved in the story. While it is a difficult subject to read about, I felt compelled to keep going because I was emotionally invested in what happened to each character. Well done."
—K. C.

Disturbing and compelling.
"I enjoyed getting inside the head of the narrator, even though his story was horrific. The story is framed as a coming of age, gang of childhood friends piece, but the heart of the story is in the abuse several boys endure and how they each deal with it. The details of the abuse are handled deftly by the author — I was able to feel the horror without getting disgusted by what I was reading. Towards the end I was cheering for a different outcome sitting in my armchair, but the characters acted exactly

as they had to given their personalities and backgrounds. The subject material and how it is presented by the narrator also provides a bit of an education on the mindset of abusers and their victims for sheltered readers like me."
—J. Morch

COPPERHEAD ROAD

BY
ROGER CANAFF

Published in New York City by the Brooklyn Writers Press,
an imprint of the Brooklyn Writers Project, LLC.

www.brooklynwriterspress.com

TITLE: Copperhead Road

ISBN: 978-1-7340973-9-9 (e-book)
ISBN: 978-1-7345724-0-7 (paperback)

Library of Congress Catalog Card Number: 2019920801

2nd Edition

Also by Roger Canaff

AMONG THE DEAD
Alex Greco Series Book 1

BLEED THROUGH
Alex Greco Series Book 2

To Gregg and Chris,
who believed.

To Bob and Clem, the Cotler and Steve
who saved me.

To every survivor of child sexual abuse
still suffering in silence.

And to the Boys of Summer, 1985.
I love you, and those days, more than words can say.

Custis Lee Mansion sits atop Arlington Cemetery, which became Arlington Cemetery when Union troops began the practice of burying their dead on the sloping front lawn of Robert E. Lee's home.

On the other side of the river, along the elegant line of a neoclassical bridge, is the Lincoln Memorial.

Driving along the G.W. Parkway with my father as a boy, he'd point them out to me, visible from the slope of the hill on our side to the basin of the city on the other.

"Look," he'd say. "It's like they're glaring at each other."

The Mansion.

The River.

The Cemetery.

This is where Virginia begins.

*I confess to Almighty God,
and to you, my brothers and
sisters, that I have sinned of my
own fault; in my thoughts and
in my words;
in what I have done,
and in what I have failed to do.
— from The Confiteor*

Contents

Introduction to
the Revised Edition

The pandemic of child sexual abuse is finally being released from darkness into mainstream consciousness with tragic and compelling new revelations every day across the media landscape. Long before there was light on the subject, though, there was terrible suffering, almost all of it experienced in silence. Male victims, especially, had virtually no resources and no means of individual or cultural expression. I was among those suffering, and it was from this private place of pain that Copperhead Road began. I never expected this story to be years ahead of its time, but I am proud that it is.

Copperhead Road centers around a group of boys who must confront not only their collective history of sexual abuse by the same predator (a well-respected community member) but also a new and terrifying threat. Younger boys begin disappearing around them, found raped and murdered. The race to stop the killing while at the same time preserving their dignity, their sanity, and their very lives is one that drives them to unimaginable extremes. The ultimate question asked is whether the bonds of adolescent friendship can survive a haunted past and also overcome a nightmarish present.

This book was my first novel, a character-driven, coming of age story that I began writing as an adolescent and refined years later. My professional work as a special victims prosecutor and expert in the field gave additional weight to what started as a fictionalized memoir. There is still much that is autobiographical about the book. Creating this second edition has taken me back, sometimes wistfully and sometimes painfully, to the original place from which it emerged.

This revised second edition will answer many reader questions I have received over the years, as well as some of my own, about elements of the book that merited more in-depth focus.

I have also been able to add a bit more background, color, and depth to the characters I love. The ones who stood by John Ray, the protagonist, are true to the boys who surrounded me and pulled me through my own darkness those many years ago. The story, although elegiac, is ultimately hopeful.

Experience, personal, and now professional, has tempered me and given me the tools to make this a better book, and that is what I've striven mightily to do. Above all, it is an expression of love. Love for the boys who carried me through, love for the children still suffering in silence, and love for a society finally coming to terms with an evil as ancient as humanity itself. It is an evil that will only be eradicated by courage, empathy, and understanding. It is my sincerest wish that Copperhead Road remains an enduring part of this effort.

Chapter One: August

"Without warning, something's dawning...listen."
— JUDAS PRIEST

1

I am a child of denial. From the age of six, I learned to be terrified of the truth, that the lie was the best friend and most sensible implement I had with which to chip away at the day-to-day existence that made up my life. There was no time for reflection. Reflection involved reality, and reality was no friend of mine. It's not as hard as one may believe who hasn't had to do it. I'm talking about the separation we make between what is and what should be. But I'm also talking about the acts themselves—yes, the acts he made me perform, and the acts I then committed.

It's not as hard as one may believe who hasn't had to do it—that is the great lesson of my life. I have seen and taken part in acts of violence, bravery, hatred, chivalry, perversion, and perfect evil, acts both heroic and demonic, and the common thread that ran through all of them is that they flowed from the actor in a way that was surprisingly easy... surprisingly natural.

This is the story of a haunting. It is not a haunting of the supernatural variety, unless we define the more mystical aspects of the human form and the often suspicious weight of circumstances as something supernatural. A ghost story would be easier to tell as the material in the countryside that surrounds my Virginia town is rich and plentiful. But we were not haunted by a ghost. We were haunted by a demon, a demon that was encapsulated in a living, breathing human being who subjected real horrors on real people for a very long time. My unfortunate fraternity of fellow victims and I were directly affected, but no less than an entire town was truly haunted while he was among us. We sheltered him. Silence was his greatest protector, and the town slept willingly, if unwittingly, as he did his work here.

This is the story of that tribulation: the stones we overturned, the corpses we unearthed, the silence we finally broke, and the people we left behind. It is a story that I can only tell through the haze of memory and the dimness of time. The tingling nonsense and angry lust of my own adolescence speak to me most clearly through the musical icons of my time: the menacing snarl of Billy Idol, the aching chirp of Madonna, the insouciant drawl of John Mellencamp. I was seventeen then, and although it is both funny and painful to reach back there, it's even more difficult to do so honestly.

The fortunes of a community are tied closely with that of its children, even in this transient age. Like any organism, a community grows and changes, suffering from and responding to infection and disease. Some surround and engulf. Some die. Some regroup and fight back. In the sweltering August of 1984, ours began to explode.

2

August 28, 1984. 8:00 a.m.

Huey Lewis and the News.

Jesus Christ.

I have died and now I'm in Hell. Sit up. Goddam. Huey, CHRIST, what? Oh. The alarm clock.

I'm up. I'm sitting up. Whoa, I'm down. Wave of nausea. Big wave. "Heart and Soul," is that what this is? I'm going to kill Vic for doing this to me.

The clock, when my eyes finally made their way over to it, read 8:01. With a heavy arm, I found the button that released me from "Heart and Soul" and sat up. I reached for yesterday's socks, put them on, and fell promptly back into the uneasy sleep of a hangover. Cotler let himself in at 8:12. He went to my room and knocked twice before coming in and bouncing a sneaker off my head.

"What the fff—? What time is it?"

"Eight twelve. Eight thirteen now. And it ain't summer no more. Get your ugly ass up."

"I thought I *was* up. I dreamed I got up to put socks on."

"You got socks on." I looked. He was right. I tried for a moment to decide if the dream had been reality, or vice versa.

"Go eat," I said. "I won't be long." He gave me a look that said I'd better not be long, but the thought of food softened him up. As always, my mother had prepared a first-day breakfast for the two of us before leaving the house with my father and sister. Cotler was a cop's kid with a long-dead mother and no woman's touch in his diet. My mother lived to feed, and Cotler traditionally ate both my breakfast and his.

In the shower. Out of the shower. Coaxing the last bit of deodorant from that plastic part that holds it in there.

A comb through wet hair. I found a shirt, dug into an emptying carton for a fresh pack of cigarettes, and headed downstairs. At the landing was a collection of school stuff my father had picked up for me at the drug store. I grabbed it all and called to Cotler.

"Ain't you gonna eat?" he asked through crumbs and bacon. I shook my head and felt my brains swish from side to side.

"If we're going, let's go."

3

Belle Ridge, Virginia was our hometown, and I leaned my head against the window as Cotler sped down the town's main drag on this bright and already blazing day, his truck alive with the smells of manhood: pine oil, gun grease, and long-dried sweat. Belle Ridge in 1984 was classic suburbia with a working class and rural edge—a string of gas stations, an aging but pleasant LBJ-era shopping mall, a painted church here and there. All in all, a real American dream machine. These things and a cookie-cutter selection of streets and houses blurred past us as Eddie Rabbit sang happily about driving his life away while my friend hummed along with him. Cotler was uniformly cheerful and alert early in the day no matter what he'd done the night before, and there were times I hated him for it. He took the morning like a lover.

Unlike many of the towns around us, named by the English for minor royal figures or tavern owners, Belle Ridge held no significance in Virginia history. It popped up early in the 60s as a housing development for college-educated government workers and assorted military support types, and no usable structure within its limits dated back to anything much before the Mustang.

But on the eastern edge of Tolland County, twenty-five miles from the District of Columbia and twelve from the battlefields of Manassas, Belle Ridge was tucked blindly into an area saturated with American history and local lore that unfortunately went mostly unnoticed by our bedroom community. This is where Cotler came in. He was an anomaly in Belle Ridge in that his entire family was of Virginia heritage, and his father's line had two centuries of roots in Tolland.

"Vic kept us out too late sayin' goodbye to summer," Cotler called out over the rush of wind in the window as we rounded that last corner before the school. East Tolland High School was on the western edge of what became Belle Ridge, and it pre-dated the town by at least a generation. Cotler's father played football there when it was still all white and populated mostly by farmer's kids who'd been drawn from the corn and soybean fields nearby.

"You seem none the worse for wear," I said, cupping the morning breeze with my hand and silently cursing his perkiness. "What about Terrance? Any news?"

"No, he said, frowning instantly. "Nothin'."

"They find his dad yet?"

"No. My dad's calling him every goddam hour. You'd think this asshole would call back if he gave a damn."

"Maybe he's got the kid. That's the hope isn't it?"

"It is, but it ain't likely. There's no evidence he's been anywhere near here."

***

Cotler's father was the sheriff of our county, and Terrance Hark was the biggest thing set on his plate since he had taken the job. The wiry, auburn-haired seven-year-old, last seen after a summer rec program let out, was wearing red and black sneakers, black Toughskins, and an oversized Flyers jersey. Terrance had been missing for nine days. He lived with his mother in the house they previously shared with Terrance's father—until the man abruptly left a few years earlier and headed out west somewhere. Parental kidnapping had been hoped for from the start, but the story was not taking shape. Terrance's father could not be located, but that was nothing new. He was years behind in child support, had switched jobs and western states regularly, and hadn't spoken to his estranged wife or child since a couple of Christmases previous. It seemed unlikely he had suddenly decided to return east and steal his son back.

The other options were much less palatable. Terrance had last been seen skirting the tree line behind the elementary school—the line that defined the beginning of the woods, the undeveloped space between our town and its nearest neighbor, which in those days was a considerable distance. In their totality, the woods cradled and nudged their way almost completely around Belle Ridge, and to the west and south were only broken up by active farmland some miles out. Terrance was a rebellious child even at that age and often led other children into the woods for war games, playful exploration, and the promise of things like discarded cigarette lighters and bottles for deposit. When no one else would follow him past a certain point, he had no problem continuing on alone.

***

A child lost in the woods in August was a better situation than one lost in February, but the warm weather was little consolation. There had been at least three serious thunderstorms in the days since he'd disappeared, not to mention eight friendless nights. No matter what kind of spin you put on that, it spelled out something very ugly. The boy could be the most resourceful and brave seven-year-old in the world; he was still seven. Cotler's father's people and the state police had been working the woods, parks, roads, and surrounding towns since the disappearance, and had no leads whatsoever. It was starting to wear on everyone involved, and Cotler was no exception.

We parked in the far student lot and watched for a moment the swarm of kids in crisp jeans and white sneakers approach the building in clusters and pairs. Out among the bleachers and the track-and-field area with the storage sheds, the men who tended to those things sauntered about in baseball caps and khaki shorts, putting down chalk lines and reeling in garden hoses. Straight ahead to the west was the continuation of the same tree line into which Terrance had disappeared. In a day or two, the well-worn footpaths that led into the woods beyond would be littered with loose-leaf paper, discarded cigarette butts, bottle caps, and wads of chewing gum.

I noticed Cotler focusing in that direction as his old truck hissed and cooled. I was uneasy for other reasons, but any prolonged view of the woods filled me with a secret and silent dread. Now as Cotler's gray eyes narrowed on them, it occurred to me that, for perhaps the first time ever, he was joining me in regarding them with suspicion.

"You think he's out there still, just wanderin' around?" he asked me, his gaze unmoved. I shrugged.

"I don't know," I said, walling back the deeper thoughts I couldn't begin to express or share anyway. It was an old habit, all but effortless now. "At this point I guess I hope he isn't."

"It's a patch of woods, that's what I don't get," he said. "Even if you're goin' in circles, you'll find a path and walk out at some point. Even if you're just a kid."

Assuming nothing happens to you while you're in there, I thought, and my heart picked up a beat. Cotler sighed, which I took with relief to mean that the conversation was over. Then he looked over at me.

"You seem more than just a little hung over, Hoss," he said, his voice lightly quizzical. "Could be a long year. You gonna make it?" I forced a smile to the surface and pulled my eyes away from the woods.

"Only one way to find out," I said.

We did find out. And Hell was unleashed in that knowledge.

4

The field before the woods seems as big as the sky, and Cotler and I run wildly to get to the center of it as if we are explorers on the rocky shores of an undiscovered continent, as if quickly beneath the soft earth we will find the glittering booty of a vicious and wealthy band of thieves. In the middle of this field, which borders some ranch homes in my town, there is nothing but more grass, but Cotler and I are five years old, and the magic and wonder of being in the center of the field is more than enough. Cotler's overalls barely cover his already oversized frame as he prods me along with an accent thicker than mine, while his sandy blond hair whips around his freckled face as he runs beside me. Dry grass crunches under small feet as a result of a hot and oddly rainless May. Cotler calls after me and grabs for assorted flying insects, identifying them with colloquial names that I do not recognize. Behind us, our mothers in brightly colored Pat Nixon dresses and tall, full hairdos call out to us in a vain effort to get us to slow down. I turn to see how far we have run, and their smiles are barely visible on tiny, feminine faces.

Finally we are there, and the two of us collapse in the tall, yellow grass and roll together under an expanse of pale blue sky that seems to have no end and no beginning. The world spins as I struggle to catch my breath, and I find myself laughing at the brightness and the freshness and the simple, royal glory of being in the middle of the field. Here, we are the tallest things in the universe. Here, we are alone, unreachable—kings of a vast plane of summery grass. Suddenly, Cotler rolls over and directs my attention to the woods that begin on the far edge of the field.

"We're Confederates," Cotler says very seriously. Not knowing what a Confederate is, I nod solemnly and wait for an explanation of just what that means. He whispers, "We're Confederate soldiers, and over there in them woods is our enemy." He peers intently into the tree line and I follow his lead. I see nothing but trees and shadows.

"I don't see anything," I say. Cotler nods.

"Ain't gonna see nothin'. You caint see 'em 'cause they hide."

"Who?" I ask. Cotler answers without removing his pale gray eyes from the tree line. "Yankees," he says. I nod and stare again at the woods. Now the trees seem to take human form, and the shadows dance and sway with movement. Twisted limbs and trunks are muscular forearms and legs. Minute spots of sunlight seeping through the brush are tiny eyes, peering stonily back at me. Yes, I can see; there are Yankees in the woods. The woods are dark and deep and full of Yankees. I know then and there that I never want to be near those woods. The cool darkness hides monsters too hideous for exposure to the light of day, I am sure. Yankees.

"We don't have to go in there, do we?" I ask Cotler, my small heart pounding at the thought. Cotler looks at me and nods in the affirmative, and I am very afraid. "But why? Why can't we just stay out here?"

"'Cause sooner or later they'll come out," Cotler says, peering suspiciously at the tree line. "Sometime we got to go in and get 'em. Then those woods'll be ours."

"I don't want 'em."

"We'll go together," he says. "We'll find all of 'em in there and drive 'em out, and then we'll own them woods." His voice lowers. "We'll know secrets about them woods we won't tell no one." He grins slyly at me, the gleam of the high sun in his eyes. Reflecting briefly on this in a boyish blur, I nod more forcefully now, feeling Cotler's bravery and confidence spilling over and supplementing mine.

"We won't tell any girls," I say.

"We won't tell no one," Cotler says, rolling over again and looking up at the endless sky. I follow his lead, and the two of us lie among the reedy grass and watch a butterfly that has floated over our spot. It flutters and bobs as if it were a loyal subject come to pay homage to the young kings of the field. We fold our hands on our stomachs, brown summer's *children, and bask in the bathing sunlight of midday.* "We won't tell no one," *he says again.*

5

If there was a last innocent moment as the year began, it was probably focused on Tamara Woolen, the girl upon whom my fluttering anxiety landed as Cotler and I crossed the parking lot and approached the school. Of all the crushes I endured in childhood and adolescence, hers was the worst. Just the thought of seeing her on a day-to-day basis as school once again got underway had been fueling vague uneasiness for days. Now it focused to vicious clarity as we heard her behind us, her voice high and crystalline on the warm air. In a protective reflex, Cotler looked over at me to gauge my reaction. I had a fleeting moment to damn the fact that my infatuation with her was obvious to him despite my foolish assertions to the contrary, and then I was lost in anticipation as she overtook us. She was gabbing with a couple of other girls about network television, fall fashion, and whatever plans they were making for the new school year. My heart paused as I waited for a greeting and promptly sank when I heard nothing. Instead, she swished ahead of us in her new jeans and yellow blouse, sailing past me as if I were a droopy-eyed freshman carrying a trumpet case.

Fuck.

"C'mon, Johnny, she's just playing first day games. Snap out of it." The voice that shook me out of this daze was not Cotler's. It was Steve's, and the two of them were standing side by side, watching me as I watched her bounce up the stairs and into the school. Steve, charac-teristically, stood dressed to kill in black jeans, a tan sport coat, and a dark green T-shirt beside Cotler, who sported a sweat-stained cap and muddy boots. Cotler was rough and unkempt, not ugly, but Steve Drillas was gorgeous, plain and simple. Greek with dark eyes, a slender but ap-preciable build, and a face straight out of the movies, he was simply one of the most beautiful people ever to come through our school.

"It's no big deal," I said, fooling neither them nor my-self. I motioned to Steve's attire. "You look ready for the ball. Who's on the menu?"

"We're seniors. No one's fucking safe this year—and I ain't taking over this dump without you and Grizzly Adams here, so lighten up, okay?" He patented this with a Steve-Drillas-Winning-Smile and held it until I finally smiled back. He turned to Cotler. "He been like this all morning?" Cotler shrugged.

"Just since she buzzed past here." From our place on the social ladder of childhood, Cotler and I would never have guessed in a million years we would be friends with some-one like Steve Drillas. Oddly enough, the peculiar thing that sparked his association with us was that he smoked. I mean he smoked for real, meaning he didn't only bring a bat-tered month-old pack of ultra-lights to parties and football games. Where he had picked up the habit I didn't know, but he smoked in the boys' room and in the parking lot in the morning, things the pretty people generally did not do. I shared cigarettes with him from time to time, a cus-tom that forged relationships between smokers of a cer-tain breed. Through that experience he'd eventually come to work at the airport with my motley crew, which since kindergarten included Cotler, Vic, Spencer, and myself. We weren't outcasts, the four of us, but we certainly weren't part of the in-crowd either. Steve was one of those kids, lucky, depending on your point of view, who had adolescent in-crowd written all over him. But he seemed to shun that envied circle for reasons that never were apparent.

Now, at the top of the school steps, we stood literally and figuratively on the verge of our last year as children, and Cotler seemed to sense what I was sensing: Steve, for whatever reason, apparently wanted to extend the friendship we'd forged at work to include our after-work lives as well. To our lingering mystery, he actually wanted to be our friend full time. He looked toward us with the slightest hint of apprehension as we pondered what to do next.

"How long 'til homeroom?" Cotler asked.

"'Bout twenty minutes," I said. "Everything starts late today. You suppose Spencer's here?"

"I'm sure he is," Cotler said, giving the big doors an appraising look. "He's got that Bible group that meets real early. Let's head down to the cafeteria and give 'im hell." He looked over at Steve. "You with us, Hoss?" I smiled at the subtlety of this loaded question, and I think Steve got it.

"Lead on," he said.

***

One highlight for the three of us this year was that we had a class together, something standardized testing had prevented for Cotler and me since we were toddlers. Emerging Issues was the class, a senior-level elective that focused on current events and was taught by a guy named Neil Bonner, probably the most talented and popular teacher in a generation. Bonner was a 60s leftover, a raging liberal, and a kind-hearted, twinkling-eyed type who seemed born to work with teenagers. Cotler and Steve had signed up for the class on a lark, both assuming they'd never get in. Emerging Issues was almost always overbooked, and Bonner and the administration spent much of the summer shaping the class mostly from the top scholar applicants and then handing out second choices to everyone else. But due to whatever scheduling glitches or administrative machinations, all three of us were admitted, and we passed the summer in anticipation of what looked like a fun elective with a fantastic teacher.

E.I. was the last period of the day, beginning at 2:30. As I approached the classroom on the second floor, I ran into Spencer, who'd been with his Bible group that morning and was spending most of his time in accelerated and college-level courses. He had taken E.I. the year before, the only non-senior in the class. Spencer had admonished me over the summer to watch out for Cotler in E.I., thinking that Bonner's debate and discussion forum might be a shock after the "read and regurgitate" classes Cotler had been forced into for most of his life. We were discussing this when Cotler and Steve, who had already been in the classroom, wandered back out into the hall and saw the two of us talking.

"Gonna be an interesting year," Steve said, shaking his head. Cotler grunted in the affirmative.

"What? Why?"

"Doug Lars," Steve said, the disgust clear in his voice. Cotler grunted again. "And fucking Vinnie Foust."

"Oh shit," I said, probably with more feeling than I intended. "Vinnie, too?"

"That ain't all," Cotler said, speaking at last. "There's some new kid. And he's already mixin' it up with Doug."

I looked quizzically at the two of them. In our place and time, a new kid was a big deal.

"New kid? Who?" Steve shrugged.

"Some hood, I dunno. Looks like one, anyway. And he obviously doesn't know who he's fucking with if he's pushing it with Doug."

The new kid, I found out later, was named Lon. An unusual name, matching well the guy who bore it. I peeked into the classroom in the minute or so before the bell rang and saw him, sitting low in his chair and absently tapping out a rhythm on his desk. Steve was right; he looked like a hood. But he was handsome, with a smooth, angular face and long dark hair. A huge lock of it covered one eye, John Mellencamp style, while the visible eye was set into his face like a black stone. I was about to turn away when that eye caught mine, and for a long few seconds we carefully regarded each other. Or more accurately, Lon regarded *me*, with an uncomfortable closeness for a stranger. He cocked his head as he studied me and his thin lips broke out into a slight grin. I turned away, oddly uncomfortable, and stepped back toward my friends.

"You're right, he looks like trouble," I said. I had a sudden strange, heavy feeling inside, deeply unwelcome and reeking ridiculously but compellingly of something out of my past. A wave of fresh anxiety moved through me and I tried to shake it off. The preoccupation I'd had with Tamara all day now seemed far away and more childish than it already was. A few seconds later Coach Bonner, as most students called him, strode past us and warmly greeted Spencer before smiling at all of us and heading into the room.

"He was in this classroom last period," Steve said, referring again to Lon. "I'm in here, too. It's an English class."

"Tamara's in it," I said, as much to myself as to any of them. That alone was weird. I usually didn't mention Tamara out loud at all. No one seemed to notice.

"Yeah, and so is Doug," Steve said. "Everyone walked in at the about the same time, and this guy Lon was already there, sitting at a desk I guess Doug decided he wanted."

"Knowing Doug, he didn't give a damn about that desk 'til he saw the guy sitting there," Cotler said. Steve nodded and continued.

"Probably. Anyway, Doug told him to move and the kid wouldn't budge. The teacher broke it up, and somehow it came up that both of them are also in Bonner's class and have the same room sixth period. Doug tells the guy not to be in his seat when he gets back—or else—and walks out. The new guy hasn't moved. Bonner's in for a hell of a first day."

At about that moment, Doug and Vinnie swaggered past us in their usual bullies-at-the-carnival manner, peering into the classroom and gauging what was going on inside. For any veteran of the American high school experience, Doug needs little description. He was a phenomenal athlete; tall, sandy-haired, solidly built, and infinitely comfortable in his own skin. Suitably handsome and a football hero, he was also an honor student, due in large part to the fact that he was a consummate cheater who benefited greatly from sympathetic faculty. In our small world he was the very definition of a high school god. Vinnie, on the other hand, was pretty much the opposite of everything that described Doug. But also in cookie-cutter fashion, he too had a role to play: Vinnie was the Bully's Little Pal.

Doug was someone we hated, and it was a righteous hatred. His looks, his popularity, and his command over all things female and social in our world were enviable, but that had nothing to do with it. Doug was shallow, at times violent and wantonly cruel, and he had been since we were little children. Even Spencer despised Doug, and he had a soft spot for rattlesnakes. Vinnie was a very different story. He was vicious in the way that the Cool Guy's Valet feels he can and should be, I guess, but he was more pathetic than anything. Undersized and possessed of a rat-like face and zero charm, Vinnie was a clever loser—quite intelligent, in fact—who surmised his options and acted rationally, in retrospect, in terms of what our world could offer him in the early 80s. I didn't like Vinnie, not by a long shot, but I didn't hate him.

And I *knew* Vinnie. I knew him, you see, from before. Vinnie was a repeat victim, as I was, of the same man over the same time period, and we dealt with the common nightmare of our childhood by avoiding each other, progressing nicely into adolescence as enemies for typical reasons. Had the events that make up this story not intervened, we would have continued on that path and probably never interacted again. But the stranger who would drive those events had found his way into our world, and *he* was the one seated at the desk Doug wanted.

At the sound of the bell, Bonner gathered us in. Doug and Vinnie walked in last, and all eyes shifted between Doug and the new kid. Bonner, who didn't yet know what was going on, looked questioningly at Doug as he stopped in front of Lon's desk. Lon had not changed his position, but he made one quick and unmistakable motion that gave me a fresh dose of dark worry and overshadowed the unfolding drama about to play out in front of me. He had focused on, and then probingly studied Vinnie with the same slightly bemused look he had used on me. Vinnie seemed not to notice and padded over to an empty desk near the back of the room. My throat went dry. Then Doug spoke the words that started everything.

"This guy," he said, a menacing touch to his voice, "is in my seat." Lon did not move, and his gaze, after having shifted back from Vinnie, now froze. Everyone waited in anticipation. Bonner was shuffling through papers and briefly looked up. His eyes narrowed as he assessed what was going on.

"There are no assigned seats in here, Doug," Bonner said. "There's an empty desk over there. Take it and sit down, we've got a lot to go over today."

"No," Doug said, his eyes on Lon. "I wanna work this out now. This guy's in my seat." The new kid continued to stare straight ahead, but now his face broke into a light smile.

"'No' is an answer I can't accept when it comes to control over my classroom," Bonner said smoothly. "Sit down over there." Doug continued to stare at the new kid, probably puzzled and annoyed at the mean, handsome smile on his face. There was a pause and suddenly Bonner's tone got surprisingly steely. "Doug. Look at me when I talk to you." Finally, Doug swung his head around. Bonner's look was cold but controlled. "I told you to sit down over there. Nothing is going to proceed until you do. Sit, now." Doug glared back but begrudgingly got moving and took his place at the open desk. The smile on Lon's face faded, and he went back to sitting silently as Bonner described the course and what would be required of us.

***

"Christ. How did they get into that class?" Steve asked, squinting at the brightness as the four of us left through the reddish steel doors and headed toward the parking lot in the shimmering mid-afternoon sun. It was 3:30, and our first day was over.

"Doug gets what he wants," Spencer said with a shrug. "And Vinnie isn't stupid. He just acts like it."

Yeah, I thought with weird clarity, my heart picking up a beat yet again. *That's always been his cover.* What I was feeling was scary, but more than that it was simply bizarre, plain and simple. At my locker a minute before, Tamara had strode over with a sweet greeting and an apology for not stopping to say 'hi' before school. I should have been on a cloud, but all I could think about was what had happened in Bonner's classroom, what it meant, and why it was bothering me so much. To say I didn't ponder the past where Vinnie and I were concerned was an understatement. I shunned it, plain and simple, and for years that had worked just fine—outside of occasional nightmares. Now, out of nowhere, I felt it creeping toward me like a spider toward something caught in its web.

"What about this new guy?" I asked, with a hint of frustration that stated things more forcefully than I would have intended. "What's he doing in there?"

"Bonner takes in strays," Spencer said with a shrug. "He probably volunteered for him."

At Cotler's truck we discussed Lon and what chance he stood in an all-out feud with Doug. The general consensus was that he looked fairly tough, but was obviously from out of town and knew little about the person with whom he was dealing. Doug Lars was not the kind of bully who would back down if you stood up to him—and I still wish Hell on whoever began feeding young boys that ridiculous myth in the first place. Doug was the kind of bully who would beat you with breathtaking savagery if you stood up to him, as most bullies will, and I had seen it firsthand. He was strong, fast, and perhaps most tellingly he simply enjoyed hurting people. Doug's superior athletic ability gave structure to his urges and, as a football star, elevated him to teen idol status no matter what else he did—and his parents were respectable people, which only helped his cause. His coaches and the other adults in his life would admit he "could be rough" but forgave him due to his respected abilities. His peers, particularly other males, knew far better. Doug often humiliated other boys because it amused him, and since childhood he had beaten others for the same reason. Cotler himself was one of the only people in our world who had fought Doug as a kid and not lost miserably.

We talked for a few more minutes in the bright heat and eventually made plans to hang out the next night on Cotler's back porch. The year was starting off well, all things considered, and my mood should have reflected that. But that weird darkness remained as Cotler and I rode back through town, the breeze whipping through our hair and the radio blasting *Alabama*. As we approached my house, it intensified as I finally realized why Lon's behavior had been so disconcerting. The fact that he had regarded Vinnie and me the same way was odd enough, yet it was much more than that. It would be weeks before I would truly know how or why, and for now I kept it safely to myself. *Vinnie was lucky he hadn't seen that look,*

I thought as Cotler backed out of my driveway and gave me a clipped wave.

I knew it now.

The look he had given both of us bore more than bemused contempt. It was laced with familiarity.

6

In *my worst dream I am lying on my back in the woods. I am on a bed of dry leaves, and in my view, behind the tree line of a clearing, the sun is setting. There is always a figure standing at the edge of this clearing. The bright red-orange light of the setting sun surrounds him, and he is visible only as a black, frozen silhouette. He has no face that I can see, no features that I can make out. Beside me is a woman I do not recognize outside of my dreams. She breathes beside me but does not touch me. Her smell is rich, feminine, musky. The warmth of her fills my space and, but for the fear, I could be very excited. I turn to her, away from the figure before me. I reach out, but she is gone and the man named Kelly is beside me. The figure at the edge of the clearing remains—it watches silently as Kelly reaches for my hand, now so tiny and weak, and places it where he wants it. Kelly's penis is hot, throbbing, and feels like lead in my hand—but I am terrified and I do what he commands. Eventually he stiffens and bites on my ear as he climaxes. His hot, fetid breath—beer and cigarettes—is on my face. I am frozen with fear, positive he will tear my ear from my head. His fluids are on my leg; he wrestles me still and begins to climb on top of me as leaves rustle beneath us. I cry out to the figure at the edge of the darkening woods—only in my dreams do I know its name. My scream is muffled by Kelly's weight. A fallen branch scratches my face. The figure, unmoved, is eclipsed by Kelly's upper body. Kelly wants to kiss me. He wants me to kiss him back.*

The dream came shortly after falling asleep, which I had done with a brand new Trigonometry book open but unread on my lap after a futile first attempt at homework. When I finally clawed my way back to consciousness, I tossed the book aside and dug in my pocket for cigarettes, lighting one with difficulty and setting the pack on the nightstand with a trembling hand. I was terrified, not so much by the residual horror of the thing but because I was afraid that some new cycle of nightmares had been triggered and would now haunt for months any attempts I would make at sleep. I opened a window in an effort to alleviate some of the smoke and leaned out of it. From here I had always enjoyed a great view of the town. My parents' house sat on a hill that sloped down my block and out onto Belle Ridge Boulevard. Craning my head around, I could see the western end of town as it thinned out past the schools and yielded to patchy darkness. This darkness was the woods that were the subject of my dream, the subject of a thousand dreams over the eleven years since it had all begun. The fresh air ushered in a weird sense of loneliness; I had never wished to utter a word about what had happened to me to anyone, but now I longed, for the first time, for someone to tell it all to.

Eventually I turned on the clock radio and rocked slowly back and forth, smoking a new cigarette and breathing deeply. From the rock station in Washington, DC, "Whole Lotta Love" kicked along quietly, the hammer-like guitar licks muffled at low volume. After a long while I stopped shaking.

***

Sleep finally found me again sometime after 4:00. At 7:30, my father was standing over me with a pack of cigarettes in his hand. He looked pissed.

"Jesus, can't you keep these goddam things out of sight? Your mother would have been in here any minute now and raised what kind of hell." I sat up in bed slowly.

"I had a nightmare," I said, my mouth thick with sleep. "Sorry."

"Listen, your mother is very upset. Please don't make things harder on her for a few days."

"What happened?"

"Terrance Hark was found this morning. Dan called here a few minutes ago." The Dan he was referring to was Dan Cotler, Cotler's dad. My father went on, punctuating each word. "He was dead, son. He was murdered, very brutally."

My mother had been a big part of a search effort over the past week to locate Terrance Hark. They put up flyers, helped to establish contacts and promote awareness of the situation in neighboring towns, and had run nightly search efforts in the area. She was also part of a church-based mothers' support group for Vanessa Hark, who lived about a mile and a half from us. I don't remember if I was surprised or not to hear that Terrance had been found dead.

"Does she know about 'very brutally'?" I asked.

"She knows about 'murdered,'" he said. "Don't say anything to anyone but Cotler, understand?" I nodded. Cotler, of course, knew anyway.

"Where did they find him?" I asked. He sat down on the bed in his slacks and cheap tie. My father was much shorter than I was but well-built and completely gray. He took his glasses off and rubbed the lenses with a handkerchief. It was a nervous habit he practiced often.

"In the woods. Those fucking woods west of the high school." Those fucking woods were the ones Cotler and I had played in all our lives, and Terrance had roamed in more recently. The woods were also the focus of the preceding night's nightmare. Cotler knew them like no one else, and I mean no one, but he had not been on any of the official manhunts. The county frowned on the use of minors for such jobs—even sheriff's sons—so Cotler had been discreet when he gave his dad some makeshift maps and hints. Maybe they had paid off. I would find out later.

"I'll be cool to Mom," I said. "I'm sorry, Pop. That's godawful."

"Dan's worried, John."

"Jesus, who isn't? I don't blame him." He regarded me sternly.

"He's worried because his oldest son likes to traipse around back there like it's the great virgin forest."

"We don't go unarmed," I said. That was true. It was also the wrong thing to say.

"There's a monster out there, John," my father said, lowering his voice. He looked straight at me, and suddenly I knew he was scared, which meant Dan was really scared and had probably given my father some details that I would not hear from him. My mother came in then, and although she had already been crying, fresh tears appeared in her eyes when they met mine.

"I'm sorry, Ma," I said, hugging her. "I'm really sorry."

"He was just a baby," she said into my shoulder, crying again. "He was just a tiny little baby. I wanted so much for us to find him. I just can't believe . . ." She trailed off and was sobbing again.

"It's okay, Ma." I was finding myself choked up as well, and surprisingly unnerved. I supposed the whole community was about to feel that way.

"I have to see Vanessa today, Johnny . . . I just . . . don't know what to say to her." I stood there pretty much speechless as she continued to hold me. "It could have been *you*, John. He looked like you, you know, when you were a little boy. All this time I've thought *it could have been you*. It could have been you out in those woods, something horrible happening to you. I thank God for that, Johnny. I thank God it wasn't you."

"Yes, Ma," I said. "Thank God."

7

Cotler was grim faced as we drove toward school. He had woken when the call came in to his father, and he'd been up ever since. Cotler's father was widowed at the birth of Cotler's younger brother Calvin, and Cotler was the parent of the house when his dad was called away. The word from him was much more detailed than I had heard from my father. A man Cotler knew fairly well named Marcus Wilham had discovered the boy's body, dumped into the remains of an ancient well, now only several feet deep. Marcus was a lifelong drunk who lived in a dilapidated shack on the edge of the woods out past the school; he poached for various edible animals in the woods pretty much year-round. He had been out late at night, ostensibly looking for squirrels—*spotlight hunting for deer, more likely* Cotler thought—and had discovered the body because of the smell surrounding the stones that made up the well. Marcus was apparently still vomiting when he phoned Cotler's father in a panic.

Cotler and I both knew the spot, but for different reasons. A well-used trail ran fairly close to it that began just after the last few backyards of town. Since way before our time it had been called Copperhead Road, presumably because of its width as well as for the snakes that were known to bask in its wide, bare path on cooler days. It was named at least a generation before us, and I doubt even Cotler knows who christened it as such. We had both been to the well, together and separately, and to me its black maw conjured up images of a giant mouth in the ground. As a child, I had believed that the well was an entrance to Hell. Alongside those stones, a few of us had experienced something very much like Hell—Hell as I'd imagined it, anyway.

Very few clues had been gleaned from the site: no footprints and no enlightening physical evidence. The boy was naked, covered hastily with leaves and brush, and at least a full week dead. We rounded the curve before the school, and Cotler waved at some kid in a truck coming the other way.

"Is your dad still out there?" I asked. He shook his head.

"Some state people and a few deputies are. The whole area's been roped off. Poor Marcus won't leave the shack, 'cept to get another quart o' beer. The man was adversely affected."

"What now?" I asked. Cotler shrugged.

"There'll be more state people involved. Feds, too, maybe. Dad'll put the word out to keep kids close by 'til he finds something.' Hope like hell the sonofabitch don't hit again. We talked a little this morning when he came back from the coroner. Your dad give you the business about goin' back in there?" I nodded.

"He'd prefer we didn't for a while. How's your dad feel about this? Any ideas?" Cotler frowned.

"Ain't shit. Just a dead kid and someone who knows how to cover his tracks. Hopefully they'll find something in the light."

Cotler drove silently as we entered the parking lot in a long line of cars, but he was noticeably uncomfortable, like something hadn't been said. As we parked I figured out what it was and why he had hesitated to mention it. Cotler wanted to do some investigating of his own . . . if not at the site itself, then likely all points leading to it. He had no plans to interfere with an investigation of his father's, but knowing Cotler and the new circumstances, I knew that he would be tempted to supplement it with his own quiet little inquiry.

"You're wanting to go out there, aren't you?" I asked as we pulled into a space. Sandra Miles pulled up beside us in her Mazda blaring Cyndi Lauper. Cotler shook the gearshift as he pulled his keys out of the ignition. He looked out over the practice fields beside the lot, and at the woods beyond.

"Gonna wait awhile," he said. "See what they come up with. It ain't been long. If Dad needs me to point out a trail or a creek, he'll ask. Chances are I won't do anything. But if they don't find nothin', after a while I mean, I may go poke around a bit." He looked over at me. "You're a lot smarter than me. It ain't likely, but if I do start somethin' I may need you to help me put it together. You with me?"

My response was wooden and instant, even though my

bowels froze at the thought of spending prolonged time out *there* looking for a killer. But I did whatever Cotler did. I had planned never, ever to tell him what had happened to me, and for the sake of my sanity I trusted him completely when it came to the woods. In any event, I was bound by friendship.

"Aren't I always?"

8

Pale moonlight splashed down among the pines behind Cotler's house, and an army of crickets sang to their mates over by the creek that ran behind the backyards in our old section of town. Steve passed me a cigarette as Cotler finished his update on the town's first murder mystery in years. Spencer and Vic also sat with us in a semicircle on the open porch. Spencer, his asthma acting up, had his inhaler close at hand. Cotler noticed it and asked him if things were okay with his older brother, Armand. It was widely known that anxiety exacerbated Spencer's condition, and Armand could be a fountain of anxiety.

"Yeah, he's been okay lately, thanks," Spencer said. His blood was African and Puerto Rican, and in that combination he looked more Asian than anything. Small and thin, he had an open, smiling face that was round and warm, and eyes a little slanted that made him look monkish and prematurely wise. It was a fair representation of him as he was both of these. "My mom finally got him to go to a psychiatrist in Leesburg. If he takes his meds, he'll be fine. If he doesn't, there's nothing anyone can do."

"He's still at the same job, right?"

"Yeah. Bob Westmon is a saint. I'm his brother and I don't have that much patience with him."

"One of the deputies saw him the other day," Cotler said. "A guy on twenty-eight got his car stuck in some mud on the median. He was about to call for a tow when Armand walked up outta nowhere. The guy said Armand told him to get in and he'd try to push him out. The guy thought he was crazy, but he did it, and sure enough your brother John Wayne'd that thing right outta the rut. The guy wanted to stop him and offer to pay him or somethin', but he just walked off, covered in mud. A cruiser saw the car paused at the median and asked the guy what happened. He said the strongest man in the world just appeared like an angel out of nowhere and heaved his car out of a bog. He couldn't believe it."

"That's my brother. All muscle and no brains."

"Most of it is his heart," I said with a slight grin. "He does that kind of stuff all the time."

"He's made his share of trouble, too," Spencer said. "Let's not pretend."

"Like what?" Vic asked, "A couple of fights?"

"*Assaults* are what they were called."

"On fucking assholes who deserved it," Vic shot back. "I remember that shit. Your brother saved our asses a couple of times. He can beat the piss outta whoever he wants, as far as I'm concerned. He never hit nobody that didn't have it coming."

Vic, actually, was right about that, although the law doesn't always recognize that kind of justice. Armand beat up bullies, he just didn't do it at the right times. And he really had saved our asses—as children walking through the wrong shopping center parking lot or digging for treasures in the wrong dirty creek bed. Belle Ridge was no ghetto, but before the slow gentrification of the 1980s, it had more than its share of violent white trash. Vic's mouth didn't help either, and there were a few times growing up when Armand's dark, hulking frame appeared from behind a building just in time to prevent one of us from taking a real beating from kids sometimes twice our age.

He was deathly quiet and usually peaceful, in many ways a gentle giant. His large, broad face and searching round eyes looked perpetually childlike. But Armand had a temper, fueled by the frustration of a host of learning disabilities and their father's cruelty. He left high school after his freshman year, went through jobs and runaway episodes and juvenile court, finally settling on a routine of wandering Belle Ridge and haphazardly looking out for his much smaller, asthmatic little brother. The job he held now was because of the decency of a man in town who owned a small metal shop where Armand worked and sometimes lived.

"Well, like everything else," Spencer said, standing to stretch, "It's in God's hands. It's after twelve, guys. We'd better get to bed."

"And listen up," Cotler said, looking over his brood appraisingly. "Be careful gettin' home. There's still a monster out there someplace." I didn't give the admonition much thought until Steve dropped me off at the end of my block. It was only when his taillights disappeared around the corner, leaving me alone in the early morning darkness, that it came floating back . . . and with an old, familiar face attached. A *monster*, I thought, gazing up at the bland, white moon. A *monster*.

9

The name of the man who raped me was James Rodman Kelly—and Cotler and I were on our way to see him at his shop in town on the afternoon of August 31, 1984. When it came to Jim Kelly, as with many things, I followed Cotler like a robot, focusing on the present, ignoring the past. Kelly owned a gun shop and was Cotler's local firearms expert as well as being a mentor of sorts as a conservationist, hunter, and woodsman.

Kelly was indeed all of the above. Unmarried at 38, he was considered to be among the most eligible bachelors for the working class around the area. He was, to all outward appearances, the quintessential southern woodsman living life on his terms. But he was more than just an image—he was a decorated combat veteran who taught wilderness survival skills both in and after the service. He knew more about weapons than many enthusiasts twice his age. He knew more about the topography of our area than any game warden. Cotler looked to Kelly as a model for his later life and, like me. had known him all of his life.

He was also a community activist and loomed large in local service groups. He coached little league baseball, taught firearm safety on his own property, and took groups of young boys camping in various places; he called himself a self-styled Scoutmaster and wanted to teach the boys what woodsmanship was really about. His personality was strong, decisive, and blunt. A natural leader in any situation, he easily took control of the local little league associations even though he was childless. Indeed he considered this an advantage: Parents, he would say, have children around for only several years. He had seen a generation of boys already, ever growing and ever re-placed by fresh faces—but all with the same basic needs and make-up. That was the grim truth.

When a local scout troop tried to take him on with a membership drive of their own in town, Kelly brashly announced that Belle Ridge already had a scout troop—and one that wouldn't waste time giving out merit badges for pigeon-raising or having a pen pal. The town loved it. Dozens of boys waited months for an opportunity to camp out with Big Jim. Cotler was one of his regulars growing up and continued to be until Cotler was old enough to go by himself. I followed right behind him. Kelly began to abuse me sexually shortly after meeting him in the spring of 1973. He never touched Cotler. I never said a word.

Some ugliness had transpired between Kelly, Cotler, and me at about the age of twelve, when I could no lon-ger bear to go away with Cotler and Jim on camping trips. I made up dozens of excuses and faked or semi-faked a ward full of illnesses until Jim finally advised Cotler that I was probably a bit too soft for the tougher camping that lay ahead for a boy of teen years. Cotler resisted this and told me so. Speechless and out of excuses, I told Cotler I just didn't want to go anymore.

I half expected to lose Cotler's friendship at that crucial point in our lives as boys, but he surprised me—and not for the last time. Being just about to the age where he could camp alone anyway, he simply told me that we'd go without Kelly, and that was that. Kelly liked Cotler and treasured his father's confidence and friendship even more. He stopped referring to me unkindly, and we rarely spoke after that. The idea that Cotler may have believed even marginally that I was "soft" was horrifying to me. I followed him out to go camping at every opportunity, even in the woods where I'd been raped. I rarely slept on these trips and stared wide-eyed into the night for hours after we lay down to sleep, staving off panic only with the sound of Cotler's somniferous breathing beside me. With him, I convinced myself, I was safe. And I always had been. Cotler never assumed that I was fond of Kelly, but he had no reason to believe that I hated or feared him either. He continued to associate with Jim, ignorant of our past, and I kept a professional distance.

We climbed out of the truck, Cotler carrying a piece of one of his hunting rifles. Jim called us over to the shed beside the store, where he was working on something.

"What's up, big 'un?" Kelly bellowed as we stepped into the musty, dark room. The walls were a veritable museum of tools and hard implements of all kinds. Pieces of firearms lay here and there in piles and groups. Buckets of differing greases and oils filled the shed with a clean, steely odor, complemented by the ever-present smell of gunpowder. The plank floor creaked under our weight. Kelly wiped his hands off and offered one to Cotler.

"Not a damn thing," Cotler said, wiping his brow. "Just came by to drop off that assembly from my three-oh-eight. Dragged Johnny along with me."

"I see that you did. John," he said, nodding to me. Kelly's eyes were blue and hard as steel. I avoided them and nodded dispassionately in reply. As was typical in his presence I began to sweat, and flashes of disjointed memory continually pulled my thoughts away from the conversation. Whenever we were with him, Cotler had to shake me to remind me it was time to go.

They spoke briefly about weapons, and then Cotler brought up the murder of Terrance Hark. Kelly's eyes darkened as he spoke of it. He had spearheaded many a search around the wilds of the area. Many believed that the loss of a town boy was as great a loss to Jim Kelly as to anyone but the parents.

"Can you believe it?" Kelly asked. We were outside now, Kelly leaning against his pickup in cowboy boots, faded jeans, and a black T-shirt. Sweat beaded on his brow and fine blond hair stuck tenuously to his skin. "Jesus, your daddy called yesterday to tell me that he'd been found and I just sat here in this empty store for the better part of the morning. Couldn't even open. You know, we walked right by where he was. We went down that trail looking for him."

Cotler nodded. "Y'all looked everywhere. Goddam chucks had to get to him before he could be found."

"Old Marcus actually got to 'im before the chucks did," Kelly said. "Goddam, that old nigger'll never be the same. And I feel for 'im, too. Christ knows I wouldn't have wanted to tiptoe into that mess lookin' for deer in the middle of the night on Copperhead Road."

"Any thoughts?" Cotler asked. Jim shook his head slowly.

"I hate it, but I think it was a drifter. We get 'em, you know—'specially out there where all the construction is. Contractors' men from all over. They stay in station wagons from Monday until payday, for Chrissake. I've told your Dad they're a menace, and he sends a car by there every night, but there's only so much he can do."

Cotler nodded grimly. No one hated the rapid development of our county more than Cotler. It would mean in time, he knew, the extinction of his woods. To think it attracted outsiders capable of something like this made it even more of an insult.

"I won't be doin' much with the boys out in those woods, needless to say," Kelly went on. "It's a shame. Something like this eats up a community."

"Keep your ears open, Jim," Cotler said. "I don't want to see us give up for a while. I hope like hell they pull somethin' off that scene today."

"Don't you worry, I will. Hey, listen, have you all met Lon? He told me he was in a class of yours, Cotler." Cotler looked at Jim strangely.

"That new guy in Coach Bonner's class? Looks like- "

"Yeah, I know. Looks like a punk. He needed sponsorship to finish high school. He came to my shop a few months ago, asked if I'd vouch for him, give him some work. The school called in July, asked if I'd think about it. He's shown up for work, so I agreed."

"Is he living here?" Cotler asked. He knew Kelly had a back room with a cot in his shop.

"Sometimes, yeah. Here or at my place. He comes and goes on his own, but this is his official address, as far as the school's concerned. Seems to live a pretty clean life. We'll have to see. Anyway, I'm glad to help him out. Watch out for him, will y'all?"

"I'll try, Jim, but he ain't the friendliest," Cotler said. "Seems like he wants trouble. Are you sure you want to be associated with this guy?" Kelly smiled and waved him off.

"I've put out a hand to worse, you know that. Don't worry about me."

"Where'd he come from? Anybody know?"

"I think he had people here once and they moved away. Not sure why he's back. I left it to the school to ask those questions. He showed up in town early this summer and ain't afraid to work. He says he finished eleventh grade somewhere north of here. Ohio, maybe . . . I can't remember. He's eighteen. That's good, 'cause any older and he'd have to enter a community college course for his high school dip. This way he gets to finish school like a normal kid. I hope he makes it. Anyway, watch out for him if you can."

Cotler thanked Jim, and the two of us turned to leave. Cotler seemed preoccupied as we pulled out of the lot and didn't notice my usual discomfort around Jim. When he finally did speak, it played on my disquiet like a snake's rattle.

"Meant to tell you something before," he said. "Bonner pulled me aside today right after the bell. Swear to God I thought he was gonna ask me to drop the class."

"I was wondering what that was about," I said. "Bonner would never do that. And don't start in with how you're not smart enough, either. You're doing fine."

"Naw, it ain't that," he said. "He actually makes me feel smarter. He's real good at it. That sound queer?"

"No. It sounds human. What did he want?"

"Well, truth is, he asked me how you knew Lon . . . this guy that Jim's helping."

"What?" I asked, fresh fear awakening in me. "What the hell did he mean by that?" Cotler shrugged.

"Beats me. Bonner said he figured you knew him from somewhere 'cause he keeps lookin' over at you all the time. I noticed it, too. You haven't?"

"No," I lied. "Not really."

"Well, Bonner said new kids tend to eyeball a good bit anyway, but it seemed strange to him. So, he figured maybe if Lon knew you, he knew me too, maybe through Big Jim."

"Well, I don't know him," I said. "And if I don't, I don't suppose you do either."

"No," he said. "Vinnie, though. Gotta wonder about that, too." Now I turned and gaped at him before I even knew I was doing it. My blood ran cold. "Vinnie?"

"Yeah," he said, turning to me and seeming to notice my discomfort for the first time. "Vinnie Foust."

"I know," I said, tasting bile in my throat. "Why Vinnie?" I licked dry lips and struggled to mask what was feeling oddly like panic. Cotler just shrugged.

"Bonner didn't mention it. It's just somethin' I saw. Lon seems to eyeball him a lot, too. I don't know why. Ain't like you and Vinnie got a whole lot in common."

"No," I said. My breaths were shallow, and I turned to the window of the truck to light a cigarette. My reflection in the glass was that of a ghost in a mirror.

"You okay?" he asked.

"Yeah. Just feel weird all of a sudden. Ate something, maybe. Can you . . . Cotler, pull over quick." He waited behind me while I vomited, the smell of road dust and honeysuckle mingling with the awful tang of puke.

"Sorry," I gasped at last.

"S'okay," he said softly. "You ate something bad, alright. Get the poison out."

Get the poison out, I thought, a horrible new sadness bursting through the sickening fear in my belly. I was turned away from Cotler so he did not see the tears, or if he did he mistook them for a by-product of the effort of throwing up. *Yeah. Get the poison out. Jesus, please. Vinnie and me. He looks at Vinnie and me. How long since I'd paired us together in any way? And why was Lon doing it?*

Chapter Two: September

"What set you free and brought you to me, babe?"
— BILLY IDOL

1

September rolled into the Ridge, sealing the tomb in which school had buried summer. The weather, of course, took notice of neither the school's nor the Roman calendar as the month began. Barely a leaf in town had lost any vitality, and most of the scrubby Tolland underbrush was still a lush, summer green. Yellow honeysuckle climbed the lengths of the old wire fence that ran down Chapel Road past Jim Kelly's shop and the town cemetery, and temperatures remained in the eighties. The body of Terrance Hark lay under fresh dirt in that cemetery, and the place where he'd been found remained roped off. Cotler's father was on the Teletype every morning working with the State Police investigations office, but as yet had turned up nothing. The mood of the town remained suspicious, and it seemed to struggle with letting its guard down as fall got underway.

Tamara continued to be flirty and friendly, and it looked as if I would have another shot at her as the weeks went on. Lon, in the hallways and classrooms I shared with him, continued to study me with the cold eyes of a

"

pawn-shop dealer. I had yet to speak to him and had no desire to. He spoke little, but when called upon he was articulate, if terse. He seemed disinterested in the subject matter and took no notes whatsoever. Vinnie and Doug kept up their guttural drone, aimed at Lon on some days, but Vinnie was quieter than usual. I wondered if he had started to detect Lon's attention as well. Doug simply regarded the new kid with predator's eyes and looked for a chance for further confrontation.

2

The second hand on the clock was moving swiftly toward the point at which the sixth period late bell would ring. Spencer glanced with frustration at it as I dug in my notebook for his physics homework, which I had borrowed to copy in fourth period. It was the first Wednesday of the month and we were at my locker, already a hapless mess of disorganized papers and books.

"For Pete's sake," he said, "if you need my homework again, get it from me in homeroom, okay?"

"I did this assignment, Spencer. I lost it." A lie.

"Bull," he said, coming as close as he ever did to cursing. "You were over at Tamara's helping her with hers. You probably did your English in homeroom. This is an important semester for colleges, John. Don't blow it."

"I know it is," I said. I did and I didn't. Finally, I produced it and he stuffed it into a book. "Thanks, Spence. I'm sorry. I'll see you at work."

He waved me off as if to say it was okay and hurried down the hall to his class. I turned to dig for my E.I. notes at the bottom of my locker and felt my heart come to a lurching halt as I overturned what looked like a discarded notebook cover. It had been folded and slipped into the vents of the locker, landing on the pile at the bottom. There were letters on the front of it, an inch high and printed carefully. In red they spelled out "I KNOW."

3

It is a late summer sleepover weekend for Cotler and me, just before the start of third grade. It is delightfully late at night, and we are munching happily on oatmeal cookies and hard candy, speaking in hushed tones for little more than the joy of whispering in the dark after our bedtime. A flashlight on the bed between us emits a beam of soft yellow light, dividing his bedroom between where we are under the open window and where his baby brother Calvin sleeps. Calvin is in foot pajamas on a blanket, his thumb in his mouth and his eyes shut lightly. His breathing is rhythmic and steady, his toddler's sleep deep and dreamless.

A breeze, warm and heavy with the smell of jasmine that grows in the woods behind Cotler's backyard, blows softly through the open window and stirs the curtains. Pale light from a brilliant and full August moon flows through the room like midday. Cotler, whispering furtively about his dream of constructing a rope ladder from his bedroom window to the ground, suddenly stops. His wide smile slowly fades. I open my mouth to ask what is wrong, but he raises a hand and shushes me. The breeze has brought along something else.

"You hear that?" he asks. I listen, and at first hear nothing. Cotler sits up on his knees in bed and looks out the window. Another breeze blows in, this one full enough to send the curtains billowing around his head, and now I hear something. I hear voices.

"There's a fire up on the Hill," Cotler says, his voice oddly uncertain.

I scramble up to see what he is looking at. Cotler's house is on the westernmost street in this, the oldest part of town. "The Hill" is a rise in the wooded area visible from his backyard, less than a half-mile from us, deep in the trees. It is a place dotted with trails and fire pits, frequented by teenagers and hippies because of the view of the town that it yields. I strain my eyes and pick out what Cotler sees—the distinctive orange flicker of a campfire. The breeze blows again, fresh and fragrant, and now the sounds are clear—and chilling. Behind us, Calvin stirs uneasily in his sleep and moans. Voices, seemingly several, or as many as a dozen, float over from the Hill, rising over and on top of one another in a surreal, fast-forward sounding cacophony. It is impossible to tell what the voices are saying—some sound as if they are talking backwards, some emit a droning, unintelligible buzz. They speak quickly, forcefully, as if they are spitting out words in an effort to recite something against a clock. This strange noise rises gradually, the sounds getting more intense, the buzzing mantras going faster and faster.

Cotler and I are frozen at the window, the interloping breeze in our faces. Our eyes finally meet, and I see that he is as frightened by this as I am. This is instinct in its purest form. We have not heard one intelligible word coming from the Hill, and yet we know without words that what we are hearing is . . . wrong. Calvin moans louder, tossing and turning on the blanket. I am about to ask Cotler what we are hearing when the voices stop. There is a pause, and then a scream comes up. It is high, piercing, and unmistakably feminine. At its end it trails off liltingly, and the chill cuts deeper as I realize that the scream may actually be laughter. Authentic laughter follows the scream—cackling, insane laughter that sounds positively evil. The swollen moon above us brushes the trees on the Hill with white light, but we can see nothing but the glow of the fire. The voices come up again, babbling gibberish, groaning and buzzing nonsensically. They rise to a pitch, fall suddenly quiet, and then the scream comes again. The scream trails off, more like laughter this time, but not any laughter I have ever heard comfortably. It is laughter that masks something wicked—the laughter of people who laugh because they would rather do that than something else. The high, crazy cackling laughter follows, as if on a loop. When the voices rise again we hear Calvin start to cry, and are shaken into our present surroundings.

"What is it?" I ask, trembling. "What's going on up there?" Cotler, unhappy at not having an answer for something going on in the woods, nevertheless shakes his head.

"Don't know. I ain't ever heard nothin' like it."

He goes to shush his little brother, but the child is frightened and unhappy. I go back to the window alone and gaze first at the pregnant moon and then at the flicker of the campfire. I am thinking of Big Jim, his strong hands and strange blue eyes, and my small frame convulses at the thought. The woods are filled with things like Jim—I am sure of that now—and this thought makes me sag with despair and dread. Not even the full moon can expose these things . . . these bad things that live in the woods. They are magical in their ability to hide until they are upon us. The firelight remains, the sounds go on. The woods are all around us. Our town is surrounded, and the only way out is to face what is in them. I place my hands on the open windowsill and press out at the screen. It will pop out easily—this I know because Cotler and I have removed it before. I look back at Cotler, singing softly to his little brother the way he remembers his own mother doing for him . . . his mother who is dead and gone. My eyes go back to the screen. My thin arms stiffen on the sill.

I could jump.

What would that be like? Is there a world beyond this one where there are no monsters in the woods? My breathing slows. I listen for the call of the thing from the other world, the invitation to go, but all I hear is the rush of the wind in the trees and the madness from the Hill.

"Johnny, close the window. Please." Cotler sits with his brother's head in his lap and his voice uncharacteristically high with fright. He is rocking Calvin and soothing his crying, but the sounds from the Hill allow for no comfort.

Shaken from my daze I do as he asks, shutting out whatever is in the night. Calvin soon falls back to sleep, but now it is the restless sleep of a man and not of a two-year-old. We watch him for a while, silent on the bed where twenty minutes earlier we were smiling and whispering. I am not aware of when a similar, bad sleep finds either of us, but eventually it does and our slumber party is through. Cotler has pledged to tell his father about whatever was out there in the morning, but does not, and we never speak of it again.

4

She brought the cigarette to her mouth, drew in lightly and then blew out, lips pursed. I took it back from her and noted with a slight rush the faint taste of lip gloss on it. Tamara would smoke with me alone, something I wasn't publicly proud of but secretly loved. She brought her hands behind her head, flipped her ponytail up and leaned back in the seat. Her feet in small white tennis shoes were propped up on my dashboard. White socks, ankle length, poked up from each one, her skin appearing and then disappearing again into tubes of soft denim.

Tamara Woolen was not stunning, dark, or particularly mysterious. She did not have the kind of face that launches ships or calls up heads on silver platters. What she did have were sea green eyes, a pixie nose, and a delicate, heart-shaped face with soft full lips that made her adorable when she laughed . . . and pure heaven to kiss. Outlined by wispy half-blonde hair and set atop a petite and well-shaped frame, her face brought her more than a few second glances among our peers and won her easy access to the upper social circles in our world.

Although we grew up together, it was complete coincidence that finally paired us up. Randomly, my family and hers happened to choose the same strip of beach in North Carolina for a week's vacation the previous July. We ran into each other in a T-shirt shop on the first day and then spent the week together tanning on the beach, walking past the bars and college haunts at night, and listening to new Loverboy, old Springsteen, and some other stuff she liked back then on a bright yellow cassette player she carried everywhere. Our first kiss was on the third night, outside of her door in the dirty yellow light of a motel hall-way. It was the first thing of its kind I had known willingly.

I can remember still the salt-beaten smell of the con-crete and the rhythmic pounding of the night surf behind us. I can remember her breath, hinting of flat soda and my cigarettes, and her skin, filling me up with the lingering scent of oils and sunblock. I can remember her pulling away when it was time to go, smiling furtively, and not so artfully collecting our saliva back over her lips. I can remember her slipping back into her room and feeling that cool rush of hotel air as the door closed. I can remember all of it, and had I left it there I suppose it would have been as fine a memory as a sixteen-year-old can have with his pants on.

But back in Belle Ridge where there was no pounding night surf, things did not fall so easily into place between us, and Tamara went quickly back to regarding me with the casual indifference and mild friendliness that had defined our relationship since we were in pre-school. Her interest in me never equaled our beach week, but it perked myste-riously from time to time, just enough back then to keep my head planted firmly up my ass for over a year. Now on Friday, September 7, the end of the night found us together in my truck in front of her house, sharing a cigarette after a movie we'd seen with Steve and a friend of hers.

"I'm tired," she said. Not a good sign. I sat behind the wheel and considered the radio station. That ridiculous "Ghostbusters" theme was on, and it sounded like it was mocking me.

"When's your curfew?" I asked, knowing full well it was twelve. That gave us about thirty-five minutes. My mouth felt dry. Tam glanced over at her house.

"Twelve, probably. I'm gonna turn in, though. I'm beat.

Aren't you? Fridays are so long." She reached for the cigarette and I passed it to her. Another girlish puff and it was back to me.

"A little," I said, now believing any possibility of romantic contact was slipping beyond likelihood. "What's your schedule like this week?"

"I'm pretty busy. We have a project due in English already. I'm helping that new guy with it. The one in your E.I. class."

"Lon?" I spurted, realizing a second too late I'd failed to mask a sudden stab of jealousy.

"Yeah. He's really smart, actually, but I'm helping him catch up since he hasn't been in school for a while. Did you know that?"

"I don't know anything about him. He doesn't do much in our class except look for trouble. Which he's gonna get if he doesn't lay off."

"With Doug?" she asked. And then liltingly added, "I don't know. Lon can hold his own, I think." White-hot jealousy tore claw marks through me.

"We'll see," I said, finishing the cigarette. Tam looked at me sideways.

"Have you even tried to get to know him?" she asked with an accusing tone.

"No, Tam, I haven't. Mostly because he stares at me like I have three heads. The guy's an asshole, sorry."

"Oh God, whatever."

Here I was, defending my suspicious distaste for a rude stranger in my own truck. Suddenly I wished she were Cotler and we were discussing his predictions for the severity of the coming winter. "Look, I'll be sure not to speak ill of the guy from now on. I didn't realize you two were so close."

Tamara made a "tsk" sound, and instantly I was sorry I'd spoken. I lit another cigarette but did not speak. It was worse than I thought. Tamara was intrigued by Lon. She was fascinated by Lon. And now if Lon wanted her, he would have her. Something dry in my throat began to swell.

"I'm going to bed, Johnny," she said. I shook myself out of a bad daze and looked blankly at her. "You should do the same."

"I will."

"No, you won't. You're on your way over to Cotler's to meet up with Steve and find out how far he got with Rachel. You don't look good. You always look like you've seen a ghost lately."

Maybe I have, I thought.

"Does he really stare at you?" she asked. I looked over at her in the dim glow on the dash lights.

"Yeah, sometimes. Why?"

"No reason," she said, but she looked genuinely per-plexed. "You've come up once or twice between us. You know, him asking if we were together." I hadn't near the guts to ask what she had said, but I could guess. "Anyway, he just seemed . . . weird about you when you came up. Weird like . . . like he knew something about you." She blinked her eyes twice, two little green lamps in the dark, and looked at me quizzically. I turned away and stared straight ahead.

"Who knows?" I asked out loud. But a tremor in my voice almost gave me away. Tamara looked at me for a moment longer, then leaned over and kissed me lightly. I didn't try to make more of it.

"Thanks for the cigarette and the movie. I'm still a cheap date. Good night, Johnny." She jumped out of the truck. I waited until she was in the house, and then pulled slowly away toward Cotler's.

5

The following Saturday night, September 15, found me at Steve's house, lying on his bed in his tiny cluttered room as he got ready to go out. We were headed to a house party, a common occurrence during the school year. This one was at the home of a friendly and kind of happy-go-lucky kid named Robert Reynolds, whose parents were often out of town. Our plan was to meet Vic and Spencer there, with Cotler making it over after his little brother was in bed. Steve looked at me in his dresser mirror and grinned as he tugged on his shirt.

"This thing should be a babe fest," he said. "Rob's one of those guys who gets around to other schools. That means different chicks. And we could both use some." He ran a comb slowly through jet-black hair and patted his face twice more with some cologne in a black bottle.

"Yeah, that's good for you," I said with a slight grin. "With my luck, Vic'll get laid and I'll still be high and dry."

"I doubt it. Tamara should be in a cozy mood, anyway. All nice and liquored up. Her crew's going, or so they promised in English yesterday."

I had a bad feeling about this night and Tamara, and I wanted to downplay it. "The hell with her," I said lightly. "I don't feel like dealing with that tonight. I'm gonna let it cool for a while." I tested the air and found that I sounded pretty good.

Steve glanced at me in the mirror and nodded. "Okay," he said, turning to leave. "Someone else then. You driving?"

6

Steve was right. It was a big event. Rob's parents had money by our town's standards and traveled to places like Singapore and Ireland, where Belle Ridge inhabitants rarely found themselves. Rob was alone a few times a year in a big house with a very big liquor cabinet and thus was a pro at throwing parties. We walked through his living room to the sound of Van Halen's first album and greeted people we knew. Vic was in the foreground on the covered living room rug, playing a drinking game with a group of guys—a couple of them assholes and one of them Vinnie Foust. We paused there for a moment, and I asked if Spencer or Cotler had arrived yet. Vic motioned toward the back of the house. Then he grabbed Steve's collar and whispered a name in his ear. Steve looked at him and beamed.

"Are you sure?" he asked. Vic smiled knowingly.

"She asked if you were coming," he said. "Word is she's single again. She really wants me, but I told her we'd give you five minutes before I stepped in and took care of business. You've got one minute left."

"Thanks, bro," Steve said, smiling and patting him on the back.

The girl Vic had mentioned was named Stephanie, and she went to Central Tolland High, our rival. She was perfectly built with chestnut hair and big, dark eyes. She and Steve had dated briefly at the end of our junior year, but she had broken it off over some boyfriend in Pennsylvania, where she spent her summers. Steve had called it quits seemingly with ease, but he liked her. He liked her a lot, as far as I could tell, so this was good news. He adjusted his collar and split off to find her.

As I was making my way to where Cotler was, Tamara crossed my path and offered something that could have been a wave, then walked on toward another part of the house. My heart sank like a load. I leaned against the living room wall and sighed. The heavy feeling intensified when Lon walked through the front door about two minutes later. He was dressed in denim and leather as usual, but was well groomed and possessed the confident, expectant air of someone not crashing a party. He looked invited.

"Check this out," Vic said, appearing beside me with a beer for each of us. "It's that new prick, thinks he's James Dean. Doug will be here with the rest of the football fucks before too long. Rob could have a fight on his hands before this is all over."

"Cotler's here," I said absently. "It'll be okay. I doubt he stays long."

But I wondered. I wondered who invited Lon. He looked around briefly when he came in, seemed not to notice us, and walked downstairs. Vic headed back to the drinking game, and I took up residence next to the stereo and watched them. The beer in my hand was warming fast and going down like so much cat piss. Around me went the tumbling, conflicting conversations of dozens of people in several rooms. Steve and Stephanie appeared once in search of the keg, the two holding hands. He gave me a wink before they disappeared again. I looked around for an ashtray and considered asking Robert if that was off limits in the house. The place didn't look like it was smoked in very often. Then Tamara was walking toward me again, coming from down the hall that led to the kitchen. I spied her approaching and stole back to my position, waiting. My heart felt as if it would burst. She was carrying a beer in her hand and would have walked right by me if I hadn't stopped her.

"Who's the beer for?" I asked, trying to sound light and gay. Tamara hated beer; she was one of the millions of women who loved the wine-cooler craze of the 1980s.

"No one you particularly care about," she said, not even slowing down. I almost lost the answer entirely over the blaring stereo. Then she was gone, past the drinking game and down the stairs. Down to where Lon was.

Suddenly I was hot, weak, and nauseous all at once. With a speed I could never seem to implement on a math test, my mind raced over scenarios, each more terrifying than the last. I was clearly *out*. Lon was clearly *in*. The difference was that Lon would stay in. Lon was mysterious. Lon had been around. Lon was not some scared sixteen-year-old moonstruck boy at the beach stumbling through a kiss like pre-teens behind the arcade. No, Lon would play Tamara. Tamara would let herself be played. He would have Tamara if he wanted her. He knew it, she knew it, and, to boot, most of our peers were about to know it, too.

About five minutes later they came up the stairs and walked past me, skirting Vic's drinking table on their way toward the back deck. Vic turned to me and gave me a queer look, and I tried my best to shrug without looking like I was reacting at all. Tamara seemed not to notice me, and neither did Lon, until they were almost out of sight. When they were about to leave the room, Lon glanced back in my direction and leveled a look at me. It was neither scorn nor sympathy, but it held an odd, accusing feel to it. For a split second our eyes locked, and whatever was in his went dead. He turned, and they were gone.

I leaned my head back against the stereo casing and

closed my eyes tight. My breath was coming in short, catchy gasps, and with something like guilt and fear I realized I was about to cry. Seventeen years old, and no further from tears than when I was eight. Or sixteen. The thought of this was supposed to make me angry enough not to cry, but it seemed to only succeed in making me feel worse. I clenched my eyes tighter and tried to turn the pain inward. It would not do well to cry in front of the dozens of children I'd grown up with. The urge to spill tears was strong, and I tried to focus on anything that would divert it. And suddenly I was concentrating on Lon.

What had been in Lon's look? And why had he looked back at me at all? I glanced at Vinnie, on the floor now and looking queasy over at the drinking game. Vic was murdering him, sending every full glass his way whenever Vic did whatever it was one had to do to make someone drink. Vinnie held no answers.

And who cares? the dark, logical side of my mind wanted to know. *Lon wants her and he'll have her. It won't be long, an hour, tops, before her pouting lips are meeting his for the first time, and her eyes are closing and wildfire is rushing up and down her middle, through her thighs and down to her toes. She'll reach for him, and his hands will find her cheeks, her back, her ass. Yes, her ass, and she'll want his hands there. You, John Ray, are Old News. You are Yesterday's Mail. You are Leftovers. You are Discarded Sneakers. You . . .*

Then why do I feel sorry for him? a new thought spoke up, and this one was so plain, so pure, and from so deep in the darkest closets of my mind that for a second I thought I had actually heard it. I looked at Vinnie's pathetic, trembling frame again. He was waving off yet another glass of warm beer that Vic was sending his way. His eyes were glassy, heavy, and . . . masked.

So what? the logical side reasserted, winning. *So fucking what? What about her panties, John? Cotton, silk? Peach, red? You don't know. Who does? Who's pulled them gently away from her skin or slid them tightly to the side to give probing fingers room to work? Was it T.C. Johnson? Did he? What about the boy from Central? Dan something. Did he? Who's given her that penetrating rush, the real rush, the warmness and pleasure that stems from down there. Who? Not you. But Lon will. So you think about that. You think about that, and you think about the only person who ever felt the urge to touch you. To have you touch him. You think about that.*

I was vaguely aware of Steve walking toward me from the hallway. I stood staring blankly at the shifting footwear moving over the carpet. Behind me a Duran Duran song I hated blared from tall speakers.

"Where's Stephanie?" I asked without looking up.

"She's around. What's going on?" He was peering at me, his concern obvious, and it frightened me into at least a calmer disposition.

"It's nothing. Go find your girl. Don't worry about—"

"John, look at me." I looked up at him, smelling his cologne and seeing his strained, uneasy eyes staring intently into mine. For a moment I was completely naked and almost burst into tears. "It's her and that fuckface, isn't it?" he asked quickly. I nodded like a moron and thought again of crying. Of *bursting.* "We're leaving," he said. "I'm getting you out of here."

"I can't leave yet," I said, a whisper. Some strength had returned. So had some good old paranoia. "I don't want to leave until I know what's . . . what's going on. Steve, I can't leave here without knowing what the fuck is happening with them." My own honesty was startling. So was his calm response.

"Fine. I'm going to check it out. You just stand here. No one is noticing you here. Just be cool and then we're gone. I'll tell you what's up, okay? No bullshit. But we ain't talking here." I nodded dumbly again.

He was gone for a small eternity. "The Reflex" was on now. People moved back and forth, a couple of them waved. Thankfully no one came over. Steve was right. I was damn near invisible in my little corner, despite what I had thought. And then he was in front of me again, filling up my world with that black-bottle cologne.

"Talking," he said. "Just talking." I gave him a look that begged him not to lie, to conceal, but he just shook his head. "No one looks like they're about to sneak off. Now let's go. You need a break from this."

"What about Stephanie? Man, please, don't do this to yourself."

"Forget Stephanie. Let's go."

"Goddamit, no. I'm not gonna screw up your night just because—"

"Stephanie's fine," he said calmly, like a soothing maternity nurse. "I told her my buddy wasn't feeling well. She's leaving soon anyway. I'll call her. Now follow me." I opened my mouth to protest, but he had already spun around and was leading me toward the door.

***

"We don't have to leave," I said, as we made our way across Rob's darkened front lawn. "I just need a break, you're right. I'll be okay in a few. Head for the park."

Steve nodded and we went that way. To one side of Rob's property line, a small park began that eventually ran over and bordered the town's golf course. With the side of the house and the back deck still in view in the distance, we found a picnic table beside a trashcan and a rusted grill. Steve lit two cigarettes, giving one to me. I drew in, breathed out, and then started to sob. Steve sat silently while the emotions took their course.

"I don't know what to say," I said finally, trying to clear my face of the evidence of tears. "She's just . . . the closest I've ever come. To anything." Steve nodded slowly and said nothing. "I guess I thought . . . if I could make her like me, I'd be . . . somebody. I guess. Somebody good." Yes, *and somebody not poisoned by you-know-what*, I thought underneath it. What I really wanted to tell him I couldn't, not then. "Christ, how pathetic does that sound?"

"That's not pathetic," he said quietly, drawing on his cigarette and shaking his head. "It sucks, but it makes all the sense in the world." I looked over at him, vaguely mystified. This was a guy who had his hands on a different girl every night. But he got it. Or seemed to. I hadn't intended to mention the other one at all. But it came tumbling out anyway.

"And that asshole, Lon," I said slowly. "He's laughing at me. Right at me."

And I believed that. Lon knew what Tamara was to me. It wasn't hard to figure out in our world anyway. Scarier was this feeling that he was enjoying her exactly because of what he knew my feelings were. When he'd flashed his eyes at me he wasn't trying to communicate something. He was taking inventory. For the first time since I laid eyes on him, I knew what it felt like, what he was doing. It felt like he was preying on me. And tonight he'd hit pay dirt. I told Steve this in so many words, and his brow knitted.

"What's with him and you? He eye-fucks a lot in class. Sometimes you . . . sometimes Vinnie, of all people. Cotler noticed it too. You've never seen him before this year, have you?"

"Not that I could possibly imagine," I said. That was only half true. I was beginning to suspect. "I gotta be honest, I don't even care. I don't know what his problem is. Right now I just want him—"

"You want him hurting."

"Yeah, I want him hurting," I said, and felt dark satisfaction. "He's doing this on purpose, going after her. He's hurting me and I wanna hurt him back. I know it sounds nuts . . ."

"Not to me," he said, and tossed a rock into a rough nearby. "Some people don't need a reason to fuck with other people. Maybe the guy's a psycho, who knows? You wanna hurt him back, I'm all for it. Let me know how, and we'll see if we can make that happen."

"I don't want to drag you into this," I said. I meant that. Steve didn't know how far this thing went, if I was right.

"Who's being dragged? We'll do what you want to do. Think about it. Then tell me. I'm on your side, here. But for what it's worth, I really am sorry about Tamara."

"Me too," I said finally. "But if it wasn't him it would have been someone else. I've fucked that one up royally. Anyway, thanks for getting me out of there. I won't forget it."

"Nothing you wouldn't do for me," he said. I chuckled lightly.

"I doubt this ever happens to you," I said. He waved me off.

"The only thing I've got over you is attitude, which means I've learned the hard way to treat 'em all like shit.

Girls like looking at nice-looking guys, but they shuck panties for attitude. My brother told me that." He stood poised to say something else, but then his eyes shifted back toward Rob's house.

"What is it?" I asked, following his gaze to the rear deck of the house as he trailed off. There was a commotion of some sort going on, and from where we sat, it looked like Cotler was in the middle of it.

"Let's go," he said. "Cotler might need us. We'll talk later if you want. We'll talk our goddam ears off." He smiled back at me and then led as we headed back to the house.

An odd but strong feeling of relief swept through me, mystifying at first. Then, as our long shadows fell out behind us and we broke into a jog, it clicked: I had been honest—close to completely honest—with someone for the first time since I was a very small child. I tossed a cigarette into the grass with a shaking hand, stunned by the sudden realization that there was someone I could tell. Someone I just might tell.

If I had to.

By the time we reached Rob's backyard things had apparently calmed a little. Spencer came out to meet us, a can of Coke in his hand, and Steve went in to see what was going on.

"How are you?" he asked, typical of him in his kind, quiet bluntness.

"Who told you?"

"I figured," he said, shrugging. "Tamara was talking to that new guy, and all of a sudden Stephanie Lawlor was alone and you and Steve were gone."

"Yeah. Some smoothie I am. Cat's out of the bag, I guess."

"I don't mean to pry. Just wanted to see if you're okay." I nodded.

"Yeah, thanks. Steve and I talked for a while." Spencer smiled at this.

"I'm glad. He's a good guy, yes?"

"Yeah. He is. He helped a lot. Listen, are they gone? Tamara and Lon?"

"Yeah," he said. I looked away for a moment before I asked the next question. It sounded dirty. Intrusive. Childish.

"They left together?" I studied the tops of houses as I waited for a reply. Spencer's initial silence was enough of an answer.

"They left the house together. It doesn't mean they went anywhere together. I just don't know."

"It's alright," I said. "What did Cotler get into the middle of?"

"Something between Lon and Doug," he said. "Guess it had to happen sometime. Doug's drunk and he's on the warpath. It had something to do with Vinnie, if you can believe that. Lon got in the middle of something between Doug, Vinnie, and a cop. Cotler knows more than I do." I stared straight ahead as all of Steve's rough confidence and hope leaked out of me. Lon and me. Lon and Vinnie. What now?

Cotler heard from one of his father's deputies that Lon had been outside smoking a cigarette by himself, a few feet away from where Doug and Vinnie were standing with two other guys from the football team. The deputy, a beefy black guy with the odd male name of Kim Wells, had driven past the group on the front lawn and saw them standing tightly together, like they were gathered around something. He saw the burning red cherry of a joint somewhere in the middle, and that was enough to merit a stop to investigate. He told Cotler that he lost sight of them for a moment while he parked the car, then called out and approached the group on foot, where he clearly smelled marijuana. He asked who had it and where it had gone. At that point, all three of the bigger guys turned their eyes to Vinnie, as if he was the one holding the evidence. Then, Kim related, Lon walked over, handed him a small baggie, and said that one of the big guys, not Vinnie, had tossed it in his direction. Kim pressed Lon on which one he had seen throw it, but Lon said he didn't know. He just knew it wasn't the little guy and didn't think it was right for him to get busted for it. Deputy Wells took the baggie, excoriated the group for what they had clearly been doing—during football season, no less—and left them with a warning rather than locking them all up. He didn't bother looking for the joint itself. After that he'd gone to talk to Rob, and the party was to break up within the next half-hour at most.

"Rob got lucky," Cotler said. Steve, Spencer, and I were gathered around him on the back deck. Inside, the party was thinning out, but we could see Doug in the kitchen, still fuming and pounding drinks with his teammates. "If I hadn't been here, he'd probably have come in the house and everyone would've been busted for the liquor. More likely he just didn't want the headache of a big juvenile bust."

"Sounds like Vinnie got lucky," Steve said. "Why did Lon stick up for him?"

"Well, that's the thing," Cotler said. "It's weirder that just that."

"Now what?" I asked, exasperation clear in my voice. My stomach was churning. The nausea over Tamara was gone, and this was in its place. Thankfully no one seemed to notice.

"Doug's drunker than shit," Cotler said, disgust in his voice. "I came out here to shut him up because he was goin' on and on about how Lon tried to set him up. Turns out, here's what happened: They're standin' out there with a bag of dope, getting ready to smoke it. Doug's holding it. Kim drives by in a cruiser and stops, so Doug grabs Vinnie and shoves it down the back of his pants. Vinnie's standing there ready to be busted, 'cause he don't play football."

"That's Vinnie's job," Steve said with a shrug. Cotler nodded.

"Yeah, it's typical. So then Kim's questioning all four of 'em, and Vinnie's about to give it up and take the blame. That's when Lon walks over, produces a bag o' dope and hands it to Kim. Lon says someone threw it, but it wasn't the little guy. That's all he knows."

"You mean . . ." Steve started.

"Yeah," Cotler said. "According to Asshole in there, Kim never found the dope Vinnie had in his pants. Lon must have had a bag of something on him, and he walked over and gave it to the cop so Vinnie wouldn't get busted. What the hell was that about?" He directed this question at me. Cotler had a tendency to ask me questions that no one could reasonably expect to have an answer for, and generally I was used to it. But this was not sitting well with me at all. I started to speak as Rob appeared in the sliding glass doorway on the deck.

"Cotler," he said, "Please. That guy is back . . . Lon. Doug's gonna kill him." Cotler got moving and we followed.

Lon and Tamara had returned to the party. When Doug heard he was back, he declared his intentions to stomp the guy and called out to him from the kitchen. We got there just as Lon was walking out the front door.

"Thank God, he's leaving," Rob exhaled, turning back to Cotler. "If he gets out of here fast, we'll be okay."

"The fuck I'm leaving," Lon said, pausing in the doorway. He looked over Rob's shoulder to Vinnie, who stood in the living room and regarded Lon like some awful god. "Tell your boyfriend I'll be in the park in ten minutes." He walked out the front door as Tamara tried to stop him. Lon walked past her like she was a houseplant, strode across the lawn and into the park, where he disappeared. Doug stomped around Rob's kitchen counting off the minutes. When ten had passed, he walked out of the house with a little crowd in tow. Our group followed with Cotler in the lead. Outside, the night was warm and fragrant. And then Tamara was reaching for my arm.

"Johnny. Please." I turned to look at her and was instantly and not surprisingly overcome with sadness, shame, and desire. Her eyes were wide and hurt. Her pouting lower lip trembled. Steve and Cotler moved a few feet away from us. I looked at my shirt, where Tam had clutched it, and then at her.

"What the hell do you want, Tamara?" I was terrified that my voice would betray me and shake. She seemed not to notice either way.

"He'll kill him, Johnny. He really will."

"And?"

"John, please don't be like this," she said. "I . . . I know what this looks like, okay? But he doesn't know what he's up against."

"That sounds like his problem, hon. I can't fight this one."

"Do you really think she wants your input?" Doug asked

loudly. Tam spun around and glared at him as he sauntered toward us. "She wants your hired gun." Doug turned to Cotler now, who stared back with a look of pure, malevolent contempt.

Tam tried to split a look between Doug and me, but she didn't deny what Doug said. It was true, after all. There was one person in my world who could make Doug think twice about a fistfight, and it wasn't me. Tam chose the ground to look at now as Doug gazed at all of us, smiling and triumphant.

"Why don't you leave the guy alone, Doug?" I asked finally. "He doesn't . . ."

"Stay the fuck out of this, you pussy," he said to me. His tone was one of effortless dismissal, the kind of cruel and deadly accurate arrow he had slung at weaker people his entire short life. In Tamara's presence, I was even more of an amusing target. Cotler, without words to describe the humiliation he had just seen me take but who felt it nevertheless, now leveled his eyes at Doug. Doug saw this and paused. He was not afraid of Cotler, but he would not trifle with him needlessly, either.

"You stay out of this, too, Cotler," Doug said, but with a more cautious tone. "I got no problem with you."

"You're about to have a problem with me," Cotler said. "Get on to where your fight is now."

Doug looked at Cotler critically for a moment, then turned toward the park where Lon could be seen already, smoking and standing beside one of the picnic tables.

"He's gonna get hurt," Cotler said to Tamara, who was now too ashamed for words. "It just ain't our problem." She looked over at me helplessly for a moment, and without the strength to ignore her I started to say something . . .

but she turned and followed the crowd herself. I was, after all, worthless without Cotler.

"Don't get a scratch over this, Cotler," Steve said as we approached the park. "Let Doug kill the fucker if he wants. If there's a God, they'll kill each other."

"Doug ain't no joke in a fight," Cotler said. "Whatever happens, we shouldn't let the new guy get hurt that bad, if it comes to it. We'll see."

Doug reached Lon, standing between the picnic table and the big trash can, and the gathered group took places in a rough semicircle around them. A night breeze picked up and blew Lon's hair in strands around his face.

"Admit it," Doug said to him, a stiff finger pointed in his face. Lon looked at the finger and did not speak. He looked solid and only the slightest bit apprehensive. "Admit it and it won't be as bad. Admit what you tried to do to us and tell me why. Maybe I'll even let this go. But either way you better start talking. Now, you fucking freak." He was feigning anger, but Doug was not angry. Not yet, anyway. Doug was lit up, pumped for the rout he expected. He had no intention of "letting this go" even if Lon fell on his knees and begged.

"I'll tell you what," Lon said, calmly and with even strength. We all viewed this with silent respect. The guy was dead, but he was holding steady. He paused, his calm now gathered in full. "Ask Vinnie Foust why I did it." Doug wrinkled his nose but smoothed out momentarily and smiled. My heart began to thud. Doug motioned toward Vinnie, who looked as pale as milk in the dim light. "All right. I'll do that. What about it, Vinnie?"

Silently, I slipped behind Cotler and tried to control my own breathing. Vinnie rolled his eyes ever so slightly out of Doug's view and stared off past the confrontation. His clothes hung off him and through their looseness we could see him shaking. He seemed to want to look anywhere except at Lon. All eyes were now on him.

"Go ahead, Vin," Doug said, a little more impatiently. "Tell us what you've got to do with this asshole trying to set us up?"

"How the hell should I know? Leave me out of it." Vinnie's quaking voice was the antithesis of Lon's. Lon looked squarely at Vinnie and slowly began to smile. Doug saw this, and for the first time that day he looked doubtful. The small crowd sensed this as only voyeuristic crowds can do and moved in closer. Doug spoke up to reassert control.

"No answers there, pal. Your time's runnin' out."

"No, Doug," Lon said amiably. "Yours is." Doug looked genuinely taken aback.

"Do I hear you right?" he asked. Lon smiled, and firmly shook his head.

"You don't see me right, either. You or Vinnie. But you'll see soon enough. How you're fucked, I mean. How we all are." Doug's face wrinkled again. Now, he was getting angry. It must have been inconceivable to him that this poor sap wasn't urine soaked and begging at this point.

"No one's fucked here but you," Doug said at a lower volume. "We're done talking. I'll give you one chance and we'll see if you're smart enough to take it. Beg, or suffer. Which is it?"

"You could ask Vinnie the same question," Lon said with bizarre, mock cheerfulness. "How 'bout I do it myself?" He leaned back now and spoke around Doug to Vinnie, still looking lost and utterly alone. "Beg or suffer,

Vinnie. What's it gonna be?" Doug stepped back now, incredulous. A weird hush fell over the crowd, and suddenly it wasn't Doug's fight anymore. Doug was an extra in this scene. Vinnie gulped hard and pushed his glasses up his nose—helpless, it seemed, to look away from the gravel and fallen leaves below him. "Everybody needs a home," Lon went on. "But this is your road, and you've got to follow it to the end. Can you do that? They don't know how it feels, do they? Never forget that. They don't know how it feels." Vinnie raised his head, his mouth hanging open, and looked at Lon as if he had been drawn to him in a trance.

"All right, fuck this," Doug said. He stepped toward Lon to strike. "You're gonna get—"

"Who the fuck was talking to *you*?!" Lon asked loudly, an oversized smile on his face. Doug, too surprised for words, stood frozen for a second. Lon turned back to Vinnie. "Watch and learn, Vinnie," he said, again with that mean, cheery tone. And then he turned back to Doug, still smiling obscenely, and spit right in his face.

Doug hit Lon so hard and so fast for the next few seconds that his face seemed to explode in blood. He staggered back and grabbed the picnic table, trying vainly to cover his eyes and nose. For a moment it seemed as if he would fall into the large trash can beside him. A few of the girls in the crowd turned away. I was aware of someone who sounded like Tamara screaming, but she wasn't alone. Doug grabbed Lon by the shirt and smiled a toothy grin at him. To most of us the fight looked as if it were pretty much over.

"Spit at me, huh?" he asked, his gleaming face pressed against Lon's bloodied one. Lon's mouth hung open in an ugly, contorted way, and thick blood dripped from a lower lip that was badly split and already swollen. His eyes looked far away, empty. He gazed at something on the front of Doug's tight T-shirt.

"Jesus, you must be high. We're gonna have some more fun, now. You are never gonna look the same, you cocksuck—"

"All right, Doug, that's enough," Cotler said, stepping forward. "The fucker's finished, now let up."

Doug turned angrily to Cotler and began to say something, and that was all the time Lon needed. Spencer saw it first and pointed. Lon's glazed eyes suddenly filled with life, and surreptitiously he reached behind him into the trash can as Doug screamed at Cotler to stay the fuck out of it. He grabbed for something and came up with it just in time for Doug to see what was coming. An iron bar, about two feet long and an inch thick came crashing across Doug's face with a whistling sound. Doug saw it just in time to pull back enough to prevent his jaw from being crushed like an egg, but it bit a sizable hole in his cheek, from which his blood jetted copiously. He opened his mouth to scream and almost choked on an incisor that came tumbling out.

He staggered backward, eyes like saucers, spitting the tooth and a whole lot of blood into the space between the two of them. Lon smiled now, a red and freakish apparition behind stringy, bloody hair. He swung again, savagely, and this time swung low, connecting with Doug's side. Doug shrieked as the blow tore through him and turned as if to run. Lon swung again and connected with his shoulder. Doug fell forward and grabbed the leg of Rob Reynolds, his former party host. Rob shrieked in reflex and began to pull away. The blood pouring out of Doug's mouth covered Rob's shoes. Doug was moaning, and it sounded unnatural and haunted.

"Christ, cut this shit out!" Cotler screamed. He was trying to position himself between Lon and the figure of Doug on the ground without getting hurt. He kept his big arms raised in front of him, preparing for Lon to turn on him. Lon looked at Cotler for a moment, and then dropped the bar. It made a dull thudding sound as it hit the ground.

"'The fucker's finished,' huh?" Lon asked. The words were garbled by the blood and torn flesh in his mouth. He leered at Cotler as he had at Doug, his face pounded into a grotesque caricature of what it had been five minutes before. He looked faceless, unrecognizable, amazingly evil. "'The fucker's finished'?! Only just begun." He looked down at Doug, still crawling away. "Only just begun!" He turned and half-walked, half-staggered through the park, disappearing into the woods.

No one followed. Doug's teammates came to his aid, slowly bringing him to his feet. Most of the gathered group followed Doug into the house. Cotler picked up the dull implement that had been Lon's deliverance and tossed it back into the trashcan.

7

September 21. We didn't see Lon for almost a week, and there was speculation that he had dropped out. Doug was in pain for a long while and missed three days of practice. As it turned out, he needed a bridge for the lost tooth. On Friday morning I ducked out of a pep rally, this one for a game against Osbourne Park over in Manassas and headed for the boy's bathroom in one of the older parts of the school.

The bathroom was silent, save for that inexplicable hum

that school buildings always seem to have. In front of the mirror over one of the sinks, I took a hard look at myself for the first time in weeks. The testimony of family and friends came back in echoes. I looked bad. I looked pallid, exhausted, and frankly perpetually frightened, much like my father's immigrant parents in all of those yellowed photographs. My hands shook slightly almost all of the time, I suppose because of a lack of restful sleep. When I did sleep, predictable dreams plagued me.

I was depressed over Tamara, who according to the rumor mill was spending a lot of time with Lon in all his dark intrigue. That was bad, but I could deal with it. It was the rocket-fueled anxiety, this faceless, amorphous feeling of doom that waited to grip me until I was in a classroom, in church with my family, or at work, that was killing me. A tuft of smoke entered my eyes as I peered at myself, and I closed them, feeling suddenly close to tears. The urge to cry was attached more to simple weariness than anything, and I welcomed it as it moved through me.

When I opened my eyes again, Lon was behind me.

I nearly swallowed the cigarette as I spun around, clutching the sink. He was clad in the usual biker's attire, and it struck me that he wore the same clothes, though usually clean, quite a bit. His hair was drooping down, shrouding his beaten face in Christlike fashion. The eyes, the mouth, the look altogether was less vampire-like but still badly swollen and bruised. He sensed me giving him the once over and smiled.

"You didn't pull the door shut," he said. "I just," he made a sweeping gesture with both hands, "came on in." He lit a cigarette, one of those filter-less Luckies that became popular for a while again in the early eighties, and took a deep drag.

"Welcome back," I managed, unsure of what else to say. Lon nodded.

"Now how do I take that?" he asked smiling, contemplating his cigarette. "Do I take it on its face or I do I assume you know how long I've really been gone?" I paused, unsure of how to continue short of running out of the bathroom, which was my true desire.

"You don't look bad," I said.

"You should see the other guy," Lon said, and I almost smiled. He finished his cigarette, pitched it neatly into a urinal, and immediately lit another one. He took a long drag and looked at me through the smoke. I waited for a chance to end this encounter. "You don't look good, John, I gotta be honest. Is it the dreams? Is it that dumb little bitch you so desperately want to call your girlfriend? Do you think I've at least felt her up by now? I mean, do you wonder? She's worth a fuckin' boob squeeze, wouldn't you say? Or would you even know?"

"No," I said, afraid, angry, and sick at the same time. "I really wouldn't know."

"So I hear."

"Look, Lon," I said, drawing breath the way Spencer did when his asthma was acting up, "maybe you're confusing me with someone else, but I don't know you. And what you do with or without Tamara Woolen isn't my problem. Can we just leave it at that? Please?" I could feel my heartbeat in my ears. He didn't answer me. His eyes, as bright and black as I'd ever seen them, looked probingly into mine. The bathroom seemed smaller now. I wanted out, and I started to leave.

"Do you know why I went after her?" he asked mildly as I made for the door. I paused there, eyes closed. The feel of him behind me was weighty and sickly warm. "I did it to show you that I could. I can do a lot of things, Johnny. All sorts of things. You remember that. We'll talk soon." I bolted before he could finish, hastily making my way toward the stairway. I wound my way up through the silent school to the second floor men's room, found a stall, and threw up everything.

Chapter Three: October

"Fire on the mountain. Run, boys, run.
The devil's in the House of the Rising Sun."
– CHARLIE DANIELS

1

The cemetery that serves the town of Belle Ridge was originally placed to serve the entire farming community of eastern Tolland County. It was not an unpretty place, encompassing a large hill and sloping gently from its summit on all sides with a view of the town, the surrounding countryside, and the Blue Ridge Mountains to the west. It sat on the left heading west out of town on Chapel Road, just a half-mile or so from Kelly's shop.

It was an interesting and frankly creepy fact growing up that there were two types of people buried at East Tolland Hill: the citizens of the area who never knew of Belle Ridge and whose lives ended as far back as the late 18th century, and the tragedies of Belle Ridge itself. There were a few older people who had come to live in town late in their lives who were buried here, but not many. Most people over fifty who died in Belle Ridge had grown up elsewhere and were usually placed back home, in a family plot or a spot next to a previously deceased spouse.

Instead of the elderly, East Tolland Hill from the mid-60s on slowly filled with the sons and daughters and spouses of the town, put there like broken toys after car wrecks, bouts with cancer, death at childbirth, as in Cotler's mother's case, and more recently, murder.

As I kid, I didn't know what to make of that strange mixture of graves from the distant past alongside graves of people who were basically contemporaries. It seemed to me at times as if the ancient inhabitants of East Tolland Hill were angry for having been shunned by the elderly of our town and reached out from time to time to claim the life of a child or a young adult to keep filling the hillside in a more proper, continuous rhythm. Or maybe it was just circumstance. Most folks came to make Belle Ridge their home and raise their children, naturally unfocused on what to do if one of them died. When they did die, there was East Tolland Hill.

October 7. We stood on the slope of the hill, Cotler and I, with two bouquets of flowers. The first we placed on his mother's grave. The second was of brightly colored flowers in Flyer's colors that we placed on the grave of Terrance Hark. Mrs.

Hark was coming here every day, refreshing the flowers and decorations on the grave. "Enshrinement," my mother called it. It was the first Sunday of the month, and the Cotlers went there with us after having dinner at our house. The sun had just dipped below the hills in the west as we turned to walk back to the truck. A stiff breeze picked up. September evenings were quickly, almost frighteningly, turning into downright chilly October weather.

"I went out there last night," Cotler said as we pulled away from the cemetery.

"I know," I said. I figured Cotler had been out to the site of the murder because he hadn't had to babysit the previous night, and he had even declined to go out with us over to Spencer's. He was not home, but his truck was. Also, I hadn't heard from him until relatively late on Sunday morning. It had been in his plans for weeks, I knew. When you converse with someone every day for all of your life, you start to recognize his patterns. "How did you go?"

"I went in behind the school and made my way along the small trails until I came to Copperhead Road. I just followed it to the place."

"That's like two miles, isn't it?"

"I couldn't well drive. I needed the walk anyway. It's best to have some thinkin' time if you're on your way to a place like that." *He went in total darkness, too,* I knew. Cotler eschewed flashlights in the woods. He believed in patiently letting his eyes adjust as well as possible to his surroundings, that way preventing his dependence on any isolated and battery-powered light source. If there was no moon or there was cloud cover, he went slower and listened more closely.

"I really wish you wouldn't do stuff like that. What if he'd been out there, revisiting the scene, or whatever?"

"I was listenin'," he said, as if he were describing wallpaper.

"Did you find anything at the spot?"

"Hell, no. I didn't go under the police line. I didn't do much of anything, really. I walked around, went down some of the other trails near the Road. I made a wide circle around the whole place, then I just sat up on a stump a ways away. I sat there a piece, and then I walked home."

We didn't speak for a moment. I knew now why he had

gone. He had gone to get a scent, a feel, something primitive and undefinable, I supposed. It felt right for him to do it, and so he had. As when he was hunting, Cotler didn't often second-guess a hunch, nor did he lament when it came up zero.

"What did you get from it?" I asked as we turned on to our sleeping town's main road. Garth Brooks, new to the music world at that time, sang softly from the radio about lost love and rodeo. Cotler fidgeted and then spoke.

"A local. A local that can get around in the woods. That's what I think. I hate it. I fuckin' hate to say it. But I think whoever did this knows this place intimately. More importantly, knows *that* place."

"What gives you this? You have a vision out there?" He looked at me with a hint of annoyance.

"No mistakes. That's what this cocksucker left us. My father's no stranger to brush and trees, and neither are those state people. They've been over that spot and all around it a hundred times. Ain't come up with spit."

"So?"

"So, it makes me think more than not that whoever did this knew the area well enough to find a good spot, do his work, and then get out of there without leaving a trace. Nothing out of place, John. No cracked branches. No spade marks. No footprints of any kind. He never so much as caught his pants on a bramble. In and out, like a ghost. Either that or he's been back there, cleanin' up. Either way he's a woodsman and someone who knows what he's doin' out there. He knew the smoothest paths, the quickest ways in and out. How to move without leavin' a single track. That's what I think."

"No offense, but that's hardly conclusive," I said. "It could be that he has been back. It could be that he knows that area. It doesn't mean that he's lived among us. There's a lot going on around here now. Construction, new roads, new companies. All sorts of people can find their way to Copperhead Road. Hell, we did with no one showing us the way." Cotler said nothing. I could tell I hadn't moved him one iota.

"That ain't the way it smelled to me," he said.

"Oh. That ain't the way it smelled to you," I said. "I forgot about your—"

"It ain't," he said louder. "I know it sounds crazy. I'm tellin' you 'cause I got a good idea of just how crazy it does sound. I don't exactly watch what I say around you, didn't feel like I had to."

"Look, I'm sorry. You don't sound crazy. Not to me anyway."

"I just can't stomach it," he said. "It's like a bad dream. I wake up, and the boy's still dead. Nothin's ever gonna change the fact that he grew up here and got stolen from here and got killed in the worst way . . . right here." The green glow of the dash illuminated his face and I could see it pulled tight, stony, and drawn.

"No. You're right. Nothing is going to change that. And maybe if you get the sense that it was someone from here, maybe it's the right hunch. I don't know."

"I sat out there, John, and I waited. I waited for it to make sense how a total outsider would come in here, grab that kid, and do it. It wouldn't come. I tried to imagine where he would come from, how he would come to know that spot. You know, the Road and all. I know it's crazy, but I just didn't feel any outsider's presence. Nothin'. I didn't smell anything that seemed like it wouldn't normally be welcome there. You know?"

I didn't know, but I knew Cotler knew. When we played 'manhunt' with BB guns out in those woods, it was Cotler who could sniff out even the quietest, most patient invading foes hiding in those gullies and tree stands. It was Cotler who could point out the chucks and the birds and the rabbits, shushing me even before they crossed our paths. I don't know if it was talent, upbringing, or some weird mix of heightened sensibilities and unshrouded perception. He was, in so many ways, simple. He was proud of being simple. Maybe this helped him to see what others missed. I don't know.

Tamara's parents' house was along Belle Ridge Boulevard, and she re-invaded my thoughts as we drove past it in the gathering darkness. Supposedly her friends were concerned that her romance with the town's bad boy was leading her astray. I had seen her wearing Lon's leather jacket one day in the school parking lot, and there were rumors that she had been absent from school a few of the days that he'd been gone. This should have been hell for me to bear, but in actuality it was scarcely a priority anymore. The dreams were getting worse, and so was the gut feeling that Lon was the delivery boy for some old nightmare I didn't fully understand. I smoked continuously, ate very little, and regularly found myself nauseous or close to tears, often with no warning at all. As Cotler pulled up to my house, I turned my thoughts back to the subject at hand.

"So, what now?" I asked. He shook his head as he pulled into my driveway. A light in the downstairs den indicated that my father was still up with a drink, engrossed in a book by one of the Watergate felons.

"I'd like to watch things around town," he said. "'Cause

if I'm right, if it is someone from here, it might happen again." Cotler's face reflected real pain and fear at the thought of this. "That's where I may need you. You're smarter. You can help me put stuff together, if we see something."

"Not when it comes to this, I'm not," I said.

"No, you are," he said quietly. "You are." He sighed and cursed under his breath. "I just cain't imagine. I cain't imagine who."

And I *could*, I thought to myself with sickening certainty. I *could*.

2

The night closes in easily around us. We are full, pleasantly sleepy, and possessed by that rich, warm fireside contentment, laced with a hint of excitement and known only to young boys—all of us thirteen—out on their own in the nighttime. Cotler's artfully prepared s'mores continue to slide from his blackened spatula onto the big rock beside the fire. Vic and I partake of them as if there will be no s'mores ever again. Spencer is wrapped snuggly in a huge quilt his mother would likely whip him for bringing out into the woods—it is a calico weave that Spencer's great grandmother, the daughter of a slave in Memphis, Tennessee, knit for her first child. Spencer's Redskins cap is pulled down around his ears, and he munches happily on a bag of chips while watching Cotler work in the fire's glow.

Then the scream comes. Seeming to come at first from the direction of the farmland, it fills the entire woods. It rises slowly, sounding like the hiss of a burst pipe at first, then swelling to a pitch higher than any of us can achieve even at that age, with the possible exception of Vic. The scream is not just a wiry shriek—it is a hellish, high-pitched wail, full and almost mournful. Absolute terror, coupled with some mysterious and unfathomable sorrow, seems to characterize it. The scream is throaty, wild and hoarse—the unbridled scream of childbirth, the scream of torture. But higher. It is a noise that, then and now, I can only identify in one way. To any reasonable person, the scream we are hearing sounds as if it is being made by a little girl being torn apart in the worst way imaginable. There's just no other way to properly characterize it. It rises in volume to a crescendo, and then falls off abruptly. For a second no one says anything.

"Jesus, what in God's fucking name was that?!" Vic blasphemes. Cotler shushes him and peers into the night. Vic's face is already drained of color, as is mine, and the many s'mores in our bellies now consider retracing their steps.

"Could be an animal," Cotler says doubtfully, more to himself than to us. He continues to peer into the dark. But I can hear a small tremor in his voice. If Cotler is moved at all now by fear, then I am paralyzed.

"Animal, my fucking ass," Vic hisses in a terrified whisper. "That's no goddam animal. That's a person—a girl. Someone's being fucking killed out there. Right out there!" Vic crabwalks a few feet away from the fire and hugs his knees.

"Cotler," Spencer asks weakly from under the quilt, "what is it? Really, I mean. Vic's right. It sounds like someone's murdering a little girl out there." Spencer looks over at me, but my wide, white eyes are fixated in the direction I think the sound came from. Before Cotler can answer, it comes again.

High, piercing—a throat-searing, blood-curdling yell from

the very mouth of Hell itself. When it dies down again, the woods are eerily quiet, as if the scream is just too tough an act to follow for any other nocturnal caller. Cotler stands up.

"Holy Jesus," he whispers, unsnapping his Buck knife. "Holy God and Jesus." Cotler points his stern look in Vic and my direction. Vic shakes with fear. I continue to stare.

"Where'd that come from?" Cotler asks. "I thought it was comin' from over there at first, but now I caint tell."

"Who fucking cares?" Vic points out, a distinctive whine now creeping into his voice. "We've got to get out. Right now."

"There's gotta be some explanation," Cotler murmurs. "This shit ain't what it seems. It caint be." Cotler's accent is stiffening, usually a sign that he is very mad or very afraid. I move back toward Vic.

"There's a fucking explanation," Vic says, the high whine now dominating his voice. He almost sounds mournful himself, as if he's relating some great disappointment. "It's fuckin' Jason, man—some fuck like that. Jesus, he takes them out here, where no one'll hear 'em scream—except we're out here. He'll be comin' for us, Cotler. You think he can't see that goddam fire? Oh shit, man, he knows we're here, and he's probably enjoying doing that girl so we can hear it. Goddam, man, we gotta get outta here. We—"

"Shut up, Vic," Cotler says. Vic shuts up but continues to make a 'mmm-mmm' sound under his breath. Slowly, Cotler moves a few steps toward the woods.

"Cotler where are you going?" I ask. He doesn't answer but is moving slowly away from the fire, toward the brush. His knife is out and ready in his hand. He holds it as he's been taught by relatives (and by Kelly), with the back of the blade resting against his wrist, running down his arm. He pauses and waits for the scream to come again.

"Cotler," I say, "I think maybe Vic's right. Maybe we oughta just back slowly outta here away from the direction of the . . . noise."

"And leave a burnin' fire out here in this little clearing? Christ, Johnny it's been dry out here for goin' on two months. Listen for it again. I'm gonna check this out."

"Jesus," Vic says, "can't we at least agree that, whoever she is, there's nothing we can do for her now? It's time to cruise, for God's sake." Cotler, scared and frustrated, turns a sharp glare on Vic.

"You want out- then go. You know the way. Go on—all of you. Go on if you want. I can get outta here—believe me. Fast." Cotler's accusing gaze does not shift to Spencer and me, but we feel it anyway. Spencer shifts under his quilt. Vic looks glumly at the ground.

Inside of me a terrible fear leaks its spreading venom, leeching through my gut and into my hands and feet. But paired with the fear is a budding resentment—of the woods, of the true character I know it is now taking on right before us. The woods are unmasking now, removing clothing.

And there is Cotler. Cotler's bravery, though honest, is to me misguided and foolhardy. For all of his knowledge about this place, he knows nothing. Not compared to what I know. In that place I come as close as I ever have to hating him, and not only for his stunning ignorance about where he calls home and where he has dragged me time and time again. I want to hate him more for his bravery—and how he can be brave, perceived as such by Vic and Spencer, even in their great fear. Perhaps the cruelest trick of the entire episode is that, for all its suddenness and raw terror, the scream does not surprise me.

"We're not leaving without you," Spencer says. "I just

don't see what you'll accomplish by stomping around out there. Please, Cotler, let's think—"

Spencer is cut off as the scream rises for the final time. Fresh and horrible, it is not particularly different in character or intensity than any of the others. Cotler, ignoring all of us, moves silently into the woods toward the direction of the scream. Vic and Spencer are clearly awe struck by his courage.

"It's not getting any weaker," Spencer says. I stare into the brush where Cotler has disappeared. "You'd think—"

"Torture," Vic croaks. "He's doin' her slowly. He knows we're out here. He wants us to hear it. Oh yeah. Sonofabitch is takin' his time, he—"

"Shut up, Vic!" I hiss. Vic gapes at me. He remarks later that my face looked as if it had been drained of color by a dreadful illness. Spencer moves closer to me, and Vic gradually joins him. Unconsciously we are moving closer and closer together around the fire, as if by some atavistic instinct.

We all imagine the girl. In my mind she is blonde, maybe three feet tall. Maybe six, maybe seven years old. What is left of a torn cotton print dress lies on the cold earth beneath her. Smeared blood makes wide, uncertain stripes across the smooth, pink skin of her belly, back, and flailing arms. Her eyes are wide and white, and they roll unbelievingly in pain and terror, taking in smudges of bark, limbs, and black sky. The beast that holds her has no face. He cuts, tears, digs into her in unholy places. She screams.

Silence. The woods have begun to seem more restive again, and various crickets and night creatures make their noises in the thick brush. Vic, Spencer, and I huddle close around the fire, dying now for lack of attention into an orange coal bed. Cotler appears out of the trees. His knife is folded and put away.

Vic jumps when he appears. The three of us say nothing and wait for his hushed order to put out the fire as well as possible and bolt. Cotler looks at the neglected fire, his face glowing in it, and then back over to us. Slowly he smiles, a tired, bashful smile.

"What the fuck is so funny?" Vic asks slowly. He is not yet amused. Cotler shakes his head and takes his hat off, wiping his brow with it.

"Bobcat," he says. "I should have known." Spencer eyes him suspiciously.

"Bobcat? You mean a bobcat made that noise?" Cotler nods and squats on his big hams before the fire.

"I don't know why I didn't think of it before. I've been told how they sound, but I don't guess I woulda believed it until now. They mate about this time of year. That's what he's doin'. Notice how the screamin' didn't really let off or change much? He just up and hollers when he has the notion. Maybe he got himself some and he'll keep quiet." Vic shakes his head.

"You're crazy. That was no animal—I'm sorry man, but—" Cotler cuts him off.

"Never heard a bobcat, have you Vic?" Cotler is gentle, and almost teasing with Vic. I can tell he is a little ashamed for the way he reacted before. The tired light in his eyes is brighter, more at ease. Cotler is unconsciously slipping into Storyteller mode- his only and rare attempt at showmanship.

"It sounds like a girl being raped," Vic says dubiously.

"It was described to me as soundin' like a woman screamin'—real high and loathsome, like that. That one sounded a little young, but I'd be willin' to bet that's what it was."

"Did you see him?" Spencer asks. Cotler scoffs.

"See a bobcat? No *way*. He wasn't gonna let me see 'im. But that's what it was, boys. And if he's still lonely in a few, we may hear it again, so get used to it."

"That," Vic says, "is the most hateful sounding God-damned thing I have ever heard. Ever." Spencer nods, even though he'd never use those words.

"It's not gonna be easy to sleep. I don't care if we know what it is."

"Oh, c'mon now," Cotler says, building up the fire again and exuding the grandfather mannerisms. "That cat isn't gonna come within two hundred yards of this fire. Let him scream. Hell, if I thought I could get me some that way I'd be whooping it up all night right beside 'im."

A pause. Then Vic is laughing, and so is Spencer. Soon Cotler joins in, in spite of himself. I smile but do not join in the laughter.

It is years before I can admit to myself that I am disappointed in Cotler's correct appraisal of the situation that night. Not because I relish in the idea of a tortured child. Because I want vindication. I want the woods to confess, and in a shameful corner of my mind I welcome and anticipate the telling of the ugly truth. Slyly, they elude me once again.

3

Monday, October 15. The night was crisp, moonless, and velvet black. Spencer had asked me for a ride home from his evening honors class at school, and I wheeled easily down the street leading toward the parking lot. The chilled, still air made everything seem sharper, cleaner. There was no summer haze left in our atmosphere. I had a few minutes to wait on him, and I planned to spend it smoking cigarettes and trying to clear my head in solitude. I parked next to the fence, the only manned vehicle in the lot, and stepped out of the truck. Within moments my eyes wandered helplessly to the woods, as they always had. The tree line was barely visible across the playing fields. Darkness enveloped everything beyond an occasional patch of lamplight.

A tiny orange dot appeared on the tree line. My heart jumped as I realized it was a cigarette cherry. The cherry bobbed lightly, and behind it a tall, thin figure clad in a leather jacket moved easily across the practice field toward the school. The walk was familiar, if only vaguely. It was Lon. He came through the opening in the fence, smiled at me, and walked over to the truck. I stood motionless beside it.

"Hello," he said. His dark eyes danced, and I felt fear, anger, and some unfocused emptiness sink through me.

"Where're you coming from?" I asked, humorless. Lon glanced over at the woods and back to me.

"Home," he said. "You don't go there much anymore." I shifted and looked beyond him. He read my uneasiness like a magazine.

"That's smart, Lon," I said, holding my composure by stiffening up and placing my hands deep in my pockets. "Hang out in the woods in the middle of the night. I know some people that may be interested in that."

"You were easy to find," he said, looking at me pleasantly. "I picked you out right away." He paused and looked me with an almost cheerful curiosity. I pondered just what made him feel like he had the right to look at me that way. The low drone of the surrounding town enveloped us. I lit a cigarette, no longer caring about giving shaking hands away. I was getting angry. "Fuck you," I said dully. "I don't have to talk to you." I reached for my keys, about to turn away.

Lon grinned, and continued in his soft voice.

"He liked you. Jim, I mean. Vinnie screamed. Jim never liked that. Vinnie screamed like a stuck pig. Painful, I guess, when you're that size. But he really liked you. I always wondered why he did. You know, I've always thought that maybe it's because you liked . . ." Lon stopped at the sight of the tire iron in my hand. In a slow blur I had let go of the door handle and pulled it from the bed of the truck where it lay loose among its company of empty oil cans and beverage containers. The tool made a screeching sound as I pulled it from under the spare. I waved it slowly in front of him now, a stranger in my own body. Cloudy breath hissed in front of me. Lon stared at the tire iron.

"Get away from me," I said, but my voice cracked and sobs were already climbing in my throat. Cold tears were welling up inside my eyes. "Get far fucking away from me, or I will kill you with this. I'm not kidding."

"He's doing it," Lon said, keeping a somewhat safer distance and a less mocking tone. "After all these years, he's making a monster out of you. That's good. It's a good time for monsters. Even you are not too late, John."

"You're the monster," I said between clenched teeth. I still held the tire iron in front of me. "Who the fuck are you? You come to this place, you stare at me like I'm supposed to get up and dance for you any minute, and now you're some long lost pal from my childhood? Leave . . . me . . . alone. I don't know you. I don't want to know you."

"You wanna kill, don't you?" he asked, his voice almost a whisper. His hair lifted lightly in the cold breeze. "It'd feel real good to kill something, wouldn't it? Why won't you?" I glared at him and breathed heavily.

"Fuck you," I said, raising the tire iron again. "It's a nightmare, that's all it is. I don't think about it. Nobody thinks about it. I don't know who you are or what you think you know, but I'm telling you to stay away from me. You want to trade memories with someone, talk to your school sponsor."

"My school sponsor," he said smiling. "That's right. Our hero, Big Jim. Are you jealous?"

"Jealous," I said in a hiss. "Jealous of you living with Jim Kelly."

"It's not really living with him. It's more like feeding off of him." I lowered the tire iron.

"So feed off him and leave me alone. None of this is my problem." Lon's smile widened.

"Oh, yes it is. Why don't you think about working with me, rather than hoping I'll disappear? You want to kill, don't you? Think about it—that desire. Think about being something besides a sniveling wet rag waving a tire iron. Go ahead if you want. Knock my fucking head off. Kill something, John." I held the tire tool tightly but did not raise it again. "You'd be doing me a favor." Lon walked slowly backwards as he spoke. Even in dim starlight, he seemed to glow. "You'd be doing this whole miserable place a big, fucking favor."

"What are you doing with him?" I asked, spitting it out. Lon smiled and continued to walk backward, his hands in his pockets.

"What's it to you? The new nightmares are someone else's. It's not your problem."

"What the fuck is going on back there?" I yelled. In a

backyard somewhere a dog barked. Lon shrugged, walking away. "I think you're letting me in on something." He turned back toward me and fixed me with a gaze evil and wild.

"I think you *want* in on something." He turned and sauntered off toward the tree line, his jacket whipping lightly around him. His tracks were dark, crushed spots in the gleaming grass. I wiped my eyes, crawled back in the truck, and waited for Spencer.

4

Friday, October 19. Vic crossed his legs and leaned back against the tree behind him, tipping up a clear bottle of rum from his father's liquor cabinet and wincing as he brought it back down. We were in Broyhill Park, the namesake of the developer who collaborated with US Steel to build our town, and drinking beside the golf course. A week of Indian summer had blown into the Ridge and Vic, myself, and Steve sat under a grove of oaks with a cooler of beer. Cotler was nearby, camped out in the back of his truck with Spencer and several other of the cross-country guys, telling local civil war stories and keeping the group mesmerized. On a night breeze, his voice floated over to us like syrup, his drawl accentuated with the telling of the tales.

"Cotler thinks it's someone from here," I said, passing a new beer to Steve.

"Thinks who's someone from here?"

"The killer. The one who got the Hark kid." Steve looked my way in the dark.

"What makes him think that?"

"Dunno. I usually can't follow why he sees things the way he does. But he's beginning to think whoever did it had to be from here. Or near here."

"It's possible," Vic said, discarding the now empty rum bottle and reaching for a beer. He smiled at me and the cords in his neck stood out from his shirt. "You think this town couldn't produce a murderer all on its own?"

"I didn't used to think so. Now I'm wondering."

"This place isn't Mayberry," Steve said. "I got my share of beatings from rednecks at the baseball field, too. But murder? This town's small time, Vic."

"Maybe," Vic said with a shrug. "Maybe it's growing up."

"Last few days I've been mulling it over," I said, looking over at Vic. "I get the feeling your brother wouldn't have been surprised by it."

Vic smiled slightly and gazed in front of him. It was okay then, mentioning Marty. I was one of a very select few who could get away with that and was happy that I hadn't pushed it, especially in front of Steve, whom he didn't know very well.

***

The legacy that was Vic's life in 1984, his cross-country team, was the legacy of his brother, Marty Moreland. Marty graduated in 1980 from East Tolland and by that time was already a cult hero for kids who were considered outsiders in Belle Ridge. It was Marty who brought cross-country to the town, and he brought it for kids like himself who seemed to have no other place to go.

Marty, like Vic, had a big mouth and a sharp sense of humor. Like Vic, Marty was only five-foot-four and weighed less than a buck-oh-five at fourteen. The biting wit that seemed as natural to him as breathing was way ahead of his peers, and in true adolescent form it won him less in confused smiles and playful retorts than it did beatings. Marty had a good heart, though, and a lot of guts; truth be told he was a lot deeper than his little brother ever would be. He also had another attribute that no one suspected—his lungs. Marty could run, relatively fast and strong, for a good long time. He developed his own method of pacing himself and his own style of heel-toe running to increase his wind power and lower his overall times in the five, ten, and even fifteen-mile runs that he footed every day.

In high school he saw a great many kids like him who were being thrust into the same pattern of apathy and isolation that he'd been able to escape because of his talent, and unlike most people, he decided to do something about it. He read books, consulted with other coaches and studied runner's techniques. With that budding knowledge in hand during his sophomore year, he began to grab as many pale 90-pound losers as he could find and made runners out of as many as he could. Over the next two years, he continued to take in whatever misfits and weaklings he could gather: some overly thin, some not so thin, some tall, and some short—making damn good runners out of a few, focused teammates out of others, and brothers of them all. After two relatively successful seasons of this, he and his strange band of bony teammates went to the school for group recognition but could find no one in the administration interested in helping them start a team under official school colors.

Close to giving up hope and quickly running out of senior year, Marty finally got a break in the spring of 1980 through our E.I. teacher, Neil Bonner. Bonner, with his own skeleton-like frame, had run track in high school and could appreciate the larger good that Marty was trying to do. He agreed to coach the team and even to finance it on his own until a budget could be worked out. With his tenure and popularity he was a powerful force, and with the help of petitions and a letter-writing campaign, the school was finally swayed. A girls' team developed quickly thereafter, and the other three county schools had teams by 1983. Marty, who never competed officially, couldn't have been more proud. In the last year of his life he had seen a dream come true.

As for Vic, his path was made viciously clear with Marty's death in the late winter of 1981. Vic entered high school five months after his brother apparently hanged himself from a tree outside of town, virtually exploding with running potential. By the end of his freshman year he was the team's leading man, a better runner than Marty ever was. This was at least partly attributable to the lucky accident of genetics. Vic was built for speed and not much else, just like Marty. But those of us who knew him, knew better. Vic had the lungs and the chassis, yes, but he ran like hell because there simply was no other choice. Running had been his brother's hope. It was Vic's god. Not only did he need to run, he needed to run motherfucking beautifully, and so he did. I saw him throw up and keep moving, piss blood-red and go back out to do four more miles, fly up hills on swollen feet and blistered ankles. The loose, excitable, sloppy child that was Vic well into his twenties metamorphosed when he laced up his shoes. Marty's final gift to his young, brash brother was to force on him the ambition and the character to do one thing perfectly, even if it killed him.

*****

Now Vic said, "There's a place up on the Hill. Like a party spot or something, where kids used to hang out. Marty took me up there once and he showed me some weird shit."

"Where on the Hill?" I asked.

"Up Potomac View from Canard's Run," he said. "Up there behind Cotler's house. Haven't thought about it in years. Saw some weird shit up there."

I looked over to where Cotler was still telling stories. I was unpleasantly revisiting the night he and I, as children, had seen the fire and heard the voices from that same spot. I thought about calling him over but then thought better of it. We had never discussed what we saw or heard after that night, and I wasn't sure if I wanted to now. It was still a terrible memory, and I already had a head full of them.

"I think I know where you mean," I said quietly.

"Probably," Vic said. "It's been around for a while. It looked like an old hippie hang-out from the 70s, maybe even earlier." He put his beer down and stared straight ahead at nothing in particular. "We were up there maybe six or seven years ago, and even then it looked like it hadn't been used in a while. There were those old beer pull-tabs on the ground. I don't know why the fuck he dragged me up there. Probably just to fuck with me. It was during summer vacation one year and there wasn't any-thing better to do. But sometimes. Sometimes I think he took me up there for a reason."

"What did you see?" Steve asked, seemingly oblivious to the creepy feeling that had seized both Vic and me. Vic sighed.

"The spot was just a fire pit with some stones and

cigarette butts strewn around. I thought that was all of it, but then Marty showed me this round concrete thing right in the middle of it with a sewer lid at the top. You could pry the lid off and actually climb down inside."

"Like a drainage tunnel?" Steve asked. "I didn't think there was any need for those. No houses up there."

"You're right, there isn't any need. My brother said there was supposed be a development built there, but the builder went broke like in '69 or '70. He dug a few tunnels and laid some drainage pipes and left them right there. The cylinder had some pipes leading out from it, but they didn't go anywhere. It was down in there that we saw the weird shit."

"What'd you see?" Steve asked. Vic frowned and took another gulp.

"Little stuff, but stuff that made you think, you know? First thing Marty pointed out was the lid to the cylinder. It had symbols painted on it, stuff I couldn't read. He pried it off and we climbed down an iron ladder to the bottom. The first thing we found was a bra. It was half buried in the mud. And it wasn't a woman's D-cup either. It was one of those strechy, grow bras."

"Like a twelve-year-old girl would wear," Steve said.

"Exactly. Like a twelve-year-old girl would wear. It was sitting there, curled up in the mud like a dead snake. There were some other clothes, too, but just pieces of stuff. An old shirt with the back missing, a pants leg from some jeans. And on the wall there were red handprints. Human handprints, like someone had put their hand in dark red paint and pressed it there. Except I'm not so sure it was dark red paint. I really don't know. The prints were all the same height on the wall, except in one the fingers were all splayed out. In another one the ring finger and the pinkie were together while the other two and the thumb were spread apart. And then in the last one there were only three fingers. The hand was there but two of the fingers were missing. I swear to God."

"What the fuck?" Steve asked, his brow knitted in confusion and disgust. Vic chuckled.

"Yeah, that's what I said, but without saying 'fuck.' If Marty was trying to scare me, it was working. I started crying and we climbed out. Once we were back on the ground, he showed me how there was a circle of stones going all around the base of the cylinder. About two feet from it, all around. And the sewer lid itself had these weird symbols painted on it. Reminded me of a Zeppelin album cover."

"Black Mass," Steve said, muffled because he was lighting a cigarette. "I've heard rumors that stuff like that went on in the woods sometimes. Is that what your brother thought it was?" Vic waited a long time to answer, shrugged, and shook his head.

"Maybe. He didn't say what he thought it was. Looking back, it might have been something like that. All I know is, when I think about it now, I just get this feeling, like he was trying to tell me something."

"About what it was—the devil-worshipping stuff?" Steve asked.

"No," Vic said. "I don't think so. Marty believed in God and the devil about as much as he did Santa Claus. It wasn't that. It was something else he was getting at, I think. Something he wanted me to see—like how fucked up people could be for even playing around with shit like that. That's the feeling I get, anyway. I guess the point is, some kid getting killed here wouldn't surprise Marty. Not one bit."

"Seems like it hurts Cotler," Steve said. "The whole thing about the town having a bad side."

"He loves this place," Vic said, looking over at Cotler. "And I get that. He's tough, and he's seen some bad shit with his dad's job and his mom dying and all. But there's some shit that goes on around here that he doesn't look for. Some stuff that goes on that doesn't make much sense. You don't see it right up, especially if you don't want to. You gotta run your finger along the bottom. Then you'll drag it up."

"Hey, John," Steve called over to me, catching me by surprise. "You okay over there?" I shook myself out of a bad daze and gave a forced smile to both of them.

"Yeah," I said. "Yeah, I'm sorry. Just thinking." I wasn't aware of why I'd become so uneasy. I told myself it had just been a long time since I'd reflected on the Hill and what Cotler and I had heard up there as kids. But it was Marty's memory, and Vic's unusually frank manner in speaking about it, that was so unsettling that night. It had been a long time since I'd thought about the Hill; a long time that was, until recently, when stories like Vic's were suddenly relevant again. But Marty was an issue I couldn't get close to, not then.

The night was getting colder and I snugged my jacket closer. Vic and Steve moved on to another topic, and I excused myself and walked over to where Cotler was entertaining the group about Lee's move back from Antietam, and his broken army's bloody trek through our county in the fall of 1862.

5

I know that I am dreaming. I am close to the surface of wakefulness, and in a slow, drunk panic I punch forward to break through the shadowy space that stands between where I am and the cool darkness that is my bedroom.

I am in the woods with Jim, beside the familiar half-moon-shaped clearing just to the west of us. This is a place he likes well because the hill with its grove of trees is higher than much of the surrounding land and provides a view of the nearby trails and brush from the inside. He is holding me down and has me bent over an old tree log. I hear the snapping sound the leather of his belt makes and the chink of the buckle against the button of his jeans as he undoes his pants. With this done, he reaches to pull my pants down and his hands are like steam shovels as they strip clothing away from me. He is silent, impatient, breathing heavily. He spits to the side. If I scream, he assures me, I will be torn apart and buried out here. I'll look like that rotten woodchuck we found under this very log the previous summer. Do I want that? No, I assure him. I do not. He eclipses me from behind and I am gagging at the thought of this . . . again.

I look up. Through the trees is the figure on the edge of the clearing. He watches us silently, and I cannot see his face because of the setting sun behind him. Even though I am disgusted and terrified at the thought of being watched, I want to call out to this figure, to beg it, screaming for help. But I do not know who or what it is—and I do know this: calling out will mean torture, maybe death. I strain to see it more clearly, but all I can see is a vague silhouette. Behind me, Kelly grasps my waist. I prepare for the worst and look down.

A rock lands directly in front of my face. Another. One strikes Kelly in the forehead behind me, and he pushes me forward, falling backward himself and cursing a blue streak.

"What the fuck?!" he screams as he scrambles up to his knees. Another rock lands beside us. Another hits him in the chest. I turn my head to see him wiping blood from his face then turn away quickly, not wanting him to see me peeking. I look instead for the figure in the clearing. Whoever it is has concealed himself now and is calling out, calling to the other boys who are in the woods not far from us. Kelly whips his head this way and that, pulling his clothes back together in a mad rush as the other boys begin slowly moving toward the sounds of this stranger's calls. The stranger is not saying anything but 'Over here! Hey! Everybody!' The sound of his voice begins to come from different places as he dodges from tree to tree in an effort to keep himself hidden from Kelly's view. Kelly grabs me by the neck and fiercely whispers at me to pull my pants up. From the corner of his eye he senses movement and hears voices, confused boys running over to a new voice. I roll over and pull up my own pants, now as confused as Jim is. Kelly's eyes are wide with rage and confusion as he searches for the origin of the voice in the approaching twilight. Something to his left seems to catch his eye.

"You stay here," he commands, and bounds off into the woods. The figure he is following whoops and hollers unintelligibly now as he bolts from the area. The voice of the stranger is vaguely familiar but I cannot say from where. Kelly follows after him for a few minutes but soon returns spent, sweating, and very angry. He now sees a group of boys entering the clearing, coming over to where I stand among the trees. Kelly assesses the situation as he stomps over. He looks at me with deep suspicion, but I am obviously as terrified and confused as he is.

"What's goin' on?" Cotler asks. "We heard yellin' . . ."

"A prank, I guess," Kelly says, catching his breath. He is aware of the boys looking at him, and I can see him containing his anger, pressing it below the surface. Please God,

I pray, don't let him see this as my fault, somehow. *"Any of you see him?" Everyone shakes their heads, including me. "Well, I was lookin' to gather everyone in about now anyway, so it's just as well. Musta been some weirdo out there, hootin' and hollerin' . . . everyone okay? Let's do a count. Who's got their buddy?"*

Everyone answers that they are paired up correctly, and we pack up and move on to the truck. Kelly's eyes find me from time to time as we walk along . . . and I wonder who the rock thrower was . . . and why Jim couldn't catch him.

6

Monday, October 29. Jeremy Bingham was a precocious, large-toothed boy of ten with sandy brown hair and hazel-gray eyes not unlike Cotler's when he disappeared after school that breezy, gray afternoon and plummeted himself into the consciousness of Belle Ridge and the rest of the area forever. He had gone with three other friends directly from school down to one of the creeks that emptied into the sewers to look for late season crayfish. According to the other two boys who had gone along, everything was fine with the exception that they had found no crayfish—until an argument over who had first found a discarded lighter sent Jeremy in a different direction than the other two. The other two boys called after him teasingly, expecting him to traipse back and walk home with them eventually, but they never saw him return. With darkness and the resultant threat of punishment fast approaching, the other two assumed Jeremy had wound his way home on his own, and went home themselves. Their story was told to Sheriff Cotler and his new FBI contact shortly after 7:00 on Monday night; Jeremy's father had called his son in missing at 6:30.

Panic ensued. The town was no longer a place where a terrible murder had occurred. It was now a place where terrible murders might still be occurring. Rain began to fall shortly after nine as the sheriff, most of his department, officers, state troopers, and game wardens from other jurisdictions, along with dozens of volunteers showed up at the Belle Ridge satellite sheriff's office to begin the search. Media descended on the town for the 11:00 broadcast while camera vans with bright, big channel numbers on the sides took in scenes of trained dogs, men with maps and radios, and the tearful pleas of Jeremy's parents. Cotler's little brother Calvin was once again lodged at my parent's house as his father prepared to work around the clock in desperation. The challenge was two-fold now: finding the boy and managing the reaction of the town. He was grateful for the volunteers but swamped with them as well. When Terrance Hark had disappeared, he had a smaller but much more experienced and woods-wise group to oversee. Tonight, the satellite office was under siege from folks wanting to know where they should start looking.

7

Cotler was at my house at 7:30. He brought some things for Calvin, allowed my mother to force a meal into him, and then sat in my basement by the back door donning hunting gear. He dressed in the dark, not wanting to arouse questions from my parents.

"You'd better not let your old man see you," I said.

"Got no plans to, don't you worry."

"Where are you going to look?"

"I'll start by the creek, but not where this kid went in. That creek runs into the woods, joins up with another, and that second one bends around toward the airport. Where it meets up with the other creek he woulda gone right. I guarantee it. Any boy would. It's a lot bigger than the first one and there's lotsa neat rocks and stuff. Even if you were lost, it'd look like the most logical choice. Bigger water usually leads to people. Dad said he was one to go back there a lot, too. If he's an explorer, he knows it eventually makes it to the airport fence. That's where I'm lookin'."

"Haven't you told your dad this?"

"Yeah, he actually asked me. There's a team goin' that way. I think Ray Fisher is heading it up. There's another one . . . probably the best one . . . with some state and federal people and some dogs, goin' in the way he went in. I'll stay away from them. I know it'll be well-covered ground. But guess what? They don't know it like I know it."

"You might freak someone out if they see you creeping around out there without a team. This is a dangerous time, Cotler. Some of the guys doing this are packing. Let's face it, there's going to be a few loose cannons out there."

"No one's got a gun outside of a cop," he said. "Not supposed to, anyway."

"What the hell does 'not supposed to' add up to?"

"I can move quiet," he said, lacing up black boots and tucking in camouflage pants, "and I can move fast. No one is gonna know I'm out there unless they got dogs. If I hear dogs, I'll come out. I'm not stupid."

My father appeared in the doorway. He had come

downstairs to get out an old rain slicker before joining his team, now assembling at the church. He looked at me and then over at Cotler, obviously not dressed for the ball. He stood silently for a moment, and finally Cotler lowered his head.

"I can't stay here and do nothin' sir," he said. "Please don't ask me to." My father looked appraisingly at Cotler's clothes and then studied his face. Cotler would not look up at him, mostly for shame. The sheriff had placed his sons in my father's care, as he had all their lives when the circumstances demanded it, and no one had to express the fact that their wellbeing was his complete responsibility. My father stood motionless in the open door, outlined in the dim light of the downstairs rec room. He did not sigh, shake his head, or exude any of the other tired, withdrawn mannerisms that were his trademark. He appeared taut and nervous, yet sure at the same time. He stood perfectly still and made not a sound. I had never seen him this way before. I had to look over at him again to make sure it was the same person.

"When you get back," he said calmly, "you come straight to this house. This one."

"Sir?" Cotler didn't know what to make of this and neither did I. Again, the man who was my father but now a different man altogether moved not a muscle.

"Go do what you have to do," he said, in the same tone, not loud, not quiet. It was as if he didn't want to wake his real self. "Don't let your father see you. When you get back, you come straight here. Whatever you need you get it here. If I'm not awake or back yet, get John up. Understood?" Cotler lowered his head again and nodded.

"Yes, sir. Thank you for letting me go." My father walked

past us, grabbed an ancient, browning rain slicker, and turned in the doorway before leaving.

"I didn't let you go. Good luck, Francis."

8

Few friendships in my experience have formed more naturally, intensely, and with more speed than the one between my father and Cotler's father. They met through the town's volunteer rescue squad in the fall of 1966, within a week of my family's settling in Belle Ridge. Both men were pushing thirty, married about a year, and expecting their first child. Both were secretly hoping for a boy and neither was disappointed. Francis was born first, in February of 1967, to be followed by me, ambling along symbolically four months behind.

Both men, their wives would testify later and often, were taken by the other after their first meeting. Dan Cotler was a state trooper at the time, and my father was settling into his new job at the pharmacy on Chapel Road. My father immediately liked the gentle giant in Dan Cotler and the easy, smooth way in which long, slow words rolled out of his mouth . . . when he spoke, that was . . . which was just often enough to make him quiet without being withdrawn. Dan represented the ideal of the modern southern man to my dad, himself a short-legged, bespectacled, Irish New Yorker. Dan was, in many ways, a pleasant surprise to folks like mine who saw the white South of the 1960s as an absolute cauldron of small-minded hatred and violence. To Dan, John Ray, Sr. was a thinker, a serious-minded and apparently very concerned man who asked questions more than made pronouncements, and this Dan respected. Dan liked the abrupt, almost jerking way that John spoke, the way he dropped his 'r's and seemed to crush everything into a single syllable. It reminded him of the cops he secretly admired on some of the TV shows. Both struck each other early on as considerate, thoughtful types who could be turned to and counted on in times of trouble and confusion, and neither was ever let down by the other. Their work in the newly formed rescue squad quickly spilled over into friendship as they put the organization together in the summer and fall of 1966.

In February of the following year, Dan's reserve unit called him to service in Vietnam, and Dan went shortly after the birth of his first son. He went first to Camp Lejeune, North Carolina, where he loaded equipment and helped to process new Marines, and then on to California, and then "in-country." He spent seventeen months total in Vietnam, with a month-long break on a hospital ship in the Philippines. In those months he wrote exactly twenty-three letters: three to his mother, nineteen to his wife and son, and one to my father. To his wife and mother he wrote pleasant, surprisingly literary descriptions of the lushness of the countryside and the eager, quiet manner of the friendly Vietnamese he had encountered. He complained lightly of the heat and sometimes the food, but assured them continually of his safety and his confidence in the eventual security of victory in his nation's objective. He closed each message to his wife with a short, sweet note to his tiny boy who, at three months, was already growing beyond anyone's expectations.

To my father, his newly found and somehow deeply

trusted friend, Dan wrote one letter in the famed summer of 1967 that mirrored neither the hope and wonder of the American pop culture or the folksy eloquence of the letters to his wife and mother. This letter was not one of literary description but instead a grim plea. He described to my father a shotgun, a Remington .870 pump shotgun to be exact, that he needed my father to send him. He described the gun and gave instructions on how to ship it, indicating that he preferred it sawed-off but could do that himself if need be. He included 100 dollars and a final "thank-you" in advance, along with an extraneous admonition to keep everything discussed there between them. He also included the names of several gun dealers in nearby towns that Dan had known most of his life; men who would fill my father's order quietly and at the best price. My father took the 100 dollars and purchased a savings bond for Dan's infant son, then went to work locating the Remington.

***

My father did not know Jim Kelly, but saw one day he had opened a gun and fishing shop in town, and in the interest of supporting a town business, stopped in one Saturday afternoon to see if the new proprietor had what he wanted. He liked Jim Kelly in an off-hand way almost immediately, believing him to be at least twice as Southern as Dan and perhaps not as complex, but friendly and knowledgeable nonetheless. He had planned on telling him nothing of what the gun was for and found satisfactorily that Kelly was not prying. But my father's inexperience was obvious, and in conversation it slowly became clear that the gun was not for him.

After determining that Kelly was also a vet and briefly assessing him as otherwise okay, he admitted that the purpose of the shotgun was for a friend serving in Vietnam. This friend apparently needed it for "crowd control" and "tunnel clearing," as he had put it. At this Kelly nodded gravely, still asking no questions, and simply asked my father to give him a week. One week, he said, and he would put together the weapon his friend needed, and at a price he swore would not be beaten, in honor of helping a local man in arms. Kelly had spent twelve months there after leaving high school in June of 1965 and had been back stateside only seven months before acquiring the money to buy the store through his GI Bill. All in all, the young man who shook Dad's hand and asked to be called Jim struck him as professional, suitably serious, and valuably experienced. He was happy for his unintended choice of gunsmiths.

Upon his return, Kelly handed him the Remington .870 he had requested, and my father handed it back with something of an admiring shiver. It was gleaming coal black with a handsome, deeply polished brown stock and a pump so well-oiled and hinged that it slid open and closed with a fine, snapping sound like a cracked whip. The barrel had been expertly and immaculately sawn off and sanded so the gun now stood at a menacingly stout seventeen inches. Kelly threw in a generous supply of shells, the finest gun oil obtainable, and a few other cleaning materials, most of which my father did not recognize but Dan Cotler surely would. The *pièce de résistance*, Kelly said in whatever colloquialism of his that passed for that term, was the pistol grip he installed in place of the butt of the shotgun. This, Kelly warned, made the gun highly illegal in Virginia and most other places, but would make it as prized as a weekend in Reno with one of those Hefner babes in the 'Nam. Kelly, he assured my father, would have given his mother's fine china for one of these during his stretch.

Kelly helped my father pack the weapon for shipment, and my father sent it off the next day along with a picture of me and Dan's own son at two and six months. The only other package my father ever received from the country of Vietnam came about five months later and was not from Dan alone but from his whole unit. Enclosed was a framed photograph of the whole group, still one of his most coveted possessions, the colors of the regiment in patches, and a short note that simply said, "*To John Ray—the slickest gun totin' country boy that ever came out of New York City. We don't know where you got it, but we couldn't live without it. Thanx, Santa.*" Every man in Cotler's group signed it.

***

My father showed the note to Kelly, who thanked my father for the business and hoped to meet the man using the gun when he returned home. My father said he'd take him by, which he did. For Dan's part, he could hardly believe his good fortune as he surreptitiously unpacked the weapon that arrived on his base in early August of 1967. He had hoped and felt pretty certain that John would somehow get him a shotgun of his description, but he had never dared to dream that the very tool he imagined needing would arrive in his hands within six weeks of his asking. The ammunition was fresh, well made, and very powerful. The cleaning materials included were the best, Dan noted. Supple rags, stiff, neat brushes, and an oil the fine consistency of which Dan had never seen.

The supplanted pistol grip was set to the stock like iron in stone, and it balanced perfectly in their grubby, sweaty hands. Easy to heft, easy to fire. They oohed and ahhed as Dan worked the smooth, sliding pump: clack-clack, clack-clack, clack-clack, over and over in the tents and storage sheds of his base. The smallest and most wiry point man in the unit carried the gun, pistol grip sticking dutifully out of the back flap of a knapsack, and it was the envy of the entire company. The gun was the absolute most precious item any of them had, and it was cleaned, guarded, and used with the utmost of care. And every mean, steady blast of the thing that sent a cloud of death into the mouth of a tunnel or the shadow of a treetop and brought an enemy tumbling in pieces to the wet earth below had every man in Dan's platoon praising John Ray's name.

Upon his return, my father took Dan to meet the young man who had constructed the weapon he had so depended on over there. Dan and Kelly shook hands, and the three men discussed the war, the town, and the politics associated with both. A friendship had been born.

9

That first dismal night of the search for Jeremy Bingham bled into the next day, and then the next. It rained, seemingly non-stop. Sheriff Cotler brought his laundry and ate what meals he would eat with us, occasionally inviting his FBI contact or a man from Richmond. The men who came to the house with him were polite, quiet, but primarily removed and subdued. They didn't talk much at all, and what they said was usually directed with forced cheerfulness toward Calvin, my sister, and my mother. My mother, happy to have a job to do, tended to the cooking and the children and the care of the men at the center of the storm.

Day Three of the search was Wednesday, Halloween. Halloween 1984 would be remembered in Belle Ridge for its absolute stillness. A few kids went around to houses on their own blocks under the watchful eyes of parents, but not in many cases. The haunted houses that adorn every fourth or fifth block, the low-key vandalism and endless horn blowing were all absent that year. The town was haunted, and somewhere in the dark was Jeremy Bingham, without his mother and without his costume. No one wanted to do anything except continue the search and keep their own kids at home.

Halloween was overcast and blustery, the one dry day in that entire week of muck. Big, colorful leaves blew in circles along sagging gutters and through front yards. Slate gray clouds moved in silent, sweeping columns across the sky. As the day darkened, houses were shut up and kids herded inside. Low-riding patrol cars, state troopers, and men with dogs appeared here and there. They gathered at the sheriff's substation to begin another long night's search. The clear day brought with it a stiff breeze that swelled into a cold wind by nightfall. As the men got to work, the wind began to whistle ominously down the blocks and between the houses. It whistled in mockery of the exasperated search crews and the trembling inhabitants of Belle Ridge.

Chapter Four: November

"You never come back from Copperhead Road."
— STEVE EARLE

1

Sunday, November 4. Cotler and I tramped in single file through a muddy, rain-soaked tangle of trees and bushes on our way back to the road. We were scouting in anticipation of the coming deer season on the property of a family friend of the Cotlers'. He went out to places he hunted a few weeks before to scout the population and get a feel for what was going on. He looked for tracks, examined scat, and assessed the food supplies. These things yielded information about the average size of the deer population and their patterns of sleep and movement.

I was glad we had gone. Cotler desperately needed a diversion from the pressure of the search, now in its sixth day. He had slept little, if at all, since the 29th and continuously wore a tortured, strained look on his face, deepening as the lack of rest set in on him. The day was breezy, chilly, and dank. The rain that had begun in the last week of October had become unusually heavy since Halloween night and then tapered off just enough for us to get out of the house. A cold mist, mostly caught by the thinning canopy above us, persisted as we made our way back to the road.

"Looks like more rain," he said, looking up toward the sky and holding out a branch for me as he stepped through a bramble. He stopped in mid-step and raised his head slightly, seeming to want to taste the air in front of him. I stopped behind him, assuming that he had detected animals nearby, and waited. He paused and turned slowly to the left, back toward the airport fence. A creek trickled about a hundred yards in that direction. We had been near it earlier, at a different spot where Cotler believed the deer were drinking. "Do you . . . smell something?" he asked. I took a deep breath, but cigarettes tend to dull smell and taste. I smelled nothing but wet wood and leaves and mud.

"Not really. What is it?" Cotler remained still for another few seconds. He lifted his head higher and waited for a breeze. None came though, just the ever-present dull mist. Around us the woods seemed to sag with wetness and quiet rot. He shook his head and walked on.

"Never mind. I thought . . . shit, I don't know what I thought. Let's get on home." He shook his head absently and I followed behind. It was 5:00.

2

I swam up from a dream as Cotler shook me, gently as he could manage. I wasn't particularly surprised to see him, except for the hour. Cotler had woken me all of my life, probably hundreds of times. This time, his face was ash white.

"Cotler?" I became fully awake at the sight of him. "Christ, what is it? You look like hell."

"I need your help," he said. He was whispering, but not because anyone would hear us in normal conversation. He was whispering because his voice was shaking. "I've been laying with this all night. I can't lay no more."

"What?"

"I need you to go check somethin' with me. Somethin' real bad. We can't go now. It's better to wait until light. We could go now, I guess, but I . . . I'm scairt." He looked away and sat down in my desk chair. For a moment I thought he might cry, which I could not have taken. But he didn't cry. It began to dawn on me, and my blood went from sleepy warm to ice cold.

"It's the Bingham kid, isn't it?" He nodded.

"I can't lay with it. Not another minute. I . . . I think we walked right past him." He looked up. "I'm bettin' I know where he is."

"Why haven't you told your father?"

"I cain't just yet. I don't know why. I just wanna check this out. Just you and me first."

"All right," I said. My heart was a slow thudding thing inside my chest. "All right, let me pull on some pants."

The sky was slate gray with the slightest night-blue tinge as we tromped through the woods from where Cotler had parked. He had played it smart. We had driven the full length of the road to the fence, and then slowly backward. He had insisted we stay in the truck for a few minutes before going in to see if anyone else would venture out. The day continued to swell with pale gray light, and after a few minutes we went in.

***

The thud, thud, thud, of my heart was back now, bigger and thicker. We were close to a place, another place that I knew from childhood and had revisited in nightmares. It was the thought of this place that led to thoughts of Kelly, and then to Lon. At that point I wasn't admitting my suspicions, to myself even, that Lon was involved with the death or deaths going on here.

"If you see something foreign on the ground, point it out to me," Cotler was saying. "Don't pick it up but show it to me. He should be right over there."

We walked a few more feet toward the creek, and then the smell hit us. It was high and foul and gassy, the kind of smell you can feel starting to stick to you, to your clothes. It was heavy and ripe. Cotler saw him first and abruptly turned away.

"That's him," he said, a little garbled. "He got buried too close to the creek. Water's washed him loose." He licked his lips. "It's bad, John. Don't come no closer if you don't want."

But I did want. I wanted to see Jeremy Bingham. I wanted my eyes to meet with what my mind could barely comprehend, that this little boy had been taken from his mother, probably abused and beaten, and then covered with red Virginia clay like the family cat. But for the grace of God, I was Jeremy Bingham. I needed to see him.

I covered my nose futilely with my shirt and began to walk toward the creek bed. The smell was overpowering and so was the sense of memory. Beside us, crossing over the creek, was a large fallen tree that made a rudimentary bridge over it. I had been here before.

"He's a mess, John," Cotler warned, his voice rising as I walked dreamlike toward him. "Don't go—"

I cut him off with a gasp.

Jeremy Bingham was a mess. Only a small part of him was exposed, but it was a key part; his head, shoulders, and parts of his arms. Later we would learn from an autopsy report on Cotler's dad's desk that the cause of death was a deep puncture into the base of the boy's brain. This was unseen, as he lay face up before us. Although he was too close to the creek, the grave should have held for much longer. The killer had simply not counted on the volume of rain since the time of the burial.

It looked as if he had been pushed backward into the hole, like a man pushed into a soft chair. His head was still embedded in the dirt, and his face was deteriorating rapidly. What skin was left sported a sick, pale, greenish color, like the back of a ripening leaf. His mouth and one eye were open, both clotted with settled mud. The water had done a job on him, too. The flesh around his mouth and nose looked loose, almost runny. A regular museum of insects played hither and yon across his face. He was naked, at least waist up.

I looked up. The sky wasn't a crisp slate gray anymore. It was pasty and white, like a big, pus-filled marshmallow. It looked too close. The world began to spin. I glanced over at Cotler. He was regarding me sternly, like a father would a son contemplating his first time behind the wheel of a car.

"Retch if you have to," he said, almost harshly. "There ain't no shame in it. Just back up some. We don't want to touch anything near here."

I did retch. I ran back about fifty feet and retched what felt like every meal I'd ever eaten. Cotler did not. Maybe a lifetime of discovering rotted woodchucks and cleaning deer had hardened his gullet enough to take this. He just stared at the embankment, taking shallow breaths with an expression of pure, grim disgust on his face. Finally, he came over to me and put a big hand on my back.

"I'm sorry, John. I'm sorry like hell for bringing you out here." I put up a hand to tell him it was okay. When the last of the spasms left me, I wiped my mouth and stood up.

"It's alright. I just couldn't hold it anymore. It's his eyes. They're full of dirt. And his mother is up right now, wringing her hands and. . ." Cotler shushed me softly. He held on to me with one hand and wiped his forehead with his hat using the other. His eyes were closed.

"Shit," he said. He held his head high as he surveyed the body and the area one last time.

"We should call your dad," I said, wiping my mouth and purposefully looking away from the body. "Call him from the Exxon. We can wait there." He nodded but did not move. He continued to survey the area, sniffing the wind and looking oddly anticipative. His feet were frozen in their tracks. "Cotler?" He didn't flinch, as if he hadn't heard me. He looked as if he would never move from that spot. "You found him," I said. "You've ended this part of it, at least for his family. You came back, and you found him. Come on."

Without turning he shook his head.

"No," he said. "No, I ain't found him. I found what he done." He turned his gray eyes on me, and I was half amazed to see a faint swell of tears there. And a wicked gleam. "I ain't found him. I'm gonna find him. I'm gonna find him and when I do I'm gonna bury him that way. . ." he pointed back toward the creek, "and ain't nobody, not even you, ever gonna know where he is." He swallowed hard and stomped past me toward the truck.

3

Something in the town broke on the day that Jeremy Bingham was found dead. Something crucial and necessary to the make-up of the community came unglued and was left to rattle and flail in the wet November wind like an old shutter in the week that followed his discovery. Panic and despair were the two new tenants of Belle Ridge, and they swaggered like bikers at a sweethearts dance through the streets and into the homes and businesses. Meetings between people in parking lots and at stores were truncated and suspicious. Children were shuttled about from school to whatever activities still convened and didn't pedal and walk the streets anymore. The evil eye was on the town. The fear had set in.

Jeremy was buried after an extensive autopsy performed by two doctors at our region's state forensics lab in Fairfax County. It determined the cause of death but yielded maddeningly little in terms of physical evidence. One thing was indicative, however, from the examination of the body: Jeremy Bingham and Terrance Hark were more than likely killed and buried by the same person. Belle Ridge had a serial killer on its hands.

4

November 12. The day of Jeremy Bingham's funeral was rain-streaked and miserable as usual. I had fallen asleep afterward, woken by my sister a little before nine. She told me a friend from school had called, no one she knew over the phone, and that he needed me to pick him up at the school at about 9:15. I had no idea who she was talking about but figured she had misheard the person, probably in a hurried rush to call someone else.

Approaching the school in the steady rain, I pulled in not knowing what to expect. *Cotler? No way. He never goes near the school after hours, and besides Susie knows his voice as well as mine. Spencer, maybe; he's often at academic meetings and banquets for the gifted and hard-working. There are none scheduled that I can think of though. Or maybe . . .*

There were no lights on inside the school and only one car in the parking lot. Beside it, his mouth standing open, catching bits of rain in his teeth, stood Vinnie Foust. I followed his gaze, a tortured, ugly look of denial and some kind of blind rage, to the wide, white wall of the school auditorium, behind the clinking, flagless flagpole. On the wall, in some sort of greasy-looking substance, someone had scrawled a message in letters approximately twelve inches high:

VINNIE FOUST AND JOHN RAY WERE RAPED IN THE WOODS BEHIND THIS SCHOOL.

Tendrils of rain rolled quickly down the side of the big wall, running over the letters but not smearing them, and for a few horrified minutes I was sure that the paint was waterproof. It looked thick, pasty. My bowels froze.

My first instinct was to get back in the truck and scream out of sight, leaving Vinnie to watch the wall with that strange, quaking look on his face. Anything seemed better than actually dealing with the situation, thus legitimizing the whole thing and making it real instead of the hideously realistic, garishly convincing nightmare that it surely was. Instead I stepped out of the truck and spoke the first serious words to Vinnie Foust that I had uttered in the better part of a decade.

"Turn your lights off, Vinnie. They're shining right on it." His head whipped around as if he'd just noticed I'd arrived, and I saw clearly the bright gleam in his eyes from tears. Rage? Shame? Fear? I didn't know. All I knew is that he looked worse even than I felt. He avoided my eyes and instead peered past me toward the fields. He got moving, saying nothing as he reached into his car to shut the headlights. He stood leaning on his mother's Camry for support and gaping at the sign. "Who did this?" I asked. My voice was surprisingly strong, and I turned to Vinnie who still would not meet my look.

"How the fuck should I know?" he asked the wall. "Someone called me, talked to my mother. Told me to come here now. Someone called me."

"Who?"

"How the fuck should I know?!" he yelled again, sending rain and spit flying from his lips. He still would not look at me but looked past me as if he were blind and led by the sound of my voice. "How the fuck should I know? But I'm getting out of here, I'll tell you that. Fuck all this. Fuck it all, I'm not staying here."

"We have to get that off there, Vinnie," I said. I had the sensation of being beside myself, watching a stranger control my body. Was this a welcome thing on some level? It couldn't be, but I also knew I wasn't as torn up as he was.

"Fuck you!" Vinnie said, still dangerously close to screaming. His eyes flew everywhere but on me, flashing back and forth to the scrawled words and wincing whenever he saw them.

"Vinnie, Goddamit, we have to clean this off before a cop comes by. I've got rags in my truck. Let's go." He went to move but slumped back against the car and muttered something under his breath. I ignored him, went to the bed of the truck and found a wet, stinking oil rag. I walked over to the wall, still terrified the paint was waterproof, and was relieved beyond words to find that it wasn't. I don't know exactly what the substance was, but it looked as if it was some sort of body paint, rubbed from a solid form like a big, greasy piece of chalk. I rubbed the rag over my name and it quickly smeared away. A few seconds later Vinnie was next to me, erasing his. We split the words below in silence and stood back to make sure the message was totally unreadable. Except for the ghost of some red splotches, it was gone.

"Who was it?" I asked, not bothering to try for eye contact with him.

"You know who it was," he said, barely audible. After a tiny eternity I decided to ask the next question, but he had turned and was stomping back toward the car. I called after him.

"Vinnie, wait. What does he want? For God's sake, it's not going to end with this! Next time we won't get a warning!" Vinnie shook his head and waved his arm back toward me, as if warding me off from behind him. "Vinnie, wait!" I was filled, suddenly, with a burning urge to get it all out. That's where the relief was, I was sure, and although Vinnie was my last choice for commiseration, he was the obvious choice right now. Vinnie, to whom I'd never spoken a serious word since early childhood. Vinnie, who was the only one who could possibly understand. Vinnie, who was apparently stuck for better or worse in the same nightmare I was. This was what I had secretly, desperately, hoped to find. That I was not alone. "Vinnie, please, let's . . ."

He jumped into his mother's car and sped away, not looking back as he tore out of the parking lot. I watched him go with frustration and budding, fresh despair. I threw the rag back into the truck and scattered some cans and other soaked pieces of trash in a childish rage. My silly hopes for relief were gone, gone with Vinnie's refusal to meet me halfway. I was alone. In the dark and the cold, wet rain Vinnie and I were truly, utterly alone.

5

"That wasn't nice," Lon said from behind me as I lit a cigarette and leaned wearily in the doorway of the smoking court. It was the dreary Tuesday afternoon of the next day. Smoking court was empty except for some younger hoods on the other side I didn't know.

He had come up behind me from inside, and in a daze I hadn't heard the door. I hadn't slept or eaten since last night's little chore. Cotler and Steve were at lunch, but I hadn't come up with a decent excuse about my absence the night previous. I jumped when I heard Lon and he shushed me quietly.

"Shhh. You'll draw stares. You don't want people seeing us together. I'm sure of that. Christ, that's as bad as pairing you up with Vincenzo Foust." He lit a cigarette and ran a finger along my shoulder, making my skin crawl. I might have vomited except that I had nothing inside to purge after last night and this morning.

"What wasn't nice?" I asked. The finger paused. "You said that something wasn't nice. What did you mean?"

"Vinnie . . . last night. Not wanting to talk to you after

that important moment you shared." I could feel him smiling, grinning slyly as he pictured the anger and surprise blooming on my face.

"Where were you?" I asked out of the corner of my mouth, as if I were a spy talking to the plant or coat tree behind me.

"I was close by," he said cheerfully, as if relating an interesting factoid to a kindergarten class. "I'm always close by. Closer sometimes than you think. You need to remember that, John. Lon is always close by."

"What the fuck do you want?" I asked. Lon sighed, and lazily ran his finger down my back to my belt line before taking it away.

"I want to straighten out this communication problem that Vinnie has. We need to talk—all of us. That's first on my list."

"Lon," I said in a croak, wiping a tear from my left eye with the heel of my hand. The last of the smoke fell from my hand and I crushed it out absently under foot. I was beyond anger now. "Lon, I don't know what's going on here, but can't you just leave me alone? Leave us alone? I can't . . . I mean I don't know what I did, for you to come after me this way, but please, if—"

"Shut up," he whispered into my ear. And, with polite matter-of-factness, "We'll meet. Soon. You, Vinnie, and me."

"I won't," I said. Lon paused, and cocked his head. "Do you think you know what pain is, John?"

"Yeah, I think I've got an idea." He smiled, turning back to me.

"You don't. But you'll find out if you cross me."

"What do you want, Lon?" A whine.

"I want your soul, and I'll get it. For now, you can do

what I say and stave off disaster, or you can defy me and suffer. There's only one other option."

"Which is?"

"You can kill. Like I told you before. You and Vinnie can make that your pet project for 1985. The two of you together. You can kill me. Or you can kill yourselves. Do one of those things and you'll escape a fate that I don't think you even want to ponder right now. Am I clear?"

"I'm not a killer," I said dejectedly. Lon's smile broadened.

"Wait for my next order. We're going to meet, soon. And by the way, don't tell Steve. I'll be watching, and I'll know." I opened my mouth to say something but Lon turned and left, leaving a plume of smoke to peter out behind him as he blew it out and headed for the door. After a minute or so I realized I was getting wet. I headed indoors, turning over excuses for last night in my mind as I walked slowly toward the cafeteria.

6

The dismal, gray corridor that was November of 1984 was leading me toward suicide. It was a path that presented itself to me slowly, slyly, as the rain fell and the wind blew and all other options seemed to rot softly and fall away in the black hours before dawn. I lay in bed at night, watching water split and run down my window while listening to the sweet, calm sensibility of the idea turn over and over in my mind as 3:00 turned to 4:00 and on to 5:00. It is, they say, a lack of perspective that makes suicide such a dangerously attractive option for adolescents, and perhaps this was my difficulty as well. But for me the idea was not born of revenge, or impulse, or vainglory. It was simply, quietly, the most logical choice given the options, and even today I can appreciate the subtle sense it made at the time.

I began to contemplate the act the night Lon almost made us celebrities on the wall of our high school and found something more and more provocative in the idea as wet, shrouded days slipped by like seconds on a senseless, plodding clock face. It began to seem less ridiculous, then somewhat viable, then downright smart as each night's unrest yielded haltingly and suspiciously toward sleep. What sleep I had was filled with dreams, dreams of flying, freeing myself, opening the tomb that was November and just slipping away. If I smiled at all that month outside of the company of my friends it was only in thinking about that release. The giving in, the going down, the great escape. I was on my way.

7

The first rumblings of impatience toward the sheriff came from a neighborhood organizer named John Olving. Olving, like Jim Kelly, loomed large in civic groups, little league, and select soccer. He had run unsuccessfully for a county Board of Supervisors position once before, but he was young, with a family, making a decent living, and expected to run again.

Not long after Jeremy Bingham's funeral, Olving, the parents of Terrance Hark, and several other families convened at the Methodist Church in town to confront the sheriff on how the investigation was being run. Sheriff Cotler, looking drained but composed, appeared with his contact from the state police and patiently answered questions about what was being done and why. What about roving patrols, they wanted to know. Sheriff Cotler asked what they meant. Deputizing enough men to walk through the town and the woods around it day and night, armed if necessary, and looking for signs of trouble, they explained. The sheriff replied that he had already organized several watch groups to patrol parks, schools, and playing fields to see to it that children were supervised at all times by someone, if not their own parents. He had increased police presence all over the town, especially at points near the woods. He had sent his men down the dozens of trails and pathways that a generation of children had carved through the woods, and had investigated fire pits, campsites, crumbling houses, and shacks that had been left to rot out there from time to time.

Not good enough, Olving said. He wanted armed patrols, an impenetrable "wire" around the town that would intimidate anyone who ventured in unwelcome, especially if they came by way of the woods. Especially at night. Cotler and his state contact disagreed. His men were the only armed people on patrol right now, and he liked it that way. He was stretching his resources as it was; some of the deputies were pulling patrols on their own time. But armed, roving groups, he said, were not the answer. Olving responded that, as free citizens, he and men like him could wear weapons in plain view and walk wherever they wanted to walk. The sheriff pleaded with the group to consider the safety of his own men and each other if they went around toting guns in the middle of the night on badly marked trails, but to little avail. Olving's idea caught on quickly, and his group grew from five men the first week to almost twenty by the middle of December.

The sheriff took what action he could to counter the designs of John Olving and his crew. He warned his own deputies about the possibility of armed men walking around in the dark in the woods and ordered a zero-tolerance policy for weapons violations. As an avid gun owner and hunter himself, he told the local press, he would not attempt to trample the rights of fellow townspeople to arm themselves legally. But he wouldn't put up with brandishing, illegal weapons, or reckless discharge either.

Olving looked for press as well and didn't have to look far. We received write-ups in militia magazines, crackpot newsletters, and some legitimate sources as well. Belle Ridge was the town where unafraid men and women were standing up to protect their children. News of the controversy spread quickly, and the eyes of the region watched us and our leaders with growing interest.

Sheriff Cotler did one final thing as the month ended and the Olving gang began in earnest: He attempted to prevent the kind of shot-in-the-dark situation he feared most tellingly from Olving's men. He warned the drifters, drunks, and loners he was familiar with who wandered around the town and the woods not to rattle around at night as they were accustomed. One of the men he spoke to was Marcus Wilham, the old drunk who had found Terrance Hark's body. A few were Latino laborers who worked on various construction projects happening on the outskirts of town. The sheriff talked directly to their foremen or brought an interpreter. The rest of the men he spoke with had homes in town or trailers nearby but were simply unemployable and spent most of their days asleep and their nights walking from place to place. One of them was Armand Lillington.

8

Wednesday, November 21. Opening my locker that afternoon, I found a plain white piece of paper with two sentences written on it: *First Meeting is tonight—9:30 off Copperhead Road. Go in by the middle school, watch for the fire on the right, and come alone.*

Vinnie must have gotten a similar invitation, because his mother's Camry was parked near the corner in the middle school parking lot bordering the woods when I pulled in at 9:25 that evening. He was poised to enter the trees when I stepped out of my truck. He looked at me briefly, then turned and headed down the trail. I caught up with him unhurriedly and walked a pace or two behind. After about five minutes of walking I couldn't take the silence any longer and mumbled something in greeting. He ignored me and kept walking. I walked up beside him.

"What's the use in not speaking to me, Vinnie?" He stepped up his pace and remained silent. He was crying, or had been, and when he saw that I noticed he tried to pass it off as a runny nose. "Say something, for Christ's sake. What sense does it make to—"

"Fuck you, faggot," he said under his breath. "How about that?" I faced off in front of him on the trail and blocked his way.

"Don't you ever call me that again, goddam you. I'm utterly serious. Are you better than me?" Vinnie eyed me savagely from behind his coat sleeve. It was the first time he'd looked directly at me in years. I don't know if I'd ever seen concentrated insanity before that, but I knew instinctively I was seeing it there.

"I got out," he said, hissed really. "You stayed in. You didn't have to stay in. You stayed in, and you let that fucker do all those things to you over and over. I think I know why, too, I think—"

Lon's fist connected with the back of Vinnie's head and sent him sprawling. How he had gotten behind us I don't know, but he seemed to appear out of the mist. Vinnie rolled over and looked up helplessly at Lon. I stood aside, mouth open.

"No insults will be hurled at each other," he said to the both of us. "That's my job." And as if to confirm that, Lon looked over at me. "No idle threats, either. Got that, faggot? Now, real threats—those you may actually carry out—are fine, as are the acts themselves. Anything can happen at one of these meetings, and I wouldn't be surprised or disappointed if one of them ended with two or more of us dead. That's all fine. But idle bullshit, macho talk, no sir. Say what you mean, mean what you say. And back it up. Now get the fuck up, Vinnie. Move."

We followed Lon further into the woods. Vinnie's eyes darted everywhere, and he jumped at every sound. He wiped his face constantly with the heel of his hand, a gesture I remembered vividly from our childhood together. We finally came to a small clearing with several crates and a dirty, much-used fire pit in the center. A mud-streaked black tarp protected a cache of dry firewood and Lon fished some out as he dug in his pockets for matches.

As he ordered us to sit down, I noticed something unsettling. He had a camera, a small but expensive looking 35mm camera half out of a black leather bag beside the stump where he would sit. The camera looked like it had been deposited there hastily, as if it had just been used.

I looked over to see if Vinnie had noticed it, but he was staring ahead motionless and would not look my way, even when Lon was faced away from us.

The two of us sat like stones while he lit a fire. I had seen Cotler light a thousand campfires and I was highly impressed with Lon's ability. It was obvious from watching him that he was no stranger to this kind of life, and I wondered what that said about where he had lived or was living. Firelight played on his handsome face as he bent over the pit. He sat down opposite us and smiled.

"Suppose I had a gun and asked each of you to suck my dick. What would you do?" Vinnie and I stared at him and said nothing. It was to be torture then? Is that what?

"I'd tell you to kill me," Vinnie said finally, half aloud. Lon deftly but quietly leapt to his feet.

"You're a liar," he said smiling. He pulled a medium-sized black pistol from his belt. It had been hidden under his army jacket. He pointed it straight at Vinnie's face. He walked over to Vinnie and stopped when his crotch was eye level with the smaller boy, keeping the gun trained on his face. "Vinnie," he said softer, "pull down that zipper there, pull out my cock, and suck. Now."

Vinnie's face began to tremble, slightly at first, gathering force, as if he were having a small seizure. His beady eyes were wide, round, and he stared at Lon's crotch in front of him as if it were death's door. He took in a ragged breath to speak.

"Th-th-they'll h-h-hear you," he said, gasping. Unsmiling, Lon pulled back the hammer on the gun.

"I know where I am and I know where they are. I'll obliterate your face and bury you out here. Make your choice."

I sat beside the two of them, wondering if I would see

Vinnie die, or if I would see Vinnie perform a sex act on Lon. The choice in viewing was less than appetizing. And then, I knew, it would be my turn. I wished, more than anything, that I could be back at home, in front of the medicine cabinet, starting the process of dying and lying down in my cool, dark room. That was an end that I could deal with. I had been a fool to come out here, I knew. I had been a fool to even contemplate surviving this . . . whatever it was.

Vinnie was slowly unzipping Lon's jeans. Lon grunted and moved closer to him, placing the gun on top of Vinnie's head. Vinnie's eyes were blank, expressionless, and I thought, *He's not far. He's not far from losing his mind in a vomitous explosion from his head.* Lon placed his gunless hand behind Vinnie's head, gripping the back of his neck. I turned away but Lon directed me with the pistol to watch.

Vinnie produced Lon's penis with his right hand and regarded it blankly. "It's not hard," Lon said roughly. "Make it hard." Slowly, Vinnie began to stroke him, still wearing a mask for a face. I noticed the clean path of a tear on the side of his face. Vinnie opened his mouth and moved closer to him.

Lon's gunless hand gripped hair on the back of Vinnie's head and pulled it back, kicking him off of the crate with his left foot onto the ground. He chuckled as he worked himself back into his pants, zipping up and regarding Vinnie triumphantly. Vinnie lay on the ground in a shaking, sobbing mass.

"Get up, you pussy," Lon said tiredly. He looked at me as I cast my eyes to the ground. *Pills,* I thought. *Lots and lots of pills.* I had promised myself I would say nothing, no matter what Vinnie ended up doing, but I couldn't help myself.

"Why would you do . . . a thing like that . . . to us?" I

asked chokingly. "To anyone? Why on earth would you do that?" He looked over at me coldly.

"Jesus Fucking Christ, John, what does 'why' mean? I can't believe that after all you've been through you're still asking *why*. The why's of this world rank right up there in relevance to the consistency of dog shit in healthy hounds. Haven't you learned that, yet? 'Why' is bullshit. *Why* did I threaten to make Vinnie suck my dick? Because he was there. And it proved a point, didn't it, Vin? It proved that he'll do it. Because he has done it. And it's just not as difficult as we might tell others. Not for me, and not for either of you. Maybe next time I won't stop him. Maybe next time it'll be you." Lon noticed something. It was Vinnie, crawling ever so slowly toward the darkness of the woods beyond the fire. Lon called over to him.

"If you leave this circle, I'll hunt you down like a dog. If I don't find you tonight, I'll find you tomorrow. Get back here." Vinnie stopped in mid-crawl, paused for a moment, and then did as he was told.

"Why don't you just kill us now and get it over with?" he asked when he had returned to his seat.

"There's that fucking 'why' again. Shut up, Vinnie. Shut up and speak when you're spoken to." Then he turned to me. "John, how old were you when Kelly first introduced you to the thing called 'love?'"

"Six," I answered robotically. Lon nodded.

"Tell us about it. Tell us everything you remember."

***

Russet brown. That, my father says, is the color of the truck that Kelly drives. Cotler, me, Vic, Vinnie, and two other boys, one I think I remember as Vernon, will soon climb in the back and Kelly will drive us out to a place in the woods where he will show us how to recognize poison ivy, tie simple knots, and build our first campfire. This is our third outing with Kelly, and he has promised us a meal prepared completely in the woods, no brown bags of any kind, for our satisfactory performance so far. Our fathers laugh and joke with Big Jim as the boys mill about excitedly around Kelly's yard and work shed. One of the other men helps Kelly load a cooler into his cab, and then one by one the fathers of the boys climb into large sedans and honk their horns as they pull away. Kelly waves at each departing father, his wave a sharp, gentlemanly chop of the hand in mid-air. He wears jeans, a large flannel overshirt, and scarred boots. It is a cool, dry Saturday morning in late May of 1973.

My father and Cotler's father call us over and hunker down, reminding us to mind Big Jim and to be careful. Cotler's father, a giant to me in his gray trooper's uniform, winks at us and tells us that if we see some pretty flowers out there we might do well to pick them for our mamas. We nod solemnly as Cotler tugs me over to the truck, shouting excitedly about getting to the woods.

Our fathers leave, waving as they back out in Dan Cotler's state cruiser in a cloud of dust. The six of us line up to pile into the bed of the truck where Kelly has put some sleeping bags and old couch pillows for us to sit on. Kelly lifts each of us up and places us in the bed where we scramble for seats. I am at the back of the line. Kelly lifts Cotler first, who goes to the back passenger corner of the truck and saves me a seat. Then Vic, whose oversized head and thin, wiry frame make him look prematurely angry and impish. He smiles devilishly, looking for something in the truck that he can throw, either out at a passing car, or at anyone but Cotler. Vinnie Foust is next, looking confused, clownish, and sad in large glasses and a grossly striped sweatshirt. Then Vernon, then another boy whose name I may never have known, and then Kelly is lifting me up. I feel his hand in the seat of my pants and think nothing of it as I am lifted in the air. Then, curiously, I feel him grip my buttocks, running a big hand down toward the back of my crotch as he sets me up in the truck bed. I feel a strange, giddy sensation, as if I'd seen my mother without clothes on. Kelly pats my butt and I move forward, taking my prized seat beside Cotler. Then we are on the road, laughing and shouting at the wind in our hair and the trappings of our hometown speeding by in slippery movement to the left and right.

After cleaning up from our afternoon meal, Jim announces a scavenger hunt. He describes several items that he's hidden around us—colored stones, small toys, bags of candy—and divides us into teams to look for them. He strictly sets the perimeters for where we should look for these items and has us pick a buddy. While I expect to join Cotler, Kelly whispers that he and I will be partners, and he sends Cotler off with Vernon.

Kelly and I walk up to a bluff where he can view most of the boys as they hunt for their treasures in the thin patch of woods. We come to a tree and Kelly tells me to sit down. He looks over the area, scanning for the other boys. Then he sits down and lets his big hand rest on my thigh.

"Wanna be pals?" he asks me. I nod and wait for instruction on exactly what that will entail. I am not afraid. As of yet I have no reason to be. Kelly's big hand runs slowly up and down my thigh, and his eyes seem to play over my small frame in a way that is curious, but as yet not alarming. He motions to Vic and Vinnie, searching for stones in the creek that is below and to the left of us, and I look over to where they are. When I look back I notice that Kelly has undone his pants. All I can see of his anatomy, though, is a tuft of hair where his jeans would normally cover his crotch.

"It's okay," he says softly, and his voice is breathy and low. "It's okay. We're pals. Just you and me. I can't trust the other boys with bein' pals, not even Francis. You understand?" I nod, buoyant and happy to be in Kelly's trust. He smiles briefly, and I notice that he is sweating. Slowly, he takes my hand and puts it on his crotch. My small hand rests lightly over this area and I can feel the heat of his body rising toward it. Now I hesitate. Something is wrong. Something feels funny, like when he was lifting me into the truck.

Kelly seems to sense this hesitation, this unease, and he says again, "It's okay, Johnny. Just . . . let your hand fall there. Just let it fall." I lower my hand, and it comes to rest against Kelly's now erect penis. I pull back—suspicious and afraid. Kelly, aroused and breathing heavily, seizes my hand and presses it against his own flesh. He places his other arm around me and pulls me to him. Panic, a new, terrifying emotion, springs up inside of me. "It's okay, goddamit," he is saying. "Just stroke it. It's okay." With his own hand he presses mine against him and forces me to stroke him. I begin to cry and Kelly simply looks around him and seems not to notice. "It's okay," is all he will say as his breathing grows heavier and heavier. He looms over me and wants to watch my hand do the work. Finally he climaxes, and rolls over on top of me. I feel a sticky wetness and smell sweat and cloth. I am seized now with wild fear. Kelly covers me with his immense size, and stays on top of me until I am quiet. After what seems like an eternity he lifts himself up, brushes me off, and puts his face very close to mine.

***

"We're pals, okay, John?" I nod, but I cannot look at him. He seizes my chin in his hand and forces me to look into his eyes. This is a moment I will never forget, and see it in dreams many nights of my life. His eyes are cold, blue and lifeless. Even at six, I can see that they are different eyes from the sleepy but sharp, confident but subdued ones that he uses to look at the land around us, the road in front of us, or the group of us together. These eyes are staring, strange, and overly focused. "We're pals, and pals don't tell on each other. Do you understand?" I nod again, more forcefully. He gently places his hand on my own crotch. "I'll hurt you down there, if you tell. I don't want to, but I will. Do you understand?" A small trickle of urine escapes into my underwear and I nod, tears swelling in my eyes. "It's okay," he says. "We're pals. I won't hurt you 'cause you won't tell, will you John?" I shake my head, unable to speak. "That's right. We just been pals, today. That's all. No one's gonna know. No one. That right?" I nod. "Tell me," he says. "Say it." I cannot, and Kelly places the hand again in my lap, this time less gently. "Say it, John. I need to hear you say it, or I won't know for sure." I open my mouth to speak, and nothing comes out. I try again and finally can utter something.

"I won't," I say, shaking my head and gaping at him. Behind him a fat, furry squirrel races down the tree, regards us plaintively for a moment, and heads off for the brush beyond. I feel suddenly naked and ashamed as the squirrel's flat, black eyes seem to flick my way.

"You won't what?"

"I won't tell. I won't. I promise." Finally Kelly nods, and smiles. He grips my crotch for a split second, and I am terrified as his fingers close around me down there. He loosens his grip and removes his hand, patting me on the back.

"Good, Johnny. That's good. Let's go, okay, pal?" He helps me up and I walk silently with him toward our campsite. The sounds of the woods which enamored and fascinated me just minutes before are now mute. The trees, shadows, rocks, animals, and birds now melt and fade into a gray field before me. I see nothing but Kelly in front of me, and feel nothing but a cold, gray emptiness that I have no words for and no understanding of. The other boys, when they return from the hunt, show me their treasures and I nod blankly. Cotler looks closer and asks if I have a tummy ache. I shake my head and force a smile, a novice at a lifelong art. Kelly's eyes are on me often for the rest of the outing and I watch my actions closely. Soon the smiling is easier and I find that, if I really try, I can sort of forget what happened today. I can put it in a bad place I don't think about, and not go there. I attempt to do this with more success as we clean and pack and head for home. I am happy that I do not think of the events of the day as we rush to meet our fathers, waiting for us as Jim's truck pulls onto his property.

***

Lon sat silently through my story and Vinnie's, which was strikingly similar, except that Vinnie's first encounter had been at a little league outing, and from what Vinnie had said, Kelly had been building up to it with strange comments and occasional caresses for quite a while. Why he moved faster in my case, and why he was borderline violent with both of us, I never knew. Most of the time, I would learn much later, guys like Kelly "groomed" their victims for some time and did not start out with threats or force. But in our cases, at least, he had chosen us quickly and wasted little time getting what he wanted.

Neither recounting had ever been spoken aloud. Lon seemed oblivious to the weight of the event for the two of us. I imagine Vinnie felt as I did as he spoke woodenly from the darkest corners of his past. Out here we were again six. We were small, weak, and scared. Lon was letting the fire die down as Vinnie finished. He sat back and gave us both an oddly sympathetic look.

"Neither of you told anyone," he said. "Why do you think that is, Johnny?"

"He threatened me, for one thing. I didn't know if he meant it or not."

"He did," Lon said, smiling slightly and looking at his cigarette. "He did." Vinnie licked his lips.

"Are you gonna . . . leave us alone now?" he asked. Lon looked over at him, the same plaintive, gentle look on his face.

"No."

"What then? What do we have to do?" I asked.

"What I say to do," he said softly. His face was darkening in the fading light of the fire and he looked like handsome evil in its red reflection. "Just exactly what I say to do."

"Why?" Vinnie asked, wincing as soon as he's spoken. He was trying hard to keep the whine out of his voice, and failing for the most part. "Why are you doing this?" Above us the rain was beginning again in earnest, and Lon stood up and pulled his jacket around him tighter.

"I'm not sure myself," he said, looking toward the trees. The rain, now intensifying, hissed in the wet woods around us. "We're going to find that out." Lon kicked some dirt on what was left of the coals and ground it in with one old boot as he dismissed us. "Good night, boys. I suggest you walk together on the way back. There are bad things out here now. Bad, bad things."

9

I sat in my truck for several minutes after leaving Vinnie silently at the end of the trail that led to Copperhead Road, and I contemplated the end of my life. It wouldn't be hard to accomplish; I already had a method in mind. I nurtured the plan as it took shape, going from a vague possibility to something much more concrete. The exercise was a neat escape from Lon, and Kelly, and the nightmare of the past that was now an even blacker nightmare of the present. There was control in it, and release. My thinking was narrow and surprisingly selfish. If Lon wanted to punish me explicitly for being in the wrong place at the wrong time, then I would cheat him by simply doing what he dared me to do—beating him to the end. My only concern for my family was with regard to sparing them whatever pain I could with finding and having to dispose of me. Vic's older brother Marty had been found in the woods by stoner kids skipping school.

I pulled into the 7-11 on Chapel Road, realizing I was out of cigarettes. Smiling was coming easier now. In my mind I could see a door, an escape route, and I was almost ready to use it. The guy behind the counter at the 7-11 we had nicknamed Moose because of his spooky resemblance to the cartoon character. He nodded to me as he rang up my purchase, and I nodded back, still smiling. I thanked him and walked out into the rain. Vic was emerging from his car.

"Hey," he said, coming over to me and squinting at the droplets. "Where the fuck've you been?"

"I was out," I said with an evasive shrug. "Everything okay?"

"Yeah, I guess. What about you?"

"I'm fine. Why?" Vic looked at me closely. He was not yet under the overhang of the store and raindrops he seemed not to notice fell on his runner's nylon jacket and sweats. Behind him, the black surface of the store's parking lot gleamed in streaks as water ran down to the street.

"You don't look right. You sick or something?"

"Not that I know of."

"You got a weird look, Johnny. Weird." His eyes seemed to search mine for something, a trait that Vic normally did not employ. There was nothing subtle or sly about it. Vic wasn't capable of that. I began to recoil. This was not part of the plan, being figured out by the least perceptive of my friends.

"I'm okay, Vic. Really. I'm tired, that's all." He cocked his head and looked at me a moment longer.

"All right. Get some rest, okay?"

"That's where I'm going. See you in the morning." He nodded and watched me as I backed out and pulled onto the road, leaving him in the rain among discarded cups and cigarette butts and the sloping, black surface of the lot.

10

November 23. Friday afternoon after school I crawled upstairs and slept. At seven I got up and packed a few things into a gym bag. I stood in front of the medicine cabinet and counted bottles. I was a pharmacist's son, and I knew what was in there and could kill me in what combinations, and at what intervals. My parents and my sister were gone, Susie to a friend's house for the weekend and my parents to dinner somewhere with the neighbors.

I shut the mirrored door to the medicine cabinet and went downstairs to the liquor cabinet. I examined what I might need in there and sat down at the dinner table with a pad and pencil. It was time to decide where, when, and how, and then to decide what, if anything, I would tell those around me. I was in a rhythm, a wind down. It was automatic. Simple.

The phone rang.

"Johnny?" It was Steve. I had a giddy sensation, as if I'd been pulled up from a dive with no notice.

"Hey. What's up?"

"Not a lot. Everything cool?" I stammered for a second.

"Sure, why?"

"No reason. Just wanted to see how you were."

"Oh. Yeah, I'm good, thanks. You going out tonight?"

"Not sure," he said. "There's a chick from my old job I'm supposed to call, but I haven't yet. She's the type you've gotta be in the mood for." He remained silent for a second. "Call me later, though, if you're up and want to talk. If I'm here I'll shoot over."

"Oh. Okay. Yeah, thanks." I hung up the phone and sat back down. I looked at the pad, and at my car keys on the table. I looked outside at the wet, gray darkness beyond the kitchen window. In front of the window was a four-colored "sun-catcher" I had made for my mother in a day camp the summer Cotler and I were eight. The panes of the sun catcher were too dark and hopelessly smudged by glue, but it had hung there for almost ten years, not catching any sun.

Tell Steve.

It was a jolt. Like I'd been slapped. This thought came to me suddenly and was gone in a flash, but in combination with the phone call it had severed the clock-like motions I'd been going through that evening, and frankly for most of that week. The feeling was strong—strong enough to make my heart pound in my ears. It seemed oddly external.

I wandered aimlessly throughout the house, developing an increasingly large headache as this new possibility gnawed into my consciousness and ate away at the things that were already in place. The feeling was not a good one. This new idea was a hulking, threatening thing that whispered of hope while reeking of deeper disaster.

There was a way out, my other voice mocked, and I was merely wasting time and a good weekend in which to do it by putting it off with these silly notions. Childish it was, this other choice. Surely that was true. I looked again at the sun-catcher, watching it twist slowly under its coat of dust.

Suicide. Tell Steve.

So this was it? When life had become its most inextricably complicated, the choices I had to deal with would be that simple? Telling Steve, I supposed, meant hoping somehow he could help. At first glance this seemed immensely unrealistic and it meant telling—telling everything—to him. It meant opening the circle for the very first time.

I walked upstairs to the medicine cabinet and stood in front of it, opening and closing the door. Benign and yellowing plastic pill bottles twitched as I opened and shut it, again and again. Suicide was temptingly easy. It could be done with complete stealth, out in my truck somewhere combining liquor, medicine, and cigarettes in an increasingly heavy blur. A unilateral event. No long rehearsals about how I would broach this subject with Steve. No awkward build-up, no terrible moment, wondering how the story would come out, let alone how it would be taken. No fearful test of friendship that maybe no one was up to anyway. Suicide was easier. Take the pills until you can't get up anymore and then just drift off to dream. Privacy. Then nothingness. Nothing to worry about really, at all.

Unless I was wrong about some things.

After some time in the bathroom, I went downstairs to call Steve. That haunted-sounding Eurythmics song "Here Comes the Rain Again" was on in the kitchen, a gift from a bored DJ commenting on the weather. I picked up the phone. It was 8:00.

"Still got someone lined up for tonight?" I asked. My heart pounded. I had decided to let fate take a hand. If Steve could talk, then maybe I'd talk too. If not, I'd let the pills do the talking. My head felt like it was swimming. A warm, demonic voice reminded me that Option Two, Plan B, the Doomsday Weapon, was always ready to be executed if this didn't pan out. If I lost my nerve. That voice was familiar. It was Lon's.

"No one I can't have tomorrow night. Whaddaya wanna do?"

"Talk," I said, "if that's okay."

"What do we do better? Yeah, that's fine. Ready anytime."

"See you in a few," I said. "Thanks, brother."

***

I picked him up, thankful to be driving for some reason, and we headed out through the county, out to roads Cotler had shown me that I remembered only vaguely, farther out to roads even he didn't cruise very often, and then finally to the highway that bypasses our county seat. I picked up Route 9 and headed up toward Harper's Ferry while Steve and I discussed girls, school, and a host of other light topics. The Virginia countryside was wet, dark, and utterly empty along Route 9 except for an occasional lonely vehicle like ours.

I reached Route 340 and headed west along the Potomac River, which geographically shapes our county along the top of the state, to where it meets the Shenandoah, Maryland, and West Virginia. At this convergence was Harper's Ferry, where John Brown forfeited his life for his participation in a slave revolt. When we reached the town, I pulled over at a favorite picnic spot of my family and Cotler's from our childhood. The spot was a small grassy area just outside the main touristy part of town, and it sat beside an active train track and the river beyond it. The tracks led to a trestle and eventually crossed the Potomac and Shenandoah on into Maryland just a hundred yards or so from the road.

"So, what's been on your mind?" Steve asked, drawing heavily on a cigarette as we walked along the tracks. The night air was wet, but there was little wind and we were comfortable in jackets. "Long way to go just to BS, not that I care."

I took a deep breath and blew slowly outward as tides of emotion and memory collided in my head. I had a sensation of breaking open, spilling forth like a fallen coconut.

We reached the beginning of the trestle and I perched on a beam, looking at Steve directly. The thousand opening lines I had rehearsed for this moment fell away like stones from a scarred hillside, and my voice sounded alien as I began.

"Do you know who Jim Kelly is?" I asked. Steve nodded slowly.

"That redneck who coaches all the teams and has a gun shop on Chapel?" I nodded and breathed deep. The world swam.

"He molested me when I was six years old. He did it every chance he had until I was about twelve and I could stay away from him. Truth is, he raped me." I started to shake, uncontrollably, and could barely light a cigarette as I grasped the beam for support. Steve stood speechless before me, his black hair lifting in the breeze.

"Are you okay?" he asked finally. I nodded and leaned over my knees to catch my breath. A whistle sounded, and we saw the light from the train, approaching us from the Maryland side.

"He did it the first time when Cotler and I were camping with him. He . . . sent Cotler with another kid someplace and told me he wanted to 'be pals' for a while. I was thrilled that he wanted to spend some time with me. I was always so jealous of Cotler for getting his favor so much. Get on this side, the train's coming."

Steve did as I told and we backed up a safe distance from the passing train. When it roared by, it filled up the world with black iron-and-steel wheels. We watched it silently until the last car had passed, its blinking magenta end light glowing softly in the gloom. After it passed I told Steve everything, everything but the nasty details, anyway, until I felt as if I'd vomited a day's worth of carnival junk food after a wild ride. I told him about the old days and what I suspected might be the resurrection of Lon. I told him about the prank at the school, what Lon had been making us do, and what I suspected he had in mind for us to do before it was all over. The only things I left out were my suicide plans, and my suspicions of Lon's connection to the murders. Those things, I figured, needed to wait.

Steve listened expressionlessly for the most part, not even nodding or 'hmm'-ing as he usually did when listening to someone. I wondered a few times if he was still listening, or if he had tuned me out either as a fantastic liar or an attention-seeking child. Was it a mistake? Had I said all of this just to be looked at sideways? Would I be humored by the charming, amiable Steve Drillas? And now it was out, all of it, spilled out on the ground like rotten beer at the bottom of a trash barrel. Lon's voice again: *don't mean to say I told you so, but...*

"Who is Lon, then?" Steve asked. I looked at him closely. His eyes were clear, bright, interested. He looked fascinated—horrified, maybe. But not incredulous. A moment of relief.

"That's the big question. I don't know, but something came to me the other night. Obviously he's someone who was involved in this, somehow. He's someone who knows what happened to us. As far as I can remember, there were six kids in our group, the group that started going out with Kelly at about the same time. Cotler, me, Vinnie Foust, a kid named Vernon, I think. For a while Vic went, too. And there was another kid I can't remember. I've lost his face somewhere over the years, and his name, but . . . it's probably my own mind making it all up, but that's who I think Lon may be. The name is sticking with me.

You don't hear a name like Lon all the time. I don't know what happened to Vernon. He moved before we got into middle school. Lon, if that was his name, disappeared too. I never saw him after a couple of summers had gone by. Vinnie and I were the ones who got the brunt of it, I guess." With this last sentence I was suddenly overcome with a deep sadness, an almost sentimental feeling. I leaned over and waited for it to pass. Tears stung my eyes and I wiped them away.

Silently, Steve lit two cigarettes and handed one to me when I righted myself. I nodded thanks and gazed out over the river. Lights on the Maryland side twinkled in whites and yellows through the trees.

"But Lon is living with Kelly, isn't he?"

"Sort of. I don't know if anyone's ever been sure where he really lives. Kelly sponsored him for enrollment at school and that's his official address. I still don't know where he came from. Even if Lon is this kid from before, I barely knew him. I can barely remember what he looked like. We talked, once or twice, as a group. I remember that. I can remember talking about what Jim was doing to us, but it was once, maybe twice. Vinnie and I talked about it more often, but he was gone from the group by the time we were nine or ten."

"What about Vinnie? He have any ideas?"

"Vinnie and I don't talk much. Not now and not then. We had one conversation before he stopped going out with us. I guess we were going into fifth grade when he told me he had read somewhere about what Kelly liked to do to us. He told me it was bad, and that it could make us sick. He said he was quitting the group, and that I should, too. I remember yelling at him, saying that he *should* quit, no one liked him anyway. God, I was so fucking scared.

He started to scream, telling me that we were becoming faggots. I didn't know what that was, but I could guess."

I had gone through the last cigarette in about three minutes, and Steve lit me another. I was crashing now, sweat was breaking out on my brow and over my lips, and I couldn't stop the flow of words. At this point I would have told anyone the story without stopping. My mouth raced to shove sentences through to the surface as fast as my mind could manufacture them. Steve stood by, the light wind in his hair, and looked me with something like heavily guarded wonder. I rambled headlong.

"I didn't know what to say to him. I couldn't get out. Cotler was still going, and I couldn't, I mean, I couldn't find a way *not* to go." I looked slowly up at Steve as my lower lip quivered and the spit there shone in the pale light of the trestle lamps. A great truth had just come forward, stinking of the time it had been buried beneath. "I was trapped. Cotler was still going, and I couldn't find a way not to go with him. He wanted me to go, and I couldn't stay away. It took me three more years, *three more*." A scream that was more of a loud retch escaped me and I turned and threw up over the side of the trestle. There wasn't much to get rid of, but I retched anyway, screams tearing through the retching until I was hoarse. The screams echoed across the river, traveling through the night like shrieking wind over the water. I pounded my fists against the trestle and cried. Steve waited behind me until I was finished. He had another cigarette waiting when I finally turned back to him. I took it, wiping my mouth and my eyes.

"Cotler didn't know," he said. I shook my head.

"How could he have? This stuff, Cotler can't even picture it."

"So I guess . . . you never told him?"

"Would you?" Steve looked at me levelly and shook his head.

"Stupid question. I'm sorry."

"Kelly was Cotler's absolute hero growing up. He still is. Cotler loves his father; he admires his father. He loves me. But Cotler wants to be Jim Kelly. He always has."

"What do think he'd do if you told him this?" Steve asked. I pondered the question for the ten thousandth time and answered as I always had myself.

"I don't think he'd believe me."

***

"Do you feel better, having told me?" Steve asked as we made our way toward the car. Not the question I expected, but I answered honestly.

"Yeah. Much better, actually. I should have done something like this a long time ago. There was no one to tell, I guess."

"Spencer?"

"I couldn't. I don't know why. I trust him, I just couldn't find the words. And there was no reason to tell anyone, then. It didn't . . . come back like it has until that fucking asshole reappeared like a ghost. Mostly I just didn't think about it. I figured I'd get away with that forever."

On the way back, Steve said very little as he had done all night, but his reticence didn't bother me as much now. It was as if he knew it was somehow proper to keep quiet in the face of such a monumental confession. And he believed me. It was in his eyes, and that was a godsend. As I drove home, I pictured the medicine cabinet again and shivered. It was not unimaginable for me to kill myself, not by a long shot yet, but it was not an idea I was dreamily stuck on anymore, either. Maybe that, at bottom, is why I was so grateful to Steve for reacting the way he did. A favorite expression of my mother's came back to me: *Joy shared is doubled. Sorrow shared is halved.* True, I suppose, but the joy part is easy. The sorrow-halving thing comes about because someone is willing to help bear the load. That was Steve on that November night. I had offered him a sagging, stinking load to help me carry, and he was shouldering it, slowly, deliberately, and with quiet contemplation as it settled over him.

"What do you want to do about Lon?" he asked as we neared the Ridge. I turned and looked at him in the gloom of the cab, and his face was expressionless.

"Honestly?"

"We've been pretty God-damned honest so far."

"I'd like to kill Lon. Because I think he's killing me."

"What if it came to that?" he asked, his face still a mask.

"Came to what, killing Lon? *Killing* him? I'm not a murderer.

"They don't call it murder when it's in self-defense."

"There's been enough killing around here," I said. Steve nodded.

"True . . . true. But killing can be random and meaningless, or it can be tactical and worth something. I'm not saying I'm up to it either, man. I just don't think this fuckhead is playing games. And if he is, he's playing a man's game. He should know he could get hurt."

"He mentioned that to me," I said. "Sort of. He said killing him was an option I had in dealing with all this. He said Vinnie and I could do it together."

"Jesus, Vinnie. I forgot about him. How's he taking all of this, anyway?"

"Not well. But I wouldn't hold my breath waiting for Vinnie to stand up for himself anytime soon. Not against Lon."

"I guess not," Steve said softly. I pulled up to his house and put the truck in park. There was an interesting shine in his eyes, how much of it showmanship I didn't know, but still I thought, *murder shared is halved.*

"Look, thanks," I said. "I don't know what else to say, I just hope that this doesn't . . . change things between us. I . . . took a chance, telling you this stuff, I guess." Steve looked directly at me with the masklike face again. "What you told me never leaves this truck," he said. "Not until you decide it does, if ever. And don't be thinking you're some weirdo in my eyes. What the fuck do I care what some shit did to you when you were little, except how you feel about it? I'm glad you feel a little better, that's all."

"I do."

"Good. You're gonna be all right, then, tonight?"

"Yeah, I think so."

"Not gonna kill yourself, are ya?"

"No," I said, hiding a grin. "No, I'm not."

<h1 style="text-align:center">11</h1>

Wednesday, November 28. "Sit down, it's good to see you one-on-one again," Coach Bonner said to me as the last of our class streamed out of the classroom at the end of the day.

"Thanks, Coach," I said. "I won't keep you."

"Think nothing of it. The room's quiet. I can concentrate on one person rather than twenty-five. What's up?" I shifted in my chair and waited until the foot traffic outside had thinned to silence. "It's Lon Chambers. I . . . I don't know if you can talk to me about him. I'll understand if you can't." Bonner put his hands on his knees and leaned forward. "He's bothering you, isn't he?"

"Well, yes. Yes, sir, he is." He nodded at this.

"I had a feeling. I went as far as to ask Cotler if the two of you knew each other; this was a couple of months ago. He did seem to study you quite a bit. I'm sorry I didn't ask you directly. I was just curious at the time I asked Cotler. It didn't seem like anything important."

"Cotler told me," I said. "I didn't think it was either. But it's gotten . . . well, weird between us."

"Has he hurt you?"

"Physically, no."

"Okay. He's threatened you, then?"

"Yes, in a sense. To be honest there are some details about this that I'd rather not talk about, right now anyway. Is that okay, or am I wasting your time?"

"Not at all. Tell me what you wish to tell me, and I'll respond as intelligently as I can. Take your time."

I looked at my teacher for a moment, his curly dark hair and mustache, the khaki sport coat and knit tie—and fleetingly considered telling him everything. His eyes were caring and focused. His features were set kindly, and his entire face was directed totally toward me. It seemed to glow with sincerity.

"I don't know where Lon is from," I said, beginning this as carefully as I could, "or how he got here. He seems to know me, but I don't know how. I'm not asking you to intervene in what's going on between him and me. I can take care of myself that way, if I have to. What I'm trying to figure out is where I know him from. Maybe that'll give me some idea of why he has a problem with me. Is there anything that you can tell me about who he is or whether he ever lived here before?"

The coach straightened up and looked beyond me for a moment. "Let me be honest with you, John. Regardless of how much I like you personally, you know of course I can't say anything I'm obliged to keep quiet about, right?"

"Of course."

"Okay. That being said I'm trying to weigh what I can say but probably shouldn't against what your concerns are. I can't stand teachers who get wrapped up in student gossip. They're people who secretly want back into high school, if you ask me. Your lives here are tough enough without the faculty getting into the act. So be honest with me. This conflict you two are having, does it involve a girl or a bet or some other fairly minor issue?" I looked straight at him and shook my head solemnly.

"No, sir. It's very serious. I know how that sounds coming from a seventeen-year-old, but it is."

"I know seventeen-year-olds," he said. "They don't normally walk around carrying the globe on their shoulders like you apparently have for the last few weeks. I'm satisfied that this is no joke, whatever it is. I just had to ask."

"I understand."

"Well, the truth is there isn't much I know. Lon is basically the equivalent of an emancipated minor, except that he's eighteen. Do you know what that is?"

"I think so. It's a kid who's been freed from his parents by some legal thing, isn't it?"

"Yes. Lon didn't have to go through that, exactly. He was eighteen when he came here and asked to enroll."

"He was sponsored by Jim Kelly. He's an old friend of Cotler's family. That much I know."

"That's true, yes. Lon's school materials go to that address. Mr. Kelly volunteered to sponsor him when he came to us, provided an address, and guaranteed that he has a place to live. Beyond that, though, I don't know and couldn't say anyway what the arrangement is between them. We called Kelly because he's been a big help over the years with mentor programs and the like. He agreed to watch Lon and care for him if he needed help. It's not easy to enroll the way Lon did. He had to have an interview with the principal and a couple of other teachers. As a matter of fact, I was one of them. That's part of the reason he's in this class. He's very bright, actually."

"He doesn't seem stupid," I said.

"He's not. He is troubled, though. I'm not sure in what way. There are other school professionals that focus on that sort of stuff. What little I do know I just can't reveal at all. Do you understand?"

"Of course, Coach. I won't ask anything else."

"I appreciate that. But we can talk about you, John, and your relationship to Lon. If there's a legitimate conflict, it can be discussed within bounds. Can you think of any reason why he's picked you out for trouble?"

"No, I can't. That's why I was asking where he came from. Does anyone know, can anyone say if he's been here before? If he ever had an address in this area?"

"I think he was local once, but I'm not sure. I didn't ask him very much outside of what his educational plans were and what courses he'd already taken. Again, other faculty members questioned him about his family life and history, but what little I know about that I cannot discuss. I can tell you that I heard nothing from him and know nothing about him that would suggest the possibility of abuse toward other students. He wouldn't be here if his responses had indicated something like that, or if there was a serious history of it. I'm sorry I can't say more. Have you tried to talk directly to him?"

"Yes. It hasn't worked so well. We do talk, though. Mostly on his terms."

"Do you fear for your safety? If you're that concerned, perhaps someone else on the school staff should know about this."

"No," I said, lying without much conviction. "I don't think that's an issue. Not now, anyway." He paused for a moment and kept his eyes on mine.

"Can I be frank with you, stilted as this conversation has been?" I nodded. "You don't look good, son. I've been worried about you, and I was glad when you wanted to speak to me. Your work in this class is fine, and from what I know your other grades are slipping, but still passing. As silly as it sounds, a student's grades do sometimes reflect some other trend in his personal life. What about Francis Cotler? Have you told him?" I'm sure he expected that to be as natural as ringing a fire alarm, which in another life it would be.

"No. It's . . . it's too complicated for that. I . . . I really can't say why. Christ, I don't want to sound like this is cloak and dagger stuff. I just . . ." I trailed off and Bonner let the silence rest between us. I hung my head and thought about sleeping.

"It's all right. We've said what we could say. I guess if I controlled anything beyond this classroom I'd be more valuable to you."

With my head still sunken, I waved my hand toward him as if to say this was okay. I didn't feel like speaking much anymore. Bonner had been straightforward and kind, but as I had feared he wasn't able to offer much. I could feel his eyes on me for a moment, and I thought about raising my head and looking less defeated, but I just couldn't. He paused and then spoke again.

"John, if I may ask, is there someone you can talk to, about this—all of it?" *All of it.* I looked up now, wide-eyed. My face must have glowed with suspicion.

"Sir? About what?"

"This problem. With Lon. Is there anyone you can go to?" He looked perfectly relaxed, but I saw that I had fully awakened the razor sharp thing that was his brain.

There was a puzzle here involving Lon and me, a Lon whom he knew more about than he could say. Something told me he had more of an idea of where I fit into this puzzle than I thought he did. I doubted that he had talked to Vinnie. I wondered if he had made any connection between the two of us.

"Yeah, sort of. I'm still trying to decide who to tell and how much. I'll work it out."

"I'm sure you will. You have an ear here, of course, for what it's worth. I've heard things over the years that have dulled my surprise reflex, believe me."

"I might," I said, getting up to leave. "I just might." He seemed to study me as I got up and gathered my books.

"John?"

"Sir?"

"Keep your circle small, if you do decide to tell anyone anything. Does that make sense?"

"Yeah. It does."

Chapter Five: December

1

Tuesday, December 4. Vinnie and I met wordlessly as we trudged down Copperhead Road to Lon's meeting place for our second palaver with him. We both made a right at the secondary trail and saw a small fire burning up ahead. Lon sat beside it with a bottle of some cheap-looking liquor and an open can of SpaghettiOs. Beside him again was the black camera bag. It was the only thing I ever saw him with that he couldn't put in his pockets or his waistband.

"Sit down, girls," he said. "Anybody follow you?" Vinnie and I looked at each other. "You didn't check, did you? I need to rethink this whole thing, is that it?"

"Rethink what thing?" Vinnie asked. "What'd I do?" Lon discarded his spaghetti can and lit a cigarette. He stared disgustedly at Vinnie through the flames.

"I don't ever want to hear you say that again," he said calmly.

"Say what again?" Vinnie whined. "What?"

"I. That word. I. Get it out of your vocabulary. You are a

team, you and your brother John. If you can't get along, we won't be able to work together. And that'll be your problem, not mine. Sit down." He took a long plug from the bottle and winced.

"What do you mean *team*?" I asked as we took places on big, well-smoothed rocks beside the fire. It was welcome heat after the walk through the cold woods. A column of smoke and ashes rose in a weaving pillar into the canopy above us and then up toward the crystal sky. Lon spit into the fire and smiled at me.

"Name someone in authority who knew you were getting banged and did nothing to stop it. Either of you." Again, we looked at each other.

"There's no one who knows about it," I said. My heart was starting to pound. Lon paused, enjoying our discomfort. He picked up a stick and slapped the ground with it lightly. He considered the stick as he spoke.

"When you were nine years old, your mother took you to Dr. Abbot because you were experiencing pain sitting down and defecating, didn't she, Vin?" Vinnie looked startled, but Lon continued to slap his stick and watch it expressionlessly.

"I don't remember back that far," Vinnie said uncertainly, shifting on his rock.

"You're lying," Lon said without looking up or changing his tone. "But I'll come back to you. If you lie again you'll suffer the consequences. Now to you, John. You were eleven, the August before you started middle school. You'd been fucked so hard that summer you couldn't pull up your Toughskins without wanting to scream. What'd your good mom do?" Now he looked up at me, his face an outwardly inquisitive and inwardly threatening mask. I glared at him just as a wet piece of pine exploded in the fire and sent sparks fluttering into the heated air.

"She brought me to Abbot. What of it?"

"You tell me. Let's hear it."

***

James Abbot was the first doctor to open an office and take up residence in the fledgling development of Belle Ridge in 1964. By 1970, he was concretely the town's doctor, and an uneducated guess is that upwards of 75 percent of Belle Ridge's first generation of children saw him at one time or another. Even when the overflow of the D.C. area finally overtook Belle Ridge and claimed it in the late 70s, dotting the landscape with a host of more modern medical facilities, Dr. Abbot's little home office snug in the heart of town was always full. He was short, nondescript, and quiet, hailing from somewhere in Pennsylvania and married to a woman who looked startlingly like him. He practiced medicine in a converted yellow ranch house right across from the baseball field.

By August of 1978, I had been camping with Kelly and Cotler three times since May and had been profoundly abused each time. Kelly had fully established his routine of sending the others off and getting time alone with whatever boy he had chosen for that day, the mechanics of which I sensed and tracked with growing terror each time.

By late July I had constant pain in my anus and bruises on my inner thighs, neither of which I would let my mother examine out of shame and outright fear. But being a mother, she saw how I walked and saw how I winced when I sat down. After two weeks of my refusals to let her look at me, she dragged me to Dr. Abbot.

I remember being utterly mad with fear as I lay on Dr. Abbot's examining table on my stomach. I can see as clearly now as then the eight-by-ten picture of the crying hobo clown with a wilted flower in his hand on the soft blue wall in front of the table. I stared at the clown, with razor stubble and a frayed green bowtie, and pondered the end of my short life as Dr. Abbot gently poked and prodded me below the waist. Doctors didn't always wear gloves then in non-infectious cases, and his hands were cold. When it was over he asked me to sit up and dress myself. After I did, he sat down in a plastic orange chair and looked at me for what seemed like an eternity. His face was long, white, and oddly flat looking. His round, brown eyes rested on mine uneasily.

"No one is . . . touching you, playing with you in a bad way, are they, John?" he asked finally. I shook my head wide-eyed and said not a word. Dr. Abbot pursed his lips and seemed to want to look further around the room. More of that awful silence passed. "Okay," he said finally. "Let's go see your mom."

He recommended hot baths and Epsom salt and told my mother that I had probably been playing rough and straddling jungle gyms and other things that made for bad seats. He didn't say another word or ask to speak to her alone. With guarded, swelling relief I left his office and vowed that I would not be observed looking sore ever again.

Vinnie's description wasn't much different from mine, except that he was experiencing absolute agony when he tried to use the bathroom, and the crying alerted his mother. Vinnie's mother was normally rather preoccupied staving off beatings of her own from Vinnie's remarkably cruel stepfather, but apparently his discomfort had been sufficiently obvious to get her to sneak enough for an office visit from the old man's pocket. Same one question from plain-faced Dr. Abbot in his examining room. Same answer. Same diagnosis to Vinnie's mother. Same treatment recommended. End of story. Vinnie and I sat silently as Lon nodded in response. He looked up from his stick slapping area and gazed at us through the flames. Around us, what night birds and animals there were in the December cold hooted and called restlessly in the blackness.

"Anal damage," he said at last. A pause. "Anal damage. That's what he put on your visit reports for those days. Nothing else."

"How would you know that?" I asked. Then it came to me. "You broke in, didn't you?" Lon shrugged. It wasn't hard to believe. There were six original models of homes in Belle Ridge, and most boys who had lived in one of them for more than a single summer knew three or four ways of getting into all six without keys. That Abbot didn't have an alarm system even for a doctor's office wasn't a big surprise either. I don't think any buildings in Belle Ridge had alarms until late in the eighties—and after Lon had been there.

"How many others did you see?" I asked with something drying everything in my throat and mouth to a tacky paste.

"Twenty, all together," he said. "From 1969 until this summer, but that's just people I suspected or knew of. Terrance Hark was one of them. Yeah, you heard me. Looks like whoever killed that kid may have done him a favor in the long run. A real favor." He paused and fixed us with a thin smile. He got up and put two more logs crisscross on the fire.

Vinnie and I were both praying for the same thing, that Lon wanted us to tell humiliating stories for his enjoyment and nothing else. There was, as Vinnie pointed out, nothing we could do about it now.

"Sure there is," Lon said. And our doom was sealed. "It's time he paid. You two are going to bring that about." Vinnie swallowed audibly. I hung my head and stared into the flames. "You'll find out how, soon enough."

2

The break John Olving was looking for came during the first week of December. His patrols had been roving around the area for about two weeks, thankfully without incident except for a few heated arguments with deputies who hated the idea of armed men walking around out in the dark alongside them. In fairness, Olving was doing his best to keep his group organized and structured. He screened his volunteers, approved the weapons that the armed ones carried, and wrote out schedules, routes, and specific tasks for everyone on his team.

Where he overstepped his boundaries was with his "suspects list," a list of people he or his group members had observed in "suspicious circumstances" as he put it to pretty much whomever would listen. A few of the nomad laborers were on his list, primarily because of opportunity, but what Olving thought about most was motive. Not so much who *could* do this, because frankly quite a few people could, even skillfully enough to leave few or no clues, but who *would* do this. Olving and his lieutenants thought about that. They compared what they suspected with who they had seen and when. They thought about who might have a history of mental illness, maybe a history of violence, particularly against children, even as a child. They thought about who might have something in for little white kids who maybe had it better than they did. They thought about all these things, and they liked Armand Lillington a lot.

***

Spencer knew his brother was on Olving's suspects list, and it didn't bother him much. Armand, at one time or another, had been on everybody's bad list for something. He was an oversized loner who wore an ugly brown jacket no matter what the weather, hot or cold, and who padded hither and yon around town and through the woods almost every day. What Spencer did not know was that John Olving received an anonymous phone call that week. The caller would not identify himself and, in fact, was never identified. He indicated he had seen Armand Lillington on October 29, the day that Jeremy Bingham disappeared, walking out of the woods near the creek bed that Jeremy had been playing in. The caller said that Armand had been carrying a sack tied with a drawstring, possibly containing clothing. Olving tried to ascertain the caller's identity, but he would not budge and, after a brief exchange, hung up. Olving considered seeing if the police or phone company could trace the call, but he did not do so. Instead, he called the sheriff, as was his duty, and assembled his most trusted team members. Regardless of what the sheriff and the state bureau would do with this information, Olving's men were going watch Armand Lillington very closely.

3

Monday, December 10. "I want Doug," Lon said as we walked through the middle school playground beside the woods. The day was gray and damp and possessed of a probing, gnawing kind of cold. A wet cold, Cotler would have called it. It played hard notes on your bones.

"You want Doug?" I took out a cigarette and noticed Lon looking down at the pack. Without really thinking I offered him one and he took it.

"Yeah. I want him on the team." I froze, stopped, and turned to look at him. I could feel what color there was in my face draining quickly into my churning bowels.

"Relax," he said. "I want him on my team, not your team. You think so little of me, John. Why do you assume my whole big life revolves around your and Vinnie's miserable, little pathetic ones?"

"Then what the hell do you mean? And speaking of Vinnie, why isn't he here?"

"Vinnie's not here because Vinnie is an asshole. And besides that, he's Doug's bitch, and I don't trust him with this part of the plan. So you don't tell him, dig?"

"We don't speak," I said. Lon nodded.

"Yeah, I've noticed. Pity. Anyway, I want Doug. What I want from him really doesn't concern you. Truth is, it's something else I'm working on, and as long as you two do your jobs and hop when I say hop, the twain shall never meet."

"What do you want with him, then?"

"I want him in bed, for starters," he said with a matter-of-fact tone. My head jerked back in shock and I looked over at him. Lon seemed not to notice.

"What?"

"I want him sexually. Why is that such a surprise?"

"I don't know. It just is."

"You've been around me long enough," he said. "You never picked that up?"

"Truthfully, I've never cared."

"I guess it's a little wild for your tastes, huh?"

"If you're saying you're gay, you're not the first person I've known who was."

"Oh, yeah, you're quite the worldly guy." He cocked his head thoughtfully for a moment. "I don't know if you would call me gay. Probably some gay people wouldn't. I don't know what you'd call me. I don't really care, either."

"I thought you . . . liked Tamara," I said, afraid of what he might say they had done or not done, but I couldn't help myself. In fact, I hadn't seen her with Lon for quite a while, and the schoolgirl crush manner in which she spoke of him and looked at him no longer appeared to be there either. I didn't know what to think, and anyway I now had other problems. Lon scoffed at me.

"You would think that."

"I saw you together. I didn't make that up."

"She's nothing," he said with a dismissive wave. "Just thank God I thought so. For now I've got Doug Lars on the brain. Smooth and hard, he is, wouldn't you agree?"

"Straight, too, from what I gather. You got a plan for that?"

"I don't need much of one."

"He'll kill you," I said, unable to suppress a dubious smile. Without meaning to I drew out the word *kill*.

"He didn't kill me last time. Since then we've become pals."

"Last time you had a pipe."

"Jesus, John, you're blind as usual. I don't expect to romance Doug Lars. But with enough substances in him I'll bet you the farm I can get him to do other things. All sorts of things." He looked over at me. "You don't believe me, do you?"

I didn't, but my conviction was already faltering. Doug Lars, sex machine. Doug Lars, pure animal. Doug Lars, no more than a six pack away from . . . well, who knew what? My head was starting to pound. Too many things not making sense anymore. Did people really imagine things like this?

"I'm taking my time with it," Lon said, seemingly oblivious to my reeling mind but slyly feeding on it as usual. "We hang out a lot, there's no hurry. I get him some great drugs. And he's starting to like them. He's starting to like them a lot."

That was true. Not long after their fight, not long at all, as a matter of fact, Lon and Doug had apparently made amends, and now Lon hung out from time to time with Doug and several others in his circle. The drugs that Lon was able to obtain from who-knew-where surely fueled the association, and there was talk—rumors, flying here and there—that Doug was becoming something of a pothead because of Lon. Light drug use in our school among athletes off-season was nothing out of the ordinary, no more I suppose than it is for professional athletes, but Doug really was flirting with an image problem. Almost imperceptibly it was threatening his heretofore-unblemished image as the talented tough guy.

Did Doug care? I doubt it. Something happens to high school heroes sometimes. Maybe it's the pressure of being a tiny god, I don't know, but sometimes they look for trouble just to shirk the image. Or maybe they've become so bloated with praise and admiration in their little worlds that they feel they can do anything and get away with it. I think there's something fun about pushing the envelope, being bad-because-you-can-be when you're on top of your game at sixteen. Vic's brother, when we were younger, told us stories about lifelong prom queens who just flipped out their senior year and whored around the class like working girls, about top-name athletes and scholars who blew it all off to get high as kites with the dregs they grew up scorning. It becomes fashionable at some point to walk over to the other side and play in the den with the thieves. Succeeding generations of hoods know this and frankly have always laughed it off. *Hey, I smoked a bowl with you'll never guess who.* It was fun, I suppose, for both parties. Maybe that was Doug's point of view, if he thought about it at all. I think he knew about the chinks in his armor, and I don't think he gave a rat's ass. And the more I thought about it, the slightly less crazy Lon's intentions sounded. Slightly.

"Doug is a tight bag of bones that'll fuck anything," Lon said as if he'd read my mind. "Football-wise, he's good, but he's probably not good enough to go pro, which means he'll waste time at a college somewhere until he finally screws up and drops out. Basically all he's got is this year, and somewhere deep down he knows it, and that it's time to fuck off. I think you give him too much credit, like you do everybody. He's had it easy so far, and he's not yearning to meet the next big challenge in his life."

"You're right," I said slowly. "Doug's more lucky shithead than he is Ronald Reagan. That doesn't mean he's gay."

"He doesn't have to be. With enough of the right drugs, you'd be surprised what people like him will do." He crushed his smoke out against his boot heel. We had come to the end of the field and were at the far entrance to the woods. There was no real wind, but the cold continued to pry and seep its way into my flesh with blue fingers. "I know Doug. We get awfully comfortable together when we're hitting the stuff really hard. I know how to break him down, and I know when to make my moves. And he'll fall for it like a woman."

"Maybe," I said dully, pulling my coat around me tighter.

"Well, when he does, I'll need you to play a part," Lon said, a touch softer. I gaped at him.

"If you think for one min—"

"It's not that, John. I wouldn't share him with you. You'll be quite hidden, but I'll need you to be there. Just one night, if I play it right. Can you handle a good camera?"

"You've lost your mind."

"At least I had one. Don't fret for now. You've got enough to worry about, don't you?" His bold, deep eyes probed mine as I stood there, quaking in the cold and the dread of Lon's plans.

"I'm playing your game, Lon," I said, and I swallowed hard to keep tears away. "I'm doing what you're asking me to do. I just wish I knew where all this was going. I'd like to know what your limits are."

"And I'm trying to find out what yours are," he said, leaning toward me. He spoke with intensity. "You think I'm slowly killing you and that's probably true, but don't you know you've got to die before you can ever dream of living? You say you hate me, John, and that's well and good, but the fact is I pay you more mind than anyone ever has in your shit-ass life. Everyone, your family, even, what have they really done for the inner part of you. The naked part? Read the paper and did the dishes while they wiped your ass and glanced at your homework? I threaten to tear you down and make you a god, and the truth is you love me for it."

"I wish nothing more than for you to fucking disappear," I said, but my own voice was hollow and inside I felt something minimal but undeniable in his words. It was anger, mostly, born of confusion and resentment of the people in my life who had failed to protect me, people I'd never thought about that way until recently. Whatever it was, it shook strong pillars in my heart.

"You don't like the lessons but you love the teacher," he said, smiling broadly now that he had me in his sights. "No child likes the chores but every human being God, or who the fuck ever, put on this earth wants to be wanted, and deep down you love the way I want you. You love the way I look at and stalk and read your every move. In my use of you I love you more deeply than you've ever been loved because I pay closer attention to you than anyone ever has."

"I'm not Vinnie Foust. I have friends." My voice shook and I cursed it. Above us it was getting dark. Lon scoffed.

"You have friends. Who? Steve Drillas? He's a pretty piece of plastic. You're some fun for now in his glittering little life. Lean on him and he'll bolt before he can crumble. Oh, and then there's Cotler. Good old Francis. Led you into the woods one day, and golly, look what happened."

"Fuck you for even saying that. I think you're wrong about Steve, but I'll admit I haven't known him long. Cotler I've known—"

"'All my life,'" he finished for me. "I know, I know. And because he's wiped your nose for seventeen years you figure he loves you. But you know goddam well Cotler's never looked inside you like I have. He's never made you quake and shiver and grow for what he's shown you like I have. He can't, for Christ's sake, he's too stupid. Sure, someone left you on his doorstep and he's toed the line, keeping you from being beaten up for picking your nose. So what? He's a big ugly kid who's happy to have something to do."

"You dismiss it so easily," I said, my voice rising, "but it's just words you're throwing at me. You can't imagine loyalty like his. I don't know why he does it, and I don't think I've ever cared. Yeah, so he's not so imaginative. Seventeen years of being there for me day-in and day-out add up to a lot more than your well-put-together little speeches. You want facts, I'll give you facts. The biggest one is that without Cotler I'd be dead, a few times over, a long time ago." Lon listened to this with a patient gleam in his eye.

"Dead is better than being banged in the ass for six summers, though, isn't it, John? You've said that yourself. And that is Cotler's fault."

"Sure, Lon. So is cancer." He fixed me with a flat gaze and spoke fast and low.

"That first summer, no. That was Big Jim. Maybe even the second. But the big news, John, the truth you've known somewhere down there for years is that Cotler *knew*. He found out and he buried it because it didn't go along with the woodsman's life, and so he let you suffer and pretended it wasn't happening. Don't look at me like this is all a surprise, John. You've spent the last ten years of your life talking yourself out of hating Francis Cotler, and yet you stand here and tell me about your friends. I'm your friend, Johnny. This is friendship. This is as good as it gets."

Something broke in me and I screamed at him, open-faced and naked like a child confronting a nightmare. I screamed and turned, running across the blue-gray frozen, past empty jungle gyms and dodgeball circles and the darkened, frosted windows like dead eyes on the face of the school.

4

Wednesday, December 12. I asked for Steve's assistance, but with indescribable temptation I didn't tell him what little I knew of Lon's plans for Doug, and maybe that made things easier when Lon called icily that afternoon to tell me I needed to be at the Crawley place at 9:00. It would only take an hour at most, he suspected. He'd be ready at nine, and Doug would be good and primed.

The Crawley place was an ancient, crumbling house located all the way out on Copperhead Road. There used to be a carriage trail that led to it from some other usable road, but both were long gone. I don't know who built or occupied the Crawley place, and indeed I can't be certain if Crawley is even the actual name of anyone who ever lived there. It was a farmhouse once, from the looks of it, and was never serviced with electricity. Wooded areas of our county and its neighbors were dotted with places like it, houses, barns, or sheds that were once the center of cleared farms that either failed or were abandoned long before I was born.

"It's not bad out here tonight," Steve said, lighting a cigarette as we walked through the woods on the way there. "No wind."

I nodded and thanked him again for walking with me. I had told him only that Lon wanted to meet with me about something, alone for some reason, and Steve had offered to walk with me and wait outside the house so I wouldn't have to trek out there two miles each way on my own in the dark. I was grateful but worried. The last thing I wanted to do was drag Steve further into this mess, whatever it was.

"Any idea what this is about?" he asked. I shook my head, which was a partial truth.

"No. Maybe it's just another shitty pep-talk about how Cotler sold me out. I loved it the first time."

"I don't believe it, you know," he said.

"I don't really believe it either, but it's making me think. What happened to me went on for a long time. A long time."

"Yeah, it did," he said. "And you weren't the first or the last, right?" I nodded. "Then why do you pick out Cotler for knowing when nobody else knew? I realize people turn away, deny stuff, whatever, but it seems obvious to me that Kelly's been getting away with this shit for years because he's fooled a lot of people."

"Dr. Abbot knew," I said, remembering the meetings, the firelight. "He knew about a lot of it and he didn't do dick."

"And he wasn't six. Or seven, or ten like you and Cotler were. Jesus, man, I can barely put a thought together now. Forget what I could do when I was seven or eight. What the fuck could Cotler have known?"

"It didn't stop until I stopped it. We were twelve. I went with Cotler every time. Kelly would send him away, but . . ."

"But what? Kelly'd send him away and off he'd go to bop around with his twelve-year-old brain wanting to squash bugs and look for musket balls. Cotler was a little kid. I know he's always been a real serious guy, but the fact is even he was a kid. His whole world was rocks and buried stuff and shit that crawled around. You should have been that way, too. But think about it. He'd have to have seen it, red-handed, to even have a concept of it. Do you really think he could have picked up hints and figured it out?" I thought quietly for a long moment.

"No. This stuff isn't in his frame of reference. I don't think he even imagines it. Unless of course he did see it, sneaked around like he's so good at doing, and ignored it. Maybe then he did shut it out, like Lon said."

"And if he did, if he was seven or even ten, would you blame him as much as you would that shithead doctor?"

"No. No, of course not." Steve paused, drew long on his cigarette, and sighed.

"It scares you to think that he might have seen it, huh?"

"It makes me absolutely sick. What scares me most is that he could have seen it and turned a blind eye to it." We walked in silence for a few minutes.

"Lon's trying to take Cotler away from you," Steve said. "All this shit he's preaching is just words, like you said. Cotler's been there for you, all your life. Period."

"I know, I know. But what if . . ."

"Oh, fuck 'what if.' 'What if' is the last thing on the spice rack you decide to put in the sauce and then it tastes like shit. My brother told me that once."

"Truth is a lot like that too, though, isn't it?" Steve smiled and looked at his cigarette.

"Another thing George told me. Truth is a funny thing. Every truth starts out the same, but we're the ones who make it important or just a little bit of something. We decide where it goes. You follow?"

"Sort of."

"What I mean is, let's say this horrible thing about Cotler is true. Maybe he's eight or nine and he sees something, or hears something. Maybe he turns around and forgets about it, can't deal with it, I don't know. If even that happened, that's probably the long and the short of it. Now take you and Cotler. Do you know what you two are? You're like a treasure. You're like a super old oak tree a hundred feet tall or a really nice old house that the town is just plain lucky to have around and everyone goes to look at it. I see people sometimes. People you two have known all your lives, people who knew your parents, back when. They see you two together someplace and they smile. What you two have is rare, man. Do you see? That truth, the two of you, is big and it's already lived a long time. That other truth—if it's even a truth, which is doubtful—well, it's up to you to decide what to do with it. Do you follow?" I nodded. I did follow.

"You can't change the mass of the things in your life, but you can make them heavy or weightless depending on how much gravity you assign."

"Exactly. Thank you. You've got enough to deal with without Lon's psycho bullshit on top of it. Lon doesn't like me much either, does he?"

"He thinks I've been taken in by your magical personality," I said, grinning a little. "Heads up. The house is just ahead."

The Crawley place came into view, and we stopped. There was a fire going in the house in one of its four fireplaces downstairs. The house should have looked lived in with a fire going inside. Instead it looked turned on and awake, but anything but comfortable and inviting.

"I'll be over there," Steve whispered. "There's a big log. I can sit and watch the place, and there's a little light. I'll see you when you come out." I noticed him fumbling with a Walkman.

"Keep that low," I said, dimly reminding myself of Cotler. "Never turn both of your ears away from the woods." He nodded and gave me a thumbs-up as I trotted off. I approached the house and waited. I looked at my watch. 8:59. At 9:03, Lon emerged. He came over to me, and his eyes were red-rimmed and glassy, but otherwise alert.

"Is he here?" I asked. My curiosity was starting to build. Lon fixed me with ruddy eyes.

"Your boyfriend's here. I can smell him on you."

"There's no one here but me."

"Mm-hmm. You walked two miles in the dark and you're not pale as ice. Bullshit. You'd be a wreck if you were alone. Don't try to lie to me, John. Where is he?" I sighed.

"He's somewhere over there and he doesn't know anything. He doesn't, Lon. Yeah, he came out so I wouldn't have to walk here alone. He'll wait and then we'll go. All he knows is that it's a meeting. You know he knows about those, it's nothing new."

Lon did not shake his head. He didn't throw up his hands. He gazed at me, simply and calmly as before. When he spoke, his words were cool and sure.

"If he fucks this up in any way, I'll kill the both of you. I'm fading from view around here as you've probably noticed, and believe me I can do it. I don't need you as much as you might think, and I sure as hell didn't ask for him."

"He doesn't know anything, and he won't move until I come out of there. You said one hour."

"You're a fool for bringing him out here, walk or no walk. Don't say I didn't warn you. You think he's Jesus. All the two of you are going to do is cross me at some point and get very badly burned. I'm watching him now. You tell him that."

"You said one hour."

"And that should be about right. But if it isn't, don't you go anywhere until the job's done."

"What's the job?"

"You go in there," he pointed toward a dark rear entrance, which I knew led through a pantry to some backstairs. "Go up the backstairs, stay close to the wall so they don't squeak. Plant yourself on the landing by the first door. I've been up there. It's sturdy, but don't go wandering around. You can see downstairs from there. Look to your right when you get situated and you'll see the camera. Everything is completely set up. It's loaded and the shutter speed is set for the light. Just focus with the lens and shoot. Don't touch anything else on the camera. Aim, focus, and shoot. It'll advance automatically. Try to get clear shots of his face and not mine. There are thirty-six exposures, so don't be stingy but don't jump the gun either. Wait 'til it gets good. It will."

"What if he doesn't go for it, or whatever? How long do I wait if you two are killing each other down there?" Lon's eyes narrowed.

"Unlike you, I maintain control of situations I involve myself in. Just do your job and I'll do mine. When you've shot the roll, set the camera where you found it and get out." He turned, walked over to the woodpile, chose some pieces, and headed in. After a minute or two I did, too.

5

From the looks of Doug, I could have walked in with Lon and waved to him as I went by. From my perch upstairs on the landing, I could see them as clearly as if I were right in front of them. I hunkered down and backed deep into a shadow. Doug was stretched out on an old mattress against the wall near the fire, which thanks to Lon was blazing. Lon sat down next to him with the pipe and methodically refilled it from a baggy between his legs. Doug saw this and grinned, a slow, sleepy smile on his face. His eyes were laughing little slits. They passed the pipe once or twice, laughed about something I couldn't hear, and then Lon put another log on. The fire was almost dangerously large in the fireplace, and the heat of it was visible on their shining faces. Doug unbuttoned his flannel shirt, one and then two buttons. I picked up the camera, the same camera, by all appearances, that I had seen in Lon's possession almost every time we'd seen him. It had a comfortably complex and weighty mechanical feel to it. The sweat on my hands made it slick and loose in them. I lifted it to my eye and focused, just for practice. The camera peeked through the slats in the railing like a nervous rodent. There they were again, up close.

Lon had his shirt off and in the fire's glow his body looked sinewy and fine. Slowly, almost imperceptibly, he moved closer to Doug's planted frame on the mattress and they passed the pipe. There was conversation, but I heard very little of it. Lon made a muscle and invited Doug to feel it. Doug did and chuckled. Then Doug made a much bigger one and Lon put his hand on Doug's arm. The hand went to Doug's shoulder. Doug stiffened for a second but otherwise did not protest. Through his grin he mumbled something like 'Wha-fuck, man?' and closed his eyes. Lon's hand began to rub Doug's shoulder, and then his neck. Shoulder, neck. Shoulder, neck. It seemed to go on forever. In sick fascination, I had forgotten to lower the camera and saw all of this through the viewer.

Lon's hand was on the move again. Quickly but effortlessly, it slithered down over Doug's chest and lingered as if sniffing for something, at a button on his shirt. Doug looked down and broke into a giggle. He put his head back and closed his eyes again. The hand opened the button. Then another. Lon's face was only visible at an obtuse angle. His mouth was set in a smooth, easy grin, but his eyes, when Doug's eyes were closed, were very much alive, watching the other's reactions. All systems go, the eyes said as the hand sprouted fingers now and played lightly, lovingly on Doug's durable and flat stomach.

When the hand went for the belt buckle, I readied the camera. The fact that Lon's face was still visible seemed problematic, but then, as if he'd read my thoughts, he turned completely away from me and went to work on Doug's jeans. I was almost too amazed to shoot the camera. Doug stretched out further, closed his eyes, and hooked his hands behind his head.

Click. The camera made a low, satisfying sound as the shutter snapped. *Click.* It was beyond perfect. Doug was facing me, almost looking up at me. His face was clearly visible, his open shirt and his cut chest beneath. In his lap was the clear figure of a bare-backed young man at his crotch. *Click. Click.* Doug grunted suddenly as if awakening, and I thought a slaughter was imminent. He tossed his head back and forth and grabbed Lon's shoulders, pushing him away and spinning him around. The next few minutes were a blur of clicks and half-horrified, half-mesmerized gaping. Doug did not reach for Lon to kill him but to mount him, which he did. As he straddled the mattress with Doug behind him, Lon put a rotten pillow by his head, again obscuring his face. *Click. Click. Click.* Doug's eyes never opened and his face was clearly visible at profile, twisted and knotted up in an expression of blunt and vicious lust. *Click. Click. Click.*

It was not a tender thing. Doug never touched Lon except to position him. He never got very close to him at all, except to do what he positioned him to do. When it was over, Doug zipped up sloppily and fell back on the mattress, spent and dreaming. His face was cherry red and beaded with sweat. Lon pulled his pants back up and got up to light a cigarette. He never looked my way.

I had taken 28 clear, sharp pictures of my hometown's generational offering to greatness involved in a sex act with another young man. I set the camera down and headed down the stairs. The whole process had taken 35 minutes.

***

"Doug Lars," Steve said to himself for the tenth time as we padded softly through a column of dark, wind-whispering trees. "I wanna believe it. I do believe it. But I can't believe it."

"Believe it. I just took a roll of film to remember it by."

"I gotta admit," Steve said like a sports commentator describing a particularly unlikely upset, "it's not as crazy once you break it down. But Goddamn. And you have no idea what he's going to do with the pictures?" I shrugged.

"Assuming they come out, I have no clue. Personally, I hope I never hear about it again. Maybe he's got some other little hell worked out for Doug. I don't know and I don't care."

"You don't really believe that, do you? That it's not all related?" Silence.

"No. I don't. All of this is related."

"I wanna believe it. I do believe it. But I can't believe it," he said again.

We walked along silently for a few more minutes until the schoolyard came into view, off in the distance.

I'd been thinking about what Lon had said about Steve, and about being a fool. Maybe I was a fool, but Steve was passing little tests. The game was far from over, but so far he had performed admirably. He had been completely tight-lipped about everything I had told him. He had not changed his disposition toward Lon, Vinnie, or anyone else involved one iota, and I suspected it surprised Lon, although he'd have downplayed it had I brought it to his attention. *Hope. Sweet hope.* I pushed it away.

"I owe you," I said. "I mean it when I say you'll never know how much I appreciate what you've done for me, especially these past few weeks. But if things get bad, I mean really bad, cover yourself, okay? Don't follow me too far into this. Lon talks big, but chances are he'll leave you alone as long as you stay out of his way. But if you really cross him, I do think he'd kill you. I think it wouldn't be his first time."

"I've never had a friend like you," Steve said. "You talk like I'm doing all the work here, but you've been like a brother to me, too."

"I'm glad. Just remember what I'm saying. Please." He nodded.

"I just don't want to leave you alone in all this." No bravado. No bullshit. A further test, passed amply.

There was another begging moment of hope, but I pushed it out. Steve had come through for me, but I had no business denying the overtly probable anymore. If I owed him the truth, it was time to deliver. We had reached the parking lot. I faced Steve and tried to bring something to the surface that seared me. I said it plainly and with little emotion.

"I don't expect to survive this. Probably Lon will kill me when he's done doing whatever it is he wants to do. He'll bury me somewhere out here and then disappear forever.

I've got to be realistic. I can't stop him and I can only protect myself from him temporarily."

"But Cotler—"

"Cotler's blind. This situation doesn't exist as far as he's
concerned, and it never will. He won't know anything until
it's too late, if it goes that far." Steve shook his head.

"It'll kill him to know you went out without a fight. It'll
kill him to know you never told him."

"You don't know him like I do. He's as loyal as the ocean
is deep, I know—but this is bigger than loyalty. Some things
are bigger than us. Bigger than anything we've built. Can
you believe that? Because you have to. Any other trial,
any other test, Cotler would be there, I know. But this all
happened too close to home. I love him too much to test
him like that. It's out of his league, my league, all of ours.
Without Lon I could have gone on living with it. That's
what I planned. But Lon's here and he's not going away."

"Jesus Christ, he's one person. Listen to yourself!" He
was angry but I stayed calm.

"He's one person who's got some tight connection to
Jim Kelly . . . and my balls in a vice. I'm living day to day,
man. I don't feel much anymore, I've got to tell you. I'm
losing Cotler. I met you too late in the game. Everything I
had to lean on is falling apart fast. My life hasn't been that
complicated. It doesn't take much to tear it apart. I think
more than anything the real reason I won't survive this is
because I don't want to."

"Then why me?" he asked. "Why the fuck am I here if
you're ready to lay down and split open?" I smiled warmly
at him.

"Because I'm afraid of these woods. And you walked
with me and I appreciate that. I'm sorry if this upsets you.

I can't afford to care much anymore, and I'm done denying things and making up new ones. I don't care how ugly the truth is, I want to be close to it. And you just heard it." Silence. Steve frowned deeply, in a rare moment of his life when he was apparently completely without words.

"I've got some thinking to do," he said finally. We got in the truck and headed over to his house. "Could you get away this weekend if I could pull something off?" He climbed out of the cab. "I've been working on it for a while, but I haven't moved on it."

"I don't see why not. What do you want to do?"

"You'll see," he said, smiling. "Give me a chance to show you something worth living for."

***

I believed what I had told Steve, and I didn't regret telling it to him. The inexplicable way life chooses to smile continually on some and shit on others confounds even the most learned on the science of probability. I was confident in my fate and drove home in a dull and listless daze.

Then the hope appeared again, a begging dog at the table, the far-off laughter of children or lovers in a park. It wanted in, and I didn't want to let it in. I rounded the corner at Cotler's block without thinking about it and drove past his sleeping house. The hope clamored on the doors of my heart now, and in a rising voice it said that indeed I wasn't so sure of my gray little view of things. If I was, the voice reminded me, the pills would have spoken a long time back. There was Kelly, and Lon. There was Cotler, Spencer, and Steve. Long odds. But long doesn't mean zero. I turned off the truck and listened for a moment as it cooled and popped and hissed in its old, hidden corners. And I thought, *I want to believe it. I do believe it. But I can't believe it.*

6

Cotler was quiet, overly so, on the day following my photography debut involving Doug Lars. Much of it, I knew, had to do with the bad press his father was suffering, the frustration of the investigation, and the nagging pressure from groups like John Olving's. But I was attuned to Cotler's moods more finely than an exquisitely calibrated seismograph, and I knew there was something going on that eclipsed all of the other stuff. Finally, he told me what was on his mind, that Armand had become a prime suspect, at least for John Olving.

"What does your dad say?" I asked.

"He interviewed Armand at work. He said he made a delivery for his boss that day out in Annandale somewhere and wasn't nowhere near that creek."

"Does it check out?"

"Sort of. The boss did send him out there, but it was early. He made the delivery, but it looks like he could've had time to swing by that area."

"Do you think he did anything?" Cotler frowned.

"Armand ain't no killer."

"What about Spencer. He doesn't know?"

"He's about to. Dad's got to check it out. He'll probably search the house, do a couple of other things." He paused. "We should tell him."

"I can do that," I said. "Let me know when it's okay."

"Anytime's okay. I should be the one to do it, I'm just . . . well . . ."

"You don't have to be ashamed," I said. "It's not your fault someone called John Olving with some information."

"That ain't what bothers me. What bothers me is that Olving and his people have already convicted him. Dad's looked at Armand. FBI has, too. He's got a decent alibi for the first one and no history of anything like this. But try telling that to old John Olving, and he'll tell you you're just stickin' your head in the sand and ignoring the obvious."

"Look," I said, "People are getting antsy, starting to see things. Armand is an easy target. He knows that. He ought to be careful where he goes by himself."

"But he goes everywhere by himself," Cotler said, his voice rising. "Jeez, he lives his whole life that way. What's he supposed to do? Buy a friend so he's got an alibi wherever he goes?"

"Your dad's got to follow up, just in case. It doesn't mean he has to like it, and it's not personal. He's not a stupid man. He's not going to railroad the guy. And believe me when I say that you are the last person, you or your dad, who Spencer will blame."

He nodded, and for a moment stared wordlessly out at the grayness of the afternoon. "I just don't like what's happening here," he said, his voice strained. "I don't like it at all."

7

Friday, December 14. "Washington College, in Kent County, Maryland," Steve said finally as we left the Beltway, heading east on Route 50. After several attempts at figuring out where we were going, that was all he'd say. He had only told me to be at his house that Saturday evening, dressed well and up for anything. Susie had fixed my hair and picked out some clothes, and oddly enough I looked pretty good.

"I hope like hell I can remember where it is," he said. "But that's all I'm telling you. The rest is the surprise."

"What the fuck kind of surprise is this?" I asked, uneasy as I watched the shadowy landscape flatten to give way to the approaching shore.

"If I describe it, then it won't be much of a surprise, now will it? Relax. Kick back. Steve's in charge."

Relaxing, though, was out of the question. As with everything one did with Steve, this adventure had a spicy, enticing underside to it, but as a lifelong loser I was utterly unable to relax when interaction with girls was likely to occur, as everything so far had certainly promised. Steve sensed my discomfort and did nothing to alleviate it; instead, he seemed to enjoy watching me fidget in my pressed clothes and gelled hair. I prodded him a few more times and got nowhere, finally settling on the blackness of the Eastern Maryland night to stare into as we sped down the highway in his old Nova. For some twenty minutes we drove in silence, listening to Prince whining from the rear speakers. I no longer tried to hide how fucking annoyed I was with him.

"I have family in Cyprus," he said finally. "Did you know that?"

"Cyprus."

"Yeah. Surprising, huh?"

"Not really. It's a Greek island, isn't it?"

"Half Greek. The other half is Turkish. They hate each other. It's a very scary place."

"Okay."

"This is interesting stuff," Steve said, trying to sound miffed. "Know what the climate's like over there?"

"I couldn't imagine," I said with a sigh.

"It's hot. And dry. And it's really mountainous. People still get around on goats."

"I see."

"Damn, you're just not interested in the trials of my people, are you? That hurts, man."

"What the hell does this have to do with anything?"

"I just thought you'd be interested. Passing the time, that's all. I thought about going over there, you know? After school or something. Doing relief work, maybe. Learning the language."

"Relief work."

"Yeah. There's a group my brother was involved with for a while before Diane got pregnant. They go over and distribute drugs and food and stuff in war-torn areas. It's some kind of a spin-off from a Peace Corps group or something. It's pretty tough work. Lots of snipers, hostile areas, that kind of stuff. George never got to go because of the kid, but a guy he knew was killed out there. Bomb went off in a camp he was working at. Pretty ugly."

"So why the hell do you want to go?" I asked. He shrugged.

"Somebody's gotta be the hero. It'd give me something to do for a while before I settle on nothing."

"Whatever," I said. Steve smiled and turned off of Route 50 onto an even darker road, and we continued on.

Washington College was a picturesque, academic-looking little place with large, colonial stone buildings and long quadrants of grass punctuated by sentinel-like light posts showing statues scattered here and there. In the cold December night, the grounds were utterly deserted, but lights were on in some of the dorms, and varying music drifted out from a few of the rooms. Steve drove past the main campus and turned into a small apartment complex down the block. He motioned for me to grab a bottle of wine he had resting on the back seat.

"Okay," he said as we parked, "Surprise time. I know you're nervous, and you don't have to be. Just kick back, watch the old maestro at work, and play along. Can you do that?"

"What do you mean, play along? Play along with what? I don't know a single thing about why we're here or who we're here to see. Tell me what to play along with and maybe I can do it."

"Hell, no," he said. "If I give you lines, you'll fuck them all up. Just play along. Act, Johnny. It's a blast. Trust me."

"You can act. I can't act."

"You can act tonight, brother. C'mon. It's a surprise. That means a nice surprise. I wouldn't drag you out here to look like an idiot. Let's go."

***

The door of apartment G4 opened up and a tall, long-haired brunette in a sweater and jean skirt threw her arms around Steve as I stood back to give them room. She wasn't as pretty as some I'd seen Steve with, but she was no dog either. She planted a quick but luxurious kiss on his mouth before ushering us both in. In the introduction I caught her name, Leslie, but not much else. She smiled at me briefly, seemed to look me up and down once, and then high-tailed it back to the kitchen with Steve's wine in tow. In the task of getting my coat off and looking for a place to put it, I didn't notice the other one on the couch.

"Drop it on that chair," she said. "We'll get it out of the way later."

***

She was tanning-bed brown, girlishly thin, and her skin looked a little dry. Her hair was long and straight, light brown and streaked with blond in wide, languid stripes. She had a small mouth, slightly pursed and painted faintly with lipstick that had been there awhile. She sat cross-legged on the couch in black shorts and a bodice-type top that buttoned up the front and gave her a slightly hippie-ish appearance. She held a can of beer in one hand and a long cigarette in the other, smiling in my direction and waving as she let a plume of smoke out of the side of her mouth. Her eyes were sharp, piercing almost, as they met Steve's and then mine, but their faded brown, or hazel tone—I couldn't tell which—softened a little under the glaze of what was probably her third beer.

"April . . ." the other girl was calling her as she hurried back to introduce us. April smiled again as I said her name in greeting, and something in me turned a somersault.

Steve ran the show with the skill of a senator's wife, commenting lavishly on the smells of dinner and the general decor of the place. The girls were leaving soon for Christmas break and were among the last people still in their building, which was mostly inhabited by college students. He stayed to spark conversation between April and me for a few moments, then went to the kitchen to fawn over Leslie's cooking. From their conversation I learned that this was a girl Steve had met through his brother George. They met when George was waiting tables at a Greek restaurant in Tyson's Corner and Steve was bussing them, but I had never heard of her.

"Johnny," Leslie called from the kitchen, "would you like a beer?" I said I could use one, and April motioned for me to stay put. She raised her arms from her lap, untwisted long thin legs with the grace of a gazelle, and jumped up from the couch.

"You sit," she said, smiling at me as she passed me on her way to the kitchen. Her voice, lower it seemed when she spoke only to me, seemed to come from the speakers against the wall. Again, the somersault. I lit a cigarette and looked around the room.

***

"How?" Leslie was asking Steve as she sipped his beer and looked into his eyes over the stove. "How did they talk you into it?"

"Somebody's gotta be the hero," he said, smiling lightly and putting his arm around her waist. "Besides, it'll give me something to do for a while until I settle on nothing."

"Go back to school, Steve. What's so wrong with doing what everyone else does?" Steve frowned, and the frown deepened to create furrows in his brow. Frustration moved across his face. He looked clouded as he took a swig from the bottle and handed it back to her.

"School," he said, a hint of disgust in his voice. "Where? Turnpike Tech again? I can't do that. Not now, anyway." Leslie looked at Steve with something so pathetically and deeply concerned that for a split second I felt the same way toward him, caught up in the moment. She shook her head and he reached for her cheek. "Les," he said, peering into her eyes, "I came here because I want to spend my last night drinking wine, listening to music, and enjoying you . . . and all of this. No business. Please?" She opened her mouth to protest, but he raised a finger and she stopped. "Please," he said. "I get it enough from everyone else. John and I just want to relax, and we want you two to relax. We've got a long-ass flight tomorrow and God knows what after that."

Leslie seemed to soften and walked back over to the stove. April got up to join her while Steve and I offered to set the table. Steve shot me a quick look, barely a glance really, to see if I had taken his signals. I couldn't look at him directly for fear of laughing or screaming.

***

We sat cross-legged around their coffee table and ate something they cooked in a wok, the wine flowing freely and some sort of soft R&B music leaking from the speakers around us. The table was candlelit, and each of our faces glowed pleasantly in the soft light as we laughed about drinking and dating and college life, the last two of which I knew very little about. I could lie, though. I was, and probably still am, very good at that, and I found that Steve's brazen act and a good amount of wine and beer bolstered me enough to say just about anything. Before long I was letting Steve lead me down paths of stories about us living together after high school two years previous and finally getting involved in the international relief-work circuit last year. What Steve lacked in geographical or political knowledge I filled in pretty easily, and we worked like an old comedy team.

With Steve it was all possible. After an hour of the girls smiling, laughing, brooding during the serious stuff, and generally sitting glibly on the edge of their seats, I felt like I could tell these two I was John F. Kennedy. Steve was masterful, I mean believable to the point of hilarity. He leaned back as I moved in to fill in parts of a story, chuckling and pointing at me as he "remembered" the car I was referring to, or the ratty apartment, or the job we both hated. We were in character, and creating a life between the two of us seemed as natural as anything we had ever done together. It was an extension of our friendship, a product of it that seemed as real as any actual memory we had in common.

As dinner wound down Steve and Leslie were getting closer, and I noticed with no small celebration that April was slowly, deliberately moving toward me also. We cleared the table, freshened our drinks, and gathered around the TV for a while. April brought me a beer and sat down beside me. Behind us on the couch, Leslie and Steve soon got very quiet, and shortly thereafter waved goodnight and shuffled off quietly to her bedroom. April turned toward me and asked if I was watching whatever was on television.

"Neither was I," she said, and turned it off. Music played again, some sort of urban sound, but jazzy—not that Quiet Storm stuff that made me think of hot summer nights at my grandmother's in Queens, listening to the city outside the open window and digging for New York radio stations on the tiny transistor I had hidden under the covers. Whatever this smooth jazz was, it poured out from the walls like syrup and seemed to make the darkened room float. April got up to light two candles on a little shelf cluttered with figurines and other girl's stuff on the wall, and I noticed a picture of her and Leslie, two bikinis on a beach somewhere. I went over to check it out. "Do you like candlelight?" she asked as we stood by the shelf in the flickering light. We both leaned toward the wall.

"Yeah," I said, smiling. My mouth was suddenly filled with words, four or five useless sentences to somehow more fully describe exactly why I liked candlelight, or to disclaim in some way my delight at the sight of lit candles, but I clamped down hard on them, remembering how Cotler's natural and Steve's learned reticence could be so disarming, and so goddam charming, too. April smiled furtively.

"Wait'll you see my room," she said. Her room. I shifted slightly in an effort to conceal an erection that seemed ready to come tearing through my jeans. With some effort, I flushed visions of April and what was probably no more than an hour away with a mental slap in the face. *Stay cool, John.*

I stayed cool.

"How long have you known Steve?" she asked me, sipping her wine and letting her eyes find mine slowly.

"We've known each other for a long time," I said, this technically truthful. "I guess we've been friends for four or five years." That was not true, and inside I prayed this estimate jived with all the stories we had spun earlier. I was pretty sure it did. Conversation with April, though, alone and without Steve, could be dangerous. I planned on keeping my answers brief while trying not to be obvious.

"You've been doing this work longer than he has though, haven't you?" she asked.

"No. Not more than a couple of months, maybe. Why?"

"Your eyes," she said, as plainly as if she were indicating how she wanted a steak cooked. She set her glass down and brought a finger to one of my eyes, tracing around it gently. The feel of her finger was soft, smooth, like a nurse's. She leaned closer. "Your eyes are so tired."

"It's been a long day," I said, again truthfully.

"That's not what I'm seeing," she said, almost a whisper. She was smiling, and her breathing was deeper, almost audible. I smiled at her quizzically.

"Tired isn't what you're seeing?"

"Not that kind of tired," she said, still tracing her finger gently around my face. "You look different. Different from Steve. Different from a lot of people. What's going on under there, anyway?"

I pulled back slightly, forgetting for a minute the intense horniness, even the barely containable anticipation of losing my virginity. It scared me, this attempt to peer into my mind at whatever dark stuff crept around in there. It was more like drawing water from a well than it was looking down into it. I could feel that stuff rising to meet the looker, like some malignant, fleshy flower at the beam of light that threatened to shine on it. The feeling had never been so strong as with Lon. This wasn't the same type of feeling, but it was still oddly intrusive. For the first real time in my life, and in this little apartment, I was dealing with a girl, a young woman really. And girls could smell things. Tam had smelled things on me for as long as I'd known her, but Tam had never detected anything particularly interesting.

But for some reason, April did. She smelled something interesting and wanted to get closer. This was a game to her I supposed—a sweaty, intoxicating game that ended as often as she pleased with some sort of tryst—but April still liked to play. Whatever was at the end of the trail wasn't nearly as much fun if she didn't play. I had no idea how lucky I was that there was something there for April to smell. She saw the change in my eyes, from dreamy, I suppose, to guarded, and purred softly.

"Ooh," she said, "secrets." Her eyes danced and she leaned closer to me, swishing her hair gently over my arms. *Jesus,* I thought, *everything she does is fluid, rhythmic, like this goddam music. Sex pours out of her like wine out of that bottle.*

As it turned out, the slight recoiling was the smartest move I could have made to make my conquest of April complete, if that was a fair assessment. Suddenly I saw the wanting there. I saw the interest. I felt April warming at the thought of whatever mystery she sensed was attached to me. *If there was ever a benefit to what I was surviving,* I thought briefly, *I guess this is it.*

"Not really," I said. "None worth talking about, anyway."

"You can't hold out on me," she said smiling, her eyes drooping lazily into bedroom stance. We were steadily leaning closer to each other. Her hair brushed over my hands, my arms.

"Oh, yeah," I said, my own eyes closing as I began to focus on her mouth, parting just barely. Her tongue appeared behind her lips like a scout peering from behind a soft barricade. "Oh yeah, I can."

"You remind me," she said, breathy and now very, very close, "of an old boyfriend." I could feel her breath, mingling with mine and filling the small space between us with the scent of red wine and cigarettes. Her eyes seemed to move in a slow circle around my face.

"Is that good or bad?" I asked.

"That's bad, Johnny. That's very, very bad." Her eyes

fell toward my mouth and we kissed, our tongues meeting with our hands not far behind. April pressed herself against me and her bodice rose up, allowing my hands to fall squarely on her bare hips. My hands felt electrified on the smooth curve of her waist. I ran a finger along the thin band of her underwear, clinging to her skin just below the black shorts that hung perilously against her backside. April's tongue ran along my teeth and in and out of my mouth, and her fingers found my hair, ears, and neck. In languid, swan-like motions, she arched and twisted and twirled herself inside my embrace, licking and biting gently on my ears and neck until I thought I could swallow her whole. "Pick me up," she breathed in my ear. "Pick me up and take me to the bedroom."

I picked her up and she wrapped her legs around me like a snug puzzle piece, kissing and biting and licking as I stumbled across the room onto a wine glass that shattered beneath my shoe, and down a narrow hallway until April pointed and pushed a door open, kicking it closed with one long leg as we swirled inside. I set her down and we were nose to nose, kissing while my hands found her breasts for the first time. The buttons on her top seemed to melt and fall away in my hands until it was just off and on the floor. With a single, angelic twist she stood on tiptoes and the black shorts fell to the floor around her feet. She stepped deftly out of them, finding the button on my jeans as she did.

***

Three candles, more lumps of wax than anything else, illuminated April's tiny, girl-cluttered room from a single black candelabra on her dresser. Shadows like spreading fingers dispersed yellow and gray streaks across the wall and ceiling as I explored a girl's nakedness for the first time. She nodded silently, her eyes closed and her hands gripped around my neck as I stroked her, and when I found the right spot she breathed fire on my neck and kicked the sheets beneath us into a storm of linen and skin.

Finally, April pulled me up and her eyes locked onto mine as she guided me slowly into her. An explosion lurked deliciously just below the surface and I struggled for words as I felt myself lowering into her like a slow train into the darkest and deepest of soft, sleepy tunnels. Strangely, I had a vivid image of myself as a little boy lying on my back in the rear of our old station wagon, smiling furtively and falling into a pleasant, cradling sleep as our car passed from the darkness of the Manhattan streets into the pale yellow of the Lincoln Tunnel that took us from the city of my parents' birth to the long stretch of night road that led home.

"April," I breathed as I found the bottom of her and she arched to accept me, "honey, I'm not gonna be able to—"

"Shhh. It's okay. You've got all night."

And that's about all you've got, I thought with eerie certainty. *So make it count.* The crescendo continued to build, and I gripped her tighter as I prepared for the inevitable. It arrived, and my whole world was her—her eyes, her lips, her breath, her hair. I saw a dozen images as I jerked and twisted inside of her. For a single black moment, I saw Kelly's face and I convulsed, nearly falling out of her. Then he was gone and my world was back, my world named April, the nineteen-year-old who found her way into the utter, never fading permanence of my memory so easily as to make it laughable.

***

"Leslie and I hooked up when I worked for my brother at Strokos out in Tyson's," Steve said as his car barreled toward the beach in the hour before dawn. He had gently shaken me awake, and we left the girls sleeping with a thank-you note and a promise to call when we could get to a phone, wherever we ended up. "I was fifteen but told her I was eighteen. Truth is, she's a sweet girl, but she's easy and she ain't too bright. But this chick April, I wasn't as sure of. I figured you'd get somewhere with her. But man, that was beautiful. I can't believe I actually worried about you. You were great!"

"You," I said. "You, dude, are a dangerous person. No one should be able to pull off an act like that. We could do anything. We could get away with anything, you and me."

"Ah, my friend, be careful. We did great tonight, no question about it. You were fucking priceless. But remember our audience. We fooled them, but they wanted to be fooled. Hell, I think April had us almost figured out." The thought of that chilled me, and I told him so.

"What do you mean April had us figured out?"

"Easy, killer. You didn't sleep alone, did you? I didn't say figured out, I said *almost* figured out. There's a difference. I just saw her looking us over once or twice when we were going on about so and so, really deep in the bullshit. There was something in her eyes; I don't know. And I don't care, because neither did she. That's the thing about chicks, man. Sometimes you're nobody. But sometimes, you're like a fucking dress they know they can't afford, but they just won't leave the store without. Sometimes, they're just buying what you're selling. And they'll come up with any reason they can find when they really, really want to."

"I'll never figure this out," I said, shaking my head. But I couldn't stop grinning, and a feeling like that hadn't alighted on me for a very, very long time.

***

We drove through the sleeping town of Ocean City, found the beach road, and made our way up past 115th Street. Restaurants, cottages, bait stores, and surf shops lay silent as stones on either side of the road. Steve, watching the hotels as we headed farther and farther north, finally turned right into an open lot and parked.

We walked over the dunes and down to a huge pile of rocks beside a jetty. The rocks went out into the surf, and the jetty beside them must have gone out another hundred yards. The early morning beach was chilly and salt-beaten, but mercifully windless. He led as we climbed the pile and found smooth places to sit. In front of us the sky continued to soften. Venus glowed just above the horizon.

"So, what now?" I asked as we smoked in the dimness and listened to the pounding of the surf below. "Don't tell me there's more. I'm out of energy."

"No," Steve said, looking with utter satisfaction and quiet delight at the expanse of gray water in front of us. He brought his jacket closer to him as sea spray floated around us. "This is the end of the line. Truthfully, this part of the surprise is for me, too, a little bit. But I wanted you to be here."

"What's here?"

"Here," he said with a deep smile, "is where I lost my virginity. This is where I went after it happened."

"You lost it right here on these rocks?"

"No," he said, pointing. "Back there on the beach, a ways up. My family's place is about a mile that way. But the girl was staying at this hotel, and after I walked her back to her room, I came out to this old rock pile. I sat out here and waited for dawn. Just like this. I wanted you to feel that . . . what I felt. That's pretty selfish, I guess. You probably had something more sophisticated in mind to do at this point."

"Hell no," I said. "This is great. I've never heard this story. How old were you?"

"Fourteen, almost fifteen. It was the summer before sophomore year. Her name was Mandy. Mandy Renker, from Severna Park, Maryland. Cute girl, a little meaty but I didn't care. She had huge tits and told me she always wore stuff she knew would show them off. She told me she was sixteen, but that's what I told her, too, so who the hell knows? It was really no storybook kind of moment. I picked her up at an arcade and wound up humping her sometime before dawn. I had a rubber that George gave me. I think half the reason he gave it to me was because he knew it would make me feel like a man. But I had to use that sonofabitch.

"I didn't even have her bra off when she asked if I had one. We were rolling around up there, and all of a sudden it was 'Hey, do you have a thingy?' That's what she called it. A 'thingy.' I'll never forget how proud I was that I did. She took it from me like it was candy and went right to work getting it out of the package. She knew what she was doing, I'll tell you that. Too bad I didn't. Then she climbed on and I thought I was going to die. I think I lasted all of seven seconds."

"Did you ever see her again?" Steve chuckled.

"She wasn't the marrying kind. I think she went home the next day. Back to whoring around in Severna Park. I don't think I'll ever forget her, though. You never forget your first.

My brother told me that. You know what the best part was, though? Seriously? The best part of the whole thing was coming out here, sitting on this fucking rock, and watching the sun come up, knowing that it was coming up for the first time that Steve Drillas wasn't a virgin anymore. You give me one hour, one hour out of my life to live over and over again, and I swear I'll live that one. It was better than any skirt I ever got my hands on. It was better than the day my niece was born. I don't think I could even picture the girl five minutes after it happened. It was just being out here that was so great. Feeling like the goddam king of the world."

Steve breathed deep as a light spray floated up over us, and he gazed out over the blue horizon. Venus was very bright now and sharing center stage with light pink and violet hues that were spreading from the horizon upward. I watched him watching the coming dawn, and not for the first time wondered how much of his grand manner and persona was an act. And then I realized I didn't care. He had brought me out here to live a moment with him, and I had never felt so wonderfully alive. The scent of April was still all over me, and I sniffed deep into my jacket from time to time to bring it out before the conflicting smells of smoke, beach, and road wore it all off. My mind still spun with the look in her eyes when I entered her for the first, and then second time. The way she arched her back, the way her hair found its way into our mouths in thin strands as we kissed and rocked on her bed. April. The word tasted like victory on my tongue. And it was possible to remember it that way for a lifetime. Blue continued to give way to gray and pink as the dull December sun climbed toward the horizon, and Steve motioned for us to leave.

"Let's check in at the Drillas family shack. I may have to

rig the plumbing, but we can crash there for a few hours before we head back. I know a great breakfast place, too. Open all year. We'll chow and get some sleep. What do you say?"

"Steve," I said, still sitting. He sat back down. The tears in my eyes were faint but obvious. I stared out into the ocean, unable to look at him directly.

"Yeah?"

"No one . . . well . . . no one ever did anything like you did for me last night. I mean, I can't . . . I don't . . . "

"You don't is right," he said. "You don't have to say anything. And you don't owe me anything. I saw an opportunity. I introduced you to a girl who thought you were fucking Prince Charming. Congratulations, Johnny."

"Yeah, but it meant a lot, you know? I mean, with girls I've always thought that, somehow, I guess, that I never would. You know? Like it wasn't meant to be, or something. I just . . ." My words broke up like the waves of foam and water against the granite below us. I was overcome, suddenly, out here on the rocks, for a love of my friend Steve, the boy who had engineered this whole plan because of what he knew about me; what unspeakable things he knew, what unspeakable things I had trusted him with.

He waited patiently as I stammered and glanced out toward the horizon. Finally, I shook my head and held my hand out for a lift-up. Steve smiled, knowing full well what he had pulled off and why, and all the more proud of himself for doing it. We cleared the dunes and encountered a beach road that now looked entirely different, pale and gray in the cold light of dawn. Behind us the sun stretched and shimmered in its rise, and prepared to bathe all America in the light of a new day.

8

Sunday, December 23. I unpacked gifts for family and friends and set them down on my bed to wrap. My mood had brightened considerably since our trip to Maryland, and the household had almost returned to its usual state of mild hostility, sarcasm, and occasional good cheer. Smells of butter, sugar, and cinnamon appropriately filled my mother's kitchen. Susie squealed with delight when I told her about

Cotler's prediction for snow, knowing his knack for "smelling" it as much as I did. And indeed, the snow began to fall in silent, thin white waves as darkness took hold over the area. Over dinner we planned midnight mass and outings with friends on Christmas day. I couldn't remember a time in the past three months where we had been a family to such an extent.

The phone rang at 7:50.

"It's Santa Claus," Lon said. "I need some helpers to deliver an early present to Dr. Abbott. I'll see you and Vinnie at the trailhead at midnight. Don't be late."

***

By 11:50 there was an inch of crystal white, unblemished snow covering and muffling the Virginia night. My tires were the only tracks of any kind so far in the big white blanket, and I was amazed, as I was every year with the first snowfall, at the absolute silence it brought about. It was ethereally quiet. The world seemed at a standstill. I reached the lot and turned my lights off after washing Lon and Vinnie in the glow of them. Vinnie's glasses were fogged up and he stood there looking like a blind mole in the snow. Beside him, Lon shivered.

"You need a better coat," I said, for no particular reason I could fathom. Lon was poorly dressed for this weather. He wore old jeans, black leather boots, a torn flannel shirt and the same tattered leather jacket he'd had in October. His nose looked red and raw. He glared at me.

"I've been living on my own since you were pissing your panties. Shut up."

"What are we supposed to do?" Vinnie whined. "What are those buckets?" Then I saw them. Two covered, five-gallon buckets, the kind filled with joint compound you found at construction sites. Vinnie and I looked them like they were filled with snakes. Beside them was a trash bag filled with small items that made indentations on the sides.

"They're presents for Albert Schweitzer," Lon said, warming his hands with his breath. "John, you're driving. I don't trust you assholes, so I'm going along this time. Let's move."

This time. The phrase hung in the cold air and settled slowly into our bones. "This time" meant, of course, that there were to be other times. Lon grabbed the bag, and Vinnie and I took the buckets. They were both filled about a quarter of the way up and they made nasty squishing sounds as we placed them in the truck.

We drove in silence toward Dr. Abbott's office. To my surprise and mild relief, there were several other cars on the road making their way slowly through town; it was just enough not to make us an unusual sight. Lon had planned well. The snow was eliminating tracks, diverting attentions and generally deadening the reflexes and nerves of the town. If you would brave the weather, it was a great night to do mischief. One block from where the office stood, Lon ordered me onto a street that dead-end-ed at the fence of the Belle Ridge Community Center and golf course. This place was popular for couples to park, and also a great place to pop a hole in the fence and get onto the golf course for all sorts of havoc and diversion as we had done back in October. Dr. Abbott's block backed up to the fence of the golf course. One could move easi-ly along the fence and behind the houses, passing to the rear of the backyard fences. Outside, the snow was falling harder, and Lon wasted no time as we came to a stop. He adjusted a bulge under his jacket and I guessed correctly, and with a chill, that he was carrying his camera. I wanted to ask what the hell for, but he spared me the chance.

"Awright. Vinnie, take one of the buckets and start walking. Move behind the backyards and stay low. When you come to his house sit where you can't be seen. There's a shed and some big trees around there. He's got no backyard fence but stay back anyway. Be fucking care-ful." Vinnie sighed heavily but quickly got in motion. Two minutes later Lon sent me scurrying through the open back yards, towing one of the sloshing buckets through the snow. I joined Vinnie behind the shed in Dr. Abbott's backyard and waited for Lon. "Give me your gloves," he said when he'd reached us, dropping his bag with a light plop in the snow.

"Gloves? Why?"

"Because I don't want to leave my goddam fingerprints on the door when I go to open it."

"What do I do then?" I asked, panicking. Lon smiled.

"Don't touch anything in there."

He took his time getting across the backyard, glancing backward a time or two, but everything around us was as still as a museum. I noticed with more relief that our tracks were already disappearing under new flakes of snow. Lon took something that looked like a steel credit card from his pocket and in twenty seconds had the back door open. He waved us over and Vinnie and I entered Dr. Abbott's office as felons for the first time in our lives.

***

The house was heavy with the odor of medicines, disinfectants, and some sort of vinyl—and in the smell's wake came the memory of being there like a brick to the head. We had entered through the kitchen, which for Dr. Abbott was a little laboratory and mini-pharmacy. I had never been so aware of my hands as I was now, turning them inward and using the backs of them like deformed claws to feel my way around the dark office. The buckets swished as we moved along. Lon led as we made our way into the living room, which was the waiting room. More memory assaulted me as I entered it. It hadn't changed a bit.

Lon ordered us to put the buckets down and I barely heard him. Instead I was picturing myself on the long lavender couch, slumping and gray-faced while my mother read a six-month-old *Better Homes* and some sniffling little girl across from us tormented her mother into giving her four sourball candies in fifteen minutes. The same two pictures were still on the wall, both prints of a foxhunt, presumably somewhere nearby. The carpet was a little more worn and still a nasty brown color, one of the original bad colors the developers had picked for carpet in Belle Ridge homes. In the sleepy darkness the room had a surreal, nightmarish quality.

"Open your buckets, girls," Lon whispered, glancing around the room. "Hurry." With aching fingers we pried the tops off, and Vinnie jumped back as an evil smell emitted from his. Instantly it was all around the room. He gagged and stepped back.

"It's full of . . . oh, God, it's gross," he hissed. "Sewage. Fucking sewer water."

"It won't bite, Vinnie," Lon said, smiling behind us. My bucket contained what seemed like a gallon or more of blood, already congealing on the sides.

"Where did you get this?" I asked, my heart pounding.

"It's deer blood, relax," Lon said. "All right. Spread it around and try not to get any on yourselves. Everywhere. The couches, the desk, the walls. Move it."

Like frightened, confused children we did as we were told, gingerly splashing the blood and wastewater in different places with looks of utter revulsion on our faces. After a minute or more, Lon got impatient and angrily grabbed the buckets, finishing the job by splatting the stuff everywhere and deftly leaping out of the way of the splashes. He dragged the trash bag in and emptied out a dozen or so ratty and ancient children's shoes, tossing them here and there among the stinking mess.

Then he paused for a minute to admire his work. Vinnie and I stood beside him, scared and disgusted. I kept glancing down the hallway where the examining rooms were, waiting for little Dr. Abbott to come bouncing out of one of them with a clipboard in his hand. The waiting room, the windows, the door, the walls, the couches—everything—looked and smelled like a cross between a cesspool and a slaughterhouse. And dotted with kids' shoes and slippers pulled from a dump somewhere, it looked absolutely horrifying. Lon smiled broadly and breathed heavily with exertion. He pulled the camera from under his jacket and began photographing the scene in quick takes. Vinnie and I squealed and shrank away from him.

"What the fuck is that all about?" I said, unable to keep my voice down.

"I've got a scrap book. Don't worry. I'm not asking you to pose." That was true, but I couldn't be sure he didn't get us in any of the pictures. Glumly, we sat and waited for him to finish. He tucked the camera back into his coat and surveyed the room one last time.

"Can we please get the fuck out of here now?" Vinnie said in a shaking voice. Lon glanced back at him.

"Grab the buckets," he said. He looked around the kitchen and found a roll of paper towels, using them to wipe up visible footprints as we waited by the door. Then we were back out into the silent night, or "Silent Night," as it was now Christmas Eve, and like ghosts we crept back through the falling snow to the truck. Lon assured us he'd be in touch and took the buckets with him into the woods, disappearing almost instantly among the falling snow and the brush.

9

Cotler woke me at 11:30 the next morning, sitting by my bed with a cup of coffee from downstairs and a plate of my mother's cookies.

"Somebody vandalized the shit out of Doc Abbott's place," he said, his mouth full as I looked over at him. He waited to see if it was registering with me. "The deputies said it was a mess. Whoever did it broke in and messed the place up bad."

"His house or his office?" I asked, rubbing my eyes and sitting up.

"The office. I talked to Bucky this morning and he said there was blood and somebody's"—he lowered his voice—"shitwater all over the walls. Can you believe that? The Doc went in today around seven to let the water in the pipes trickle so they wouldn't freeze, and Bucky said he called the office in a panic. I think he threw up some before they got there."

I blinked and looked doubtfully at him. Inside I felt fairly comfortable. Cotler telling me the story excitedly at close to noon the next day meant no cause for alarm. I stretched and yawned, slowly coming to light.

"Why the fuck would somebody do that?" I asked through a yawn.

"Don't ask me. But you ain't heard the best." Something tightened in my gut.

"What's the best?" Cotler grinned, a tight, unfunny grin.

"Dad went over there after the call came in to check it out. There was shoes, too, kids' shoes, thrown all around the place. Bucky says my dad took one look at the scene and right away figgered it had something do with the murders." He waited for this to sink in. I waved a hand toward myself and nodded. "Well, Bucky didn't really see any connection and was afraid that dad was just graspin' for straws and thinkin' everything was attached to the killings in some way. But Dad told him to gather up all the shoes. He wanted to look at 'em. And guess what?"

"Jesus, what? Tell me."

"One o' those shoes my dad recognized. He couldn't

miss it 'cause of how many times he'd read the description. A black, kid-size Reebok with red laces. That ring a bell?" My throat went utterly dry and I scrambled to collect myself.

"It can't be," I said, gathering the sheets around me. Cotler nodded.

"One o' them shoes belonged to Terrance Hark."

10

The duty fell to Steve to talk me down from absolute panic once I realized Lon had somehow gotten possession of a shoe from Terrance Hark, and then forced Vinnie and me use it as a prop in Dr. Abbott's Office of Horrors. The worry was, correctly, that this find would be considered a break in the investigation. It was considered exactly that, but as Steve pointed out, unless one of us left fingerprints or other obvious clues in there, the investigators were going to be hard-pressed to identify anyone. His other strong admonition to me was that Vinnie and I were—and I had to get used to this—the last two people anyone would suspect of something like that. Only Lon joined us together. I had to remember that, he insisted. He was right, but it was tough. We discussed the issue in the common area after Midnight Mass while both of our mothers milled around and talked to the priests and fellow Catholics. Then the two of us headed over to Cotler's, as was my family's tradition.

Once there I settled down under Steve's watchful gaze and allowed myself to unwind a little bit with my friends. Vic, Cotler, Steve, Spencer, and I traded stories of awful gifts and family fights at Christmases past while Cotler spread out a table full of chips, cold cuts, sweets, and such. Outside the temperature was holding steady at thirty degrees, and more than three inches of fairly fresh snow was adorning the town like a great big ornament. The Cotlers' Christmas tree, cut fresh by father and sons every year in the mountains west of us, glowed stately with colored lights and faded balls and filled the house with the aroma of Blue Ridge Pine. Even Cotler's father, with the weight of the world on his shoulders, seemed relaxed and comfortable upstairs talking with my dad and some off-duty cops over beers and ham sandwiches.

Spencer was smiling and happy, the situation with his brother not deterring his Christmas joy one bit. Armand had cooperated with the sheriff and his people willingly. His car and the house had been searched with no results, and, for now at least, the sheriff had no further reason to examine him. It was still unclear whether John Olving's group would leave him alone or not.

I felt better about the incident at Doc Abbott's after talking with Cotler about what his dad and his investigatory contacts intended to do about the discovered shoe. I was not out of the woods, I supposed, but Steve's point that I was not a suspect in any way, shape, or form was beginning to sink in. *Maybe real criminals develop a kind of technique to remind themselves of that from time to time,* I thought. I had no idea.

Better still, despite the persistent unease and the clawing guilt, was being among the boys I loved for yet another Christmas. In my own state of disarray it was especially good to be with Spencer, walking through the world in his usual state of wonder and joy at being a child of God. Christmas was a deeply personal and spiritual time for him, and he was even happier this night, having taken his brother and mother to an evening service at his church for Christmas Eve. He and Steve argued with gusto and laughter about the NFL playoffs and Reagan's second term. Even Vic, who didn't believe in anything but his legs and the soles of his feet, looked enraptured and oddly peaceful, as if something he hadn't thought existed was nudging him subtly anyway to show Its presence. In this atmosphere of comfort and love, I let myself unwind from the horrors that had been 1984, and quite suddenly it occurred to me that for Christmas there was something foolish but maybe worthwhile I needed to do. Vic smiled crookedly as he caught me pondering this, and in recognition I patted his arm and smiled back.

11

At 12:30 on Christmas Day I was dialing the numbers to Vinnie Foust's house. At his sullen "Hello," I confirmed what I'd suspected since last night: Vinnie was alone or might as well have been. Either way he was trapped in the cage of his being with no one to release him and no one to attend to his wounds. Christmas, at least in our culture, is hell for the lonely.

"Hello?" he asked again.

"Vinnie, it's John."

"John? What do you want?"

"Nothing. I just wanted to . . . say Merry Christmas." Silence. I waited for the bitter retort. Seconds passed. More than ten of them. I heard Vinnie breathe out on the other end.

"Thanks," he muttered. And hung up. I held the phone out in my hand.

"Johnny," Susie was calling from downstairs. "Johnny, come down. The Cotlers are here and, oooh, they brought goodies!" Slowly I replaced the phone and headed downstairs to greet our guests.

Chapter Six: January

1

"I can't protect you," he is calling to me, wailing really as I run away with my hands over my ears. We are in a park, Marty Moreland and I. Pullen Park at the bottom of Cotler's block. It is a quickly darkening early March day and a dry, brisk wind scatters and gathers the trash, leaves, and child-pounded dust of the playground in random, gusty lurches. "Please, Johnny," he is calling. His voice is hoarse and horribly pained. "I can't make it stop by myself."

There are garishly bright smears of orange and red in the twilight sky, and it is at these clouds I stare as I come to a stop on the gravel strip that runs between the playground and the boulevard. Cold, reddening hands are still over my ears, but now I stop the maddening hum I have employed to drown out Marty's pleas. He stops a few feet behind me, watching me cautiously.

"Johnny, please don't run away. I'm on your side. Please. Listen to me. We have to talk about him."

"I don't know what you're talking about," I say. The words are dead and flat, and now I drop my hands to my side but keep my tear-stained face pointed away from Vic's big brother. "Why are you bothering me, Marty?"

"It's not supposed to be this way," he says from behind me. On the boulevard in front of us cars rush by, women on their way to hungry families and men to waiting dinner. "This isn't supposed to be happening. None of it. But it is. I can't wish it away and you can't either. I know what he's done to you." He pauses as if to see how this will sit with me. The wind picks up and sweeps through the park, emitting a tiny drone as I start to cry harder.

"He's not doing anything anymore," I say, choking on sobs. "I don't go out with them anymore. It's like it never happened."

"It did happen, Johnny. I'd give anything for it not to have, but—"

"So what? So what if it did happen? It isn't happening now. Can't you leave me alone?"

"It isn't happening for now. What about later?"

"What about it? I told you, I don't go near him."

"You're Cotler's friend," he says gently. "You can't avoid him forever." Now Marty walks over to me, pauses behind me then sits down in front of me on an old airplane tire that now serves as a favorite spot for children playing hide and seek. I turn slowly and it is painful to look at him.

"What do you want me to do? I didn't want it to happen."

"Johnny, please. I know that. It's not your fault. You've been thinking it is, haven't you? He told you it was your fault, didn't he?"

I nod, unable to utter a sound. My face feels as if it may burst with tears and sobbing, and it is all I can do to keep from crying out. But I no longer wish to run. Horrible or not, I have been waiting most of my life to hear someone say that it wasn't my fault, after all.

"Well, it isn't," he says. "You didn't do a single thing to cause him to hurt you. He . . . just likes to hurt boys. Jim Kelly is a sick man. He needs help. He needs help to stop hurting boys. Do you understand, Johnny?"

"I don't care if he needs help," I say, casting my eyes downward to the darkening gravel below my feet. "I wish he was dead."

"Me, too, sometimes," Marty says. He is wearing a tattered gray sweat suit, and the outline of his whippet-thin frame becomes visible when the wind blows the material tight against his body. "But killing is wrong and we couldn't do it anyway."

"So, what do you want? I can't do anything to him. I just don't go out with them anymore. I told you, he can't hurt me now." He hears me and pauses, biting momentarily on his full lower lip.

"I've talked to someone about this," he starts to say. Panic seizes me and I jump backward.

"Who did you tell?!" I scream. "Who?!"

"Not about you, Johnny, not about you. Please. I would never, ever tell anyone about you. Do you understand? Never." Marty's deep, kind eyes burn in mine and slowly I calm down.

"Please don't tell," I whine softy. "Please don't ever tell."

"Never. Never. I won't ever tell. I told someone about me, that's all. About how he hurt me. You don't ever have to tell anyone. I just know about you because . . . well, because I just know. I've seen him looking at you. I've seen him around you. There was a time at the clearing that I tried to help, but, but..." Now Marty is on the verge of tears, but with a hard swallow and a shake of his head he banishes the urge and his face tightens with the strain of it.

"I heard you once," I say quietly, something brand new dawning on me as I turn away from him again in shame. "You threw rocks." He nods and we are silent for a moment.

"This person," he says, "this person I talked to is someone I can trust. He's the one who told me that it wasn't my fault . . . that Jim is sick. We talked about what I could do about it. About how to stop it. We decided that I should tell some people. Well I did, Johnny. I told some people." He looks away at the boulevard, now lit up momentarily by passing cars cruising by in the gloom of the evening.

"What happened?"

"They didn't believe me," he says. The weight of this silences us.

"Why not?"

"I don't know. I guess it's too hard for them to believe that Jim would do it. That anyone would do it. But now I'm in trouble, John. I'm in big trouble, because one of the people I tried to tell is bound to let Jim know that this was said about him. I'm afraid. I'm really afraid."

"But what can I do?"

"You can help me. Come forward with me. Help me find some of the others that he's done this to. We can do it if we all band together. They'll know we're not making it up if we . . ." Marty trails off because he has seen the look in my eyes. It is a look of horror. Of denial. Of resolute, rock-hard refusal. I start to back away from him.

"Wait, please, think about what he's doing, think . . ."

"I-I can't. You can't make me."

"I'm not making you. I'm asking you. You're a good guy. People believe you when you say something."

"No one believes me," I say, backing away and regarding this desperate, kind boy as if he were suddenly revealed as a snake in a woodpile. "You want me to say this because I'm friends with Cotler. You think that'll make them believe us."

"That's not all of it. There needs to be more than just me. We need people to come forward. We need to stop him."

"I don't need to stop anything. He stopped bothering me. I just need to stay out of his way. Why don't you just do that?"

"Because he's still hurting boys. He hurt you. He's hurting some other boys, right now. What about them?"

"I don't care about them," I say, terror awakening hungrily in my belly. "I'm not telling anyone about this. Please. Please don't make me."

"John, think. Think about the other ones. Think about the ones not even born yet. Please."

"I can't do this," I say to him. "I can't and I won't." Marty's eyes are searching, swaying lanterns and he sweeps them across my face in half circles, looking for the courage that he has already summoned. He will not find it in mine. "Maybe you should go away for a while. Maybe then it'll be okay." He shakes his head with sadness and stares at his worn sneakers on the dark ground.

"No. It'll never be okay again."

"I'm sorry," I blubber. "I just can't." There is a long silence with only the wind and the rushing of wheels nearby.

"No," he says, looking at me again in that paralyzing, candid, and mothering way, "I'm the one who should be sorry. I had no right to ask you to do this. I'm sorry. I'll never tell. I swear it."

"Maybe no one will tell Jim," I say, my first experience at offering meaningless tidbits of consolation after refusing the course of action that might have made the real difference. "If they don't believe it, they won't bother Jim with it."

"Maybe," he whispers. He stands up, seeming finally to notice the deepening cold. "You'd better get home," he says. "It's cold out here. Let's just forget this, okay? I'm sorry I bothered you with it." He turns to leave and I am tortured, wanting to offer something in place of my cowardice. There is something in his eyes that I do not like and have never seen before. It is a look of emptiness—the way emptiness is reflected in a man's eyes when he stands before it. It is the call of death.

"Please, just go away for a while. Go away until no one cares anymore. Please?" He turns to face me and his eyes are soft and warm, not burning like before. The wind blows his hair in finger-like strands around his face. Some touch his oversized Roman nose and mouth.

"Don't worry, Johnny. It'll be okay."

"I want it to go away. I just want it all to go away."

"So do I."

"You can talk to me, about it. If you want. I don't mind."

"Thanks," he says. "I guess you're okay, then."

"Yeah. I guess." He pauses, looks away, then back at me.

"Do you like girls, John? Do you want to go out with them, be with them?" His question makes me burn with embarrassment and fresh adolescent ache. I nod, looking away. Marty smiles, knowing that I am telling the truth. He seems happy about this. But in his eyes I see why he has asked me. I see that Marty does not feel the same. He seems to search himself for a moment, and then seems to see that he can only pose questions on this subject that I am powerless to help him answer.

"That's good," he says finally. "You'll get your chance, soon. So long, guy."

"So long," I say. A croak. A dozen things leap to my lips as he turns and walks away, heroic, daring things. But they die there, and in awful silence I watch as Marty pads softly away into the dark.

2

Thursday, January 3. I woke in the dark, got up, and walked to the window. The night sky was indigo and moon dusted. High over the frost-covered rooftops, trees, and cars, it made monochrome of the whole town.

Courage.

Marty had had courage. Cotler had courage. I did not. The question was why, and what could one do? Cotler was almost all the courage I had known, and because it flowed from him like water from a well and seemed as natural a part of him as his accent, I had regarded it like a genetic gift. Cotler had courage; I simply did not. I lifted the sill and clean, cold air began to seep in from outside.

Marty was different. Marty had had courage, but it was something unlike Cotler's. I had known Marty for most of his life. Marty had been a child much like Vic, loud, rambunctious, silly. Before adolescence he had been a wealth of bad jokes and pointless excitabilities. He was neither steadfast nor brave. But Marty had changed. His courage had . . . what? Emerged? Broken through? *Or had he learned it?* I opened the window a little wider and placed an ashtray on the sill. The smoke formed a gossamer, ghost-like path out through the screen. How did one learn courage? I had always heard that courage was something one summoned, which implied that something inside had to be present first in order to make that summoning possible. I had nothing inside to summon. Nothing useful, anyway. Nothing at all, except . . .

"Use the tools you have," Cotler was saying to me. In my mind's eye we were in a patch of woods near his grandmother's farm in Henrico County. It was a bright and crisp late fall afternoon, and he was leaning over me as I announced with frustration that the tent would not stand without the joining rods I had forgotten to pack before we'd begun our hike out to this spot. He had taken the poles from me, examined them, and with thin-gauge wire from his pocket and sturdy tree branches, he'd fashioned rods of his own. *"Good planning will keep you comfortable,"* he'd said. *"But resourcefulness will keep you alive."*

The tools I had. What were those? My five senses, for starters. The common sense that I had never bothered to nurture in the slightest degree. I could continue to quake and cower in Lon's presence like a hog awaiting slaughter, or I could endeavor to keep my senses alive and take in something other than what he was offering. That could mean taking in something that Lon didn't intend to give up. That something was knowledge, maybe. And knowledge was power.

Maybe power gave birth to courage.

3

Lon never returned to East Tolland High School after the winter holiday. The unconfirmed but firmly believable rumor was that he had dropped out. Bonner would only say that he had "not returned" from the holidays and didn't know when or if we'd see him. I didn't know where Lon had spent

Christmas or New Year's, and I didn't care. It was an immense burden off of me to see that he wasn't in class anymore.

Cotler and I, in fact, knew that he had dropped out because the sheriff had gleaned the information from the school. Had he not dropped out he may very well have been asked to leave; his grades were all incomplete and his attendance had fallen sharply through November and December. Cotler wouldn't go so far as to say that his father was considering Lon a serious suspect, but the fact that Lon was an ill-dressed, ill-mannered young man of strange circumstances who had come into town about the time the killings started didn't exculpate him in any way.

There were a few fleeting, hopeful days in early January when I thought Lon might have left the area altogether, but he was in touch with both Vinnie and me by the end of that week. He planned our third meeting for January 8, a bitterly cold Tuesday night lit only by a brilliant sliver of moon in a brittle, crystalline sky. Vinnie and I arrived in silence to the small fire pit where Lon waited for us by a roaring fire. It was a welcome relief from the stalking, penetrating chill of the walk along Copperhead Road. Our bowels tightened and our throats dried up as Lon's cold, probing eyes found us among the trees, trudging through the brush to his glowing circle like lost children.

"Sit down," he said. We did as we were told and waited for what was next. Minutes passed and Lon said nothing else. The firelight played on his face and he stared into it, apparently content to sit quietly and neither ask nor say anything. Vinnie and I sat motionless, but for the first time I sought to see through the tunnel of fear and uncertainty to take in what I could.

Lon sat on a neat, flattened stump and hooked his

arms around his long legs in front of him. He looked bored, almost petulant as he stared into the fire and smoked. He also looked unkempt, more so than usual, his hair dirty and long. There was something in his eyes I had seen before but never tried to define. It appeared usually just as he was dismissing us and just when we arrived, sometimes brightest when we hadn't yet settled in around the fire. The brow was knitted, the deep-set eyes turned inward. I had seen this look on Cotler, on Vic. It was human, it was unfulfilled, it was . . .

"What the fuck are you looking at?" Lon snapped. I jumped in my skin and turned my face into a mask. *Loss.* He peered suspiciously over at me through the flames.

"Nothing. We're waiting for you to say something."

"I'll talk when I'm ready to talk. You'll wait until I'm ready to talk."

"Fine," I said. Vinnie looked at me with suspicion as well, but I ignored him and tried to focus less obviously on Lon. *It looks like he's lost something.* In time Lon found his slapping stick, lit another cigarette, and gazed over at us.

"The sheriff before Dan Cotler. Who was he?" he asked either of us.

"His name was Wilson," I said. "Ron Wilson, I think."

"Correct," Lon said. "He was the chief law enforcement officer in this county, that sound right to you?"

"I guess."

"What do you think he knew about what was happening to the boys in this town? Either of you?" Vinnie and I looked at each other and back at Lon, both of us shrugging.

***

Ron Wilson was a lumbering, low-talking hulk of a man universally called R.W. by those of his age and importance. He had been the county sheriff for twenty years before Cotler's father was elected in '81 and had all but handpicked his successor. Now he lived on a small farm between the airport's west fence and the southern entrance to Leesburg.

"What did he do?" Vinnie asked.

"It's what he didn't do," Lon said pleasantly, looking at his cigarette. "Much like the good doctor, he did nothing. Just like the good doctor, he needs to be punished. You'll get orders soon." There was silence for a moment. I lurched something up from inside.

"What is it you want, Lon?" I asked. "Ultimately?" Vinnie looked over at me with alarm on his face.

"Watch your tone, cabin boy," Lon said. "I don't answer your questions. You answer mine."

"We broke into a house on your orders," I said. "We trashed the office of the town doctor, and from what I hear he's thinking about packing up and moving away. I think we've earned a stripe or two."

"Shut up, John," Vinnie whispered, his voice wavering.

"You shut up," Lon ordered. "Don't you dare inhibit this growth that John's displaying. He's asserting himself. That's what I've hoped either of you would do. I'm here to bring out the devil in both of you. It's the devil that wasn't around when it could have done you some good."

"What do you mean by that?" I asked, my breath announcing itself in white bursts. Lon glared at me through strands of dirty hair.

"You know goddam well what I mean."

"I don't. Tell me."

"Shut up, John," Vinnie half growled, half whined. "You can't play games when both of us are here."

"One more word from you Vinnie, and I'll kick your teeth out," Lon said. He spoke calmly but he was heating up. I could feel it, and despite a rising tide of dread I forced myself to press on.

"What is it you want?" I asked. "What is it we have to do to make your plans complete? Is it Kelly you want, or us?"

"I want it all," Lon said, his voice rising. Something in my heart leapt. For the first time I felt like he was at least partially off guard and it was thrilling and terrifying to see him this way. "I want this whole miserable town, and I won't sweat one drop taking it. You're an exercise for me. You and this whole place, an exercise in destruction and that's all. I'm doing what I'm doing to this place because it deserves to die."

"If you thought you could destroy it so easily you wouldn't be so angry at it," I said.

"Watch me work," he said through clenched teeth. "Watch me work and learn something." His face was reddening, visible even over the firelight. I listened to him with as much calm as I could muster. I listened so I could remember later. It was a monumental task.

"You're angry at us. Why? What did we do?" I kept my voice low, backing off now, backing down. The thought of Lon shoving something either metal or anatomical in my face was still a palpable possibility. He looked at me squarely.

"It's what you didn't do, when you had the chance. A chance to stand up and be counted, and you . . ." He stopped in mid-sentence and seemed to check himself.

Then he let out a long breath and seemed to sag. "Aw, fuck it," he finished.

"We were children," I said.

"We were all children," he said. He was catching himself and calming down. His rude, humorless smile returned. "We were all children. Get out, both of you. I'm done with you tonight. Don't worry, I'll be in touch."

***

"What the fuck were you thinking?" Vinnie hissed as we walked back toward the park.

"I'm thinking we should start looking for a way out."

"Not interested. I'm trying to survive this and you're playing around with our lives. We don't hold any cards!"

"That's because we're not taking any," I said, catching up with him and trying to look him in the eye. I could feel the same energy as the night Lon had written our names on the school, both hopeful and hurtful at the same time. "Maybe if we started working together and focusing on him, we could do something."

"Get exposed," he said, shaking his head and walking ahead of me. "That's all we'll do. We need to go along and hope he dies. If you go too far, I'll side with him and turn on you, I swear to God."

"Vinnie," I said, shaking now with emotion, "I had a dream a while ago about something that happened when we were about thirteen. Someone approached me. It was someone older than we were. Someone we knew. Someone who . . . tried to help us, a few times. Do you know who I'm talking about?" Vinnie squeezed his eyes shut.

"I don't know . . . "

"The rocks, Vinnie. He threw rocks, and Jim Kelly went nuts and ran after him. You remember this. I know you do. We talked about it." Vinnie sagged and let out a long, rattling sigh. His already drooping shoulders fell even further.

"Yeah. He threw rocks. Jim got pissed and left me alone. So what?"

"What do you mean, so what? It worked, for Christ's sake. He helped us. He's the only person in the whole goddam world that ever did one single thing to try and help us."

"He should have helped himself."

"Did he ever try to talk to you? A few years after? Just before he died?" I stood behind him, much as Marty had stood behind me as I refused to face him. Vinnie froze as I spoke and remained facing in the other direction.

"Yes."

"You . . . you didn't agree to stand with him, did you?"

"Neither did you."

"Of course not. I didn't bring it up to throw blame around. But don't you see? He must have gone to Lon, too. He must have talked to him like he talked to us."

"But . . . who is Lon?"

"There was another kid who went out with us—he had the same name, I'm almost sure of it. Lon. The kid's name was Lon. Don't you remember?" Vinnie turned to the side but would not face me. His silhouette and breath were visible in the chilled air.

"I don't remember anything from that time," he said. "Really. Not much of anything. There were other kids, I remember that. You, Vic, and Cotler, and . . . yeah, there was someone else. But I can't picture him now."

"I've given this a lot of thought. Lon knows us. He's

always known. He had to have been involved, and the name thing is too much of a coincidence."

"It is if you're right."

"I may not be right. That's my point. I need you. We need each other. Knowledge is power, and we don't have much. We need to start putting two and two together."

"Why? What's it gonna mean if we figure out that he was one of us, or something?" He lowered his voice and peered around us into the woods. "It doesn't matter where he came from, or if he was a kid here once. What matters is now. And right now, he's got nothing to lose."

"That's starting to change." I dropped my voice a notch as well and moved closer to him. "FBI and state investigators are going to start focusing on Lon. This isn't a great time to be a strange kid living on your own in Belle Ridge."

"No matter," he said, shaking his head. "Maybe they'll get him. We can't. Maybe he's some other kid who got abused. So what? We could have his whole biography, I don't see where it gets us anything. We have to go along to get along, and you need to accept that. We're in over our heads."

"You think you're gonna survive this the way you've gotten through your whole life, don't you? Go along and kiss ass. Maybe you'll be left alone."

He shook his head and smiled toothlessly. "You make me laugh. You, who's had a built-in bodyguard your whole life. I've been alone . . . " He trailed off, drew a breath, and jogged ahead of me on the path.

"He's killing them, Vinnie," I called after him as softly as I could. I followed to where he was, almost to the parking lot where our cars stood frost-covered under the lamps. Vinnie stopped, his chest heaving. "He's killing them and he left one of their shoes in Doc Abbott's waiting room. That's his revenge! That's his plan! There's more at stake here than us!"

"You can't be sure of that."

"I'm pretty goddam sure and so are you."

"Did you learn *anything* from Vic's brother?" he asked, turning around. "Listen to yourself. Marty tried this. And he's dead."

"Marty was dealing with someone else."

"Only in a sense," he said, calming down and now standing perfectly still. "Marty was dealing with some-*one* else, but not really some*thing* else. You haven't had to make your way like I have. Laugh all you want about what I do to get by. I can survive on my own and I can make decisions that aren't clouded by stupid do-gooder bullshit. What you do is your business, but don't think for a minute I won't give you up if you threaten my way out of this."

"Jesus, I'm *offering* you a way out of this! I'm offering you the chance to fight. To you, every fight is foolish, which is why you have the life you have."

"No," he said. "Your fight is foolish. You have an idea. So what? My judgment says you're a loser, John. I'm sorry, but this isn't a game."

I was paralyzed by this and stood on the trail behind him like I'd been punched. Vinnie waited for a second, as if understanding this last insult deserved a chance for a retort, but I didn't have one. He walked out of the woods to his waiting car.

4

"So, what's the bottom line?" Steve asked as he filled mugs with fresh coffee in his darkening kitchen the following afternoon. "Lon is that mystery kid you all used to go out with, is that what you think?"

"Yeah. I'm pretty sure now. I may ask Cotler about it. He may remember the name. One of our fathers might, too. They might also know who his father was, or at least who brought him to Jim's house when we used to go out together."

"Well, whatever you do, take it slow. Have patience like he does."

"If he's killing kids, I can't wait too long," I said.

"Tell me this," Steve said. "You said he stopped himself while he was accusing you of not standing up for your-selves somehow. What was that about?" I paused for a moment, revisiting it.

"Marty Moreland," I said quietly. Steve looked at me with raised eyebrows. I told him about Marty and his visit with me at Pullen Park. If he was surprised that Vic's brother had been involved, he didn't show it.

"Marty talked to Vinnie, too, you think?"

"Yeah. Vinnie gave him the same answer I did." We were silent for a moment. "How long after that did he . . . you know?"

"About a week."

"Oh."

Outside of Steve's mother's kitchen, a cold wind blew across the side of the house and whispered of snow. We sipped our coffee and listened to the wind, and I wondered where Lon was weathering the storm.

5

When a lanky, sandy-haired redneck named Shawn Warren found out that John Olving was putting together a group to help protect the town, he was among the first to respond. Shawn was a lifelong resident of the area, his parents having put down roots as farmers in eastern Tolland County long before Belle Ridge. At first, Olving was resistant to utilizing Shawn. He didn't come from the best of backgrounds and had a reputation as a troublemaker while growing up. That was an understatement. He lived with his parents on the outskirts of town in a former farmhouse where his dad now sold tires and car parts. The farmland had long since been sold to developers, the money long pissed away, and the Warren family now scraped out a living selling things and doing odd jobs for different people. Olving interviewed Shawn and decided to bring him on. He had no criminal record, and Olving felt that his less-than-pampered background shouldn't hurt his chances at defending his town. As for what he may have done as a child, well, boys will be boys, after all. Olving made Shawn a part of his group and resolved to keep a tight leash on him.

What Olving didn't know going into the New Year was that Shawn had a special taste for the destruction of one Armand Lillington, "half-breed nigger" that he was to Shawn. There had come a Saturday afternoon in the spring of 1975, shortly before meeting Cotler and me, that Spencer Lillington crossed the path of Shawn and a couple of his friends on the way back from Broyhill Park. Spencer, concentrating on riding his new bike as eight-year-olds often do and not looking carefully enough at where he was headed, almost collided with Shawn riding down the path.

He came to a stop inches before the three boys, all twice his age, and froze, looking up slowly. Shawn smiled rudely and punched Spencer with the heel of his hand in the chest. The boy went flying off his bike, which Shawn picked up and smashed against a nearby tree. Spencer looked on horrified, too afraid even to cry. He saved his crying for later. The bike had taken his mother months to save for on layaway and wouldn't be replaced anytime soon on their meager income. Shawn and one of the other boys with him worked the bike over until they were pretty sure it was trash. Then Shawn kicked him on the ground, this small boy with a slightly Asian-looking light brown face, accused him of being a half-breed, and walked on with his friends.

His brother Armand spent most of the next week trying to repair the bike, but his heart sank as he realized he had neither the tools nor the know-how to save it. It was a lost cause, and the broken bike in the Lillingtons' small basement was a constant and painful reminder of his inability to help his brother or, in the long run, to do anything right.

As luck would have it, Armand encountered Shawn Warren a few weeks later, alone on the same path where Spencer had encountered him. He then pounded Shawn into the color of heavy storm clouds on a summer's day. Shawn made up a story to his father and brothers about what happened that day, mostly because of his shame in being bested by a half-breed two years his junior. Thereafter, he kept his distance from Armand, but he didn't forget him. Indeed, he didn't forget his stinking half-nigger mud face one bit and looked forward to the day when he would let Armand know that in just those vile words.

6

Tuesday, January 15. I was turning to go back into the house when I heard the familiar screech of the tires on Cotler's truck begging for purchase around my corner. He pulled up to the house and I gave him a questioning look as the truck came to a purring rest. He had dropped me off from school not twenty minutes before.

"What time you got?" he asked me. Something weird and potentially wild was in his eyes.

"Three thirty-five. Why?"

"Calvin ain't home. Ain't been home from the looks of things. No note. No nothin'... I called the usual places and he ain't there either."

Without a word, I jumped in beside him and we wheeled back down the block, Cotler's quick eyes scanning for playing children as we gunned it toward the boulevard. There was no reason to articulate Cotler's fear. He knew Calvin and I knew Calvin, and the Calvin we knew came home directly from school—without fail—and never, ever went anywhere without a note to his brother. Fair or unfair, Cotler did not allow his brother to live the life he himself had led as a child, making his way alone hither and yon through woods and over fields and beside highways, catching rides and hoofing it home in the dark. Cotler knew where his brother was, had a vague idea anyway, all the time.

Especially now.

"Does your father know?" I asked and was immediately sorry I'd asked it. Cotler seemed to take no notice and shook his head.

"He's in Leesburg. I could page 'im, but I ain't gonna worry him over what isn't nothin' at all. We'll find 'im. And when I do I'm gonna throttle 'im for not telling me where he was."

But Cotler's normally dulcet and sleepy eyes were awake and maddeningly keen. The kind of eyes he wore hunting. Cotler was afraid. His little brother was unaccounted for in a town that was haunted for young males, and he was very, very afraid. The fact he had hightailed it over to my house upon ascertaining that his brother was indeed "missing" belied his scolding, "boy-this-is-some-inconvenience" tone. Shamefully, I reveled in that for a moment, happy on some childish level that Cotler had come to me before beginning his search. It was one of the precious few times in our long life together, and I can count them on one hand, that I knew Cotler, for all of his stubborn and cold independence, also needed me.

***

Within an hour, we had covered every part of the town where we might reasonably expect to find him. "All right," he said as we paused in front of Pullen Park, the small, roadside park from our childhood with the short sloping field and the jungle gym at the bottom. "All right. Where haven't we looked?"

"We've been just about everywhere," I said, my tone careful. On the crest of the hill that defined Pullen Park, naked trees stretched jagged branches into the pale sky like drowning swimmers waving for help. "Maybe we should . . ."

Cotler slammed his big fist against the steering wheel and squinted into the dry orange of the setting sun.

"GOD DAMN IT, CALVIN, WHERE ARE YOU?!"

"Let's go back to the school," I said, after he had sunken into a scared, breathing silence. "That's where he was all day. We'll figure it out there. C'mon."

It was still early to prod Cotler into calling for backup, but that time was drawing near. The last thing that Cotler needed was to feel powerless in this situation, not to mention how far telling his father's men would go toward fully solidifying this nightmare, but the first thing Calvin needed was to be found. Circumstances of the town aside, January was January in Virginia, and it was in this time of year that one began to swear that she was no southern state. Although the days could be mild, as this one was, the nights got cold. *Cold.*

As we crested the hill on the boulevard before the turn we would make, I noticed a figure running alongside the road, clad in dirty sweats and an ancient navy wool cap. It was Vic, doing his afternoon twelve around town, and without really thinking I told Cotler to pull over to him. Cotler looked at me sideways but did as he was asked.

"That's Vic," he said. And the underlying tone that rode piggyback on every terse sentence Cotler ever spoke said, *That's Vic and I don't feel like dealing with his nonsense right now, okay, John?*

"Yes, it's Vic," I said, still thinking on some half-conscious plane. "Pull over to him."

"Why?" Cotler asked as we slowed to pull alongside him. Vic had not yet noticed us and he ran on toward the top of the hill, his pace strong and unbroken, the soles of his beat-up runners appearing second by second as he pounded the pavement in sharp, rhythmic steps. And then perhaps I knew.

"Because he can run."

Red-faced and puffing, Vic turned to me as we pulled

up to him on my side. He recognized us, and his face relaxed into a half smile. For a second I wanted to tell Cotler to go the hell ahead, to just wave at Vic and keep moving. He was not, after all, known for his tact or his ability to handle serious or potentially serious situations. But thank God for small favors.

"He's what?" Vic asked, hands on his knees as he caught his breath. He did it quickly, and was soon, very soon, breathing normally.

"He's . . . well, we don't know where he is," I said. "We need to find him before dark." I sat in the truck after I had told Vic what was up, not knowing what to expect from his breathing silence. He looked at me blankly for a moment and jerked his head slightly to the side, as if he'd been motioned by someone to his left. When he righted himself I saw with some relief an evenness in his eyes.

"Move over," he said. Without a word we were moving again.

Vic said nothing as we approached the school. Not a single question or suggestion passed his lips. Maybe our faces told him that we had checked everything—everything—already.

***

Belle Ridge Middle School, like all of the schools in town, sat on the western edge of the development at the end of a side street and backed up to the woods. The side street ended in a loop in front of the building where buses paused and official vehicles sometimes parked. To the rear of the school was a field that bordered the woods and a series of aging, weed encroached blacktops marked for dodge ball and other kids' games. As we parked in the front loop, Vic noticed a group of boys absently kicking a soccer ball in the front parking lot. He jogged over to them. Cotler walked over to the front school doors, checking each and peering into windows. After a few minutes, Vic hoofed back over to me.

"What did you get from the pimple brigade?" I asked. He shot me a dark look.

"Nothing good. Those kids said there's a rumor floating around that a boy got bagged today. They told me there's some other kid who hangs out here after hours and claims he saw it. Get Cotler, follow me."

"What?"

"You heard me. Get him and follow me. If that kid's still here, he'll be around back."

With Vic's explanation, Cotler sagged visibly and his eyes moved in meaningless patterns on the ground below us. I got him moving and saw that Vic had spotted the kid already when we turned the corner of the building.

He was perched on an air conditioning unit and looked to be roughly middle school age, dressed in torn jeans and an oversized denim jacket with a dirty sheepskin collar. A light wind blew his long, blond hair over his eyes from time to time, and he smoked nonchalantly while a group of three other boys watched him scrape his name or some neat cuss word or an anarchy symbol into the aluminum skin of the unit with a screwdriver. The three watching were smaller, somewhat better dressed, and only one other was smoking, and not doing much of a job at it.

"Hey, whatcha doin?" Vic asked as he approached the group. Sheepskin looked up, revealing pale blue or blue-gray eyes not unlike Cotler's and a ruddy, slightly predatory gaze that reminded me of Doug Lars. Sheepskin looked like a mean kid.

"What the fuck does it look like I'm doing?" he asked, amiably enough. Now the others moved back a little. I made eye contact with the other pseudo-smoker and he looked away. Cotler looked poised to speak but Vic put his hand out, as if to say *let me handle this*. We hung back as Vic came to a stop in front of the A/C unit.

"Look, kid. We don't mean any harm. But we also don't have time to waste. I may need your help, if you're the one who saw what I heard happened here earlier. I'm looking for a kid about your age—his name is Calvin. Calvin Cotler. Do you know him?"

The look in Sheepskin's eyes said that he did indeed. The reaction from the other three was more telling, though, and Vic saw it. They literally shrank away at the sound of the boy's name and looked at Vic with new suspicion. Sheepskin looked beyond Vic to Cotler and me.

"Calvin Cotler's the sheriff's son," Sheepskin said, looking down at his carving work. "Lots of people know him."

He was keeping his cool, better than the other three anyway, but he was guarding something. Vic knew he was close to pay dirt and it was time to get the kid to talk. The sun was only a sharp red afterglow in the western sky. He turned to the group of three. When he spoke, there was unfamiliar iron in his voice and something else that sounded high and wild. It was a half-mad and sharply unsettling tone I had heard in Vic a few times before, usually fueled by a slender white bottle and always, somehow, connected to his brother's memory.

"Find somewhere else to hang," he said to them. "Now." The kids looked from Vic to Sheepskin for a moment, and back to us. Sheepskin's eyes did not leave Vic, and he had nothing to say to his companions. They got moving, slinking away toward town. Sheepskin was tough for his age, but "for his age" was the key phrase. There had been more than gruffness in Vic's voice. There had been something that smelled eerily like danger, as if wires in Vic's head were glowing through his skin, red and bright orange.

But Sheepskin continued to smile. *Guys who look like they could be in college don't beat up sixth graders*, the smile said. *Not in this pussy-ass town, they don't*. It was a safe bet, actually. By the mid-eighties in Belle Ridge, boys who looked like they could be in college didn't beat up sixth graders, as a rule. Vic, however, had been born in 1967 and grew up in a Belle Ridge where guys who looked like they were past college age beat up sixth graders regularly for infractions as small as a chuckle over a lost pinball game. Behavior like what we were seeing from Sheepskin was unheard of when we were eleven. It would have been suicide.

"How long you been here?" Vic asked him. He was checking his voice now, bringing it down a notch. Cotler and I recognized this as an opportunity we would never have been given on the streets and schoolyards of the Belle Ridge of the 1970s. Not after that reception. Vic was giving him One Last Chance. Sheepskin said nothing in response and looked away, still employing his light, mean grin.

"I'd guess since school let out, is that about right?" No answer. "I think you have," Vic said. His voice was lower now, conciliatory. "Now I don't care what you're out here for and I don't pose a threat. But it's getting dark, and I hear you may have seen something today. I need to know if it's true. This is no joke. Help us if you can, okay?"

Sheepskin seemed to ponder this for a moment. He chuckled lightly, tossed his head back and lazily shot Vic the bird. With slippery speed, Vic reached forward and grabbed the offending middle finger with his left hand, pushing it back until it looked as if he would break it off. Before Sheepskin could even form a shriek though, Vic's right hand, a loose fist, swept backhanded into the side of the kid's face. Sheepskin dropped the screwdriver and went tumbling off of the A/C unit. He rolled over, holding his cheek and staring with absolute terror and surprise at Vic. Vic reached over and grabbed the kid's smokes from the A/C unit. He motioned for a lighter and I tossed him mine. He tucked one of them jauntily into the side of his mouth and lit it. Sheepskin, a heaving and lightly bleeding mass on the ground, continued to hold his face, staring at Vic in pain and utter disbelief. Vic regarded him like a rotting bird he had almost stepped on and smeared over the sidewalk.

"Calvin Cotler," Vic said, his voice now brimming with that greasy, wired energy. "Where did you last see him? Give me an answer, or I will put this out somewhere on your body. Now talk."

"H-he d-didn't leave until a while after everyone else," Sheepskin said through his swelling cheek. His eyes were wide, glassy circles wanting to cry. Cotler looked away, uncomfortable with Vic's methods surely, but he listened. "He came out the back doors, right there, and a guy called him over to the main path that goes into the woods."

"What guy?" Vic demanded, "What did he look like?"

"I don't know." A moan. "I don't know, he was too far away. He was w-white, and he had on some dark stuff. I think he had long hair, but I couldn't see that far. I just spotted him because he was older but he wudn't no teacher. P-Please."

"What time was this?" Cotler asked from behind Vic, speaking for the first time.

"I don't know. I ain't got a watch. It was maybe fifteen, maybe twenty minutes after everyone else left. There wudn't no one out here by then 'cept me and some other guys way down there. Please. Please, mister, don't burn me." Now Sheepskin did begin to cry, haltingly at first until he could contain it no longer.

Vic seemed less than moved. "Where did Calvin go? Speak, Goddamn you, I don't have time to listen to you blubber!" Sheepskin pointed to the path that led into the woods.

"He went over to talk to the guy. The guy kept calling him so he went over. And then, then . . ."

"Then what?" Cotler asked, stepping forward. "Then what?!" The kid looked up and the sight of Cotler standing over him brought out another moan.

"He grabbed him and forced him to run, *run down the path!*" Sheepskin half screamed. "Another guy came out of the trees and followed them. I didn't see him at all except from the back. He was white, too. He looked about y'all's age maybe. They ran and then they were gone. That's all I saw. I swear. There wudn't nothin' I could do. I swear!"

"God damn it," Cotler said, smooth and low. His eyes played over the tree line. His words fell on me like stones. "It's got my brother."

"Who do we call?" I asked. Cotler's eyes seemed to clear and he looked at Vic.

"Eric Buckman," he said, his voice controlled. "He should be patrolling the mall right now, making rounds. We need to get to him. That'll be quicker than dispatch, and I don't want my dad to find out that way . . ."

"Go," Vic said, gesturing toward the woods. "Find Calvin. I'll get Buckman." Cotler and I nodded and turned to leave.

"Vic," Cotler said, turning back as we broke into a jog, "do you want the truck?" Vic looked levelly at Cotler and shook his head. In my unquiet writer's mind I was vaguely aware that Vic was living one of the few very great moments of his life, the kind of once-or-twice-in-a-lifetime gestures that would make him somehow bigger, somehow better.

"You might need it," Vic said. "And I don't." He turned, ignoring the crying figure of Sheepskin on the ground and bolted like lightning toward another path that paved a short cut through the very easternmost patch of the woods to the mall, a little less than a mile away.

***

5:00. Cotler and I approached the trail leading into the woods side by side, Cotler already scanning the ground for clues. It was a trail Cotler knew well but probably hadn't used much since our middle school days. When we came to the entrance he stopped in his tracks and bent down, fishing a dull penny from a patch of dead and much stampeded leaves.

"Oh shit," he said, and his voice was higher than usual, a step away from a sob. "This is his. It's his lucky penny from Grandma. It's a wheat, or something." He handed it to me and I studied it. The penny was ancient and worn to a dull almond color. The date on it was 1912. I handed it back to Cotler and he jammed it into his pocket.

"I cain't," he breathed. "I just cain't. I cain't go in there."

"You have to. He's depending on you. Look, he's a smart kid. Maybe this penny didn't get here by accident. For all we know he dropped it here when he realized what was going on. He did it in case you got this far. Now come on."

"Come on and what? Where is he? How far have they taken him? Goddam, John, it's getting dark, I cain't see!"

"I've seen you track in darkness. I've seen you track in the rain and the snow. Besides, we've got a full moon tonight and it's as clear as a bell out here."

"Jesus, you want me to track my fucking brother?!"

"Now! Now, God damn it. Let's go!" Cotler licked his lips and peered ahead. We got moving, Cotler ahead of me, moving low and slow the way he did when in the woods and in search of something. He was skittish at first, constantly backtracking and cursing himself, but after a minute or two he began to smooth over, mumbling to himself and moving his head in patient sweeps across his field of vision. I watched this with relief. He spoke as if he'd read my mind.

"To your left," he said, his breath announcing itself in little clouds, "there's a broken twig. Any prints beyond it? We're looking for a few at a time. A turn with a boy in tow would mean a lot of shufflin' if they were still runnin'. Ground's hard but it's wet. If we try, we should be able to make out footprints." For a moment I saw only green and brown, melting together in the coming dark. Then I saw it, a snapped twig with a muddy smudge over it. But beyond it the foliage looked undisturbed by feet. I related this to Cotler and he nodded, moving on.

We moved farther along the trail, Cotler reckoning that we were heading northwest toward another trail that would run over to Copperhead Road. He spotted something else on the ground and picked it up, holding it up to the last of the daylight. It was a blue candy wrapper.

"This is him," he said, examining the wrapper closely. "Taffy from a bowl in the living room. He's been here. He's been this far."

A hundred yards farther we found a smooth rock with a face drawn on it in pencil. A quarter mile beyond that a folded coupon for a collection of baseball cards. Boys' things. Calvin Cotler was his father's son and had the survival instinct of a warrior. He was leaving us a trail.

"He's emptying his pockets," Cotler said, reading my mind. "There's other traffic on this trail, but not this far, at least not this time of year. I don't know how much he had to drop, but I hope he spread it out. We'll need it if they went off the path."

We moved on, feeling the darkness wed around us as we wound deeper into the woods. The trail led on to another, as he had predicted, and a freshly broken pencil piece to the left led us in that direction. I was vaguely thankful that Cotler was dealing with his terror by delving totally into the task of following The Trail, now unconsciously disassociated with what might be at the end of it. Did I remember coming out this way with Jim Simons and that fat redneck he hung out with once to look at *Playboys*? he asked. I vaguely remembered we had.

Other memories were also cascading back. There were doubts at first; everything in the woods looked foreboding to me, especially in the dark. But the lay of the land and the proximity to the school were too familiar. We passed a huge, hulking oak with a knot that looked oddly like a baby's face. Kelly had stopped here and urinated on this tree. He had pointed out the knot as he zipped up his jeans. I remembered how it had seemed to stare at me as he pulled me along again. I had been dragged down this trail once in life and had walked it a thousand times in nightmares.

We made our way primarily by the wedding white glow of the moon. It painted everything in stark, naked relief. We could see well enough, but the clues left by the boy had ceased to appear. The cold pried into our psyches and our flesh, seeking a way in. Cotler paused for a second to get his bearings. Desperation flashed in his eyes from time to time and I could see him pushing it back, shaking his head and trying to stay clear. He sighed and peered in both directions. Suddenly I had a picture of a place nearby.

"Where are we?" I asked, and a thickness formed in my throat.

"Up ahead is Copperhead Road," he said, breathing heavily and scanning around. "I guess they may have taken him that far. I just don't know. Fuck. I can't do this much longer. Moonlight is fool's light, it's nothin' to depend on. To the right is only woods until I don't know how far. To the left is—"

"A clearing. That right?" Cotler looked over at me.

"Yeah. How'd you know?"

"It's probably where we looked for Civil War stuff with Vic's brother that day in fourth or fifth grade," I lied. Cotler, his elephant's memory aroused, opened his mouth to correct me and I shushed him.

"The clearing," I said. "Is there a path that goes to it from where we are?"

"I doubt it," he said, his voice rising. I was losing him again. He blew warm air into cupped hands and swore under his breath. He whispered to no one in particular. "It's so cold out here. It's so goddam cold."

"The clearing," I said. "Show me where you think it would be easiest from this trail to get to it." Cotler looked around at dead trees and encroaching brush. Precious few sounds were heard around us, except for the dull rush of the wind through husks and fallen trees. He walked slowly up the trail and came to a stop between two large birch trees.

"Here," he said. "This goes out to it, I think."

"Lead," I said, hoping the memories and the fear weren't plain in my eyes. Cotler peered at me in the dark.

"What, John? Why here?"

"I don't know, just go. Something tells me, that's all. Since when do you question hunches?"

"When they ain't mine," he said curtly. His unintended cruelty, typical of him sometimes when we were in the woods, cut me like a knife, but I pushed it aside along with my own fear. The challenge was not losing Cotler to the beckoning madness of this situation. Petty resentments weren't going to help. Cotler studied my face, must have seen resolve there, and softened.

"All right," he said. "We'll look. Stay close."

He stepped through the birches and onto the soft leaf bed beyond. He sensed more than saw brambles and hanging branches, and he held them away from me as I moved behind him. He stopped and peered closely at the ground. He turned his head sideways and rested his ear on the dirt, a classic tracking technique that allowed the viewer to see an area as light was hitting it from a different angle, thus illuminating what would be missed from viewing it straight on. He reached down to check what he thought he had seen, and then looked back at me.

"Tracks!" he whispered. His eyes were tiny blinking lanterns in the dark. "This's been walked through. Stomped through, the way people do. It couldn't have been long ago." We moved forward and Cotler continued to feel and look at the same time, sweeping his hands through the floor of the woods below us. "There was more than one. They cut a regular path through here, they—" He stopped abruptly and spun toward me, putting a finger to his mouth. "Johnny, do you hear that?!" he hissed. I shook my head. All I could hear was a chorus in my mind, a chorus telling me to get the hell out . . .

"It's him!" Cotler hissed again, rising to his full height. His "him" came out "hee-im."

For a moment I thought I had lost him completely. But then I heard what Cotler was hearing. It was not an owl, or a lark, or a cruel trick of the wind. Cotler knew how those things sounded. It was singing. It was a boy, a woman I thought at first, his voice nervous and high and cracking, singing something that sounded like "Jimmy Crack Corn," that ancient song that never made any sense to me as a little boy. The sound was deceivingly far away, maybe a hundred yards or more through the brush. Far up ahead, through crisscrossing lines of black branches looking like tattered mesh against a dark blue sky, was a brighter, open backdrop. The clearing.

". . . my master's gone away . . . Jimmy . . ." There was exaltation as I recognized Calvin's voice fully for the first time, and then I was gripped with a terror that was draped in despair. I froze with it and gritted my teeth as Cotler rose to his feet.

The boy sings, yes, and the sound of his voice is as violently beautiful to you as perhaps the sound of your mother's would be, but maybe now there is something inside the boy, something cold and dark that was forced into him that has rendered him bad and empty. Maybe now something lives inside of him that has caused his voice to rise in what is not song but a creative scream. And this is assuming he is alone—that they have left him. Because if they haven't, and you are still a minute or more from reaching him . . .

In the second that Cotler leapt to his feet, I wanted to grab him back, pull him by the collar down to the hard, wet earth and tell him this, but I was too late. There was no stopping him now, sagely wise or not, no one could just listen to his brother singing pathetically in the dark and not call out to him in a yell. Cotler gathered his breath in a panicked, half-mad whoop. Then he clamped his mouth shut and looked at me, falling to his knees.

"What if he ain't alone?" he whispered, his breath in my face. His eyes were huge and alive. I regarded him with something like amazement. "What if they've got him still, or what if they're just . . . nearby?"

"I was thinking that," I managed, stifling the most unfit and useless smile that had ever threatened to leap to my lips. *Cotler old buddy*, I thought, *you are indeed the best. I want to hate you sometimes because you are so much better than me.*

"We'll follow their path," he said, looking toward the clearing. "It's already smushed out for us. When we get up to the clearing, if that's where he is, I'll make a sweep around him. You stay close."

"I'm afraid I'll make noise," I breathed. Cotler shook his head.

"Do like I taught you. Stay low and place each step you take. Don't panic if you hear a crunch. It ain't a church out here. Just follow behind. We ain't that far from him. If you see anything, anyone, that I miss, throw something at my back." He glided silently ahead through the brush.

The singing stopped when we were a hundred or so feet from the edge of the clearing, and Cotler stopped with it. There were some muffled sniffling and crying sounds, and then it resumed, high and cracking with fear and fatigue. It was heart-wrenching, and I marveled at Cotler's ability to keep his silence.

Twenty feet away, Cotler saw him first. He was sitting alone on part of an overturned tree and facing the clearing at its edge. His L.L. Bean knapsack was still on his shoulders. Cotler waited until I caught up with him.

"Stay put," he whispered. The wind picked up and blew a dry rustle through the trees. "I'm goin' around first. If it's clear I'll go in from the other side. I'll scare him, but I'm not takin' any chances." I nodded and he was gone.

The clearing. It was exactly as I remembered, small and vaguely semi-circular. To the right was the little hill from which it was possible to survey the area, atop it a small grove of trees. The little boy sitting on the tree stump and rocking back and forth against the cold was a mirror image I thought I would never see in reality. His face was pointed away from me and I silently cursed this, knowing that if I could just see his eyes I'd know if he'd been touched.

The glow of the moon rendered the scene a ghastly, pale blue-white. Calvin, his arms crossed tightly against his chest, rocked and sang, rocked and sang. I moved up a step, wanting a chance to assess the boy before Cotler got to him. I leaned forward and rose on my aching hamstrings. It was no use, he was facing . . .

Calvin spun around on the log and peered in my direction.

Jesus, I thought, *I haven't made a sound. He smells me. Christ, the kid really is a Cotler.* And on the heels of that thought as his eyes peered in my direction: *He's not hurt. His eyes are clear, even. He's scared, plenty scared. But he's not hurt. Not that way.*

"Francis?" the boy called softly, the hope palpable in

his voice. His lower lip trembled and he leaned forward on the log. "Francis, is that you?" The hope seemed to vanish from his gaze and he buried his head in his arms, sobbing stiffly. "Francis, please," he called through tears, "Francis, please come and get me. Francis, I'm cold and it's dark and, and . . ." He broke off and cried again. He was calling habitually for his brother, repeating his name over and over, the way lost and frightened children call for their mothers. I felt like my heart would burst. Then Cotler stepped quietly from the brush where he'd been squatting after his loop around the clearing.

"I'm here, Calvin," he said, his voice deep and warm against the hollow, screeching sounds of wind and forest. Calvin whipped around toward him and for a moment just gaped at his older brother as if his grandest wish had just manifested itself at the behest of a wizard in a puff of colored smoke.

"Francis!" he breathed, "Francis, wh-wh-where?"

Cotler shushed him and took the boy into his arms, holding him as if he were a life preserver. Calvin clung to his brother and hooked his feet around his waist, sobbing heavily. I did not move. I stayed covered by the brush for some amount of time, watching them and collecting my emotions. I stayed there for quite a while.

***

On the way back to the school, Calvin admitted, much to Cotler's chagrin, that he had been talked into approaching the path to the woods by a young guy with long hair who claimed to know me. Calvin described how this guy had drawn him farther down the path simply by talking in a low voice and backing up a step or two every few seconds, so that Calvin had to step toward him just to hear. After a few steps, Calvin said another guy he'd never seen before came out of nowhere and pushed him forward, ordering him not to turn around. Calvin walked between the two guys as he was directed, and they left him in the clearing. His orders were to stay put until they came back, and that they would be nearby and would hurt him if he tried to leave on his own. By the time we reached the school, I was positive that Lon had been behind this, somehow. It would soon be known all over town as a cruel hoax.

Calvin was examined by a paramedic in a waiting ambulance as we reached the schoolyard, and blankets and hot soup were handed to all of us. A search party had already formed with the sheriff at the center of it. He gave us heartfelt thanks as we were cheered by dozens of cops and the other searchers gathered there.

"Thanks a million," Cotler said as his soup cup sent a veil of steam around his face. We were perched on the warm hood of a squad car. His voice was gravely and deep and his eyes gleamed.

"You found him," I said.

"No," Cotler said, shaking his head and casting his eyes down in an unconscious gesture of apologetic admiration. "You did. And you kept me from crackin' up." He raised his eyes, and what I saw there beneath the gleam of emotion was sly, probing, and still admiring. "That was a hell of a hunch. I'm goddam sorry I doubted you. I'd just love to know how you knew."

"No, you wouldn't," I said smiling, knowing the remark would be ignored. Cotler looked at me quizzically for a second and smiled to himself, turning back to his soup. Behind us engines cranked to life, headlights shot white light in every direction, and laughter and catcalls filled the air, making the playground alive with the sounds of exiting men and cars.

***

The call came at about 7:30, within ten minutes of my getting home from our adventure in the woods. "Today was a warning," Lon said flatly into the phone as soon as he'd recognized it was me. He was at a pay phone as usual. I wondered where. "I suggest you chew on it a bit before you get any more big ideas."

"I wanna talk," I said, hoping I was hissing with anger. "I wanna talk tonight."

"You don't call meetings," he said.

"Cut the shit, Lon. I wanna talk to you and I wanna talk tonight. Nine-thirty."

"Okay, John," he said after a long pause. "I'll indulge this. I'll even make it easy. Nine thirty. Trailhead at the high school. Be alone."

***

My feet made crunching imprints in what passed for grass on the practice field as I headed for the tree line at 9:28. My face tingled and my ears sang with the cold. This was not going to be a long meeting. Besides, I had no idea of what I was going to say.

I peered into the woods from the trailhead and saw nothing. Without warning, I was blinded by the flash of Lon's camera. I cursed under my breath and waited for sight again while he set the camera down beside him. He was perched on a stump about four feet to the right, deep in the shadows.

"You went too far today," I said. Lon munched absently on some bit of food I couldn't see, then cast the wrapper aside.

"I'll be the judge of that."

"No," I said, my heart now thudding in my chest. "I'm drawing a line here. I didn't do anything that invited this."

"Oh no?" Lon said, cutting his eyes to me in an understated glare. "You think I didn't know what you were trying to do the other night around the fire? You think I couldn't smell you, trying to get a rise out of me?"

"Best I remember, it worked," I said. Lon smiled thinly.

"I know what you suspect me of, John. It doesn't take a genius to figure I'm a big part of what's going on around here. But I tell you this now: If I have to alter my life one bit because of you sending the sheriff or anyone else my way, you'll be sorrier than you ever thought possible. Don't play so far over your head."

"I can't live with what you're doing much longer," I said, fighting to back the words with conviction. I was frightened and trying to maintain a focus. He picked up a bottle of some cheap-looking wine beside him and took a long plug. His hands were gloveless, and I could see that they were pink and swollen from the cold. *Focus,* I thought to myself. *Focus.* "Do you understand me, Lon? I can't live with it much longer."

"Live with what? Say it. Let me hear you say it." The word weighed my tongue down.

"Murder."

"Murder," he said, chuckling. "That's a legal term. I prefer euthanasia. That's a big word. Ever heard of it?"

"It's still illegal, last I heard."

"Don't lecture me, John. Anything you could offer me is well-covered territory. You can't live with murder? Learn to. It hasn't stopped."

"How many more?"

"How many more are there?" he asked. I looked at him, my brow wrinkled.

"Kids?"

"No. Places. Places to leave them, like calling cards. Terrance was found by the old well. Jim liked that spot, told us the legend and everything. Jeremy was found by the log bridge. You remember that place, too, I'm sure. There's a couple of other places, John. Familiar places, safe places. Places well known and well grown over. Places to be revisited, with sacrifice."

"I won't let you kill again," I said. "Whatever it takes, I won't let you." He fixed me with a look of pure, menacing disgust.

"Don't ever threaten me. Don't, unless you want the real medicine. You got lucky today—you and your butt-buddy are big heroes. We would have dropped him at the school a little later. Maybe about now. Maybe later. Did Cotler ask how you knew where he'd be? Did he?"

"I knew this was useless," I said, shaking my head. "I'm out of here."

"You little faggot!" he hissed, and there was an eerie wildness in his voice. It was deeper somehow, croaking even, and I wished I could see him better. I listened close- ly to the voice. "That's what you called me out here for? I came out here in the fucking freezing cold to hear this?"

"You've *been* out here in the freezing cold," I said. "You think I can't tell, Lon?" I was scared, scared of pushing him too far, but the words were too many to keep behind my lips. "Your hands are raw. I don't know where you got that food, but my guess is you probably stole it. And why are you hiding? I can't really see you in there, and I think that's for a reason. Maybe you don't look so good. I don't think you've got a steady place to stay these days, do you?" I could feel him calming, settling back on his stump.

"Clever, John. Clever, but not smart. There's a distinction there you couldn't possibly fathom. Keep it up and you'll see how far this little game of yours gets you." The hiss in his voice was no longer dominating now.

"You're not living with him anymore, are you?" I asked. He smiled.

"I like it better on my own. I always have. Don't worry about me, John. What I need I can get—very easily."

"From Jim?"

"Sure. Among others."

"Does he know who you are?" I asked. Lon smiled wider.

"Who do you say I am? That's almost a Bible verse."

"I don't know."

"Neither does Jim. He's a stupid redneck who thinks he's a smart redneck. It works out well between us. Anyway, I don't bother him much. He doesn't need to know who I am, and neither do you."

"Who was the other one today, Lon?" I asked, changing the subject. "Who was the other one with you on the trail? I know it wasn't Jim. He's in West Virginia until next week, and Cotler's father talked to him on the phone there tonight. I know it wasn't Vinnie either. He couldn't run from here to there, let alone be any help with something like that. Who was it?"

"Who do you think it was?"

"Doug Lars comes to mind. You've got him on the team, haven't you?" He shrugged.

"Maybe yes, maybe no. Maybe I've got more friends than you believe, Johnny. Just remember what happened today. If you cross me again, it gets worse. Much worse." He scrambled up and backed into the woods away from me, tossing his wine bottle. "And by the way, don't you ever call me out here again for nothing. That counts as crossing me, too." He turned and walked swiftly between the trees and was gone.

Stupid, I thought, as I hiked back to the truck, warming stiff hands with my breath. *I was really stupid for doing this.* And another part of me: *But you're warmer than he is. You have a home and he doesn't, if he ever did. And that counts. Don't ask me how, but it does. Despite what he wants you to believe, time is no longer on his side.*

Maybe, I replied to myself, marveling at the brilliance of the moon now straight up in the naked, frozen sky. *Maybe.*

7

The call that Sheriff Cotler received late on the night of January 17 from John Olving was one that, in the back of his mind, he expected sooner than it came. Armand Lillington, he told the sheriff, had assaulted one of his "patrolmen" that night, and Olving wanted a warrant. The sheriff asked who was assaulted. Shawn Warren, Olving said. Shawn had come to Olving's home about an hour earlier and said that, while walking a perimeter in his area of the woods, he, Shawn, had come upon Armand Lillington creeping around out there alone. Shawn asked Lillington what he was doing, and Lillington lunged at him, brandishing a knife. Shawn ducked, and a brief struggle ensued. Shawn was able to disarm Armand, and punches were thrown. Shawn swore, though, that he did not strike first. During the struggle, Shawn admitted to reaching for his weapon in fear, and that he had possibly struck Armand with the butt of it to defend himself. When Armand finally saw the gun, Shawn said, he stood back and told Shawn to mind his own business. He could come out here whenever he wanted. In addition, Warren said Lillington made statements to him like "I can come and go as I please. You all haven't caught me yet." What did the sheriff think about that?

Sheriff Cotler wasn't sure what to make of the statements, but he agreed to have a deputy take a report from Shawn Warren or to take him to Leesburg to swear out a warrant for assault. That was the problem, Olving said. Shawn didn't want to swear out a warrant. He felt the situation didn't merit the involvement of the law. It was Olving who wanted the warrant. He had been trying to talk Shawn into getting one all night, but the kid was refusing and that worried Olving. He didn't want Shawn to take matters into his own hands. He certainly didn't want his group to get a vigilante reputation.

The sheriff informed Olving that no magistrate would issue a warrant based on second or third-hand information. Unless Shawn would swear it out, Olving could forget about an 'A and B' charge. Cotler asked if Shawn was injured at all, and Olving said Shawn looked fine to him, but he was understandably shaken up. What about the statements then, Olving wanted to know. The sheriff assured Olving he would personally take a statement from Shawn Warren with his investigators the next day. He

hung up, took his gun, badge, and keys, and went searching for Armand himself.

8

Spencer wasn't able to help the sheriff with the whereabouts of his brother. He hadn't seen him in several days.
Armand hadn't been at work, either. In any event, John
Olving didn't wait for Armand to be found. Instead he
went to the media and began to create fervor for his arrest. The sheriff responded that he and his fellow investigators had in fact been monitoring Armand Lillington
and several other people as suspects for months. Armand
didn't appear to be a particularly likely suspect, but he
was taking the alleged statements seriously and was looking for Armand to question him.

The public wanted more. The first organized protest occurred outside the sheriff's once quiet office in
Leesburg, a three-hundred-year-old town that had been
a part of two major wars, but hadn't seen much protest
since the late 1850s. Rumors raged that the sheriff was
turning his head because his son was a friend of Armand's
brother, and these rumors did not abate even when
state and FBI representatives echoed Cotler's opinion of
Armand as a suspect. There were also rumors about the
abduction of Cotler's own son. He was, after all, the only
boy who had come back alive. Was this because the per-
petrator, possibly Armand or an accomplice, recognized
his latest capture and decided to release him because he
was the sheriff's son? Some of it was fear, some of it stupidity, and some just plain human meanness. The sheriff

was accused of everything from gross negligence to participating in an actual cover-up.

Hate mail arrived at Sheriff Cotler's home and office, the worst of it racially motivated and accusing him of being a "nigger-lover" and "half-breed apologist." The sheriff turned over the particularly dangerous-looking hate mail to the postal inspector, answered the protesters as best he could, and went about his business. The Cotlers' home was vandalized twice in January, once with eggs and once with a brick that went through their living room window. Calvin was sleeping quite a bit at our house, and Cotler, despite his father's admonitions, was sleeping with a rifle.

9

"Hey, slick," Lon said over the phone. It was Saturday, January 19, a cold, gray waste of a day. I had been up for about fifteen minutes when he called. "Rise and shine. I've got plans for us tonight." I looked down at the sandwich I had just made and now no longer wanted.

"Please," I said. "Not tonight. I've got plans that are too hard to get out of."

"What the fuck do I sound like, a volunteer coordinator? I say it's tonight, it's tonight."

"A cousin of Cotler's is having a party tonight for his Marine Corps graduation. We've been planning it for weeks, and—"

"Why am I listening to this? Are you telling me no?"

"Jesus, it's gonna be too hard to explain my way out of!" I could feel panic edging its way into my stomach and spreading.

"That's your problem. Vinnie's friendless. It sucks, but he's got less scheduling conflicts."

"Lon, I can't." Silence.

"You all haven't found Armand Lillington yet, have you?"

"No. Why?"

"I was just thinking. The sheriff knows Armand didn't kill anyone. This dipshit town'll figure it out eventually. It's been fun to watch him get lynched, though. I tickle myself sometimes. So, who do you think is doing it?"

"You know goddam well who I think is doing it."

"It sounds like you've made up your mind. But you know, John, a young man like yourself with a troubled past could be a murder suspect if the right people stood up and pointed fingers at him. What if something like that were to happen?" The panic now walked casually through my groin, arms, and legs, and made me numb and loose.

"That's ridiculous," I said, my hands shaking so much I almost dropped the phone. "You think Cotler's father would ever believe something like that?"

"Cotler's father needs a killer or he needs another job. It'll be unfortunate, yes. Break his heart, maybe. But it may make too much sense to ignore. What with Vinnie and me doing our duty, putting the pieces together. Abuse. Anger. Rage. Opportunity. Think about it. Armand'll look like a local hero. It'll be a civil rights victory for the town if they can pin it on the white kid who really did it instead of the black kid no one likes. Have you truly asked yourself if you were capable of it?"

"You're crazy. This is all crazy." On the other end I could hear Lon smile.

"The day Terrance Hark disappeared, you were alone. August nineteenth, remember? You were supposed to go with your friend Francis to pick up a car part but you missed his call and stayed home. The night Jeremy Bingham disappeared, you were on your way to pick up Steve for work—but he couldn't go, could he? You went alone. You had plenty of time. And who found his body after all that time? Wasn't it—"

"It was Cotler who found him," I said through clenched teeth. My head was swimming.

"I'm not sure he'll remember it that way. Are you? I'll see you at midnight."

10

"Flower run," Steve said, crushing out a cigarette in an old planter of my mother's. "That'll be our excuse as to why we have to leave the party around midnight."

"You're going to say we're going on a flower run?" I asked. A flower run meant stealing flowers from various gardens or greenhouses around town and dropping them on the doorstep of a girl one of us liked. It was a fun late-night outing, but usually reserved for the warmer months.

"We're going on a flower run at midnight, just you and me. We'll leave the party and come back. Simple as that. When we go, you split off and do what you have to do with them. We'll meet up again later and go back to the party."

"It may not be that easy," I said, whining in spite of every effort not to. "Whatever he's got planned could take all night. And it could be news by tomorrow morning. At the very least, Cotler'll know about it. I've done this before. It's not going to be throwing toilet paper in someone's maple tree."

"We'll cross that bridge when we come to it. Maybe we got caught pulling flowers in someone's greenhouse and had to talk our way out of it with some old guy who befriended us and made us a pot of coffee. Maybe we got a flat and had to walk back to town. Don't worry. I'll figure it out."

"You and I will be missing whenever this happens, this thing that Lon wants me to do. You'll be a suspect, Steve." He shook his head.

"You're thinking too much. No one suspects you or me of anything. If nothing else, I really will leave flowers somewhere. And you were with me the whole time. Believe me, this'll work."

"Where will you leave flowers? Which girl?"

"None of them. I'll pick a new girl. It'll work, and it's the least of your worries right now."

"I want to believe that," I said.

"Right now, you have to."

***

At 12:15, Vinnie and I were driving in silence on a dark two-lane road six miles west of town in his mother's Camry. After years of driving or riding in trucks and big, American cars, the low, smooth, and compact inside of the Toyota was a weird sensation. Vinnie's glasses reflected the red dash lights in a neat, rounded pair as he watched the road and fields ahead of us.

Between my legs on the floor was what Lon had given us to perform tonight's task. It was a plain white kitchen bag filled with raw meat. Vinnie made a turn at a lonely-looking stop sign, and then we were on the road that ran past R.W.'s farm. I motioned for him to slow down as we approached the mailbox that bore his name and route number. We parked some distance off the road.

Outside, the night was equally cold and dark. The clouds had moved away, and a brilliant cover of stars shone above us as we crept our way across R.W.'s wide front yard. His long, red brick ranch house was dark and quiet to our left. We moved along the side fence, praying for no traffic to pass us, approaching the small corral where R.W. kept his prize possessions in old age; three purebred Great Danes. The meat, Lon had told us, would make the dogs sick for three days, thus making R.W.'s life a frightened hell for the better part of a week. He'd assured us the dogs would be inside because of the cold, and they would find the meat when R.W. let them out early in the morning. How Lon observed this process I didn't know, but then I also had no idea how Lon spent his days or nights since leaving school.

Vinnie kept a lookout as we approached the fence that marked off the corral. In a neighboring field a dog barked, making us freeze, but the sound was distant. I emptied the bag onto the ground in a corner of the corral and looked over the pen as the meat fell with a dull thump. We made our way back toward the road. R.W.'s house sat on a rise, and in front of us the fields and patches of woods rolled downward to yield a beautiful view of the Dulles terminal, glowing on the eastern horizon.

"That meat's gonna kill those dogs," Vinnie said as we plodded through the cold, stiff grass. In his glasses the airport glowed like an apparition. I had thought the same thing since Lon had first given us the bag.

"Go back and get it if you want," I said. He grunted and said nothing. The wind began to pick up across the open field, and our steps, crunching the frosted grass, were the only sounds as we trudged away from R.W.'s sleeping house to Vinnie's waiting car.

11

I could have dealt with hearing from Cotler that someone had poisoned Ron Wilson's dogs. I expected that anyway. What was unexpected and unbearable was seeing that man in Dan Cotler's kitchen on Sunday afternoon. R.W. was a man whose shape made him appear even larger than he already was. He was about Cotler's height and had a large head, long face and deeply defined jowls. His eyes, even for an older and politically experienced man were large, searching, and perpetually innocent-looking. His shoulders now drooped with age, and a fine, large belly protruded from his middle, but these things only served to accentuate his size. He was one of the few men in our part of the state who wore a cowboy hat as naturally as pants, and now he held that hat in big shaking hands as his eyes washed over me and he nodded in greeting. His eyes were red-rimmed and haunted. He had been crying.

"Do you know R.W., John?" the sheriff asked.

"Not personally. It's good to know you, sir." We shook hands but R.W. looked tortured and far away. He was un-comfortable with me there and I made no move to stay. Cotler called from upstairs and I shuffled off after giving a polite good-bye. Cotler and I took our usual places in his room, me on the bed and him on the desk, glancing occasionally out the window with perpetually new interest at the same yard he'd seen for eighteen years.

"Why's R.W. in your kitchen? He looks like hell." I knew what I was going to hear, but in spite of myself I braced for even worse news; something like R.W. had cooked the meat in some moment of madness and killed his wife. Cotler shook his head with grim disgust and related the details.

"I'm sorry," I said, with more feeling than I intended. "Does he have any idea who?"

"Naw, he can't think right now. Bucky and Rich went over there this morning and didn't find much in the way of clues. R.W. was a big man around here for forty years, pissed off a lot of folks. I guess it could be a lot of people. But what *kind* of a person? What kind of a person poisons a man's dogs?" He looked at me with such feeling and wonder that I had to force myself from turning away in burning shame.

"The world's full of them," I said. He nodded.

"Oh, one thing I meant to ask you. Who did y'all drop flowers to last night?" There was no suspicion in his voice, but I tightened anyway as I told him the name of some fictitious girl Steve and I had decided on. "Well, we got a call this morning. A guy named George DeWitt said his daughter got flowers thrown on their doorstep last night. He wanted us to know in case it was related to some vandalism around town."

"George DeWitt? Is he . . ."

"Yeah. Callie DeWitt's father. George didn't know what to do about it. Callie DeWitt ain't exactly the type of girl to get flowers tossed on her doorstep every night, poor thing." That was sad but true. Callie DeWitt was a sweet, gentle-hearted girl with the face of a goat. She was a brilliant budding mathematician, though, and more than a few students sought her advice in Senior Commons during lunch. Steve was one of them.

"That's true," I said. "What did your dad say?"

"He told him to let his daughter enjoy the flowers. Apparently the girl's walkin' on a cloud because of it. There's someone for everyone, I guess."

"I guess," I said slowly. "I guess."

12

Armand appeared at the Cotlers' house late on the evening of January 21 in need of a shower and still bruised from where Shawn Warren had pistol-whipped him. The sheriff cleaned him up, gave him a hot meal, and took his statement. After he heard it, he decided to keep Armand at his house for the time being and told no one of his whereabouts except for his own investigatory contacts.

Armand admitted to encountering Shawn Warren on the night of January 16. The area that Shawn was patrolling was a thin part of the woods that bordered the old street where Armand's metal shop was. Armand walked home from work every night, sometimes to his mother's house to sleep, and sometimes just out to grab something from the store before returning to his back room behind the shop. The path that cut through the woods, Armand said, was the easiest way to get anywhere. That was true. Getting to his mother's house or to the stores nearby was much quicker by way of the path through the woods than any other way.

He told the sheriff he had left his room behind the shop at around 10:00 p.m. on the night of the sixteenth because he was hungry. He knew it wasn't smart to cut through the woods, but there wasn't anything at the shop and he hadn't eaten since lunch. He was walking on the path when Shawn Warren shined a flashlight in his face and told him to freeze. Armand panicked and turned to run, and Shawn threatened to shoot him in the back. Shawn walked over and told Armand to lay face down on the ground. Armand refused, and Shawn hit him in the back of the head with the gun. Armand turned to fight him, and Shawn was ready. He used the gun on Armand's face like a hammer and threatened killing him for not obeying his commands. Armand stayed quiet, afraid for his life, and Shawn finally walked off. His left eye was dark black and badly bandaged. He had lost a front tooth, and it caused him to lisp pathetically. He had heard about the things he had supposedly said to Shawn. No, he hadn't said anything like that. He offered to take a lie detector test.

The sheriff considered the stories of the two men involved in the incident. Armand, he knew, was a troubled young man with a generally bad disposition and a nasty temper. He had known Armand all the young man's life and had been to his house as a state trooper working domestic calls between Armand's mother and father before Willie Lillington had been sent to the downstate prison where he eventually died. He also knew Shawn Warren, and indeed had known the Warren family all of his own life. The Warrens had been native to Tolland for as far back as he could remember. They had also been nothing but trouble-causing white trash for that long. Shawn was a liar and a bully; the sheriff knew this well. He had managed to avoid a criminal record by keeping his mischief and other pursuits below the level of legal scrutiny, but he had been interviewed and asked to testify by deputies and by the sheriff himself on a few county-wide drug cases and had lied through his teeth every time. Armand, on the other hand, was violent and withdrawn, but he was no liar. No law enforcement officer, judge, social worker, or probation officer who ever worked with Armand could say that he was ever anything but nakedly, sometimes cruelly, honest. Whether he was incapable of lying or just unencumbered with the pressures that tempt others to lie, he simply did not do it. He admitted to probation violations when confronted with them. He admitted to drug use, soliciting a prostitute once or twice in D.C., and to being drunk one night when stopped for a DWI. He had also admitted, to various authorities, his desire to kill several people, from his own father to various boys who had picked on him and his brother for being 'mixed' children and the sons of a convicted felon.

***

The sheriff had Armand retell his story. He asked for details and watched the young man's face. The story was consistent. It jived with the injuries that had been sustained by the parties. It made solid sense and he believed it. He also knew that, given Armand's past and the current mood of the town, it was going to be important to keep him very close. Afterward, the two men talked about the day Jeremy Bingham disappeared. The sheriff listened closely.

13

Once John Olving and his group heard that the sheriff was "taking Armand's side," as they termed it, more protests were held and a petition drive was started to remove the sheriff. The county attorney determined that it lacked enough signatures, though, to merit a recall election. The last time anyone had faced the removal of a sheriff in Tolland was the royal governor Lord Tolland himself, who had dismissed one summarily in 1760 from his office in London.

The next person Olving's people sought out was Stewart Delbridge, the county's seventy-year-old, eight-term Commonwealth's Attorney. Delbridge was a rotund, crusty, stooped-over country lawyer who had a sharp tongue and a proclivity for profanity. He favored off-white linen suits and spoke with an accent that few people in Tolland County still had. He was, to the transplanted denizens and progressive new residents of the county, an embarrassing anachronism. He had helped to enforce segregation in Tolland in the forties and fifties because it had been the law, although since the laws had changed, even his greatest detractors admitted that he was above reproach in his dealings with minority defendants.

John Olving also longed for the day when Delbridge, with his pocket watch and tobacco slur, would retire quietly to his farm outside of Leesburg, but under the current circumstances, he was happy to have him. Delbridge wouldn't fall prey to this ridiculous political correctness that Cotler seemed wedded to, if that was what it was. Delbridge was immune to the politics of the new Tolland. He was an old boy headed for retirement who wouldn't give a damn if the rest of the region thought it distasteful to be going after a black man for the murder of white children.

Olving was right in one respect: Delbridge was immune to politics, or any other opinion for that matter. On the last Tuesday in January, Olving and his group went to the Commonwealth's Attorney's office to meet with him, asking for an investigatory grand jury that would compel producing Armand as a witness. Delbridge replied that such an investigatory grand jury was not allowed in Virginia. They demanded direct indictments of Armand, then, before the regular grand jury. Delbridge refused, citing not nearly enough evidence on what he warned was becoming a "witch hunt" out east, which meant the eastern part of the county. The group staged another protest, and the media came running.

It turned out to be one of our county's finest moments in retrospect. Here, after all, was the white-suited, slow-talking country lawyer from still rural Virginia looking like an overseer and yet declaring that he would not seek indictments against a black man on flimsy evidence just because some angry white folks wanted it. Cameras and boom mikes in his face, reporters tried to hit the hot buttons as they questioned him—and must have been mad with joy at his responses. Didn't he feel the pressure here of a race-related prosecution? Wasn't it true that he had to think twice, given his own past, before going after a black man accused of this crime?

"Hell, no!" Delbridge responded in a growl, his bulbous, red nose like a lantern on his round face. He stood on the steps of one of the prettiest courthouses in Virginia and shook his hat in front of a grateful bank of cameras. "When we find who killed those babies I won't give a damn if the son of a bitch is coal black or snow white. We'll go for his head. But a prosecution for these crimes won't go forward until I have more to chew on than what I've got!"

Chapter Seven: February

1

There was a school-wide pep rally on Valentine's Day for the boys and girls track teams, which under the guidance of the coaches and team leaders like Vic, had progressed further and further toward a state championship in recent years. The 1985 season was set to begin in a week, and with the talent the school had to offer, it looked like a great one was in the works. Early March, just a few weeks away, was also the time of the annual Moreland Invitational, a twelve-mile cross-country run around Belle Ridge that in its third year now attracted fifteen schools. It was a proud day for Vic, and in his senior year with most of his hopes for his team realized, he had reason to be prouder still. He sat quietly among his teammates in a dirty, oversized flannel shirt while Coach Bonner outlined the team's accomplishments and gave a short and heartfelt tribute to Marty. It was in the middle of this that Steve grabbed my leg from under the bleachers.

"What the fu—Steve? What are you doing?" Cotler saw it, too, and waved down to him.

"Risking my ass by sneaking into a pep rally in front of the whole fucking school," he hissed up at us. "Get down here, quick. Meet me by the trophy case. There's an emergency."

"It can't wait ten minutes? This is Vic's big show."

"No," Steve said. "Believe me, it can't wait ten minutes. Hurry."

Steve was standing in front of the trophy case when we came into the front hallway, a look of pure, unadulterated disgust on his face. He was standing in front of the portrait that hung there of Marty Moreland.

"Shit," Cotler whispered when we reached the trophy case. "How did that get in there?"

"I don't know. I came in late to catch the tail end of Vic's thing and I saw it. I don't think anybody else has seen it, but everyone is going to if we can't get it out of there." Steve swore under his breath and stared past his reflection to the sign under Marty's picture.

The trophy case at East Tolland was like most school trophy cases, built into the wall and protected by sliding glass, locked in places with steel bolt mechanisms that turned with a key. In one section of the case was a collection of cross-country memorabilia. Among the trophies was the school's first uniform and photos from the first meet. There was also a 12x18 portrait of Marty. Someone had managed to slide a piece of poster board between the glass doors where they met in this section of the case, and had pushed it far enough so that it sat, crooked but readable, on the shelf in front of the portrait of Vic's smiling, gentle-eyed brother. In red letters it read "Marty Moreland. Dead Faggot." The three of us looked at it for a few seconds until distant sounds from the gym got us in motion again.

"We've got to get it out of there," Steve said, looking at his watch. "In about eight minutes the whole school is going to pour past here and see this. That can't happen, least of all today."

"Let's go get Roland," I said. I meant Roland Washington, our principal. None of us would have ever called him by his first name, but for some reason we tended to refer to him that way. "He's got to have a key."

"No good, I thought about that. Principals don't walk around with keys to trophy cases. Coach Carrington probably keeps one on him, but he could be in the fucking softball field putting down grass seed. That'll take too long. We need to get it out *now*."

"How, dude? It's locked, remember? We can't slide it back out."

"What about the lock?" Steve asked. "Cotler, can you pick that?" Cotler examined it briefly, then went sprinting out the door to his truck. He was back in less than a minute, a long screwdriver and a hammer in his hand. Steve and I looked at them and grimaced.

"Can't you use a wire hanger or a hair pin or something that won't break it?" I asked. Cotler shook his head as he examined the lock again with his tools in hand.

"I ain't that good. It could take ten minutes, and we don't have ten minutes. John, hold the glass out a little ways. Be careful, I'm gonna swat it now." Steve stood back and I held one pane of glass out from the other one as best I could while Cotler prepared to jam the sharpest screwdriver he had into the lock. "The whole world's gonna hear this," he said under his breath. He grimaced and swung the hammer. BAM. The glass shook violently in my hands, creaked eerily all the way up to the ceiling, but did not break. Inside the gym the noise had risen to a fever pitch, which was a blessing. Cotler whistled a sigh of relief and turned the screwdriver. The lock turned and he slid the case open.

"Now what?" I asked as we held the poster and the tools in the darkened, quiet hallway.

"I'll take the rap for the lock," Steve said.

"The hell you will," Cotler said, closing the glass back up and putting the broken lock back in place. "Let's take that thing down to Roland. We'll all take the rap. I'm thinkin' he'll understand as long as we pay for it."

"All right, fine. Thanks, guys. Let's get this outta here before Vic sees—"

"Vic sees what?" Vic asked, standing at the front of the hallway by the gym doors. "I saw you guys leave and I told Coach I needed to take a whiz. What the fuck is going on?"

We all looked at him, ready to smile and say in unison, "It's nothing, Vic," but the words died in our throats. We stood instead as guilty as whoever had put it there in the first place. Cotler's tools and the folded poster hung like bodies in his hands.

"Something happened, Vic," I said carefully. "But it's all right. No one is going to see it. No one has seen it except for us."

"Seen what?" he asked, coming toward us with a weird, loose look in his eyes. They shifted to the framed image of his brother in the trophy case. "Seen what, goddammit?!"

"Vic," Steve started to say, "someone . . ." but Vic had grabbed the poster board out of Cotler's hand and read what was there. He winced and pure, naked hurt filled his eyes. He tossed it to the side and stared up at his brother's unflinching smile behind the glass.

"We're taking it to the office," Steve said, speaking as he would to a mental patient.

"Taking it to the office," Vic said, still staring up at his brother's face. He turned to us, the anger in his face transforming it into a mask. "For what? Fucking fingerprints?" He turned again to the glass and slammed his fist into it before Cotler could stop him. It shook to the ceiling and creaked again but, woven with wire mesh, it did not break. Vic seethed, let out a yell and pulled back again. Now Cotler reached out deftly and caught his wrist.

"Vic, no! Don't let this get you kicked out of school!"

"What the fuck do I care?! Let go of me!"

"Vic, please," Cotler pleaded, still holding his arm with difficulty. "We'll find out who did it. Somebody had to have seen something." Vic seemed to calm, but his face was still tortured with rage. Carefully, Cotler released him.

"You're goddam right I'll find out." He pointed with his finger and started to say something else but a sob caught the next sentence. He bolted down the hall and out of sight.

"John," Cotler said as the pounding of twelve hundred pairs of feet on the bleachers marked the end of the pep rally. "Go find him. Make sure he doesn't hurt himself." I nodded and split off. Cotler and Steve headed to the office as the gym doors burst open and the first noisy, boisterous students began to pour out.

***

I looked for Vic but didn't find him for the rest of the day. That made for more of a shock when Coach Bonner, leaning in the doorway and watching the traffic in the halls after class, suddenly called out to Cotler. Cotler darted across the room with us close behind. Out in the hallway. with a growing legion of students beginning to notice, was Vic, blocking the path of none other than Doug Lars.

"It was him," Vic said to our group as Doug stared grimly back at him. "It was this sonofabitch right here."

Vic had spent the day at school but hadn't attended classes. Instead he had spent hours investigating, with the help of his teammates, who had been responsible for the prank. By the end of the day he had his answer. Two people saw Doug Lars attempting to place something in the trophy case during the pep rally, although neither was close enough to see what it was. That was a relief, for it meant that no one outside of our group had gotten the message. Both people who saw it figured that Doug, an athlete anyway, was doing what he was doing with permission, and neither gave it much thought. One had been a mousy sophomore who had been setting up something for a play in the auditorium with the drama club. The auditorium was across from the trophy case, and she had seen Doug tinkering with the glass and holding something in his hand a little after nine. The other had been a good-for-nothing pothead named Jim Stevens who had wandered into school late not knowing there was a pep rally. Jim Stevens's little brother Ricky was a ninety-pound freshman and one of Vic's newest team members. The mousy sophomore was a girl named Tina Draper who Vic had spoken to after getting Ricky's story.

"Vic," the coach was saying in a careful, measured tone, "what are you talking about? I need you to back away from Doug right now."

"Let him do what he wants," Doug said, but his usual swagger seemed to flag. In his eyes I saw something that looked clearly like guilt, but more importantly I saw that the prank had not been his idea. Lon had found more use for the pictures, it seemed. Doug turned to Vic. "What's this about? I didn't do—"

"He's dead, you fuck!" Vic screamed. With that he jabbed at Doug's face, and not expecting a punch, Doug took it harder than normal. His head snapped back and he screamed in pain and surprise. A thin trail of red ran from his upper lip over his teeth and down to the lower one. Bonner moved in between them and shouted something at Vic. With Vic's attention diverted Doug eyed him keenly and prepared to strike.

But Cotler saw this first. With terrific speed he grabbed Doug's punching arm and quickly put him in a hold with Doug's arms behind his back. Bonner secured Vic in a similar hold; now the two combatants were like bound animals seething at each other.

"Let me go!" Vic screamed in Bonner's struggling grasp. "I'll get kicked out, I don't care! You can't stop me from doing this!"

"Doing what?!" Doug yelled back, still in Cotler's grasp, "Getting your skinny ass kicked? Go ahead! Let him go! I'll take his ass out with my hands tied behind me!"

"Shut up, Doug!" Bonner roared. Vic seethed, and spit flew from his lips.

"You hung that poster under my brother's face! Why?! Tell me why!" Coach Amen, from the football team, was sprinting toward us through a crowd of eyeballing kids. "TELL ME WHY!"

"I didn't do nothin'!" Doug screamed back. "Prove it, if you're so sure! Goddammit, Cotler, let me go! He's going psycho and he's blaming it on me, like I'm the only person in this town who knows his brother was a fucking FAGGOT!"

For a moment there was stunned silence. Doug had incriminated himself and as yet didn't realize it. Coach Amen moved toward Doug and Cotler to try and neutralize the situation when Cotler did something I didn't expect. He loosened his grip like he was going to give Doug over to Coach Amen, but just before releasing him he twisted Doug's arm up savagely. Doug shrieked and, sensing he was being released, spun in Cotler's grasp and got ready to strike him. But it was Cotler's trap and it worked perfectly.

Cotler's big fist flew like a cannonball and seemed to knock Doug's head clean off. The punch landed, there was an awful sound from Doug's mouth, and he staggered backwards. Someone screamed. Another landed, straight into his left eye, and Doug fell. He grabbed his face with his hands and for a second lay there motionless. The two coaches were too stunned to move. In Bonner's grip, Vic was silent and watched Doug's curled up form on the floor.

"I'll get my books," Cotler said quietly to Coach Amen, "and then I'll go with you to the office." He glanced down at Doug, who was still covering his bleeding mouth and slowly thinking about making his way back to his feet. "You had that comin', you son of a bitch."

2

While Armand lay upstairs asleep, the five of us spent Valentine's night feeding the fireplace in Cotler's cozy, wood-framed basement. Around us, the heads of unfortunate white-tailed deer stared blankly from every wall. Outside, intermittent waves of flying sleet slashed against the windows. It had long since gone beyond cold in Northern Virginia to that netherworld of frozen temperatures that made ice-skating possible in local ponds for two or three weeks at a time.

We were trading stories and talking about warmer weather when Vic slinked over to the bathroom, peed, and ducked into the laundry room presumably to pass out on the cot in there that Cotler kept for just such occasions. After about five minutes though, we all noticed a distinct chill creeping in from under the laundry room door. Cotler and Steve looked over at me as if to say it was my turn to check on Vic, and begrudgingly I got moving. He was on his hands and knees, half out of the open back door to the house, throwing up on the back step. He had icicles forming on his bangs.

I pulled him in and dried him off as best I could, covered him with an old blanket, and set him on the cot. I put a bucket in front of him and sat down to watch him until he fell asleep. The final tool of his undoing this Friday night, an empty bottle of Sauza tequila, lay over by the door. He caught sight of it and winced.

"Shouldn't-a-drank that shit," he breathed. I nodded. Thus began a ritual between Vic and me that had been repeated dozens of times since middle school.

"You'll be all right. Just breathe deep and think about Donna Reavis's tits." He smiled weakly and seemed to doze. The line about Donna's boobs was an old standard between us, and often sent Vic into a semi-sleep state that lessened his woes. Tonight it seemed to do the trick again, but what emerged from Vic's delirium is something I will likely never forget. We sat in cold silence for a few minutes before he suddenly lifted his head.

"Marty?" he whispered, seeming to come directly from sleep into curious wakefulness. He eyes were blank, though, and I guessed he was still asleep. A chill cut through me like a blade.

"It's just me, Vic," I said, glancing toward the door and wishing I wasn't alone. In the other room they were laughing at a skit on a show called *Friday's*, and their laughter seemed blocks away.

"He was sitting on that chair," Vic mumbled, settling back on the cot. Now he was smiling, a sleepy, contented look on his face. I looked over at the chair he was referring to and the chill cut deeper. It was an old kitchen chair that had been used in training Cotler and me to eat at the table when we were toddlers. Thanks to Vic's suggestion and the gloom of the laundry room it looked oddly stationary, as if there was weight on it. More hard rain hit the windows above us.

"I guess he came to check on you," I said, not wanting to do anything to remove the comforted smile on Vic's wiry, slack face.

"Came to check on me," he repeated, still smiling. "He says you always take care of me, Johnny."

"That's my job." The chill would not leave me alone. I was hoping his easy smile would fade back into sleep, but soon his brow knitted and his face clouded over.

"You know my brother wasn't no faggot, John."

"Of course. I know." Vic's face clenched and a tear ran from his closed eye down onto the cot.

"You weren't no faggot, Marty. I know you weren't."

"Nobody thinks that. Don't worry, okay? Nobody thinks that." Outside the wind howled freshly past the house and instantly sent its cargo of flying ice hurling in a different direction. Vic seemed not to notice. His face softened, the features relaxed.

"He said he was sorry," Vic said, his voice clearing and steady.

"Sorry for what?"

"I don't know. He said, 'Tell John that I'm sorry. Tell him I'm really sorry.'" My throat went dry.

"Sorry about what?" I looked over at the chair.

"Don't know. He didn't say what. Only that it was Jim's fault. Some guy named Jim."

"He . . . he said this just now?" I asked and jammed shaking hands into my pockets. Vic shook his head and made a face like I was being ridiculous.

"No, no. Before he died. The night before. That's why I remembered it now. He had all his stuff, pictures and ribbons and stuff, on his bed. He had his box out, too. Our granddad's ammo box. He kept all his secret stuff in it, and he had it out on the bed like it didn't even matter who saw it. I shoulda known he was gonna do it. I shoulda known when I saw that box and he didn't even care, like it was nothin'. He'd threaten to beat the piss out of me when I got near that box, but he didn't care that night. I shoulda known. I shoulda known but I'm so stupid. I'm so goddam fucking stupid." He broke off and started to weep with his eyes pressed shut. He tried to draw a breath and it turned into a tortured moan instead.

I looked away, the fear gone and some terrible sadness in its place. "You were thirteen. There's no way you could have known."

"No. I should have known. I saw the box. I saw it in his face. It was in his face." His breathing deepened and he motioned for the bucket. I placed it below his head and without opening his eyes he leaned over and retched. When it was over, he settled back onto the cot and seemed to doze. "I saw it your face once, too," he said. "You were gonna do it." I froze.

"What?"

"I saw it in your face, John. That night. That night I saw you alone in the parking lot."

That night in November, I thought. The night I ran into him at the 7-11 after talking to Lon. The night I planned it. The night it had felt so good just to think about getting it over with.

"Yeah," I said, just above a whisper. "I remember." Now Vic smiled furtively, the smile of nestled children on Christmas Eve.

"I was gonna' call Cotler and tell him to go talk to you. But you know what?"

"What?"

"I had a dream about Marty, and he told me to call Steve instead." Silence.

"He did, huh?" Vic nodded.

"He called you, and you didn't do it. But I saw it. I saw it in your face." His brow knitted once more. "You're not gonna do it now, are you?"

"No. I'm not gonna do it now." The face loosened and the smile was back. "That's good, Johnny. That's real good . . . Hey, John?"

"Yeah?"

"What happened to my brother? Do you know?"

"He did a lot of things for a lot of people," I said, trying not to stammer. "A lot happened to him, good and bad."

"But why was he sorry for you, though? Why did he say that?"

"I . . . I don't know. I just don't know." He seemed to ponder this for a moment, his brow wrinkled, but it finally smoothed out and he went limp.

"You been sad a long time, Johnny. Long time. I know." His speech petered out to a low slur.

"I guess," I whispered. He lifted his head and looked over at me blindly, his eyes still shut.

"Is that Jim's fault, too, like with my brother?"

I drew in a breath and started to speak but only air came out. I tried again but found I couldn't make a single sound. Then I saw that Vic had collapsed into a slack, uneasy sleep.

<h1 style="text-align:center">3</h1>

February 27. "Armand asked that I bring you here tonight," the sheriff said as we sat at the Cotlers' kitchen table on a wet Wednesday night. "He says there's someone who can confirm that he wasn't near Belle Ridge on the day Jeremy Bingham was abducted. The person, he says, is someone you know, or who knows you." I looked at Armand, who stared at his big, dark hands. He was wearing a blue work shirt and still bore a couple of marks from his run-in with Shawn Warren. His hair was long, nappy, and badly braided.

"Who would that be?" I asked. I honestly had no idea. Then Armand raised his head and spoke. His eyes had a sleepy, heavy-lidded quality to them. They curved downward, and with his full lips seemed to complete a sad circle on his face. "That girl you like. You been out with her. And that guy you don't like. He been out with her, too. I saw them." I pictured Tamara and Lon. My gut tightened.

"Where?"

"Lake Lind. I was looking to smoke some. I was lookin'

for some to buy, and they seen me there. I waited a long time. That guy sold me a little bit."

"A little bit of what?" I asked. "Pot?" Armand looked at the sheriff.

"Tell him, Armand," the sheriff said gently.

Armand had made his delivery for the metal shop a few towns over near Tyson's Corner. On the way back, he stopped in a town called Lindway, a planned community just to the east of us. Lindway featured a man-made lake and waterfront area named for the developer, Maurice Lind, which over the years had become a substantial open-air drug market for middle class teens. Armand stopped there and parked his company truck in view of the lakefront at about 3:30 that afternoon. He looked around for his usual contact but did not see him. After a while he noticed a guy looking over at him from the driver's seat of a beige Mustang II. The guy was with a girl, a girl that Armand had seen before with me, and they were smoking. Armand ignored them at first. But the guy kept looking over, smiling, even. He had a different face, that dude. You didn't forget a face like his. He had a weird, intense look. After about a half hour, he got up his courage and walked over to the car. The girl was giggling; she was really high. The intense dude offered him a joint for five bucks. He took it and drove off. He didn't get back to the shop until almost 6:00 because of the traffic.

"Tamara Woolen and Lon Chambers," I said. "That's her car. I know them. Her better than him."

"They're who I thought it was," the sheriff said at low volume. He looked very tired and seemed almost apologetic. "I wanted to see if you thought so, too. Neither of them went to school that day." He wasn't a stupid man, and it wasn't hard for him to smell how much this hurt me to hear. "I tried to talk to Tamara today. She wouldn't say anything even though I was clear that the marijuana means nothing to anyone. I think she's afraid to come clean for obvious reasons. But it would mean a great deal to Armand and help him very much if she would be honest with me. I was wondering if you could talk to her, John."

"Sure," I said. "For Armand's sake, sure. What about Lon?"

"I talked to Jim Kelly today about Lon. Jim hasn't seen him, and of course he's not at school anymore. I'll worry about him. But if there's anything you think you could say to Tamara that might get her to talk to me, I'd appreciate it. I know Armand would also."

4

The next day I appeared at Tamara's locker after the last bell. I had agonized about how to approach her all day, and in the end decided to dispense with the small talk.

"Why didn't you tell Cotler's father about who you saw at the lake?" I asked when she turned to face me. She looked taken aback, but in an instant smoothed and turned around.

"You haven't spoken to me in months and that's the first thing you've got to say?" she asked, walking away.

"I want you to tell the sheriff the truth and set Armand Lillington free," I said, catching up with her.

"He's not in jail. And I'm not going to jail just so—"

"You're right. You're not going to jail. For anything. So why are you sitting on your hands while the town is ready to lynch Spencer's brother?" Tamara stared back at me, the corners of her mouth starting to quiver. She led me into an empty stairwell, blinked her eyes and ran a hand through her hair. And I was, for a moment, lost in desire.

"Don't you dare accuse me of causing trouble for Spencer's brother!" she hissed. "I'm not the person who told someone he was walking out of the woods carrying clothes in a bag. How do I know it wasn't him?!"

"Because he was buying a joint from your boyfriend when the kid was getting grabbed!"

"He's not my boyfriend. And so what? Who's to say he didn't leave there and . . . and . . ." she was starting to cry, but she sucked it up. "Leave me alone, Johnny. This isn't my problem."

"And if they convict Armand Lillington for—"

"Oh, stop being dramatic. It's in the news; they don't have anything on him. He'll go back to wandering around and beating people up before you know it. No one needs me to—"

"Tarnish your sterling reputation," I said. She shot me a look which might have cut me to ribbons if looks could do such a thing.

"God damn you," she said, and I had never heard a girl say that to me before, not that way. Dripping with calm hatred. Not like she was seventeen; more like she was thirty-five. It was an expression from Tamara's future, I thought later. Maybe a well-used expression from her future, whatever that was.

"This isn't a game, Tamara."

"Yes, it is. This is about you, John, admit it. What you really want to know is what I did with Lon. Well, I'll tell you. Nothing. He didn't even try to hold my hand. Wanna know the truth? I think he's in love with you." She turned to leave, but I blocked the door. "Let me by," she said, her voice rising. "I'll scream, I swear to God!"

"Go ahead," I said. She drew in a breath, and then slowly let it out. A whine crept into her voice.

"God, why can't you leave me alone?" She was shaking with anger and regret, and I knew that most of it had to do with liking Lon in the first place. That should have made me feel better. But it didn't.

"Come clean with Cotler's dad and the town lays off Armand. It's that simple."

"How about the guy who sold him the joint? How come no one is badgering him to do the right thing?"

"No one knows where he is," I said. She paused, trying to collect herself again. Slowly, the tears came, hard as she had tried to hold them back.

"He came after me. Yeah, I thought he was cute. He is cute. But none of it was my idea. So I smoked some pot. So I skipped school a couple of times, I'm so fucking sorry."

"I didn't want to meet him, either," I said, mostly to myself.

"What did you say?"

"I said I didn't want to meet him, either. He came after me, too."

"What does he want?"

"I don't know. What did he want from you?" She seemed to ponder this for a moment.

"Nothing. I think that's why I liked him. He never said much. I found myself talking all the time around him, trying to fill in the spaces. But I liked being with him. I don't know why. He's interesting, I guess." There was a pause, and words came into my head. They were words I wanted more than anything not to say, but they came tumbling out anyway, searing me even as I listened to them.

"Was that my problem? That I liked you? That I did want something from you?"

"You didn't like me, John. What you liked was the idea of—" she stopped herself before she could say "going out with me," but a Tamara at 25 or 30 would have said it boldly. And it was true. Her outward pompousness was just an honest expression of something people like her felt, and the rest of us knew. We were kids. We knew our places. She started to backpedal, murmuring something to pad what sounded pretty snooty, but I spared her the chance.

"Whatever it was, it was. Okay? I don't expect you to understand it, and I don't want to make this be about you and me. I just need you to do the right thing. Please." She shook her head more forcefully now.

"I don't want any part of this. I just want to live my life and forget I ever knew that person. That's what I'm doing."

"Then please, before you do that, help Armand. He's innocent and you owe him the truth."

"I don't! I don't and you can't make me!"

"Fine. Live with yourself, then. Armand'll continue to live in fear and this stupid town will continue to clamor for his head."

Tamara's eyes grew wide and the guilt she had been straining under for days began to scratch through like a moth from a cocoon. I felt a twinge of guilt. I've always had trouble playing hardball with a girl on the verge of tears. But it was a tough old world, and we were learning that fast. She tried to calm herself, breathing deeply and leaning against the door.

"I don't want to tell my father and mother that I skipped school to get high with some loser. Can you understand that?"

"Yes. Believe me, I can understand that. But I can't believe that would stop you from doing the right thing here. It's plain awful." Tamara scoffed.

"I'm the most evil person who ever lived, is that it?" I smiled thinly at this.

"You don't make the little leagues of evil. Trust me, I know. But this is low, Tam." She took on a wild-eyed, paranoid look.

"I won't answer to you," she said, her voice rising. "Not for anything. And this isn't about fucking Armand Lillington! It's about you! It's about you, and me, and Lon, and it's sick, John! It's sick!"

"Yes," I said. "It's sick. But it's not about me."

She paused, collecting herself. Then she looked straight at me with a wicked grin and showed me what hardball really was.

"You wanted to know about Lon and me. That's what matters to you. And I told you. We didn't do anything. But you know what?"

"What?"

"I would have." She turned and left.

I watched the door shut slowly, heard the echo in the empty hall. I slumped in the stairwell and cried.

Chapter Eight: March

1

Tuesday, March 5. Lon was sitting on the concrete post of the bridge over Canard's Run, a feeder creek to the swatch of water that ran behind Cotler's house, and where he and I had searched for creek-dwelling creatures before either of us could read. The road that traversed the run up here on the Hill was called Potomac View, a two-lane, county blacktop that ran just west of town and along a high ridge. In places it yielded a view to the north of the river itself, a glittering dark ribbon moving slowly toward Great Falls and the city beyond.

"What are we doing up here?" I asked as I stepped from the truck, the usual slab of lead in my stomach. He had left a note on my truck earlier, instructing me to meet him at this place after school, no later than 3:45. It was sunny and deceivingly warm. Days like that one were common in the early weeks of March; light, bright, wispy days of gentle sun and warm breezes that lull one into believing winter must finally be behind him. Lon smiled, and something in his smile—something almost childishly excited and gleeful—gave me an even stronger feeling of distrust and dread than normal. "And why are you so goddam happy?"

"Follow me."

We walked off the road onto a trail, through the woods toward the ridge of the hill that faced the town. The trail twisted and ran vaguely parallel to Potomac View Road. Through the trees I could see the town spread out before us as if on a picnic blanket. Farther to the east I could see most of Herndon, Lindway, and beyond to the great sprawl that was the rest of Northern Virginia. The trail wound west and bent to the south. I could see my block, my house, and then Cotler's, the westernmost and oldest residential block of town, almost directly below us. As we approached a small bare spot in the trees I stopped.

"Where the fuck are we?" I asked, a bad tingling sensation beginning in my groin. I had never walked this part of the Hill, and there was a reason for that. I was looking down onto Cotler's house, down onto his bedroom window, where as a terrified child I had looked up to the evil flicker of the campfire. The fire that had been where I was now.

"It's just a little bit farther," Lon said, not seeming to notice me or even look back. When he realized I wasn't following him, he stopped and turned around. "Christ, do I have to hold your hand? It's four o'clock in the afternoon."

"I don't like it here," I said, flat and sour.

"I doubt it likes you here," he said, smiling again. The smile disappeared. "You don't have a choice. Let's go."

We arrived at a small break in the trees. To the right was the unmistakable sewer cylinder lid that Vic had described coming upon with Marty. An old fire pit was next to the lid, and Lon sat down beside it on a smooth, charred rock. He motioned to another large rock on the other side. I didn't move.

"I told you I didn't like it here," I said. Lon looked at me, his brow knitted.

"That story Vic told you guys spooked you that much? C'mon, John. Even you're tougher than that." He waited for my eyes to widen at the thought that he'd overheard that conversation, but I was used to that now.

"I have my own reasons for not liking it here. I don't know how long I can stay."

"Don't worry," he said. "I don't mince words. This is about your limits. We talked about them at the middle school in December. Do you remember? You wanted to know what mine were. I was curious about yours. I think it's time we found out." I put my hands up and moved backward.

"Don't push me, Lon. Not here. I can only take so much. What do you want?" He looked around him at the tamped out clear spot, the baleful-looking cylinder lid, the dead fire pit.

"What was it you saw here?"

"A campfire. We saw it from Cotler's bedroom, right down there. We heard some . . . voices. I didn't like it at all. And I won't describe it, either. I doubt I can."

"You don't have to," he said. "I've lived out here longer than you know. Did you ever hear it again?"

"I never listened again. What do you want? Please." He looked up, set his stick down, and fanned his hands out in front of him. He looked at me with big, dark eyes, sleepy and content.

"Your future's unwritten. I'm giving you a choice. It's a choice I'm not offering to your cohort Vinnie Foust, and I expect you to keep it between us."

"What do you mean?"

"I mean you can stop this. All of it. Have your life back. Your town back. For one price." Now I did sit down.

"What do you mean, Lon?"

"I've told you, I know what you suspect about me. I'll do nothing to allay your suspicions. We're of the same cloth, you and I."

"God forbid."

"God forbids nothing. To God it's all a big, fucking joke. A joke on you. On me. On Vinnie. Whoever God is, he's watched us suffer and beg him for mercy and all he's done is sit back and cackle. You wonder, you and Vinnie, why I've come back. You wonder why I've tortured you. It's because torture is the only way to cleanse you. To get you ready."

"Ready for what?"

"Ready to accept responsibility for what you didn't do. For how you crawled. That's why I came. And with me there seems to have come a plague. I'm offering you a chance to make the plague disappear, just like you wish for in your diapered little mind."

"How?"

"Cotler," Lon said, and his eyes locked on mine, no longer dulcet and sleepy.

"Wha-what do you want with Cotler?"

"He's your price. Give him to me, and our business is through."

"Jesus, Lon, what . . ." He stood up and produced the same black pistol he had used to threaten Vinnie's life back in November and handed it to me, butt first. I shrank back from the gun in terror and wiped tears from my eyes.

"Take it," he said, his voice never rising a notch. "Take it, John. It's not loaded. For now, anyway. Take it." With a trembling hand I did as I was told. The gun felt heavy and lethal in my grip.

"What, Lon? What?"

"I told you I wouldn't mince words. I won't. Cotler is a penance. If you have any sense at all you'll see him as a victory. Either way, I'll see him as a ransom, and I'll be on my way. You'll bring Cotler to the clearing. Our clearing. I'll have everything ready, and he'll never suspect a thing, because he'll be with you. You can lower his guard. We'll meet. I'll have the gun. You'll shoot your friend in the face with it before he even knows what's happening. I'll make it so you'll never so much as be questioned about it. You should know by now that I can make that happen. It'll make perfect sense. Local tough guy goes looking for trouble in bad place and finds it. When they finally uncover him, he'll be the last of the boys of Belle Ridge who wandered away forever. I will be gone along with him."

"But, Cot—Why?!"

"You'll get no further explanation from me than this. You must lose something to gain your freedom. You must feel that kind of loss, that kind of betrayal, to be the same as me. Then I'll let you go. If you're smart, John, if you truly want to live, then you'll view this as the opportunity of a lifetime." I was sobbing now, quaking with the ugly, black weight of the pistol in one hand, the other hand balled up into a childlike fist.

"Cotler has nothing to do with this! Any of it!" Lon listened to this without a single change in his cut, handsome face. When he spoke his words were calm and quiet, almost sympathetic.

"Cotler deserves this, and you know it. Cotler sold you to the devil, and you know it. He took what was good of your lives together and left you what bled and stank and lay there rotting. Go to that hate, John. Go to that truth. Cut him from your life like a cancer and take charge, for once. For you."

"Jesus, please," I whispered. "Please." Lon looked around at our surroundings.

"I don't believe you'll find Jesus in this place," he said. I set the gun down and stared at him.

"What if I don't?" I managed finally. "You said it was a choice." He shrugged.

"Then your fate is in my hands, as it's always been."

"What about Vinnie? How come he has no fucking choice?"

"I didn't say Vinnie had no choice. Vinnie doesn't have *this* choice. Don't worry about him. This is about you."

"I can't," I breathed. "I can't, I can't, I can't." Lon did not react to this. Something raw and hungry like terror woke in me. I turned to him and my eyes must have glowed with it. "What does that mean, 'your fate is my hands?' What?" Now he stood up and walked over to me. He didn't raise his voice a notch.

"I told you back in October there was a way out of this for you. I invited you to become a killer, either of myself or yourself. You were either unable or unwilling to do that, and so I've done my work. Your fate is to be blamed, John. You'll be blamed for what's happened in that pathetic little town down there, and to its pathetic little boys. I'm sorry. That is what must be." I recoiled, almost falling backward. Lon didn't react at all.

"How can I be blamed?!" I screamed up at him. "HOW?!" He paused to light a cigarette and glanced out over the town as he answered, projecting a touch as he quoted me.

"'I don't think time is on his side anymore.' Remember telling that to Vinnie a couple of months ago? Did you think I didn't hear that? You're such a fool, John. Month after month you and that rat-faced little fuck do nothing to stop me in any way, and then you think time must be running out for me because my hands look cold and my nose is running. Congratulations. All you've done is given me the time to spin a wonderful web, and now you're all caught up in it." He shook his head and smiled, then shifted his eyes back to me like guns. "You've got one chance to avoid a fate that your fragile sanity simply cannot bear. Otherwise I go forward with what I always had planned for you anyway. When the right people come forward with the right information, there'll really be no question. Just a broken-hearted sheriff with a terrible, terrible job to do."

"You . . . can't do it. You can't, you . . . . . .railed off and realized that I couldn't breathe, or that I had forgotten how. I kept sucking for air but couldn't seem to bring it in. Lon seemed not to notice.

"I can't do it alone, that's true. It'll take corroboration. Cooperation. The right people will have to come forward and be willing to give the right information and make the right sacrifices." He kneeled down before me. "And that, John, is part of someone else's choice."

The world swooned, the sky, the trees, the setting sun now streaming lovely yellow bands of light through the leaves. Suddenly it was all clear: the enslavement, first of Vinnie and then of Doug Lars; the camera that followed us everywhere; the meetings in the woods, and my truck, parked at the trailheads at all hours; my image, in a dozen places back there, late at night, early in the morning, my hands covered with dirt and ashes. I could feel the eyes turning stonily toward me. I could see the fingers pointing me out. I fell over and looked up, a helpless mass. Lon was a blur. I turned and vomited, then rested my face in it, lacking the strength to move. I spoke to the ground.

"Lon, please," I breathed, still trying to get enough air. "Please, what else can I do? Please." He stood up and retrieved his gun.

"We're not negotiating. You've heard my offer and you have one week to make your choice." I watched him with one eye as he paused at the edge of the brush, looking at me curiously. "Give the devil his due, John."

2

Thursday, March 7. On the fourth anniversary of Marty Moreland's death, I stood in front of his grave, a simple gray headstone on the low rise of the hill that made up most of the cemetery. Marty's mother had been by early and laid fresh flowers. On behalf of our group, that morning Spencer had laid a bundle, which included flowers of our own, a pack of cigarettes from me, scripture on a card from Spencer, and on Vic's behalf a pair of laces from his newly discarded winter running shoes. Vic, as usual, would have no part of coming to his brother's grave, but he gave Spencer the laces, which was his way of thanking us for the gesture. From behind me I heard a car door shut, and I saw Steve emerge from his Nova below me in the little parking lot. He pulled his coat around him tighter as he made his way to where I was, the wind blowing through the stones.

"Christ, it's cold out here," he said when he reached me, glancing around at the gray, winter-dead slope of the hill. "Any chance you're coming in soon?"

"How did you know where to find me?"

"I'm getting to know you, I guess. I don't know if you heard, Tamara finally came forward."

"I heard. It's in the paper today, without her name. She's a little star around here now. What's Armand going to do?"

"He's going south. They've got an aunt in South Carolina. Place called Elmo, or Irmo. Irmo, I think. You know where it is?"

"No."

"Well, that's where he's going. I think Spencer'll be relieved to have him out of here for a while."

"What about Lon? Anybody heard from him aside from me?"

"I talked to Cotler about that today," Steve said. "Cot's father found him last week, loitering some place. He said Lon was cooperative. He admitted selling to Armand but said he didn't come forward because he didn't trust anyone."

I turned to look at Steve and saw a discomfort there that bordered on fear, but I could not remove it any more than I could his nose, so I let it sit there and offered no smile.

"So Lon's a suspect, at least," I said. "He still has some credibility being associated with Jim Kelly, even if Kelly's given up on him as a runaway. That'll buy him some time."

"John, please come back with me," Steve said. The pleading tone in his voice was unsettling. "You can't sit out here all day." I wiped my eyes, sat down in front of Marty's stone, and began to cry.

"This is too much," I said into my hands. "It's too much

to handle. I don't want to do this anymore. I just want to sleep. I want to rest. Don't you get it? I'm not even depressed. I'm just tired, and I want to sleep! I can't fight it anymore. It's fatigue that makes people kill themselves, man. It's the motherfucking feeling that you just . . . can't . . . do it anymore." Steve swallowed hard and collected himself.

"It could be a bluff. It could be anything. You're losing sight of the big picture again. It's not as easy to do this stuff, what he says he'll do, as he wants you to think. Listen to me, man, you're not thinking! You're doing exactly what he wants you to do, give up!"

"That's not half of what he wants me to do. Steve, listen, what's he been doing the last seven months? He's been watching Vinnie and me. Tracking us with that fucking camera. He knows about stuff I did that I can't even remember doing. He's got Vinnie's and my whole history to spring on everyone if he wants. God only knows what kind of lies they could dream up from it. Do you think Vinnie won't bury me with that kind of thing if he has to? If that's his choice? What about Doug? There are pictures of him fucking another guy in front of a big fireplace somewhere, Steve! Doug will do anything. Anything! Both he and Vinnie will get a better deal than me, and they'll jump for it. I'd do it, too."

"No, you wouldn't."

"Yeah, you're right. Know why? Because I'm a fool. Vinnie was right when he called me that. He'll live longer than I will."

"Why do I not think that's true?"

"What about the illegal things I have done? What kind of evidence has he kept on any of that stuff? What if he took pictures of us at R.W.'s place? What if he recorded us talking about Doc Abbott's place? What if the next time a child dies in this fucking town the killer leaves a clue, starts getting reckless, sloppy? What then?" Steve looked at me blankly and did not reply. "I know goddam well it's not easy to do what he says he'll do. I also know what he's capable of. This is end-game here and now. It's finished."

Steve opened his mouth to protest but shut it slowly and instead stared down at Marty's grave. I looked around at the other stones, stark against the hillside, and the town beyond it. The stone for Jeremy Bingham had just been put in and it was smooth, gleaming black with gray carved letters. In the distance the Blue Ridge Mountains reclined along the western horizon. Steve was silent for what seemed like a long time.

"What do we know about Lon?" he asked finally.

"Why?"

"I don't know. Something tells me that it matters who he is. Something tells me we've got a shot at him if we know that."

I had little to offer. I had broached the subject once with Cotler late in February, after the conversation with Armand and his dad about his side trip to Lindway on the day that Jeremy had disappeared. Cotler, with his steel-trap memory, did remember the name from childhood outings with Jim, but it was a dead end. There was a Lon who went out with us; Cotler's father remembered him also. But that Lon had died of some rare brain cancer that took him out less than a year from when he was diagnosed. The family moved just after he died, and their ties to Belle Ridge ended with him. I explained this to Steve and he listened quietly.

"Doesn't get us much, I guess," he said. "For now, anyway."

"No. It really doesn't. Whoever Lon is, he hasn't left much of a trail." We considered this for a while and listened to the stiff wind of March blow over the hill.

"What do you think he feels when he kills them?" Steve asked. I thought for a moment.

"I don't think he feels anything. The town deserves it. That seems to be what he thinks. He's about as hateful a person as I've ever come across. He's given himself his own reasons for killing them. That's all he needs." We were quiet for a while and sat still until the cold simply wouldn't let us rest any further. Then a strange energy came over me. It was not hope; I must clarify that. Hope usually produces energy, but the presence of the latter alone is no guarantee that the former follows. This was just energy, a frankly annoying and seemingly directionless drive that I had felt before and that seemed to fill me at the most inappropriate times. But maybe that was the point. "Who he is," I said slowly, turning to look at my friend full in the face for the first time that day. Steve almost smiled at the change he must have seen in my face. Maybe he thought it was hope. "Finding out, I mean. You think that's worth something?"

"It can't hurt," he said, shrugging. He watched me closely, happy for whatever it was he saw come alive in my eyes. "Knowledge is power. I didn't make that up, but I believe it." I nodded and felt the energy pulse through me. I tasted it as it passed for traces of hope, but it was unclear.

"Maybe," I said, turning away, for now, from the graves of the boys behind me. "Just maybe." We walked back to his car, and the wind followed us out of the cemetery like an impatient usher at the end of a performance.

3

Tuesday, March 12. Neil Bonner sat on his desk and I in the one in front of it as the last students padded past us after school. I had asked him if he could talk and something about my tone must have indicated that it wasn't about my dismal March report card. He studied me carefully as I watched the traffic in the hall dissipate down to nothing. When the halls were all but empty I shifted my eyes to him.

"I'm not going to waste your time, Coach. I'm trying to do what you said to do. Keep my circle small and use good judgment about who to tell. I'm taking a chance even being here." I stopped and forced myself to look at him directly. "I'm betting that someone came to you about four years ago and told you something very disturbing, before he died. I'm here because he came to me, too. He came to me because I was a part of it right along with him. If you can't talk about this let me know now and I'll get up and leave and never bother you again. But if you know what I'm talking about, then you know how serious it was. I'm here because it's become serious again." Bonner looked straight at me for what seemed like an eternity, vaguely reminding me of bland Doctor Abbott. Around us the school hummed serenely, emptily, in the darkening afternoon.

"Who came to you, John?" he asked after that little forever had passed.

"Marty Moreland. He'd been . . . abused by someone local and he knew that I was, too. He came to me and told me that he'd spoken to someone, someone he trusted. I'm guessing it was you. I'm betting it was you. If I'm wrong, tell me I'm wrong and please forget that I ever mentioned this to you. But if I'm right, I'm begging you to talk to me about it. I'm looking for answers and you may have the only ones." The coach looked down at his hands and then up at me again. In his eyes were guarded wonder and something that looked like respect.

"I don't know much more than what you've just told me," he said. "Marty came to me, yes, that's true. He told me something very disturbing. That's true, too. What he never told me was who."

"He never told you who it was?" I asked, my eyes widening. I don't know why I assumed that Marty had told him, I just did.

"Never. We talked about it several times, right up to the time he died. But he wouldn't tell me who it was. He said he didn't want to burden me with knowing. He felt that if I knew who it was, that there'd be pressure on me, my ethical responsibilities to report it, all that stuff. He felt he could tell me more and get more help in a general sense if I wasn't caught up in all those issues."

"Pretty smart," I said.

"Smart indeed." And he added with a sardonic grin, "So I guess you're not going to tell me either." I thought about this and answered truthfully.

"No. I guess not. Not right now, anyway." He nodded, accepting this without protest.

"If what happened to Marty happened to you . . ."

"It did," I said. He looked away.

"Do you know how many others?"

"At least twenty, maybe more. I don't know for sure." He closed his eyes and put his hands in prayer formation around his mouth. He stayed that way for a while.

"Are you physically secure now?"

"Yes. Nothing's happened to me for years. I can't say what's happened to other kids, though. No one knows, except for Steve Drillas. I told him a while ago, and I don't regret it."

"I'm glad," he said, and rubbed his eyes. "John, I like you. You are a brilliant, kind, and forthright young man. And so I'll be straight with you as you've been with me. Marty came to me actually about five years ago with a question. Over time that question turned into a revelation and it sickened and frightened me. I'm not a professional in that area. I tried to get Marty to go to people who were, but he didn't want to go down that road. We . . . tried to think of what he could do. In the end he decided to put his own recovery aside and go after the person who abused him. He thought the best thing to do would be to tell some authorities and try to bring the guy to justice, and maybe to seek help for himself later. He told a couple of people, and frankly those people did nothing. They fell short of calling him a liar and did nothing. I had my doubts about what he was doing, but I didn't try to stop him, either. About a month later he was dead. That's about how much I helped him. That's about how much help I can be."

"He told me," I said, "just before he died, about talking to some people. He told me about coming to you, although I didn't know it was you then. It wasn't your fault."

"I can't accept that," he said, looking at the window again, and I noticed that his eyes were reddening and swollen. He composed himself quickly and looked back at me. "But this isn't about me. I can't help you, John. Even if you told me who it was, I'd probably be powerless. All I can tell you is what I tried to tell Marty. Go to a professional. I can recommend some people who are extremely thorough and very skilled and can open the doors that Marty couldn't."

"I'm not worried about me right now," I said. "I've lived with it all my life."

"I'm not talking about your psyche, son. Yes, that's important, too. There'll be time for that. But putting a stop to this—it's not impossible. Marty went about it the wrong way, that's all. There are people who will listen; they just need the right people doing the initial talking. Please trust me on that."

"If I didn't trust you I wouldn't be here," I said. "I'm trusting you because Marty did. I'm looking for some information about Marty because I'm trying to figure out why something else is going on, something that's related. It's confusing, I don't know where to start."

"Is it Lon? Is that why you asked me about him in November?"

"Yes. Lon. He's one of us, I think. I'm not sure. That's what I'm trying to figure out."

"You said he was bothering you when we spoke in November. What does he want from you?" I sighed and thought for a moment, a series of possible decisions and consequences rattling through my head. I forced myself to take it slowly and then smiled up at him.

"I have to plead the fifth on that one," I said. "I guess I'm being like Marty, but I really don't want to burden you with all that. It's ugly, I can tell you that. I think Lon was one of the boys who was with us when we were abused, a long time ago. I think he's back, which is why I wanted to find out where he came from. I don't know exactly what he wants, but he's . . . well, he's making things complicated and I think he might be dangerous."

"You're scaring me, John."

"That's because this is scary."

"What is it I can tell you?"

"Marty. Did he confide in anyone else but you? Do you remember anyone else he would have trusted with this?" The coach sat back on his desk and looked at the ceiling. He seemed to be going through the same process I'd just gone through.

"Marty had a close friend. Very close, his senior year. I never met him. Marty wouldn't bring him around."

"A boyfriend," I said quietly. Bonner levelled a look at me.

"A companion, yes."

"I knew about Marty, Coach," I said. "Not in the way the whole damn town knows, or Doug Lars knew when he made that poster. I just knew, from a long time back. I don't care. We loved Marty because he tried to take care of us." He studied me for a moment; he seemed to be at war with himself. Finally, he sighed and looked away.

"Marty fell in love when he was seventeen, or thought he did. I suppose if I were to believe a teenager about what he thought was love, it would be Marty. The boy was from outside of town. Local, but not from here. This boy, Buddy was his name, but that's all I knew, had been in and out of trouble. I didn't know much about him, but I knew Marty had let him sleep a few times in the shed in the Moreland's backyard. Marty sneaked him food and some clothing. He had a bad home life, but I knew nothing beyond that. I'm not sure how they met or when exactly they started a relationship."

"Did you ever ask Marty if he'd introduce you to this person, this Buddy?"

"Yes, I wanted to meet him. Marty wanted me to, actually, but we never did. I don't think Buddy ever agreed to it."

"He must have known how close you and Marty were."

"Maybe. I can't blame him, in any event. Being seventeen is hard enough without . . . other complications. When Marty died, Buddy died along with him, as far as I was concerned. I half expected, half hoped, actually, that he'd introduce himself to me one day. I went as far as to look around at the funeral, trying to guess from the faces. I think some of that was just wishing for a part of Marty to be alive, somewhere. Thankfully I got that when Vic came to my office the year you all were freshman."

"You never told—"

"His family? No. I thought about it. His parents asked me questions, and I answered truthfully. I told them that Marty had been spending time with another kid about his age. I told them I didn't know exactly what the relationship was. They had suspicions, I guess, but they never asked me about that part of his life. It seemed to me like they didn't want to know very much. Based on that I made a decision to let the few details I knew about Marty die with him. I don't know if it was the right decision or not."

"And Vic?"

"I've never had a conversation with Vic about his brother. I doubt I ever will. He came to my office his freshman year wanting to run, and I let him. He said nothing about Marty and neither did I. It took me a year to get to where he'd let me teach him anything, and longer than that before I even mentioned Marty. Now he's beyond my ability to teach him. I'm looking forward to seeing him run in college, if he can get there."

"We're all hoping."

"John, please tell me you wouldn't—"

"I'd die before I'd tell Vic anything that we've discussed. Believe me on that, too." He nodded and looked relieved.

"I wish there was something else I could tell you. Marty kept a journal, I know that, but I don't know what became of it. A few weeks before his death he asked me where I thought it would be safe to keep something like that, and to be honest I told him to hide it."

"Do you know where?" I asked, and was immediately sorry I'd asked it. Bonner seemed unaffected, though, or at least unsurprised, and thought for a moment before answering.

"He had a place in the woods he went out to quite a bit. It was kind of a retreat, from what he told me. A clearing, somewhere off of a running trail."

"Copperhead Road," I said, looking down.

"I think so, yes. On twelve-milers the distance runners use that trail. Marty started them on it. He found the spot while he was resting one day and liked it because you could see out from where it stood. There was a grove on top of a little hill there or something. It gave him privacy and a sense of security at the same time, I guess. He might have kept the journal there. He said he kept a few things there, but I never knew for sure."

"Do you think he gave it to this other person? This Buddy?"

"It's possible, but I doubt Marty told him about it. He was a very shy person in that regard. I don't think he would've shared it with him." He studied me again, watching as the gears in my head turned on finding that journal.

"John, if you do find it, please handle it carefully, okay? Marty's not here to defend himself."

"I understand, sir."

"I believe that. Is there anything else I can do for you?"

"No, I don't think so. Thanks for listening." He nodded and paused for another small eternity, looking at me the whole time.

"Can you stop him?" he asked finally. It took me a moment to realize it was Kelly he was talking about, and the sex abuse itself.

"I don't know," I said. "I don't know."

"Will you come to me if you don't think you can do it alone, or with Steve's help?"

"I don't know that either, Coach. I'd like to say yes, but . . ." He nodded and sighed.

"But you can't. Thanks for your candor. Just know I'm here for you. I don't want another Marty Moreland on my heart. I don't want the world deprived of another Marty Moreland, either." My heart swelled, and I fought to hold back the emotion.

"I'm not fit to hold his shoes," I whispered. The coach's eyes danced, and he smiled at me until his whole face lit up.

"Ask around, Johnny. I'll think you'll hear differently. Be careful, son."

<h1 style="text-align:center">4</h1>

Saturday, March 16. Clouds, now a heavy, swollen blue like bruises on the belly of the sky bore down on the treetops and gave the woods a corpuscular, shrouded feel as Steve and I made our way out to the clearing where I had been raped and Marty had intervened and young Calvin Cotler had been left to wait for his brother. The rain that had stopped only hours before still hung off the leaves and branches and dulled and absorbed the sounds of squirrels and insects and deer on this late Saturday day morning. Fog in lazy, billowing rolls appeared here and there, creeping across wide places on the trail, tunneling through the narrow spots along our path, and splaying flat and silent against the wet earth.

"This reminds me of *American Werewolf in London*," Steve whispered as we walked along. "These woods give me the absolute creeps."

"Cotler and I used to come out here on days like this," I said, "He used to wonder what it was like to have been a scout for John Mosby, trekking along this path beside an army, watching their movements. Seventeen thousand men, barefoot and bleeding, trudging through a place like this, rattling tin cups and telling stories, cursing and farting and laughing. They came through here on their way to make history with their own blood. That's what this place should have been to me. That's what it is to Cotler. A beautifully, honorably, gloriously haunted place."

"That's what Virginia is to the Cotlers of the world, isn't it?" Steve asked. I looked over at him and smiled, forgetting for a moment where I was and what I was looking for.

"Yeah. That's about right." We walked in silence and enjoyed that moment.

"I guess if you look at it a certain way, ghosts aren't really scary," he said. "They just run around, lost and sad, or something. That's the difference between ghosts and monsters, I think. Monsters are really built to scare you." I thought for a moment.

"Right about the time I turned six, just before this whole thing began with Jim Kelly, I started having vivid nightmares about monsters chasing me and I couldn't run away, or if I could it was that syrupy-slow dream running. Maybe it was a movie we saw, I don't know. I remember asking my father if there really were monsters, anywhere. He stooped down and looked straight at me. It's so funny now, I can remember him having to hunker down to look in my eyes. He said the only monsters that were real were in people."

"What the hell is that supposed to mean to a six-year-old?" he asked. I shrugged, peering down the trail to the west. We were close to the forked tree that marked the spot where we would turn to go out to the clearing.

"That's my father. He said sometimes people had so much bad in them they became like monsters, but they would never grow horns or get really big or anything. He said when I got older I'd understand what he meant. The sad thing is I found out within the year." We had reached the forked tree and I motioned for Steve to stop.

"Your dad's a great guy, but he's a little spooky sometimes, isn't he?" I nodded and looked up the trail and back down from where we'd come.

"He's a straight-talker, a lot like Spencer. That is spooky, sometimes. But I remembered that conversation. It was the only thing that made sense to me when I thought about what Kelly was doing to us."

"Did it make you feel any better?"

"No," I said, stepping into the brush that led to the clearing and holding a branch out for Steve. "But it taught me something about my father. For better or worse, I knew I could believe every single thing he said."

In the gray gloom of the late morning, the clearing

looked much as it always had. The log where Calvin Cotler had sat, the rise to the right side with the single grove of trees where Kelly had pinned me underneath him. They were all there like props on a stage that hadn't seen a production for many seasons. Heavy clouds seemed to bear down on the treetops with aching weight.

I didn't have to shush Steve as we approached the place. He was dead silent all the way to the edge of the clearing, the same one that I had described to him with the stuff of nightmares. When we arrived I looked around, wondering if we'd been followed. It didn't seem possible, but I didn't have Cotler's senses. I had chosen this time for a reason. Lon, I knew, was in Sheriff Cotler's office in Leesburg, providing a written statement to him about seeing Armand at Lake Lind on October 22. Tamara was to be there separately with her father, and the whole process was expected to take most of the day.

"What's the plan?" Steve asked. I looked across to the other side of the clearing and shivered. We both spoke under our breath.

"We pretend like we're Marty Moreland and we need a place to hide an ammo box. I'm hoping he hid it out here, anyway. Where would he do that?"

"If he buried it, we're screwed."

"Maybe," I said. "Let me think for a while. If we haven't found anything by one-thirty, we're out of here." Steve looked around, taking in the grayness, the fog, the trees.

"Do you believe he really came out here to think?" Steve asked. I shook my head. "No. He told Bonner that, but it was bullshit. He came out here to see if he could thwart Jim's little episodes."

"Jesus," Steve whispered.

"Jesus is who I thought Marty was the first time he stopped Jim," I said. Steve shook his head and looked with awe over the area where Marty had staked out his hiding place.

"How many times did he pull that off when you were here? Marty, I mean?"

"For me, twice. The second time was the last time Jim ever tried anything with me. I was probably twelve. I think I was nearby once when he did it for Vinnie, but I can't be sure now."

Together we walked up to the grove on the little hill. The log that I'd been bent over by Jim was still in place, covered now with moss. I hunkered down before the log and leaned into it. Behind me, Steve stood silently and kept watch. I looked out over the woods and closed my eyes, trying to remember the rocks and which direction they'd come from. Smatterings of memory came and went. I waited. And waited. When I opened my eyes again, I had an idea. This was the position I was in, that I couldn't mistake. I remembered the view in front of me like a condemned man would remember the faces of the jurors passing sentence on him. The rocks could have come from vaguely straight ahead, and to my right. I tasted this and closed my eyes again. Yes. Straight ahead and a little to the right. I looked down, and over. The creek that defined the north end of the clearing and gave it its half-moon shape had burrowed a tiny canyon beside and under a large oak tree. Straight ahead and to the right. With uncharacteristic patience I waited and tested this vision again and again. The wind picked up and moved the clouds farther along. Bare branches on trees rustled and whispered and scraped against one another behind and above me. I nodded toward the creek and motioned for Steve to follow.

The creek had cut a wide spot beside the oak and a huge root of the old tree created a cavity above the water flow. We walked along the creek until we'd found this spot, a spot wide and deep enough to conceal a small man. Under the large root was an entanglement of smaller ones in a mixture of earth and root endings and grass. Deep in that groove, under the large root, was a pile of rocks. The rocks had shifted but remained loose, having been stacked at some point in a rough pyramid.

"Here," I said. "If he left it in this place, we'll find it here."

5

It is an uncharacteristically lovely afternoon in early March. Vic Moreland, Cotler, and I, eighth graders, are lounging in Vic's backyard, kicking over large stones in his mother's neglected garden and occasionally looking to see what we've uncovered, careful not to show childish interest at what may be in the dirt. Vic's brother Marty has been missing for almost four days and his parents suspect that he has left the area. Vic is not altogether concerned. Marty has run away before, spending the night at friends' houses and once on the golf course in town.

Vic digs beneath his lawn chair for another rock, takes aim, and then lowers his arm. Someone is walking toward us. It is Dan Cotler, who in his trooper's uniform looks dark and vaguely menacing, and even larger than he actually is. Vic tosses the rock to the side and slowly rises. Dan removes his hat and walks over to us. Cotler and I crane our necks and can see that other cars have arrived at Vic's house: the brown Crown Victoria of the sheriff, as well as another county car.

"Mr. Cotler?" Vic asks, his voice uncertain. Cotler and I look at each other. Dan is looking only at Vic.

"Hello, Vic," the trooper says, and his voice is steady but pained. Vic stumbles backward and kicks the chair over. My heartbeat is wild inside my chest and I look over at Cotler, who shrugs and reflects the fear in my eyes.

"Where's my brother?" Vic asks. "Where?!"

"Sit down with me for a second, son," Dan says carefully. His eyes do not so much as flick our way.

"No. No, sir. Where's my brother, Mr. Cotler? Where is he?!" Suddenly, there is a sound—a wail from inside Vic's house. It is Vic's mother, and in a million years I would never have believed that she could make such a sound. The wail rises again, it is pure agony and shock and terror, and it comes through the kitchen window like a siren.

"Vic, your mother's going to need you now. Something's happened to Marty. Please come with me for a moment, okay?" Vic shakes his head spasmodically and tears leap to his eyes. The trooper moves toward him, but Vic is too fast. He turns and bolts over the Moreland's back fence as his mother wails and screams anew. In seconds he is gone, through another yard and out onto a different street. Trooper Cotler watches him run off and rubs his eyes with his thumb and forefinger.

"Francis, find him, please," he says quietly.

"I cain't catch him, Pa."

"I know that. Just follow him. Find him and try to get him to come home. John, help him. Please."

"Yessir."

"Is Marty dead, Pa?"

"Yes."

Cotler's father turns away and heads for the house, and Cotler and I jump the fence and hurry in the direction in which Vic has fled. Above us high clouds swirl thinly in a sea of blue, and a warm sun continues its descent into the western sky.

6

From the journal of Marty Moreland, dated October 21, 1980:

His name is Buddy. I found out today. He was looking at me. I was right about that. I was running past the Deli and he was hanging out there with some friends of his. I was gonna run by like before but I made myself stop. He nodded and I nodded and we started talking. I think he's sixteen, but I'm not sure. The truth is I was so nervous just talking to him I don't remember a lot of what he told me.

He's beautiful.

I wish I didn't think it, but I do, and what makes it worse is I think he might like me, too. This sucks. If I knew he was into girls and I could just look at him, it would be so much easier. But he wanted to talk to me. He wanted to know about what I did, and where I hung out. He was looking at me, and there was something there. Oh God, I'm just making it up. I know I'm just making it up, but I think he likes me. I'm going to tell Coach. He'll know what I should do.

I want to see him again. I want to see him, and when I do I've got to ask him if we can hang out, sometime. Is that how it's done? If it were a girl it wouldn't be so bad. This is torture.

Jim is on to me and I'm worried. I've stopped him eight

times now, but I think he's starting to figure out my moves. Last week I saw him walking the trail and measuring the distance between trees. He's going to try and trap me, which means I have to find another way out of that spot, but I don't know any. The other trails are too narrow to run very fast. If I trip on a root back there I'm dead. As it is he's got to suspect it's me. Last time I did it there was a blond-haired kid. I think I know his name but I won't write it here. I hit him in the shoulder with a rock and I lifted my head to see if he was okay. He saw me, I'm almost positive he saw me. If Jim finds out it's me he'll come for me, he won't wait. I have nightmares where he comes for Vic. For my mom.

I don't have much longer. I don't have much longer.

I'm going to sleep. Buddy's his name.

***

Steve and I found the ammo box after about an hour of digging in the dirt behind the rocks. At home at my desk, I read and re-read passages from Marty's journal with guilt-laden wonder. There were five accounts in the journal of him hiding out and throwing rocks at Jim Kelly and his victims. Neither my name, Lon's, nor Vinnie's were ever mentioned, but Vinnie was described fairly well in one account. There was further description of Buddy, and various passages about how their relationship progressed. At some point Marty told Buddy about Jim Kelly and Buddy told him that he, too, had been abused by someone. It didn't take long, by Marty's account, to figure out that they were talking about the same person. Buddy had apparently met Jim through a little league in a neighboring town, although the town itself wasn't named. Marty didn't say much about Buddy's background and never wrote about going to Buddy's home at all, wherever that was. Their friendship seemed to center on the trails, the woods, and the Moreland's shed, where Marty had spent the night with him on various occasions.

I wondered if Vic had ever seen this boy. I couldn't remember anyone who might have been him, but after high school Marty had become withdrawn, and had spent more and more time away from home. He worked nights in a photo lab a couple of towns away and slept mostly during the day.

Beside me as I read further, the wind rattled the windowpanes and whipped around the house in eerie, baying throes. The radio was calling for gusts that would bring driving, pelting rain by nightfall, but as yet it was dry.

In guilt and discomfort, I darted through his thoughts about getting together a group to come forward. Again, he never mentioned us by name. The only names that were mentioned were Dr. Abbott and R.W., the old sheriff, along with painful descriptions of how Marty had gone to them in vain. R.W. threatened Marty with a mental health evaluation, if the journal can be believed. Dr. Abbott simply cited patient confidentiality and wouldn't talk to him regardless of what he said.

The last entry was dated two days before his disappearance. It described talking to the coach, and then with Buddy. There was an argument with Buddy, the resolution, if there was one, was not described. The journal simply ended there. There was no suicide note, no last thoughts or testaments. I got to some news clippings in the back and unfolded them.

They weren't news clippings.

They were want ad pages, folded around two photographs. In between the pictures was a folded photocopy of a handwritten letter. The photographs tumbled out onto my desk and lay there under the desk lamp like prisoners under a searchlight. In both pictures were two boys, smiling and holding up beer cans. They were dressed for the cold and standing in front of Marty's old Dodge Dart. After a long time, I reached for my jacket and car keys and headed downstairs.

***

The parking lot of the cemetery was empty, darkening, and swept clean by the wind as I emerged from the truck and pulled my jacket close for warmth. The wind whistled and screamed around me as I walked, head down, from the truck up the hill past Marty's grave. I walked over to the tree line that marked the beginning of the woods and the end of the cemetery and dug around until I'd found what I wanted. At Marty's grave I left them: four smooth gray rocks against his headstone. I knelt beside the grave marker for a few moments, but the wind stole and split my thoughts and concentration. After a short prayer I made my way back to the truck.

***

Cotler has warned me about the wind. Windy days, really windy days, are not easy ones for one trying to hunt, or keep from being hunted. The wind creates illusions to eye and ear; the movement of trees, branches, and grass beckon toward nothing and alert falsely. Screams, shrieks, howls, and hoarse scraping and scratching sounds seem to come from everywhere. Even the trained ear can be deceived easily. Maybe because of these things, I did not see that Kelly had pulled in and parked on the other end, and I did not hear him closing in on me from behind. He reached me as I got to the driver's side door, slamming my head with his forearm against the door window. He talked above the wind, directly into my ear.

"We need to talk, boy," he said, pinning my left arm behind my back. He lifted it to my shoulder blade and I started to scream. "Scream like a woman and I'm liable to fuck you like one, y'hear?" Kelly's breathing was audible and close, a cauldron of memory and old fears.

"Wh-what do you want?" I asked, bewildered. Kelly hadn't approached me in years. My eyes flittered this way and that, but nothing greeted me on either side but empty fields and an empty parking lot.

"You've been talkin'," he said. "You've been leadin' people down paths that don't add up to nothin'. Am I wrong about that?"

"I don't know what you're talking about." Kelly twisted my arm viciously upward and I yelped, thinking surely that it was broken. He let it go slowly as he composed himself.

"What the fuck have you been telling them?" he asked, his own voice rising. "I've kept my ear to the ground in this town for goin' on twenty years. I know what people think around here, and I know what people think of me. I got a good name. I run a business. Now somethin's up, and I don't like it. There's people lookin' at me and then turnin' away. Some of them ain't so quick to say good mornin' anymore. Daryl down at the cement plant is talking to me the other day and says one-a-those feds runnin' around here was asking some questions about me. Says there's some bad rumors floatin' around, wants to know how long he's known me. So I call the sheriff and he says 'just calm down, Jim, you know those federal folk got to do their jobs.' But he don't say he don't believe it, that it's all a lot of horseshit. He don't say much of anything. The goddam sheriff who's my fucking friend talking to me like a goddam politician! Now you tell me what's been goin' on, boy. You tell me, and you better by God hope I like your answer."

"I don't know what you're talking about. Please, don't break my arm. Just listen to me a minute. What rumors have been going around? Just tell me that."

"Rumors I touched some boys. Rumors I been too friendly with some of 'em, and is it just coincidence that I knew the two that been took? Rumors like that, John. Where'd they come from, goddammit?!"

I swallowed hard and thought wildly, *Why does he suspect me of this, after all the boys he has touched? Why me?* I wasn't about to ask it directly.

"Jim," I said breathlessly, trying to speak without screaming over the wind, "what in hell makes you think I'd do this? Who would I tell . . . Cotler?"

"There ain't nothin' to tell," he hissed into my ear. "And even if there was, Cotler wouldn't believe you. You know that."

"I've known it for years, Jim," I said, expecting another glancing blow to the head or neck. But none came. "I've known it for years and I've kept quiet all that time. I've kept quiet because there's nothing to tell. Why would I start talking now?" I had a peripheral view of Kelly and I could see him, hands on his hips, staring in lookout toward the town.

"Because now some fucker is grabbin' kids and killing them out there," he said, pointing to the woods and lowering his voice. "And it 'ain't me! But you think it is me, don't you, you little prick? You think it is me."

"No," I said, truthfully. "I don't think that. Why would I tell lies and get myself in trouble with you? Why now?" Very slowly I turned around and faced him at an obtuse angle. He eyed me with suspicion but I could see that he was beginning to believe me.

"Shit," he said softly, staring out at nothing in particular. Something lurched up in me. It was as if I was vomiting words. I was scarcely aware of speaking them.

"It was Lon," I said, over the wind. To me, my voice sounded strangely flat, foreign in my own ears.

"What the fuck did you say?" he asked, with a jerk of his eyes that should have made urine trickle down into my jeans. But it did not. I was oddly calm.

"Lon. Lon Chambers. You should know that, Jim. You above anyone else." Now the blow did come. Quick as a snake, he stepped toward me and slapped me backhanded across the mouth, splitting my lip against my lower teeth. I did not flinch. The pain went through me like a sharp knife and it was gone. I could feel a thin trail of warm blood roll down my face. When Kelly stepped back, I read much more than anger in his eyes. I read doubt. And fear.

"I'll kill you," he whispered, most of it lost in the sound of the wind. A thin smile formed on his face. "I'll kill you for even thinking something like that."

"I'm not the one you oughta be thinking about killing," I said. I could no longer feel the wind, or anything, precisely. The whole world had gone a sleepy shade of gray.

"What do you know?" he asked. I caught this from

reading his lips. The howling around us had picked up and the sky was darkening. Rain was coming. Kelly's clothes whipped around him and made him look surreal, like an apparition in a dark hallway.

"Enough to know he's beating a path to your door." He stepped forward again and half slapped, half punched me, not once but twice, coming across my face again from the other side. More pain. More blood. I did not resist. I didn't move. When he was done he peered at me, looking into my eyes and smiling an amused, fascinated smile. But there was no amusement in his eyes. They glowed with anger and malevolent distrust.

"He's gotten to you, hasn't he?" Kelly asked.

"That's not your concern. You wanted to know who's shining an ugly light on your life, and I'm telling you. Go ahead and beat me to a pulp if you want. But then maybe we should figure out what to do about him. For both our sakes." He seemed incredulous at first, then stopped smiling and fixed me with a look cold and straight.

"You want him dead as much as I do," he said. "Don't think I don't know it. I don't know what the fuck he's got you doing but—"

"And you need him dead," I said, interrupting him for the first time in my life. "You do if you're smart, anyway. I'm not making any judgments about you. But like you said, some fucker is killing kids out there. I think it's Lon, and he thinks he can pin it on you. And he's in a perfect position to do that. I don't think you want to know just how much I do know, but I'll tell you this: He came after Vinnie and me primarily to recruit us in bringing you down. The two of us balked and he's given us some grief, sure. But it's you he wants, not us.

"There's a lot I don't know, too. I don't know what his connection to you is. But I think the smart money says he's a dirty piece of laundry you left behind somewhere, and now he's back to stink up your life. If that's true, you'd better think about doing what you have to do before he stinks it up real bad."

"Well, well," he said. "This little piggy went to market . . . and this little piggy," he jabbed a finger into my chest, "has decided to get all grown up. You really think you're up to this, son? Killin' a man ain't like trashin' a doctor's office in the middle of the night. Yeah, that's right. I got an idea who did that. It's bad medicine. Bad."

"I'll do what I have to do," I said. And I meant it. Kelly seemed to digest this. He gazed out over the rooftops of town, around the hills and the rises of the cemetery, and back to me in long sweeps. His pale blue eyes flickered this way and that.

"Can you get him back there someplace?" he asked, his thumb toward the woods. I nodded. Another idea had come to me. It was one that would either save me or see me murdered.

"Yes," I said. "I can get him to the clearing. But he'll be armed."

"I know the gun he has," Kelly said. "No matter, I'll be hidden. As soon as I have a shot, I'll take it. Call me at the shop. Tell me what time. I'll be ready when you both get there. You won't see me until it's over. Can you do that?" I nodded again.

"Good. And don't fuck this up, or I swear to God I'll take you out, too. It's all the same once you start rollin', believe me." As he spoke he turned to leave, walking toward his truck, parked on a side road that led along the cemetery's east end. He wrapped his arms around his upper body against the wind with his head down.

7

In the clearing I could hear branches twisting, popping, as the wind tore tunnels through the trees. Cold bits of rain spattered my face. The sky went from slate gray to blue gray. At 6:42, Lon came trudging through the woods, folded over against the gusts. He looked thoroughly uncomfortable.

"Where's Cotler?" he asked, peering at me. I had found Lon at one of the strip malls in town a few hours before, smoking and hanging out with some older black guy I'd never seen. I had told him I'd arrange for Cotler to meet me in the clearing, as Lon had demanded, and that he should be there at 6:30.

"He's on the way," I said, my face a mask. "I couldn't walk out here with him. It's too much. But he'll be here. I talked to him less than an hour ago." Lon glared at me, his senses alive with suspicion.

"I don't like this," he said, as much to himself as to me. "He's got five minutes. Otherwise I'm leaving. And if I leave before he gets here, our deal is off. Is that fucking clear?" With my life depending on a nightmare from my childhood hidden somewhere in the woods behind us, I shrugged and looked at him squarely.

"Yes," I said. "It's all very clear now, Buddy."

He gasped and leaned closer as if believing what he'd heard had been a trick of the wind. But knowing it wasn't, he glanced upward at me and prepared to strike me in the face. I had been struck before and was getting adept at seeing them coming. I dodged his fist and stepped back a few feet, bouncing lightly on my heels. The person I had known as Lon grunted with hatred and frustration and gaped at me. The expression on his face was that of a child who'd just walked into his first open casket viewing.

"I know who you are," I said over the wind. "And I know what you are."

"You know nothing, you pathetic freak. You know nothing." His breathing was heavy, labored. We moved in a slow circle like two boxers in a ring, the dead grass and blown twigs of the clearing breaking beneath us.

"What do you feel when you kill them?" I asked. I was waiting, surprisingly unafraid, for Kelly's shot, or for Lon to produce the gun he had. "Terrance Hark's mother looks like a Holocaust survivor. Was it worth it?" I was starting to scream and the wind screamed with me. He shook his head, first slowly, then faster. He dove at me this time and caught me at the knees. We both went tumbling, and for a moment it occurred to me that if Kelly were out here waiting to take a shot at Lon, I wasn't making it any easier for him. Then it occurred to me that I may have been just as much a target as Lon. Maybe Kelly was setting us both up. Lon's fist under my right eye brought me back to reality. The pain went through me like a needle and I fell backward. I looked up at Lon with one open eye and smiled.

"You're nothing," he said, wiping his mouth. "You're a blind worm in the dirt and you think you've got this all figured out."

"Somebody loved you," I said. "Probably the best person who ever came out to this shitty place, and this is how you repay his memory." He kicked me on the underside of my thigh and I crabbed back from him. His jacket flapped in the wind and his eyes were huge and wild. He pointed at me and screamed like a child.

"Don't you bring him up! Don't you so much as speak his name, you sick piece of shit! He came to you begging like a dog and you told him no! It's you that's responsible for Terrance Hark! It's you that's responsible for Jeremy Bingham! Talk to me about how to repay someone, you goddam piece of . . ." He dived on me and I scrambled to get back, but he was too quick. His knee found my groin and I screamed in pain. It was the move he'd planned. In my agony my hands went toward my crotch and Lon's found my throat.

"You're wrong," he said to me, growled really, as his hands clenched around my neck. His eyes were white holes of rage and mine were swelled with panic. I whipped my head back and forth and felt hot blood trapped behind my face. "You're wrong and you think you've got it all figured out, don't you?" He took one hand off my neck and reached toward the back of his waistband for the black pistol. He produced it and pointed it at my forehead.

"Do it," I garbled. I was crying, laughing, panicking, and thinking with bitter clarity all at once. It was oddly exhilarating. "Do it, it's a fucking kindness. You're still gonna get what—" I stopped myself and his head darted upward. His black eyes searched the trees, and then a small smile appeared on his lips.

"I'm gonna die out here, aren't I?" he asked without looking down, still keeping one hand clenched firmly on my throat and the gun trained on my face. I stared red-faced back at him, my heart pounding. He chuckled and bore down, choking me harder. His voice was soft and calm as his hand dug into my throat.

"I'm not gonna shoot you. I'm gonna let you live, so you'll see the day when you wish I had. Listen close. The well. The creek bed. The clearing. That's three. Are there four places or only three? If you survive this and I don't, ask yourself if you can remember the fourth. Thank you, Johnny. Thank you so much. You had a choice to make and you made a fine one indeed. You're in league with the devil."

"You are the devil," I croaked. He lifted his head, stared straight up toward the trees in front of us and smiled grimly, drawing a breath as if to yell. Then he gurgled as a dark red flapping hole appeared in his throat. There was a clap, and the echo of a clap that was quickly eaten by the wind. His eyes widened and he dropped the gun. His other hand left my neck and went to his. He gurgled again, a hollow, spitting sound, clawing at his torn throat with red hands.

Buddy's eyes slowly fell down toward mine and I heaved him off of me in a panic. He fell to the side, his legs moving back and forth along the ground crazily as if he were trying to climb an invisible ladder on his back. I crabbed away from him just in time for the second shot, which made most of the top of his head disappear, and a puff of earth explode beside it. The climbing legs stopped in mid-step, and he was still.

Splayed flat on the ground, he looked like a Halloween prop. What was left of the boy's head looked a little like a smashed piece of soft fruit. I staggered back from him, turned, and threw up. I rose to my knees and threw up some more. Maybe a minute passed, I couldn't be sure. The world began to swoon and I started to fall forward when Kelly grabbed me by the collar.

"Get up, you shithead. If I'd a dug-a-bigger hole, I'd a killed you both."

8

The rain stopped around midnight. The wind reasserted itself less violently and the clouds began to break up and move toward the east, exposing bright spots of night sky in their retreat. I slowed as I passed Spencer's townhouse and saw that his bedroom light was on. He came out wrapped in an oversized coat of his brother's.

"Dear God," he said, looking me up and down. Kelly had given me a sweatshirt to wear and had taken my bloody shirt and burned it after our cleanup and burial of Buddy. My hands were still stained with dirt and there was a blooming shiner under my eye. The cigarette in my hand twitched accusingly. "Where have you been?" I opened my mouth to say something and nothing came out. I tried it again and got the same result. Amazingly, Spencer just put up his hand and shook his head. "No matter. Are you okay?" I hesitated for a moment before answering.

"Yeah. Yeah, I'm okay." He nodded slowly and seemed to ponder my face in the cold light of the streetlamps. But he did not prod. I was still on the brink of tears and trying to keep my voice from shaking. "Spence . . . I can't . . . I mean, there are some things I've been dealing with lately that I can't talk about. Not right now, anyway. But I wanted to see you, anyway. Is that ridiculous?"

"No. No, I don't suppose it is. Why can't you share this with me?"

"I just can't. It's so complicated. If I told you . . . I don't even know if you'd believe me."

"Is that what you think? That I wouldn't believe you?"

"I've lied before."

"You can't lie to me, John," he said. And that statement

was so true I almost smiled. Cold wind blew from around his row of houses and lifted the collar on his jacket.

"I'm so sorry," I said, a whisper. "I'm so sorry I can't tell you."

"It's okay. I'll be here when you can." I nodded and looked at the ground between us, remembering finally why I had come.

"Spencer, pray for me tonight. Please?" He looked at me with quiet, steady eyes that seemed to narrow for a moment incredulously.

"I pray for you every night, John."

9

A letter from Marty Moreland to Buddy, undated.

Buddy:

I don't expect you to be happy with what I've decided, but I hoped you would understand. I can't leave, and you above anyone should be able to accept that. He's still here. He's still hurting them, and there's no one in this miserable place who cares about it. I have to care, Buddy. Do you understand that? I have to care. He knows. He knows it's me and I'm running straight out of time. If my stand is to be here, against him, then I'll take it. If he gets past me to my family or anyone else at least I won't have to rot in my grave knowing I didn't try to stand in his way.

You have a freedom that I just don't have. It may be the only thing in your life that's easier for you than it is for me. You've told me yourself, the nothing you have leaves you nothing to lose. But please, forget your stupid stubbornness for a second and read this carefully, because I say it out of love. I'm worried about you, what this life in the woods is doing to you. It's making you wild and cruel, Buddy. It has to do that. You're becoming something different, something like a beaten animal, and it hurts me. I've tried to understand you. I think you know that. I have a mother and a father and I can't imagine never having one and then losing the other, but I know there are people who have gone through what you're going through and they haven't given up like you have.

What's this about not wanting to be called Buddy anymore? Why do you hate your name? I would feel the same about you by any name, but why? You're scaring me. You're spending all of your time trying to think of ways to recreate yourself. I think you can disappear, just like you say you want to. I think you can fake papers, move away, become another person. The very things you do well scare me about you. I know you're proud of it, but I'm begging you not to give in to it. To become invisible is to lose your soul, Buddy. That's what you want, isn't it? I know. Do you see? I know what you're trying to do. Please don't. If you give in to that, you're no better than he is.

You've wanted to know why I am the way I am, why I want to stay here and fight him. I'll tell you now, since I've dodged it every other time we've talked. There was a kid I knew. His name was Lon. Lon something, I can't remember his last name anymore. He was Vic's age, and he was the first of the boys I ever saw with Jim. I was at the track behind the middle school one day, right next to the ball field, and I heard them talking. Jim was his ride home from baseball practice and they were picking up bases and equipment. They were looking for baseballs. Jim called him into the trees, and I knew God damn well what he wanted. I crept in closer and hid behind a tree. But I couldn't do anything. The boy, Lon, saw me. He saw me and he started to scream. Jim slammed his hand on his mouth and went to work on him. I saw it. The kid was looking at me and I watched until I couldn't take it anymore and then I ran. I ran. I panicked and I ran, and he got raped, because I wouldn't stop it. He died a year or so after that. It was some childhood cancer I'd never heard of. And I couldn't have been happier because I couldn't stand to see his face anymore or even to know he was in the same town. I've seen that boy every night that I've closed my eyes. I can still see him, reaching for me and staring with eyes like saucers.

This is my place. It's my penance to stay here. The only good thing I will ever do is to stop this from happening as much as I can. You should go. But go to Ohio and live with your uncle. Give it a chance—the real world. Live, Buddy. Live for both of us. I have a bad feeling about this year. I don't know how much longer I can do this.

I said just now that the best thing I will ever do is to try and stop Jim from hurting boys. That isn't true. The best thing I will ever do is to have found you and to have loved you. I know you can't say it back. You don't even have to feel it back. I love you, Buddy. I'm making a copy of this letter before I give it to you, so

*I'll know I really did have the courage to say it to you,
at least once. That's all the truth I need. It's all the life
I need. Good bye.*
Always, Marty

10

I didn't expect them to be so vivid. The dreams, I mean. Awful, Technicolor playbacks of the events in the clearing, they marred the months to follow. The gun clap, the blood, the way Lon's head simply disappeared above his nose. During the day, too, I saw it play out in front of me while teachers' words droned unintelligibly and the print on my test papers swam out of focus. On worse days, my preoccupation was harder to conceal than anything I could remember, which of course compounded my paranoia. I was oddly uncomfortable around Cotler's father and waited with hidden impatience to leave his presence when Cotler and I were on our way out somewhere. I was jumpy to the point where a simple tap on the shoulder would send a shock wave through me that, on top of everything else, I had to learn to conceal.

But on better days, I did savor the rich, warm relief that Lon's absence was leaving me, and although his death had spawned another set of anxieties, I still preferred them to his stalking tyranny. As the month wore on I reminded myself, as I knew well, that a human being could get used to anything.

I sat up in bed on the last day of March and rubbed my eyes. Sunlight from the window above me had warmed a patch of bedclothes and woken me gently. There was the shadow of a dream, a recurring one in which Buddy sim-ply stood, headless and blood-covered, atop the little rise beside the old fallen log and pointed in a direction that meant nothing to me. Around me the light of day rushed in to chase the shadows away and I lay there, my hands behind my head. My father called from downstairs; mass was in forty-five minutes, and I answered while I threw back the covers.

Lon was dead.

More than two weeks now he was dead, and I was get-ting used to it. I smiled and stood to dress.

Chapter Nine: April

1

Friday, April 12. "Johnny, can I please talk to you?" she asked as I considered pulling a long-ignored English book from my locker. I froze, but without the intensity of the past.

"What is it, Tam?" I said, leaning against the locker. She was dressed in a polo shirt and jeans, her hair pulled back with a pink ribbon. She looked adorable, and I should have been electrified at the obvious curiosity with which she was studying me. Instead, she looked faded, an image of something I had wanted a lifetime ago.

"I owe you an apology," she said, looking down, "for saying some cruel things to you. I'm sorry. You were right about talking to Cotler's dad. I felt awful until I finally did it."

"I'm glad you did it," I said. She hesitated, then pushed forward.

"Lon talked me into doing stupid things. I don't really know how. I hate myself for having liked him at all. I was kind of scared of him, to be honest." She looked at me uncertainly, studying me in the dim afternoon light of the hallway.

"It's okay. He was—is—a scary guy. I don't like him either."

"You're not the same, you know?" A furtive smile broke over her face. "You look like you've aged ten years since the fall."

"It was a tough year," I said. She nodded, as if she understood. She found something on the cover of her Spanish book more interesting to look at.

"You made me feel special, for a while. I know it never really went anywhere, but I think we made each other feel that way, sometimes. I just . . . didn't want us to leave school without one of us saying it." She eyed me and waited for a reply. I was at a loss. I had dreamed of a moment like this, and in typical fashion it had now found me too late.

"It wouldn't have been me," I said. "I guess I'm glad you did." She looked puzzled and seemed not to know what to say next. The puzzled look shifted and settled into something like disappointment. I don't know what Tamara wanted from me; I only knew that I was too tired, too far past it to try and figure it out.

"Well, take care of yourself, Johnny. Maybe we'll run into each other around graduation."

"Maybe we will. You take care."

She nodded and walked away, doubtlessly more taken by me than she ever had been or ever would be again. I felt a flutter of regret, but little else as she swished away into the annals of vague and unimportant memory. After all, a brief period of her attention is all I could have ever hoped for. Tam was occasionally bored, occasionally curious, and I was occasionally interesting. I was interesting again because I wore the look of a flood victim of late, and I hadn't talked to her in a couple of months. But by that

April I knew fully why it had been a lark to her and the very universe to me. There is a place for losers, and then there is a magic place where once, maybe twice in a lifetime they find themselves. They play there for a while, giddily and furtively as if they know that somewhere a great god has made a terrible mistake and that only time stands between that warm, tingling place and their cold, virginal reality. With Tamara at our beach week I had found myself in that place. I had played light and I had played ignorant. Ignorant of the inimitable twists of circumstance that had brought me there, and unmindful of the wrath of the great god who would in good time show me back to where I belonged.

2

Sunday, April 21. Doug had been following me for the better part of a week. His eyes had been all but glued to me for at least two weeks. He knew. He had found out, somehow, and I was about to get it between the eyes. He followed a respectable distance behind me now in his Bronco on the boulevard. I turned into the town golf course parking lot and drove all the way back to the last spaces by the fence that bordered the back nine. He stopped a few car lengths before me, pausing like a suspicious animal that has at last a view of the food it's been smelling. I climbed out of the truck, lit a cigarette, and faced him as he drove over.

When he finally emerged from the car, he looked straight at me for a second and then wrenched his eyes away. It looked painful, that wrenching. Doug's fine, strong face was sunken and sallow. I had never seen him look this way, so beaten and confused.

"What is it, Doug?" I asked when he was within striking distance. "Let's hear it." Slowly, he pulled a crumpled piece of paper out of his pocket. His breathing deepened. A second later he lunged at me, throwing me solid against the door of my truck. His face was perilously close and I should have been in terror. But Doug wasn't so scary anymore in the context of things. "What's on that paper? What does it say?"

"You," he said, panting. "I should kill you." I laughed, a slithering, mean sound. Then I pushed him. Not much, just enough to put some space between us.

"Kill me if you want to," I said. "Or tell me what it is you need to tell me. But don't waste my time." He reared back and made a fist, and for a moment the fear was back, bright as lightning. It shook in the air before he brought it to his own jaw, swiping it across his face savagely.

"He poisoned me," he said, looking at me at last. His eyes begged for the purchase of his words in mine. "I didn't know what I was doing." He closed his eyes and his mouth hung agape. "I . . . I was tricked. I couldn't have done those things otherwise."

"I'm not judging you."

"Then take your fucking eyes off of me!" he screamed into my face. He looked savage and sad at the same time. "I didn't realize it before but now I know! You've been looking at me. Staring and staring!"

"Bullshit, Doug. You're the one who's been looking at me since you found out I took pictures of you and Lon Chambers together. Well, he forced me to, just like he forced you to do a couple of things. Let's put our cards on the table. When did he tell you?"

"He disappeared," Doug said, his voice childishly

curious. "I don't know where he is." He examined me more closely and, as well as I could, I ignored it.

"Neither do I. What did he tell you?" He glanced at the paper in his left hand as if seeing it for the first time. Absently, he handed it to me while his red-rimmed eyes examined pavement in circular patterns. I unfolded it and beheld for the first time Buddy's neatly clipped handwriting.

> *Dearest Douglas:*
>
> *If two weeks have passed and you have heard nothing from me, then feel free to read this message, as it is your right. For I am either dead or gone for good, but most likely dead. If you're jumping the gun on me, I will find out soon enough, and so will you. But I trust you, lover.*
>
> *I've written this letter as a parting gift. Not to you, you bastard, but to my friend John Ray, my only friend at the end of it all. You see, Doug, John is the third party here. It was John who took the pictures of you and me together. It is John who holds those pictures now that I am gone. If you wish to retrieve them along with his everlasting silence in this matter, I wish you good luck. He hates you, and with good reason. But I would suggest as a first step showing him this letter. Somewhere in it he may see what will move him to pity, or a deal.*
>
> *I want you to know, Doug Lars, that I am tearing you apart for the simple pleasure of destroying something more destructive than me. I'm doing this for every face you senselessly beat black and blue. For every whimpering girl you sent waddling home*

with blood between her legs. For every fat kid who never quite found the will to really laugh again in the same way he used to because you humiliated him. For all these empty people you drank from I say fuck you very much.

And to you John, I say thank you for being my friend. I know you hated me, but I need not make a cliché here to remind you that all emotions at those levels are pretty much the same. My only hope is that you will one day find the courage to see me killed. Maybe if you're holding this letter, you finally did.

That was it. It was unsigned and undated. I, of course didn't have the pictures of Doug or any knowledge of where they were. Instead I had something of deceivingly unequal value. I had Doug's belief that they were in my hands. My head buzzed with the possibilities as I pretended to look the letter over one more time. Doug snatched it out of my hands.

"He told me about this letter, where it was, a while ago. He told me if I ever didn't hear from him for two weeks I could go and dig it up. Two weeks, he said, or else. I waited three. So where is he? Did you kill him?"

"Do I look like a killer to you?"

"You look like a pussy to me," he shot back, but it was the last echo of a long clanging gong. Doug's oft-used, crass but cutting aphorisms sounded flimsy and childish in his new slick, pale skin.

"You seem to forget who was on the business end of that camera," I said softly. Doug's eyes lit up with hatred and wonder and he sucked in a breath as if he'd been hit. He made a fist and tightened it, but then let it unfold, watching it all the time as if it were not his hand making the movements but some long trusted friend gone astray.

"I'll kill you before I'll let you get those pictures out, John. That fucking psychopath," he jabbed a finger at the letter in his pocket, "showed me I could do it."

"Fuck you," I said dully. "Kill me. I'm tired of bullshit. Show me what he taught you."

"Goddamit, what do you want?" he moaned. Doug didn't want to kill me. Doug wanted this nightmare to fold up its traveling wagon and move on to another town.

"He showed me the pictures a few months ago. I don't even remember it. I thought it was someone else."

"It was you."

"Fuck you, all right?" he said through clenched teeth. "Like I said, I was poisoned. It could have happened to anyone. That guy is the fucking devil."

"Whatever."

"All right. I'll tell you what I've got. I think you killed him. I think you're fucking crazy enough to do it. And you know damn well I'm not the only one who thinks you're walking off the deep end."

"You got pictures?" I asked brightly. Doug winced, but went on, one stiff finger pointed at me.

"You were a part of him, too. You and Vinnie. Yeah, I know a little about that." He watched for a change in my eyes, but to the best of my knowledge I showed him nothing. He wasn't dealing with an amateur, after all. If Doug had more than vague suspicion, I'd have heard it awhile back. "I don't know what he had on you two, but I'm not stupid, John. The both of you have looked like rotten apples since he came here." His voice lowered. "And a couple of times when we were really hitting the stuff hard he talked about you two."

"What'd he say?" I asked with the mildest of curiosity.

"Enough to let me know that something happened to the two of you, a long time ago. I don't know what yet, but you know what? I'll find out from Vinnie."

"I wouldn't try that," I said, dead serious. Doug perked up. The sniffing, plodding mind had stumbled upon something.

"I run Vinnie's life," Doug said, his eyes brightening, his harbor in sight. "I know it's there and I'll find it. He's ready to crack anyway."

"I'm going to tell you this once. You're barking up the wrong tree. If you think Vinnie's losing it, you're right. But it's because of Vinnie, not Lon. Don't push him. He's at the point where he'll push back."

"Vinnie Foust is the biggest pussy that ever lived."

"Vinnie Foust *was* the biggest pussy that ever lived. Now he's a time bomb. Leave him alone."

"Why? What's he to you?"

I thought about this. What was Vinnie to me? A miserable prick who had never provided me with the slightest commiseration throughout this whole nightmare. Regardless, I could never help pitying Vinnie, and maybe he knew that and hated me more for it. More importantly, something common ran between us. Our connection was like a slimy steel cable through a sewer of human refuse, but it was hard and fast.

"Let's talk business," I said. "I'm giving you this offer. Back off of Vinnie and back off of me, and I'll sit on your dirty secret forever."

"What about Lon?"

"Maybe he's dead. He hasn't contacted me in a while either. Either that or he's been run out of town by someone else, but regardless I wouldn't worry about him." Doug cocked his head and studied my face. Eager and fumbling, he smelled purchase. Around us the sweet, budding scent of April rose from the golf course and made its way around the lot.

"The pictures. I get them and we have a deal."

"You get them and I've got nothing. No, I'll be sitting on those for a while. I've done it so far, haven't I?"

"That's only because Lon wouldn't let you blow it. He wanted me for his dirty work. No deal."

"No deal? Where are you at this bargaining table? You've got vague suspicions of nothing. I've got glossies." I checked my voice then. I had no glossies. I had the tenuous hold of belief, ever so fragile when it's supported by nothing. It had to sound simple, easygoing. Trumpets and lights and megaphones usually mean there's nothing behind the curtain. I was almost too late. His eyes lit up. "That's only what this letter said. If you've got 'em, show me." I smiled my best Cotler sleepy smile and shook my head.

"I don't generally carry them around. You don't believe me? Fine. You haven't got first strike capability here. I do. I'm offering something that leaves us both unharmed."

"I was poisoned," he said after a pause. "They'd know that." But he said it to the fence in front of the cars. I wanted to laugh.

"Yeah, right. The only thing the world loves more than a hero is a disgraced one. Do we have a deal or don't we?" Doug looked over as if shaken from a dream. He was imagining the poisoning excuse, imagining it working. Or maybe he was imagining his other life, the one before Lon Chambers. There was a lot of that going on in Belle Ridge.

"When do I get the pictures back?"

"At the five-year reunion," I said, and I liked the way it sounded. It came out quick and smooth, and it was as logical a common point in the future as any we would have had. I sounded like a man who had been making plans, speaking softly and carrying double prints. I could see the success of this fill Doug's raw, tired eyes.

"Five years. Fuck."

"A deal, then?" A short eternity. He nodded.

"Five years."

"Yes," I said. "In silence." He looked over my shoulder into the lush, spring-woken fields beyond. Haunted, bewildered eyes found mine again in a slow, muddy sweep.

He said, "You know I'll kill you. I'll try anyway, if you welch on this deal and try to ruin me."

"If I welch on this deal I will ruin you," I said. Slowly, with strange sincerity, he nodded.

"I know. And maybe you don't even care anymore, but I will. I should do it now, but I can't. I'll admit that. But if you let this out about me and you think I still won't murder you, you're wrong. It won't matter then. Nothing will. Do you understand what that means?"

"That's what he's been trying to teach us all along. What that means. That nothingness. It looks like he's done a good job with you."

"You know, then?"

"Yes," I said. "I know."

Doug had just uttered the four or five most meaningful sentences he would ever speak to anyone, and I guess it's fitting that they were among his last. His eyes swung to the field, then back to me again, in many ways a mirror image of him in terms of the effect 1985 had had on us so far. He stared at me coldly, stubbornly for a few seconds and his face softened, caved really. He looked as if he were on the verge of asking something, then of crying. Finally, the face smoothed and seemed to take on new life. He turned and padded softly back to his waiting Bronco. The Bronco looked as if it were a confused horse that wished it knew why its rider smelled of defeat and despair. He drove off, not looking back. I never spoke to him again.

In retrospect, I was glad that he had been given a whiff of Vinnie and me. I suspect sometimes that Lon engineered this as part of the game. This tiny bit of knowledge still allowed me the upper hand, but it helped to balance the bargaining table. Unarmed, Doug would actually have been more dangerous, and I would have supposedly had a trump card on him with no reason not to play it.

But what made me uneasy was the last thing I'd seen in his eyes. Resolve. Doug wasn't finished. The deal I'd given him wasn't bad, but there was a nagging window of vulnerability that he didn't like and that he was going to try to close just a little. He was going to probe Vinnie, just a touch, to see what he could find.

3

Monday, April 22. On the most beautiful day of the year, I held my second-to-last conversation with Vinnie Foust. At his request we met beside the baseball field where a little league team was practicing. Their bright curses and calls danced in the air alongside the crack of wood and the smack of leather. Around us the world looked as if it had recently rained liquid gold; everything seemed to gleam and shimmer in the afternoon sunshine. Below our feet, the new grass was tender and nakedly green.

"Doug knows," he said. He looked straight at me for the second time since we were children and there was something curiously loose in his face. I shook my head.

"He talked to me, too. He knows nothing. As long as we keep quiet it'll stay that way. Believe me, Vinnie."

"You don't know Doug like I do," he said. "He knows more than he told you. Lon fucked us hard this time."

"No, no. You don't know the half of it, I'm telling you—"

"Where is Lon?" he asked, cutting me off. I could see it in his eyes now, the wildness.

"I think he's gone," I said, trying to sound vague and certain at the same time. "I haven't talked to him in a while. If we're lucky, he hit the road." Vinnie shook his head.

"He's been using Doug and now he's using him to finish us off." There was a distinct and frightening whine creeping into his voice.

"Doug doesn't know anything. Vin, please."

"He doesn't know yet. Lon's feeding him a little at a time. Eventually Lon will use him to expose us to everyone. Maybe even set us up for the killing he's been doing. Have you considered that?" I sighed and tried to throw him a lifeline.

"Yes, I have," I said, metering my voice carefully. "But I think Lon is gone. I haven't heard from him in a while and I . . . I think he may have had some problems somewhere else." Vinnie looked at me blankly.

"What the fuck do you know about his problems? Did he tell you that?"

"Of course not. But . . . I just think he's gone. And I know Doug's harmless. He came at me, too. He's fishing for something. Just ignore the hook, for Christ's sake."

"He's not fishing. He doesn't need to fish. This is just what he does. He'll torture me slowly just to see if I'll admit something. In the meantime, Lon'll give him a little more each time. This is the grand finale. Did you really think he was just gonna pack up and leave?"

"Just hang on, Vinnie," I said. I had tried, but for Vinnie I would go no further than this. "You've done it so far." Vinnie looked down.

"I'm all alone," he said to the ground, and it was a cracked moan. It was a heartbreaking sound, not a cry but a whimper of despair. "You've got lots of friends. Everybody loves you."

"If everybody loved me, I wouldn't be in the same exact position you're in."

"I never had a single friend," Vinnie said, and he said it with the common wonder of the truly friendless who ponder that sad fact endlessly. I understood why my father had forever admonished me to pity the true assholes of the world, and not to hate them. *They reach a certain age, he said, and then they spend the rest of their lives sitting up at night and honestly wondering why no one likes them.*

I had little to offer Vinnie. Perhaps if I'd known how he was going to react I would have tried to come up with something short of incriminating myself as a co-conspirator and accomplice to murder. But my father, as usual, was right. Vinnie was friendless because of something crucial and un-teachable that had been left out of his upbringing, and in his superior intelligence and bizarre circumstances he was perhaps reaching that age of endless pondering earlier than most. Probably it wasn't his fault. But it wasn't mine either.

"You've come this far," I said at last. "You can hang on a while longer." He didn't seem to hear me. His eyes were moving about our surroundings, bathed a lovely red-orange in the declining sunshine.

"There's been a way out of this," Vinnie said. "Lon told us months ago what it was. Remember? He told us to kill him if we wanted it all over with. He fucking dared us. Why didn't we have the balls, John?"

"Is that what you want?" I asked, anger and resentment rising inside me. "To be a monster? Because that's all Lon wants. To make you a fucking monster like he is." Vinnie stared back at me, his face empty.

"I don't need Lon to make me a monster." He turned and walked off. He seemed to float, bob, really as his narrow shoulders rose and fell with his footfalls and his hair flew in wisps around his head.

4

Tuesday, April 23. Lunchtime. The cafeteria was its usual bleach-smelling, bland-looking self. The voices were legion, 300 kids speaking, squealing, laughing unintelligibly over one another. Cotler and I nodded to other students we knew as we made our way to our usual table. Spencer was already there eating a sandwich and contemplating another matter as if utterly alone.

"Are we getting together at your house tonight, John?" he asked as we sat down. I nodded. My parents were away with my sister at a Junior Ambassadors convention in Philadelphia. Cotler sat back in his chair and glanced at the lines, deciding on what to eat. He waved at Steve, coming out of the a la carte line with two rectangular pizzas and some peach cobbler. Steve took a seat beside Spencer. Vic walked over a minute later, shaking two small cartons of milk. Greetings were exchanged and everyone took their places. Cotler stood up, embracing the whole atmosphere of the table with his size, and walked off to the a la carte line. Spencer and Vic exchanged news and rumors about the track team. Words, muffled by food, flew brightly, and around us the cafeteria roared.

***

Vinnie walked in. I saw him enter the cafeteria, but I would be a liar if I told you that I read anything about him at that moment. He walked in alone, stood at the door beside Coach Lyons who dutifully kept watch over the 'C' lunch shift, and walked over to where Doug, T.C., and the rest of his ruling class were. Oddly, it was Vic who first noticed something amiss about him.

"Is it me, or does Foust look like he just ate a handful of sleeping pills?" he asked, his eyes moving from Steve to myself.

"Don't get my hopes up," Steve said. But we all watched him walk evenly toward his usual table. Vinnie reached the table, the last one before the doors on the other side, and stood before Doug, who sat on the end, facing the rest of the cafeteria. We heard later that Vinnie asked Doug to return some homework from a previous period.

"Yeah, hang on," were Doug Lars' last words. He turned in his chair and bent down to fish the papers out of his knapsack. Vinnie lifted his oversized golf shirt and pulled his stepfather's Army .45 out of his pants. Without a second's hesitation he pointed it squarely at the back of Doug's head and pulled the trigger.

Screams. One. Then fifty. Then two hundred. T.C. Johnson, Dennis Campbell, and a few other football players caught some of the red blast that was Doug's head as his body went sprawling forward into the aisle. Mercifully he was face down, but above Doug's fine, sinewy neck there wasn't a lot left. A pool of blood started to form like a corona around his shoulders. The incredible clap of the shot rang in the heavy air. Vinnie considered his victim for a brief second and then whipped around, facing the rest of us.

"Nobody moves!" he screamed and waved the gun over the crowd. "Shut the fuck up!" The screams stopped. Carefully he stepped over to a table nearby where fifteen mortified underclassmen had been eating their lunches and grabbed a chubby freshman in a blue sweat suit up from her chair. She had a fair, rosy-cheeked complexion and curly blond hair that was styled in probably the exact same way as when she was in fourth grade. He shouted something unintelligible at her, pulled her by the arm, and locked her head underneath his arm. She screamed, and again the cafeteria joined her.

"Shut up!" Vinnie roared, spit flying from his lips. His eyes were wild white discs behind his glasses. The gun swept over the table and back to the chubby girl's head. "Shut up or I'll kill her!" They shut up.

Vinnie dragged himself and the girl in headlock back over to Doug's body. The girl stared straight down into the pool of Doug's blood and didn't move a muscle. The two coaches in the cafeteria were still too shocked to speak. Vinnie spared them the chance.

"Nobody moves," he said, still forceful, but lower and with an odd composure. "Nobody talks. Anyone runs for the doors and I'll fucking kill them. Anyone moves toward me and I'll kill her." No one moved. Only whispers could be heard above the occasional clinks of trays and discarded silverware. A few people eyed the doors hopefully, but there were no occupied tables close enough to make it worth the risk. Vinnie had thought this out. People who had been walking across the cafeteria stood frozen where they had been when the shot went off. Vinnie ordered them to sit down where they were and told the coaches to stay put if they valued the chubby girl's life.

"I've got some things to talk about," Vinnie said. "I've got some things to get straight." His voice had lost much of its wiry squeal and he sounded almost authoritative. On the dark side of some faraway, tumbling coin this may have been his finest hour. He adjusted his grip on the chubby girl and lowered the gun to his side. And then he called my name.

***

It's hard to describe what my heart did when I heard this. It sank and did not leap into my throat or clench like a vice, as one might expect. Truth be told, I wasn't entirely surprised that he had called me. This is not to say that I wasn't scared. My skin tightened, my penis shriveled, and I let out a small gasp. Suddenly every eye that wasn't too afraid to look away from Vinnie or too fixated to look away from Doug's ruined head and the growing pool of blood surrounding it was on me. Steve, in a gesture that would have been deemed inappropriate between men in any other situation, put his hand on mine. Maybe he wasn't altogether surprised, either. Spencer leaned across the table and looked into my eyes. Tears were welling up in mine, and I fought for control. It came again.

"John! John Ray! Get the fuck over here or I'll blow this little bitch to pieces! Now!" Vinnie's voice, for perhaps the first and only time in his life, had steel in it. His breathing was audible over the eerie silence of the room.

Beside me, Vic whispered, "John, Oh Jesus, John, man . . . you . . ."

"I'm gonna do what he says. I'm going."

"He'll kill you," Vic breathed. "He'll kill you and then he'll kill Cotler too, because you know as well as I do he's gonna try and—"

"There's nothing else to do. Cotler won't try anything, yet."

I got up on wooden legs. I pulled my hand out from under Steve's and patted his quickly. He was almost crying now. To my amazement, he wasn't alone. Quite a few people were crying. Silently, for fear of certain death or dismemberment, quite a few of us as hostages, cried. Spencer's eyes followed me in a slow swaying motion. Steve couldn't take his eyes off of Vinnie. Spencer was praying.

The sound of my chair moving across the floor as I rose from it brought out a few choked sobs from somewhere close by. I began to walk down the aisle between the tables and then left, down the center area to where Vinnie stood, the blue-faced chubby freshman still in headlock. The girl stared wide-eyed and breathlessly at the ground, and at Doug's wasted blood.

I walked like a robot toward Vinnie. I wanted to urinate. I wanted to vomit. I felt crazily like an infant, like I could let loose all over myself and not give a damn. My very organs seemed to swish inside me, everything just loose, sloppy, bloody.

And my mind moved like lightning. To the blood, for

starters; the blood that now swirled around Vinnie's cross-trainers. My eyes went from Vinnie to Doug, from one child whose life was struck down to another whose life was surely over by any other definition. I stopped when I was five feet from him. I could hear the girl now, whimpering. Her mouth hung open and a bit of drool gathered on her lower lip.

"Vinnie," I said, startled at the sound of my own voice. He studied me for a moment.

"You hate me," he said. He moved his head as he enunciated "hate" and said it with a weird certainty. I again felt a tremendous urge to foul myself. I tried for a breath. The gun hung large at his side.

"Vinnie, I—"

"Deny it and she dies, right here. Go ahead. Deny you hate me." I was silent. My mind raced and raced. *Christ, someone with talent and poise could talk his way out of this and save the girl. Christ, please.* No smooth words. No slick posturing. Nothing but tortured, bloated silence. Vinnie's face softened and he looked down at the chubby girl.

"John's here," he said. "I don't need you now."

"Don't kill her, Vinnie," I said at last. I was suspiciously happy at the strength of my voice out of the gloom that was my body. Vinnie's eyes shot up into mine. The world reeled, but I didn't look away.

"I may not kill her," he said evenly. "I may kill you." With that he raised the gun to my face. A trickle of pee now escaped into my shorts. I constricted as tightly as I could and it stopped. As weird as it sounds, that was a real relief.

"Just don't kill the girl, Vin," I said. I wanted to sound tired, weary, like somehow this was all something to be discussed over cocoa on throw pillows. Vinnie looked again at the girl, then back to me.

"Tell me why I shouldn't kill her," he said. "Tell me."

"She's done nothing to you. She's done nothing to us. Killing Doug, maybe that's what you had to do. I understand. But she's not a part of all that. Do you understand me?" This was the only angle I could think to play. Either Vinnie would respond favorably to my attempt at the *we're the same, you and I* ploy, or he would laugh and kill us both.

"What's us?" he asked, peering at me. "What are we?"

"Two people who know about wanting to live. Haven't we come this far?"

"You never cared about me," he said, his chin lifted. "You and everyone else. No one cared. Everything I've got I had to get myself. No one ever cared."

"I tried, Vinnie. I tried to help you. We helped each other, didn't we?"

"He made us," he said, and I wasn't sure if he was talking about Jim Kelly or Lon. I shot for the larger concept.

"'He made us' is right. He made us everything we are, didn't he?" Vinnie grinned slowly and for a second I thought I was as dead as dirt.

"You're trying to trick me," he said, tightening his grip on the chubby girl. She gasped and spat up a little on the drying blood underneath her. When her feet moved they made a sick, tacky sound in the blood, like wet paint. "You're trying to trick me into trusting you."

"No, Vinnie. There is no trust, in either of us. We don't know how to trust, but we know how to stay alive, don't we? We've done what we had to do, you and I." I motioned below him to the body on the aging linoleum and lowered my voice. "Like this here." Vinnie's face scrunched up momentarily and he wrinkled his nose, as if wanting to know how this all smelled to him. Sweat soaked through his green golf shirt and ran down his arms.

"They won't understand," he said, mostly to himself. "About Doug."

"Maybe not. But I will. Maybe only I will."

"I didn't do it for you."

"I know that. But I'll understand. You won't be alone. There'll always be someone else who knows why. This isn't about trust. This is about understanding. I understand you, Vinnie. I know how you feel. I'll always know."

Vinnie looked as if he wanted to ponder this but was suffering from a terrible headache. He teetered a little under the weight of the situation, the silent crowd, the blood, the whimpering little girl. The gun swung largely at his side and his eyes clouded over. *This is it,* I thought. *In a second his eyes will clear and that .45 at his side will tear my arm from my shoulder or my spine from my hip in a smoky red glaze.* But instead he started to cry. Almost imperceptibly, Vinnie started to weep, and when he did the fear that had been like an alarm in my ears swam out of focus. It was muffled by sadness, and some terrible longing.

"He's eaten enough of you," I whispered. "Don't let him have any more." Vinnie heaved and sobbed. He glanced down at Doug's ruined, half-shattered face and grimaced. The chubby girl continued to drool.

"It hurts," he said. "It hurts . . . so bad."

"I know," I said, fighting for every word. "We know. Let the girl go now, Vin. This is between us, isn't it?" He looked up until his eyes rested in mine, but rest is all they did. They did not bore, like moments before. There was no real anger left. There was no wildness, no passion, nothing. *Sanity has returned to him*, I thought. *And it's left him cold.* From behind us, I felt the eyes of 300 terrified children. Beneath their fear, like the high wire man, I felt their curiosity. But for the remaining threat, it must have been quite a show.

"Somebody else has to die," Vinnie said weakly. He was breathing heavily, wet with sweat. "It's gone too far to turn back." He glanced down at the catatonic chubby girl.

"Not her," I said.

"You and me, then," he said. "How about it?" It was to be the two of us, then. Even after all this. Or maybe because of it. Me first, then Vinnie. My body quaked and seemed as if it were coming apart from the inside out. The shakes were coming from deep inside. The memories. I called them back and asked them for the infinite sadness and ageless disgust that would make death something I could face without begging.

"Just not her," I said. I closed my eyes. Vinnie raised the gun and held it there. There was a moan from close by and a collection of gasps and whispers. The longest few seconds of my life passed in silence and darkness while I waited for the explosion that would be my existence ending. He lowered it again.

"No," he said, shaking his head. My eyes opened and with a shock I beheld a soft-faced, almost angelic Vinnie Foust. It was as if he had put on a different face in the seven or eight seconds my eyes had been closed. He looked calm, restful. He had lost all of that perpetual distrust, that ever-present hostility. His features were smooth, unlined. He seemed to glow. "You stay here, John."

"Okay," I said numbly.

"I'm going to go alone."

"All right."

"I'm sorry I wasn't a friend to you."

"I'm sorry I wasn't a friend to you. It wasn't supposed to be, I guess." Vinnie nodded, his transformed face now warm and knowing, as if he were an old man listening to his grandchild describe a failed attempt at stealing second base. He looked at me one more time, loosened his grip on the girl and actually smiled at me. He glanced down at Doug once more and wordlessly put the gun into his mouth, pulling the trigger for the second time.

***

Vinnie's face seems to cave in and another ugly, red spray bursts from everything in front of me. He falls, and the chubby girl falls with him. My knees are suddenly dead and rubbery, and I fall forward onto the two of them. The chubby girl is heaving beneath me; the gun has fallen with a plop into the blood that is all around us. There is a crashing sound and men surround us, hands on us, brown uniforms. The chubby girl is clutching me as they pull her away. There are badges, guns going back into holsters. Kneeling beside me, a handsome man with large, searching eyes is looking into mine.

"You all right? Son?"

Then Cotler. My only cognizant thought is wondering how he has broken into this circle. But there he is, the smell of him, his arms around me, mumbling something southern and unintelligible. Pulling me away. Blood all over me. All over him. My feet leave the ground and I am in his arms, carried like a child out into the hall. Men around us, a face too close to mine. Somewhere in the hallway as we move in a tight group I turn my face to Cotler's stiff flannel shirt. Buried in his chest, it smells like—wood. Blacking out as I toss with Cotler's big steps toward the nurse, I am sobbing.

5

"Did you see Doug get hit?" I asked Cotler. I had woken a few moments before to his snoring. It had a taken a few seconds for the school nurse's office to take shape around me. I was in the back room, dreary and without decor, where vomiting children and the better fakers reposed in cool darkness and on coarse, sterile sheets. He shook his head.

"I was in the line waitin' for a goddam piece of pizza. I heard a noise. I knew it was a gunshot. It was weird, you know? A gunshot goin' off in school. It was like somethin' I was used to hearing goin' off in some place that just didn't fit. I didn't know it was Vinnie, not then. I figured maybe it was some asshole, brung a gun to school and it went off. I wondered if anyone was hurt. Then I heard Vinnie start rantin'. Most of the people in the lines and most of the cafeteria staff bolted out the back. Damn smart of 'em, if you ask me. They went to the office, gave word. The first county car was here in four minutes, but there wasn't much they could do 'cept sit outside the doors and watch. The state got here with my dad, and they were talkin' about snipers and stuff, but it was over too fast. All anyone could do was watch you and Vinnie and that poor girl. All of that while Doug Lars let out his blood all over the fuckin' floor." He shook his head and stared at his shoes.

"How the hell did you get in to where I was?"

"I didn't think much. I just did it. I thought you'd had it when he raised the gun to your head the second time. Then he lowered it and started talkin' again. I couldn't take much more, I'll tell you. I looked away for a few seconds. I think I saw my dad and some troopers looking in at the far door. Then Vinnie took himself out, and you all fell in a big heap. I didn't expect it. It was after that second shot that cops came in from every door. I looked over and saw you and him and her all tangled up, blood everywhere. I didn't know what'd happened. I ran over. There was a trooper standing there and I said my buddy was in there and I was goin' to get him out. Maybe he recognized me; I don't know."

"Probably he saw the look on your face and gave up any plans of stopping you," I said.

"It was stupid," he said. "I shoulda let them get hold of you and look you over. They had enough problems with crowd control."

"No," I said. "It wasn't. I knew you were there. I didn't see you exactly, but I knew you were there and it was a good thing. I would have wigged out if anyone else had tried to touch me, I think. I knew it was you and I didn't care so much." Cotler nodded but did not look up.

"Vinnie's dead. Doug is dead. Damn."

"What about the girl? Does anybody know?"

"She's at Memorial. She's in bad shape. They were gonna take you, too, but . . ." he trailed off.

"But what? Did I do something?" I was suddenly very worried. For the life of me I couldn't remember anything after being carried to where I was. The prospect of me blacking out and saying whatever was on my mind was damned unnerving.

"Well, you wouldn't let go of me for a while. My dad came over to the bed and you were just sorta holdin' on to my arm. Wouldn't let go. You weren't screamin' or nothin', you just wouldn't let go, not for anything. Dad said it was okay, that I could go there with you, but you just shook your head and hung on. Finally, he told the ambulance to go, and they got a doc from the medical center to come over here and clean you up. My dad gave permission since your parents were out of town. That doc ran some checks on your eyes and stuff and watched you 'til you fell asleep."

"I didn't say anything? Anything at all?" He shook his head.

"Nothin' that made sense. A few times you said stuff about Vinnie, but we couldn't make sense of it. Somethin' about the woods. He went out there with Jim and us when we were little."

"Yeah," I said. "He did. I guess it's what he remembered about us." Cotler studied me for a moment, and for the first time I saw the look that I would see on others faces for years. *Why you? Why did he pick you out for the miracle mile?* An uncomfortable silence fell over the room, something horribly alien to Cotler and me. I didn't like it at all. But it took thought to come up with something believable to feed him, and my head was still heavy and dull. I remembered that a detective would be here for a statement soon, so I switched painfully over to high gear.

"If I had to guess, I'd say Vinnie killed Doug because Doug treated him cruelly for years," I said. "He grabbed the girl for insurance. That was smart, I guess. Why he called me over . . . Christ, I don't know. We spent some time together when my mom and his were friends. We were maybe seven or eight. I can't remember."

"We were about ten when Vinnie stopped hangin' around," he said quietly. "I think, anyway."

"That's about right. I guess he was fixated on it. We were similar in some ways. He was scrawny and a loud-mouth, and I was chubby and a loudmouth. The difference is I had you and he had nothing, not even a safe house to go home to. I never thought he gave you or me a second thought, except to throw an insult in the hallway. I guess I was wrong." Cotler nodded solemnly and I knew he was hooked. I knew the cops and even his father would be hooked, too. The story was a good one and I was pleased with myself. I lay back, spent from the exercise.

"And all that stuff, what you said to him when he had the gun on the girl. That was all . . ."

"Bullshit. That's all it was. I was trying to come up with anything that would make him pause, make him think. I didn't even think about the connection between us for a couple of minutes. I didn't know what was going on. Then it hit me, Vinnie and I were almost friends when we were little kids. To me he was an annoying brat that came over with his mother, but maybe to him I was all he had, and he expected us to stay friends. I don't know. I don't think any of us will ever know."

What I told Cotler about my relationship with Vinnie is what I told a young detective named Matt Murphy who came in a few minutes later to take my statement. It is what I told Cotler's father, my parents, three local news correspondents and two national networks, and it is what I still say today to many who ask. Thankfully, no one but the chubby girl heard absolutely everything that was said, and I don't think anything was registering to her. The story made perfect sense, and what I have realized since then is that it would have worked regardless, so long as it contained no more than an iota of believability. There was no one by that beleaguered April who wanted to hear about any dark conspiracy involving me, Vinnie Foust, and some buried town secret. What I gave them is what they wanted: confirmation that Vinnie had acted under extreme mental stress. That he had shot one abusive, current friend and then tried to make some last minute amends with a very old former friend. It was a closed case in less than a week, and I didn't dare stand in its way.

6

Vincent Edward Foust killed another student and himself on Tuesday, April 23, 1985. School commenced again on Monday, April 29. Roland Washington sent letters to all of our parents expressing his sorrow and noting that counselors would be on the premises for as long as was needed to help anyone who felt affected by the events of April 23. They were well-used throughout the rest of the year. Principal Washington visited my house on Thursday night with Sheriff Cotler, and from what I know he spoke with the chubby girl's family during that time, and Doug and Vinnie's people as well. Through my parents I was encouraged to meet with a psychologist paid for by the school about what had occurred, which I dutifully did and to whom I disclosed nothing. He was a kind, professional man, well qualified to counsel on his subject, and he spoke with me two or three times before reporting me suitably stable, but not yet willing enough to enter continuing therapy.

Vinnie was taken away by his mother and presumably

buried where her family is, somewhere in Pennsylvania. I never heard his name again except in connection with what he had done. No one connected with his family, such as it was, stayed in Belle Ridge or to my knowledge ever returned. I don't think Vinnie would have minded. Belle Ridge for him was mostly a stink-hole where he had lost his innocence, sold his soul, and then gotten absolutely nothing in return. I don't expect Vinnie's in Hell, but even if he is, I'll bet he sees it as a damn sight better than the rat-trap life he played out here. I think of him often and wonder why he spared me after all.

April 30. Doug Lars was buried in the cemetery the Tuesday after his murder and his funeral was attended by most of the town. His father, a lean, good-looking man who might well be what Doug would have looked like in middle age stood sobbing beside his casket, clutching a football jersey Doug had worn to practice his senior year. Doug's mother was a terribly wilted flower of a woman who sat beside him stunned into some awful, unbelieving silence. She looked pretty and petite covered by a black veil and adorned in a dress that looked as if she were ready to be buried alongside her son. I had never seen either of them, even at football games where they had surely been every week, and I wondered how many more sets of parents I would see for the first and last time on this overworked plot of land. Doug had no brothers or sisters. The family consisted of their boy, the pride of Belle Ridge, the darling of homecoming, and the school's patron saint of speed and power.

At the conclusion of the burial, Cotler, Steve, Spencer, and I were walking back to Steve's car when Dennis

Campbell, one of Doug's teammates, caught up with us and blocked my path.

"Where's Vic Moreland?" he asked, his chin high and uncertain hostility in his eyes. I looked around the grounds and back to him. He looked sad and funny in a stiff, undersized blue suit, and he was a walking metaphor for my town.

"His brother's buried back there, Dennis. He's had his share of this place. He's not coming back."

"I think he stayed home to throw a fucking party. Is that where you're all going now?" Around us a small crowd was forming.

"Dennis, have you lost your goddam mind?" Steve said, checking his voice. "There are people everywhere."

"There's a lot of people who don't belong here," he said, looking around. "Most of all, you assholes. What are you doing here, anyway?" Cotler stepped in front of him.

"We're payin' respects," he said. "We're here for Doug's family. We're here for our school."

"You never gave a fuck about him," Dennis said, pointing a finger at the group of us. His lower lip was trembling, and I wondered what or whom exactly he was mourning. Maybe it was Doug after all.

"And there's a lot of people he didn't give a fuck about either," Cotler said, advancing on the other boy and raising his voice just a touch. "But I'm here because he was someone I grew up around. We fought, Doug and me, and we fought hard. And we walked around each other like we knew it well enough. I'm here and they're here 'cause you don't always have to like someone that died. Sometimes you go 'cause that's just what a man does. Get used to it. You go mourn your teammate now and leave us alone, you hear?"

Dennis looked stunned for a moment and became aware again of the crowd he'd created—the same one that had just watched Cotler hand him his ass. Steve and I exchanged a glance that communicated superfluous praise for Cotler, and got in the car. Cotler waited until Dennis and the crowd dissipated, then climbed in, sullen and silent in the front seat. The rain spattered against Steve's dirty windows as a lonesome wind blew between the cars in line to leave the cemetery.

Chapter Ten: May

1

Thursday, May 9. "Did you ever find out anything else about Lon, or whatever his name was?" Steve asked. He was beating me at chess and crushing out his nineteenth cigarette of the day. It was late in the evening and we were sitting in his parents' rec room after *Hill Street Blues*, wondering why Cotler hadn't shown up and what we would do with the first normal weekend in quite a while.

"No. Cotler's dad has been looking for him, though."

"Well, he won't find him now," Steve said. "I guess Lon chose the name because of Marty's letter, huh?"

"Yeah. That, and I'll bet he figured Jim Kelly would recognize it. Lon is a name you don't forget easily, and I'm guessing Kelly remembered it being attached to one of the kids. My guess is Buddy posed as this dead kid Lon and got into Kelly's life through blackmail. Probably a little like how he played Vinnie and me."

"So, we don't know much of anything about who he really was."

"All I know is what was in the journal and the letter. He was some homeless kid who grew up somewhere around here, left for a while and came back. He came back for blood, I guess. Marty was afraid of that. Buddy got a birth certificate, lied his way into our high school, and there he was."

"But if he wasn't from here, how did Jim get to him?"

"Jim got to all sorts of people. He's done plenty of community stuff in other towns. Spencer says his thing is to constantly put himself in places where he'll be around boys. He says he's probably had dozens of victims, maybe hundreds."

"He's been reading up on this stuff, hasn't he?" Steve asked. I nodded. I had added Spencer to the small circle of those-who-knew a few days after Doug and Vinnie's death. He took the information from me in his typical quiet and kind way. I think he suspected something was up for a while anyway; he didn't seem unusually surprised at anything he heard.

"Yeah. He's been reading a couple of books about this stuff, what guys like Kelly do and how they're able to get away with it. He wants me to read them when I'm ready."

"Guys like Kelly just don't stop, I guess," he said.

"No. I don't think they ever stop."

"Then I guess he's still doing it, maybe," Steve said quietly and was instantly, I could tell, sorry he'd said it. This did not sit well with me. The idea of Kelly still hurting kids was not something I had thought of dealing with yet, not to mention the fact that Cotler's father would never have a collar for the murder of two boys. I was still on vacation. Not wanting him to feel uncomfortable, I shook it off and changed the subject.

"What's up after school for you?" I asked. He shrugged.

"Dunno. College, someplace, I guess. Turnpike Tech to start, I'm sure. What about you? Heard from any schools?"

"I didn't apply to any," I said, somewhat sheepishly. That was true, and deadlines were flying by. "I haven't had much time to think about it."

"That's understandable. Your parents aren't going to pressure you for a while. If I were less of a guy, I'd tell you to milk this shooting thing for months." He smiled, and lit number twenty. "What about Cotler?"

"What about him?"

"I don't know, I mean, what's he doing after it's all over?"

"I haven't given it much thought," I said, and sounded genuinely perplexed. "What's ahead for Cotler and me are probably two different worlds. I'll always care about him. It's not like I'm gonna forget him. But I'm thinking I need to branch out, you know?"

There was a guilty satisfaction I was taking in having weathered the entire storm without once leaning on Cotler and his endless reservoir of strength and brute logic. Lingering nightmares and visions aside, I felt pretty damn good about myself given what I'd dealt with over the course of the year. A survivor in a brutal chess game involving Doug, Vinnie, Lon, and myself, I had been straight, but shrewd, with all of them. And other than Jim, they were dead and I was alive.

Because of this, there was a feeling birthing in me that perhaps I should leave some of Cotler behind after school was over and move on to other challenges by myself. Perhaps I had leaned on him too much, some provocative new voice inside me whispered. Perhaps his stiff concern for me had been too constricting, had done more harm than good in some areas. I was bound for college, this voice said, and Cotler, God love him, was bound for work. Perhaps there was life beyond Belle Ridge that I had to explore alone. Perhaps. Steve studied me as I explained this.

"Yeah, but is it Cotler's fault," he asked, "that he couldn't be a part of what happened this year?"

"No," I said, "but it's not mine, either. I've learned a little about what makes people what they are in the last few months, and one of the things I've learned is that people get squeezed together and apart for all sorts of reasons that aren't their fault. But you know what? That doesn't make a goddam bit of difference. I'll always love Cotler. He's my past, and I owe him. But we got separated by a hell of a wide gulf and I don't know if I can get back there anymore."

"I get that," he said. "But think about what you're saying. You did handle a lot of this by yourself. But how were you able to do all that? Who helped make you the guy that faced down all that shit?" I lowered my head.

"It's just hard, going back to that life. It was all fine when we were Cotler and Johnny and we had our little roles to play. I don't know if I can do that anymore. I don't know if I want to do it anymore."

"The only bad thing I thought about when you and I started becoming friends," Steve said as he poured himself the last of a two-liter bottle of Coke, "was that without meaning to I would maybe end up taking you away from Cotler, even a little. I never thought Cotler would say anything but it bothered me just the same. I know this isn't about me, but do you see how important the two of you are?"

"Sure. But we're eighteen now, almost. We've never been eighteen, and we'll never be twenty or thirty before they happen to us. I don't know what's supposed to happen to friends you had when you were a kid. Maybe I've got more in common with you than with Cotler. Maybe I'll go away to college someplace and meet people there that I have more in common with. I just don't know." Steve heard me out this time but frowned.

"I'm no older than you are," he said, pondering his glass, "and God knows I'm no smarter. But the truth is . . . I think you're talking your way into burying the last body from your rotten goddam childhood, John. I wouldn't say that if I didn't think it had to be said, man. Tell me if I'm crossing a line."

I looked at him for a long moment and said nothing. Steve held my gaze for a while with a guilty look and finally looked away. That's when Cotler knocked on the sliding glass door and walked in. His face was flushed and his chest was heaving. He had been running. It took him two sentences to destroy the peace that had been palpable the last six days, along with every ounce of hard-won confidence the events of the last two months had instilled.

"Chris Forrester," he said, out of breath and with something close to panic in his eyes. "He's a fifth-grader at Bull Run Elementary. And he's been missing since four o'clock today."

2

Chris Forrester lived in a section of Belle Ridge unaffectionately known as "Bray's Alley" because of an unemployable redneck named Curtis Bray who had murdered his wife and daughter there in a drunken rage in the summer of 1973. The "alley" was actually made up of four streets just south of the mall and across from the baseball field.

On those streets stood a townhouse development named Belle Mews that probably looked shoddy when it opened, let alone after twenty-two years of neglect, vandalism and constant turnover.

Chris Forrester was one of the children of the Alley. There were a frightening number of them there, mostly underprivileged. Many were victims of a sharp, post-divorce decline in their standard of living. Chris and his little brother were such children: latch-key kids whose mother worked until long after school was out, and who spent most afternoons hanging with other kids of similar age. Although his mother forbade Chris's entering the woods for any reason to the same extent that she would forbid burning the house to the ground, Chris did so often—and by the testimony of his brother and his friends had done so around 3:00 that afternoon.

"I know what you're thinking," Steve said, crushing out a smoke from a new pack and looking me over. We were outside the sheriff's substation where an army of volunteers, police officers, and search dogs waited, once again to be coordinated by the sheriff. "And you can't do this to yourself."

"Where is he, anyway?" I asked glancing around the crowd, looking for Kelly and feeling increasingly ill. "I haven't seen him here."

"His truck is over by the fence. He probably left with the parties that went out before we got here, or the one Cotler just left with."

"If I could see him, I'll bet I could tell. I'll bet I could see it in his face."

"All you'd see if you got a look at him is what you want to see—confirmation that he is doing this—so you can torture yourself some more. The truth is, we don't know.

Copycat stuff happens all the time. Cotler said as much. It's one of the things they've been worried about. Are you gonna take responsibility for everything awful that happens in this town from now on?"

"I know what I've done. I took an arrogant bet that it was Lon, and now we're all paying for it. Chris Forrester, whoever he is, is paying for it."

"Maybe you did and maybe you didn't. And anyway, whatever happened to Lon, Lon had coming. Don't look at me like that, you know it's true. He played dirty and got in the way of that bullet all by himself."

"I should have known," I said. "I should have picked it up when Jim found me at the cemetery. The look on his face, the dead-ass willingness to set Lon up and bury him out there. Jesus, I'm so fucking stupid."

"You acted on the information you had," he said. "And you bought into it because Lon was selling it. He gave you all those sick hints. He wanted you to see it that way. I'll tell you this. If he wasn't doing it, then he knew about it. He had to have known to drop all those clues. What about those shoes he threw around at the Doc's place?"

"He had twenty-four hour access to Jim's house. I'm guessing he found them there, somewhere. Or maybe in the woods. He was trying to tell me when he died. Or at least I think he was. I don't know. I don't know anything anymore."

"Listen," Steve said. "You told me Lon talked about leaving kids like calling cards. Leaving them in places that were familiar to the guy who was killing them, places he knew well and could get in and out of. When Lon died, he mentioned three places, right? Three places where you guys had all been and where you thought Lon was bringing those kids to make a point. The kids were found at the first two. The third was the clearing where they took Cotler's little brother. He told you to think about a fourth. Is there a fourth?" My head spun and I sat down on the pavement to clear it.

It came to me slowly. Yes, there were four. The first was where they found Terrance Hark, in that ancient well that Kelly had told us some squatters dug before the Civil War. Cotler and I found Jeremy Bingham in the creek at the place where the fallen tree made a log bridge. Kelly had all but drowned me there once when I scratched him badly out of sheer agony. The clearing was where Calvin was found and where Lon died. The only place left that was repeatedly familiar to my memory and the others' was the old bird-watching shack off of Switch Road, not far from the clearing. It was a squat, gray building with thin slits in the wood for viewing the birds that nested nearby. Inside were a simple bench, a shelf, a dirt floor, and nothing else. We had been there too, all of us, I was sure. It was out of the way, private, and hard to find. Kelly and a generation of troublemakers had called it the Snake Pit, and the very image of it in my mind was enough to send me into a spasm of shakes. He only took us there if we'd been difficult, recalcitrant, or if for any other reason he thought we would scream.

"The Snake Pit," I said, mostly to myself. Steve had been lost in his own thoughts and now he looked at me quizzically.

"The what?"

"That's what it's called. It's an old shack not too far from the clearing where we found Calvin back in January. It was some sort of bird-watching place, kind of dug into the side of a hill, but kids used to call it the Snake Pit because someone got bit by a copperhead there, once. At least I think that's what happened. It'd be a good place to hide something—or someone. It's a spot he knows well."

"Sounds scary," he said. "Do you know for sure it's still there?"

"No, but they'll know. Cotler knows it."

"All right," Steve said, "think about this. Just in case, we send an anonymous message tonight—they set up that tip line. We can call and tell them to look there. If there's a God, maybe he's still alive. Anyway, you can follow up afterward with Cotler and go from there. At some point you have to tell him, brother. You just have to."

"You're right about the tip," I said. "Let's do that now." Steve made the call from a pay phone while I waited and smoked. True to how it was advertised, the female deputy who answered the tip line didn't ask any questions, just thanked him and hung up.

"Okay, he said. Now we wait, I guess. You feel okay?"

"Not really," I said. "But I'll live, for now at least. You're also right that I need to tell Cotler. But you're assuming that he and his dad will take all of this like some wonderful new lead they hadn't thought about before." Steve looked down. "I don't know what to tell you about that. Personally, I think you're giving way too much to how Cotler feels about Jim. If he is doing it then he's left a trail, somehow. Maybe he's Joe Woodsman and all, but he's not immortal or whatever. If he's doing this, all it'll take is a real look at how he's spent his time these last few months and it won't be hard to make him a prime suspect. Those out-of-town investigators have been looking at him, haven't they?"

"They have, but it's not going anywhere that I can see. The bottom line is Cotler won't want to believe it. His father won't want to believe it. You'd be amazed at the power of that, Steve. You really would."

"Maybe. But I think Dan Cotler is sick and fucking tired of losing his voters' kids, one by one. This goes beyond friendship. You said it yourself, it's bigger than we are, all of us. And anyway, this investigation doesn't just belong to Cotler's father. If they find a body where you told them to look, those other government guys are going to listen to you a lot closer, and it's not gonna matter what any of the locals say."

<h1 style="text-align:center">3</h1>

Friday, May 10. The rock hit my window at 4:33 a.m., shaking me out of a light, broken sleep. Outside, the cover of night was making its last offensive before giving way to the dawn. It seemed unmercifully dark outside. It was still hours into the search and Cotler stood in the grass below my bedroom window, his face a mask of pain. I girded myself for the worst and opened the window.

"They found him," Cotler said. "Stabbed in the back of the head. Probably raped. Like the others." I nodded. My throat felt papery. "Where?"

"That old bird shack, west of the road. It's over by—"

"I know it," I said, glad that the darkness was obscuring most of my face. "I'm sorry."

"Yeah," he said, sounding gravelly and hoarse. "Me too. Turns out someone called in with a tip. God dammed if anyone knows who, though, or why. It was too late, anyway."

"Wanna come in, get a cup of coffee or something?" He shook his head.

"Naw, thanks. I got to get back. Is Calvin okay?"

"Asleep, far as I know." He nodded and breathed out hard, staring blankly at the darkened siding of the house.

"I don't understand this place anymore," he said, whispered really. He closed his eyes and rubbed them with thumb and forefingers. His boots were muddy, and brambles and seed packets stuck to the lower part of his trousers. I searched for something to say in return, but in the cool black of the early morning nothing came to mind. Nothing at all.

4

Friday, May 17. The town turned out for the burial of another of its minor citizens—the fifth in eight months, not counting the hasty job that Kelly and I had done with Lon—mourning with collective eyes of reddened glass. The day was clear and warm, and under the glare of an accusingly naked blue sky I began to backpedal from the promise I made to tell Cotler what had lain between us for most of our lives. Every resolve I tried to keep in place met a volley of fear, nausea, and revulsion. My head reeled with every imaginable worst-case scenario a confession might bring. Even the best-case scenario, with Cotler being a model of understanding and Kelly on his way to the electric chair, was not altogether comforting. For a million reasons, I wanted Cotler to have no part in this area of my life, and in the back of my mind an even greater fear was brewing: telling Cotler might mean having to tell others.

Spencer, Steve, and I discussed the situation for hours the day after the boy was found. Jim Kelly's search party was in the sector that bordered the area where the body was found, and from what I understood Jim stayed with the search group and the officials involved until the body and all the evidence had been removed. Pretty much all night. Nothing from Cotler indicated that Jim's participation was in any way out of the ordinary, and he mentioned him only in passing when I asked who had stayed for the duration. His gun shop was closed the day after, but most of the men involved in the search took off work that following day if they could afford to do so.

Steve's point was that, based on the long periods we were seeing so far between the killings, I almost certainly had time to see how the investigation played out before he might strike again. They had found the boy without my help. Maybe it was only a matter of a few more weeks before they started looking in the right direction all by themselves, particularly the non-locals. This made for small comfort, and Steve knew it.

Spencer had said very little but reminded me that there always was the chance that, despite the circumstances, I could be wrong. The shack where Chris Forrester had been found was a good place to kill and bury someone, and it was possible that my prediction had coincided nicely with someone else's strategy. I had clung to that for two days, but like Steve's argument it was given consideration only because it offered me a back door. For the second time in my life I was confronted with a chance to help end a great evil, but now the stakes had gone up considerably. And no Marty Moreland was there to walk point. My head throbbed.

You could be wrong, a condemning voice said, *and then you' d be exposing yourself for nothing and falsely accusing a man who is a child molester, but not a murderer. If that happens and it's determined he's innocent, then anything truthful you might have also said about him goes out the window. You'll be alone then, until he figures out a way to do you in for good. When Marty approached you, you were sure about what he said. You are not sure of this, and you know it.*

No, the other voice answered, damning and confident, *you know goddam well who's doing this, and you'd come up with an explanation of vampires and green men from Mars at this point to avoid standing up to it. Let this go, and someone else, some tiny creature a lot like you were not so long ago, dies. And then another. And another.*

I sweated, sick under my dark suit, and felt the voices gnaw alternately inside my head. Being wrong meant making much more than just a fool out of myself. It signed my own death warrant, sometime, somewhere down the road. And being right didn't even get me to first base. First, they had to believe it, and they wouldn't want to. Then it would have to make sense to them, and who knew what or how long that would take. There would be inquiries and explanations. Kelly would have plenty of time to maneuver, strategize, maybe even disappear altogether. This was something I really hadn't considered but needed to if I knew what was good for me.

Jim Kelly knew a hundred hideaways in nearby villages, hollows, hillsides, and remote areas where he could survive for as long as he needed. He had bought and sold weapons and pieces of firearms in lost trailer communities and inbred squatter settlements down dirt roads that would never see a map. He spent his days away from the store driving the northwestern counties and the Shenandoah Valley, gossiping with old-timers, misanthropes, loners, and woodsmen, searching out shotgun shacks and Appalachian trapper camps on the rumor of a flintlock for sale or a silver-plated musket stock to be had. Indeed, Kelly didn't need a town, a settlement, or even a well. He had survived on his wits and the land around him on two continents, in war and in peace. He could fan out into the wilds of the mountain-studded spine of the Commonwealth of Virginia and never be seen again. Until he came for me, that was, somewhere, sometime down the road.

The thought of this, the weight of my friendship with Cotler, the idea of yet another march up this little hill to a crowding cemetery, all of them leaned like the cosmos on my shoulders. Even Cotler in his own private hell stopped me and asked if I was okay. I nodded and we trudged on with the crowd toward the bright green canopy with Nelson Funeral Home on the side that marked the final resting place of Chris Forrester. The family had filled in the seats under the canopy and waited in awful, stunned silence while the rest of the mourners made their way up the hill. Chris's mother and father sat together again, the mother clutching her ex-husband and staring straight ahead at her son's box as if he were trapped inside and she was powerless to free him. Beside the family, across from where Cotler and I took our places, was Sheriff Cotler, his back arrow-straight and his hat in his hand, facing the multitude that he was inch-by-inch failing to protect. I learned to respect the man more that day than I thought possible. It would have been easy for him to duck this nightmarishly humiliating experience under the guise of working on the case. But Sheriff Cotler knew the investigation was as much the state's and the FBI's now as his, and that being where he stood was more his job than anything else. His presence here seemed to complete the now familiar atmosphere of horror at the sea of wreaths and flowers surrounding a small and pale casket in the center. On this bright and miserable Friday, it was clearer than ever that what the town was really burying up here every time this happened was a little bit of itself.

It was the sight of Chris Forrester's younger brother that finally sent me over the edge. He was five or six at most, dressed in black shorts with a tiny black bow tie and his hair slicked and combed over the side of his head. He glanced nervously through the crowd, then over at the ghostly figures of his parents. He began to cry and another relative scooped him up. He twisted in the arms of the quietly cooing woman that had lifted him up, craning his head around with the heel of his hand pressed against his eye, still trying to catch a glimpse of the mysterious place where he had been told his brother now lived.

Stop it, I thought as spears of guilt and pricking mental torture bored through my head. *The boy will survive. This day is hell but tomorrow is another, and eventually he will go on without his brother. He's not the first or the last sibling who's had to do it. Eventually he'll be a boy again, a typical boy. He'll be happy sometimes, sad sometimes, and he'll go on wanting to do what boys do. He'll play baseball. He'll hunt for treasures buried in the dirt. He'll go exploring . . .hiking . . . camping.* The world began to swim. I spun around, green-faced, and sprinted away from Cotler's side, headed for the woods.

I went about 40 feet into the trees, found one to lean on and threw up. After it was over, I sank down and clutched the sides of my head in a vain effort to stop the screaming there. My eyes closed, and for a few minutes I tried to doze. I never saw Jim Kelly, who'd been watching the funeral from the edge of the clearing, maybe twenty yards from me.

"Got a bad stomach, do you, boy?" he asked. I rolled over in shock and for a moment looked at him from all fours. Kelly chuckled at this, a low chest-born sound, and I scrambled into a sitting position as he walked toward me. "What's wrong, John? This ain't the first burial you been to." I tried to say something but found I couldn't utter a sound. "You can't even scream, can you?" he asked quietly, standing in front of me with the tree line and the cemetery behind him like a complete vision of Hell. Again, I tried to draw a breath or exhale but found I was paralyzed. "You should have found a better place to puke," he purred. He stepped toward me. "I see snags ahead because of you, you big-mouth little queer, and that's about over with. Do you—" Kelly stopped and whipped his head around. The true woodsman, he had heard Cotler's running footfalls before I had. "I'm comin' for you soon," he said, smiling happily. "I'm comin' for you in your bed." Cotler was calling my name as he ran through the trees. Kelly bolted off into the thickening brush, Cotler neither seeing nor hearing him.

"Hey, are you all right?" he asked as he approached me. "I waited ten minutes and you never came out. I thought you were . . . John, what's wrong with you?"

He came closer but I had made my way drunkenly to my feet and I lurched past him toward the cemetery. I stopped when I came to the edge of the trees and retched again, expelling thin and bitter bile. Turning back, I scanned the woods for signs of Kelly and saw none. Cotler walked over. When he was close enough I grabbed the lapels on his brown suit. His head snapped back at the look in my eyes but I held him fast. And in the cool shade of that May morning, I broke open and told him.

"When we were six," I said, breathing heavily and

punctuating every word with terrible slowness, "I . . . was . . . raped . . . by someone we both know. It went on for a long time. Long time. I'm not the only one he did it to. He's done it to others, except now he's killing them, too. Do you understand me, Francis? I know. I know who's doing this. It's the same person who made me do . . . horrible things. It's Jim Kelly, Cotler. It's Jim Kelly." Cotler's hands gripped mine on his lapels and slowly he brought them away.

"What are you talking about?" he whispered. I glanced around again, sure that Jim would appear behind us wielding an ax, but the woods were empty.

"I'm talking about a massacre," I said, my eyes boring into his. "It's a massacre I'm partly responsible for because I've known this for a while. I thought it was Lon for a long time but now I know. It's Jim. It's been Jim all along, it's—" I stopped. Something very bad was in Cotler's eyes. Something nightmares had warned me about for years. It was not shock or anger but disbelief. I whispered, "Jesus Christ, you don't believe me, do you?"

"Believe you? What are you saying, John? Raped? What do you mean *raped*?"

"For God's sake, are you going to make me explain it to you? I was raped by him, Cotler. Forced to do things. Bad, bad things." My voice was rising in panic and something like rage. Cotler staggered.

"B-But, what? Where? What's this killing stuff? Jim Kelly? He's been out on patrols with us, for God's sake, he's—"

"He's a fucking murderer. He's been molesting kids on his goddam camping trips and baseball teams for years, and now he's killing them. He'll kill again if no one stops him. That kid's life," I pointed toward the cemetery, "is on my head."

"John, please. Slow down, you're not making any—"

"God damn you, you don't believe me! You think I'm lying, don't you? He raped me. He did it when you were gone. He'd send you away. He did it to Vinnie, too, and Marty Moreland. There's a lot you don't know. I know you look up to him but I'm telling you after ten years, he's a monster. And you don't believe me? You think I'd lie about this?"

Cotler looked past me into the woods. A vacant, abysmal look was in his eyes and I could see the word "rape" turning over and over in his mind. And the word "killer." He answered by confirming my worst fears. Ever.

"No. I think you believe it," he said regarding me sideways like an approaching shark in a swimming pool. "But you need help, John. You're not making any sense. It's been this way for a while now. You've gotten worse and worse." I let out something like a moan.

"I knew it. I knew it would happen this way. I wanted to keep it from you. I wanted to keep it from you forever and I would have, but now he's killing them. And pretty soon he'll kill me. If you don't believe me then for God's sake stay away from me because now I'm a target." With that I bolted past him and out through the emptying cemetery, across Chapel Road, and beyond the schoolyard of Belle Ridge Elementary, hearing only for a moment Cotler's woeful calls behind me.

5

May 23. I did not see Cotler Saturday or Sunday. On Monday and Tuesday, I semi-faked an illness and stayed home from school. Cotler was absent on Wednesday for reasons I didn't know, and on Thursday we managed to avoid each other in class and during lunch, which I spent in smoking court. By that night, six days had passed without a word between us, the longest period in our natural lives, even counting vacations not taken together and when I'd had the chicken pox at age four. Then, he had come every afternoon and sat outside, talking to me through the backdoor screen and bringing me news from the neighborhood as if I were incarcerated. With the guilt, the disgrace, and the sheer terror of Kelly out in the world waiting for me, I was amazed I still had so much room left to miss him. I sat wounded and listless on Spencer's living room couch Thursday night while he attempted to quiz me on British literature.

"The repeating theme in *Tale of Two Cities*," he said again, waiting for my answer. "C'mon, I told you this five minutes ago."

"Life's a beach," I said, and smiled weakly. Spencer shut his book.

"You're gonna fail this test," he said. He wasn't being funny, but he wasn't admonishing either. It was just a fact. He looked at me squarely. "The reason Cotler hasn't spoken to you is not because he doesn't believe you. It's because he does believe you."

"He didn't that day."

"He does now. He's had time to think about it. That's all he's done since then. You can't expect Cotler to swallow something like this all at once, I don't care where he hears it. That's not him. He believes you. He doesn't know how to deal with it." From his seat on the easy chair Steve gave an "Um-hum" as he perused the May *Playboy* in place of his chemistry book.

"I don't know if that makes me feel better or worse."

"I'm glad you told him," Spencer said. "I'm sorry it had to be under those circumstances, but I guess you wouldn't have told him any other way."

"You gave him a lot to chew on in two minutes," Steve said. "He's been thinking it over, and it's a load full of shit he has to swallow now. He needs time, that's all."

"He watches you," Spencer said. "Did you know that?" Actually, I didn't. Spencer nodded sagely. "He knows where you've been, I could read as much when I talked to him at lunch Tuesday. I think he's trying to find a way to approach you again. The guilt he's dealing with is pretty awful."

"I'd bet a million dollars he's watching Kelly, too," Steve said. "Cotler's no idiot."

"Kelly'll smell that and then we'll all be dead," I said. Gnawing fear was churning its way to the surface again. "There's a lot Cotler doesn't know, and I've got my sister and parents to think about. And you guys, too."

"Maybe we should talk to Cotler," Steve said to Spencer. "What do you think, John?"

"I don't know what to think. I gave up thinking some-time last month."

"I do think we need to be together on this," Spencer said. "We're a lot stronger that way."

"I can't take much more of this," I said, feeling a whine creep into my voice. Vomiting was again close at hand even though I hadn't eaten for most of the day. Steve came over and put a hand on my shoulder.

"Hang on, Johnny," he said, as I closed my eyes and fought to swallow a bulge in my throat. "Just hang on."

6

Friday, May 24. Cotler was absent again, and I had no idea where he was. Outside, it had rained, as if from buckets, for two days. These weren't just rainy days. Dense showers were moving across the area in slow, gray sweeps and muffled thunder rolled down from the sky. The rain coated everything, spreading and seeping until the ground it fell upon began to gurgle it back up. On the way home from school I stopped at the 7-11 for cigarettes, stepping gingerly through puddles on my way to the store. I covered myself with the collar of a windbreaker and looked neither right nor left as I ran from the store, tossing the pack into the truck as I pulled the door shut and shook myself off.

The air was different.

The cigarettes hit the thigh of Jim Kelly, soaking wet and grinning. He'd slipped into my vehicle as I awaited my purchase in the store like a zombie. I drew a breath as if to scream and he jammed a small, stout revolver into my crotch.

"Don't," he whispered. "Just back out of the lot and turn left toward my place. Now." I looked straight ahead, but sheets of water made it impossible to see in or out of the car. I put the truck in reverse and did as I was told. Kelly directed me down a gravel road to a rotting warehouse, known as Powhatan, about half a mile past his shop off of Chapel Road. Powhatan was the name of a company that once processed animal feed before Belle Ridge existed, and its remains were a sagging, baleful-looking building with a badly rusted tin roof and rotting wooden walls and floors. In recent months it had been thoroughly searched because of the investigation. The woods had mostly reclaimed the back half of the warehouse. Lush, climbing weeds in the fullness of spring clung to the bulging walls and crept into open windows. There were truck bays on the opposite side from where I parked, and in front there was one large set of double doors, boarded over like a mouth sewn shut.

"Look what I got here," Kelly said into my ear as he led me into the decaying side door of the Powhatan. "Look at what I got here."

Inside the dim, rot-smelling building, he pushed me into a corner where I curled up like a ball. I had been in this building at least once with Cotler and some other kids on a summer's mischief outing, and it hadn't changed much. The large wooden bays along the walls that used to hold bags of feed were now mostly collapsed because of time and idle teenagers. Empty feedbags, broken timbers, and bent nails were scattered everywhere. It was divided into two large rooms, the back half being a loading area. Kelly and I were in the front room, not far from what must have been a manager's office. Dust-filtered light from various windows streamed in from outside. No real furniture or fixtures were left that scavengers hadn't long ago absconded with, but a couple of mismatched chairs had been brought in over the years. Kelly pulled one of them up and sat down in front of me. Beside him was a coiled length of rope.

"Look at me," he said quietly. I could not. "Look at me or I'll stomp your head to mush." Slowly I turned and faced him. Gloomy daylight from the window beside him painted him shadowlike. His usually well-cropped blond hair was disheveled and dirty. His t-shirt was smeared with gun grease and left untucked, slightly torn in one or two places. His skin looked bad. His eyes looked positively mad. The only real impression I had of him was that he wasn't going to be living two lives much longer. His disguise was starting to wear very thin.

"I always worried you'd be a problem, John. There's one every couple of years. Just like Marty, that skinny little faggot who couldn't keep his mouth shut. Couldn't keep outta my bizness. I wasn't hurtin' nobody. I didn't mean no harm. I like some of you differently than others, that's all." He got up and walked over to me, and I covered my face. "I liked you differently. That's all. So why do you have to fuck with me? Huh? WHY ARE YOU FUCKING WITH ME?! Answer me, queerboy, or I'll cut you to pieces!"

"Because you're killing children!" I screamed back and was immediately horrified I'd actually said it. Kelly kicked me hard in the thigh.

"I'm getting rid of stupid little problems before they start," he said through clenched teeth. Now he spoke with the sneering tone of a taunting little girl. "I'm tired of waitin' around for one of you silly little pussies to decide it's time to come back on me like a plate of bad chili. I ain't done nothin'. I run a bizness. I help kids out, lots of 'em. Ever'body knows that. Ever'body!"

"Kill me," I moaned. "Please, just kill me." Kelly walked over to the rope and picked it up.

"Get up on this chair. You're gonna hang yourself like that other faggot who couldn't keep outta my way. Get up!" I started to move, to uncoil myself, but found I couldn't lift my head. Instead I spit up a little on the old floor in front of me and groaned. He reached out to grab me and stopped dead. He had heard it, too, the thick, solid *click* of a gun. Kelly's head snapped left. From the rear room, literally out of a shadow, walked Francis Cotler, dripping rainwater from every inch of his big frame. At Jim Kelly, he was aiming his .44 magnum Smith and Wesson Model 29 revolver.

Kelly dropped the rope. Both he and I gaped open-mouthed as Cotler slowly made his way across the creaking floor. He moved with that weird, sliding grace that was simply unbelievable about him until you saw it. He had moved most of the way across the creaky floor without a single sound. For a long moment no one said anything.

"If you give a shit about what's left of your life," Cotler said, breaking the heavy, dusty silence with dead evenness, "walk over and stand back against that wall."

"You fire that in here and the world'll hear it," Kelly whispered. "We're not three blocks from Chapel Road." He was collecting himself, slowly and carefully. Sanity seemed to fill his eyes again.

"I'd do it in front of the courthouse," Cotler said. "You heard me. Against that wall. Now." Kelly watched his former friend and protégé with rage, but he did as he was told, without a sound. It was the first order I ever saw him take, and seeing it made my heart leap with a feeling I can't describe. Cotler stood perfectly still, the gun aimed dead at Kelly's face, and he looked oddly anticipative behind it. Kelly knew guns. The .44 would, as Clint Eastwood had indicated in a long-ago movie from my childhood, blow his head clean off.

"Who the fuck do you think you are, Cotler?" he asked. Cotler had nothing to say. Same steady aim. Same unbreathing, unflinching posture. "Come off it, son," Kelly said. "You forget . . . I know you. I've seen you, even when you haven't known I was there. I used to follow you when you went out camping at night. Did you know that? Did you know that I saw you out there, pissing in the woods, putting out your fire, laying down and beating off before you went to sleep? Did you know I saw that?

"What about your buddy, John? Where were you when he needed you? Huh? You knew I had a weird side, boy. Maybe you didn't know what, but you got the smell of it soon enough. You knew it when you brought him out to me. Did you ever tell your buddy John that, Cotler? Huh? Did you ever tell him that he was a gift from you to me? Did you, Old Hoss?" Kelly smiled broadly as I looked with horror over at Cotler. More worrisome, though, was that Cotler could be vulnerable to this kind of ploy. More than likely, the prevailing emotion in his life this week had been guilt. *Maybe*, he had probably asked himself in bed when sleep would not come, *I did know. Maybe I did smell it.* Cotler had failed, if he believed Kelly, at perhaps the most important task of his life save the care of his brother. Kelly bet now that Cotler would crumble, slip up, maybe lose his concentration. Then Kelly would look for an out. Any out.

But Cotler simply smiled wanly and shook his head.

"Don't even try that psycho bullshit on me," he said in his pleasant farmer-to-farmer voice. "Ain't gonna work, Old Hoss." Kelly's face fought a grimace. His eyes flashed with agony and frustration as he saw this effort sink like a stone.

"I coulda," he said, breathy and deep. "I coulda had you. I waited outside your camp some nights until you fell asleep. I came all the way to the edge of your campsite. I coulda had you like a *bitch*." Cotler's smile disappeared.

"And I wish you'da tried," he said with a frightening hiss in his voice. "Cause I'da emptied your throat right there, you yellow fuck! Hurtin' kids! Killin' innocent little children, you filthy yellow fuck!"

"Then kill me, if that's how you feel," he said, admirably

unflinching before Cotler's temper. He hadn't moved, but he was leaning out, ever so slowly, from the wall. "Usin' strong words, sure you are. But I think you'da done it by now, if you meant to. Truth is, you been killin' deer and squirrel so long and wasting ammunition on trees and targets that a gun isn't really anything but a play toy to you. I want you to think about what's gonna happen when you squeeze that trigger, son. I want you to think beyond me, if that don't bother you, to them out there. To your father, to his men. To your community. What are you two gonna do, bury me somewhere out here? You think he'll be any help? Trust me, boy, your friend John is two steps from the funny farm and when he gets there all those drugs they fill him with are gonna have him shittin' out the mouth just tellin' everybody everything. Do you hear me? Cause maybe you and me should talk, away from him. Maybe we should forget some of this silly hero bullshit and talk about reality, yours and mine." Kelly leaned out, a little more. He still didn't move forward, but he was adjusting his position against the wall, relaxing now. He was standing more like a man and less like a cornered rat. He was trying to talk sense, and hoping that the cold, prodding thing that was Cotler's brain would bite. "Do you see what I'm sayin'? There's a way we can all walk out of here, you and him one way and me on my own, gone forever. I know your pride's hurting, but it's high time you started thinkin' like a man. You've got baggage here, with your friend John. It's fact, son, and it ain't all my fault, either. He needs you more than you need to take me back to town, and he ain't gonna be any help to you if you and I have it out." Kelly finished this speech and leaned back against the wall. He looked at me, and at Cotler, waiting for a response. I could feel the blood pounding against my head from all sides. Cotler rolled his eyes minutely and smiled once again.

"Keep talkin'," he said with a shrug. "Talk until Tuesday, Jim. All your bullshit ain't nothin' to me. Maybe I'm too simple. But move one step toward me and I'll just blow your face to black little pieces—or maybe your balls, if I really ain't no killer. That's the long and the short of it, *Old Hoss*." Kelly's last hand now played to no end, his whole body shook. Soon, very soon, something was going to happen. Cotler's face ran with sweat, but he didn't move a muscle.

"Talk all you want about wounding me," Kelly said. "You know goddam well that cannon'll blow me in half at this range, no matter where it hits me. Do you really think you have it in you to lay a human life to waste—even mine? Think, boy. Think about the door you're gettin' ready to walk through." He eyed Cotler keenly, and something in Cotler's eyes seemed to shift.

"I've heard enough of this cocksucker," he said. "Can you get that rope?" I nodded feebly and reached for it. Still unable to speak I looked up at him stupidly. Cotler licked his lips when he looked at me and his eyes widened. I don't think he liked what he saw. "Tie it in a slip knot like I showed you. Can you do that, John?" Again I nodded. He turned back to Kelly. "Jim, if you like you can call this an arrest. I'm gonna start moving toward you and I want you to put your hands out for me to tie. I'm gonna bind you up tight, and then I'm gonna take you back to my father's office. If you stand still, I'm givin' you my word you'll live to see a trial. If you fuck with me, just one little move, you'll die where you stand. Got another card to play? Go ahead. I'm comin' now." Kelly glared at the boy but made no movements as Cotler approached. The old floor creaked under his weight. "Put your arms out," he said when he'd reached Jim. Amazingly, for the second time, Kelly took an order silently.

"I don't know why he thinks you're worth this," Kelly said to me. Then from out of nowhere the butt of the gun in Cotler's hand smashed across Jim's mouth with a savagery that was as startling as it was chilling. Jim's head whipped around spraying blood, and when he brought his head back to center Cotler had the gun pressed tightly against his temple. Cotler was shaking, and his wide, pale face was almost purple. Kelly looked at Cotler sideways with one huge and staring eye and did not move so much as a finger. A large gash in his cheek leaked blood liberally over his shirt.

"That's the last thing you ever say to him. The last. Say one more thing and I will pistol-whip your eyes out, one at a time. YOU GOT THAT?!" Kelly nodded. He was scared, very scared. I was too, now of Cotler.

"Throw me the rope," Cotler said to me. He knew, of course, that I couldn't get near him. Cotler held the gun on Jim with one hand and slipped the rope over his outstretched hands with the other. He pushed Kelly into the wall by placing his foot against the man's abdomen and pulled the rope tight. Kelly breathed out hard and screamed as the rope choked his wrists.

"Jesus, loosen that! Please! It's too tight!"

"I'm hurtin,'" Cotler said dully. "Lie down." Kelly's eyes grew wild.

"Cotler, please, you're a fair man at least. This is like a tourniquet, for God's sake! Please!" Cotler looked angrily back at Kelly, who was slowly, inchingly making his way backward toward the entrance to the loading area. He was moaning and, by all appearances, starting to panic. Cotler was disgusted with himself. He had let his rage get to him and had pulled the rope unmercifully tight across Kelly's wrists. Kelly had moved maybe ten feet, still babbling and moaning, when Cotler ordered him to stop, or else. He stopped and fell to his knees. His face had broken into a cold sweat. He still held his bound hands out in front of him, a desperate look in his eyes. Cotler looked down at him. Getting close to Kelly to re-tie his hands, even after his legs and feet were bound, was a risky proposition. It meant getting awfully close to him. It meant a possible struggle.

"I'm sorry, Jim," Cotler said, evenly and without malice. "I can't loosen that rope without getting too close to you, or while holding this gun, which I ain't puttin' down. Maybe if we can get you good and bound up, I'll take another look. Otherwise we'll just have to move it."

"What about him?! Have him hold the goddam gun, he wants to shoot me more than you do!" Kelly's voice was rising. For my part I sat curled in the corner, unable to utter more than a few words at time. The gun at that moment would have been useless in my hands. Kelly knew that and was counting on taking it from me and shoving it well up my ass if he could get past Cotler—a long shot, but a possibility. Unfortunately for Jim, Cotler knew it, too. The look in my eyes was probably melting toward serious instability at that point, but even at my strongest Cotler would never have given over command of that situation, which in other words was command over the gun.

"Nooo," Cotler said slowly, like a storyteller answering the excited question of an enraptured listener. "Guns aren't his specialty. Let's move, Jim. The more you cooperate the faster we can get those makeshift cuffs off of you."

It was then that Cotler stepped toward Kelly and fell through the floor. It was a soft, rotten spot in the wooden floor. Kelly knew about it and had been able to maneuver around it. Cotler either never knew about it or had forgotten it was there, and in his path to Jim he walked right over it, and it had given. One second he was there, walking, and the next there was a flesh-like tearing sound, and he was gone without so much as a puff of smoke. There was a short, curdling scream that was really the word "fuck" along with the sound of the .44 going off. The clap from the gun filled my whole world and brought tiny clouds of sawdust and dirt down from the ceiling.

"Well, at least I know the fucker was loaded," Kelly said calmly, as he stepped around the hole and toward me. "Maybe it caught him in the mouth." His face on one side was bloody from the gun butt. His hair was coated with dust. His eyes were red rimmed and utterly mad. "Now untie me."

I wanted to scream. I wanted to run. I wanted to know if my friend Cotler was dead of a gunshot wound, or a paralyzing fall. I did nothing. In Cotler's absence, my sanity was an open wound being dragged across a dirty sidewalk. I turned away from the apparition of Kelly and began to shut down, piece by piece. I came face to face with the bottom of my being. I had crossed over. Kelly screamed at me to look at him, which in his unending cleverness knew would be my total undoing.

"Untie me. Untie me or I'll beat you to death with my hands tied together and cut this rope on what's left of your—"

He was interrupted when Cotler emerged from the hole and grabbed his ankle. Kelly squealed—he actually squealed—and whipped around. Cotler was covered in some ancient black soot, and his face looked monstrous as he hoisted himself up, his eyes glowing like lamps in his head. He had grabbed Kelly's ankle for support as much as anything else. Finally he was halfway out of the hole, one arm wrapped like iron around Kelly's leg and the other splayed out on the floor, still holding the gun. Kelly looked like a farm animal, whipping his tied hands together up and down in front of him while he kicked in Cotler's grasp.

But Cotler did not let go. His face was a black grimace, and with the fingers of his right hand he was fiddling with the revolving chamber of the gun. He cursed as he did so. Kelly looked down in horror as he realized the boy meant to hold him with one arm and blow out his underside with the other.

The kicking proved too much for one arm, so Cotler let the gun go and grabbed the man's leg with both hands, pulling himself out of the hole. He got one leg out onto the floor but found more rotting wood. The leg fell through again and he screamed as it struck a gnarled timber under the floor. Kelly gave a heaving kick and Cotler was forced to let go, grabbing for purchase on the floorboards around him.

Kelly backed away from the hole and gaped at Cotler's black, bruised form. He turned and began to run for one of the huge, broken windows, his bound arms out in front of him. Cotler picked up the gun, fiddled with it for another second, and fired it at Kelly's head.

The shot hit the wall inches from his left ear, and Cotler let out a string of curses that would have shamed the most seasoned whore. Kelly dove face first through the remains of the window, knocking out a few pieces of window frame as he went through. He hit the ground with a thump and was up running through the brush like a startled deer. He never made a sound—and for a moment we could hear nothing but the echoing of the gun blast, still in our ears.

Cotler looked over at me. He ran to my side and crouched there, trying to look into my face, which I tried desperately to hide from him. I was balled up in the corner, trying to shrink as if by magic into the old walls.

"John," he said, shaking me, "for God's sake look at me. Are you hurt? He didn't . . . he didn't *hurt* you before I got here, did he?" I shook my head and was instantly horrified that such a thought had to travel through Cotler's tough, innocent brain to his lips. I began to weep and turned back to the wall. "Johnny," he said, screamed really, "look at me! Look at me goddammit and tell me you're okay!" There was something in his voice I had never before heard. It was beyond fear, which I'd heard once or twice. It was panic. His hands were rough and powerful on my shoulders, and in his grip I shook like a rag doll. I felt drool below my lip, on the left side. "Johnny, please!"

I turned to look at him full in the face and saw for the third time in my life a tear there. Just one tear, alone and very strange on that ruddy face. It forged a clean trail in the black dust. I reached out for it with one hand, barely touching his cheek where the tear was, then bringing my arm back in retreat.

Cotler got up, seemed to steady himself for a moment and walked over to the rotting side door. There was an old pail filled with fresh rainwater and Cotler cleaned his face and arms with it. He gathered the gun and shoved it into his belt, then came back over to where I lay. Without another word he lifted me up and carried me out into the rain. We left my truck where it stood and walked through the woods to another dirt road where he had parked, my body bobbing over his shoulder like a sack of potatoes. I could see the trail, the leaves, the floor of the woods, bouncing in and out of focus.

"Where . . . where are we going?" I asked when we'd reached the car and the world had begun to swim back into focus.

"A doctor. I'm taking you to a hospital." For the last time in what I consider to be my childhood I came alive in his grasp and leaped out onto the ground.

"No!" I screamed at him, standing and grabbing his shirt. "No! Not there. Please, not a hospital. I'm not crazy, Cotler, I swear it. Please don't take me there." He looked at me with conflicting fear and frustration. I'm sure he doubted my sanity, but I also knew he didn't want to admit it, particularly to himself.

"Home, then. I'll bring you home."

"Listen to me. I'm not crazy, but I think I'm headed that way and being anywhere near that town now or a goddam mental hospital—"

"It won't be a mental hospital."

"It will be soon enough. You're more hurt than I am. Cotler, please. Not a hospital and not Belle Ridge. I can hang on, but I need help. I need your help. Hide me. You can do it. Hide me somewhere. I don't care where. Just hide me and let me . . . sleep. Sleep is what I need. I need to sit somewhere and sort this out. A few days, that's all. Please."

"Hide you? Hide you? What the hell are you talkin' about? Where? How? Jesus, at least let me take you home."

"Home will eat me," I said, as smoothly and convincingly as I've ever said anything. My voice lowered. "Hide me for a while and I've got a fighting chance. Please."

Cotler pondered this, and I could see the indecision moving across his face. The more seconds passed, the more I knew my chances were improving. I could see it already, the relief he felt at the fact I was at least within shouting distance of lucidity. And underneath that I saw what was even more promising: the wheels turning in his head about where to take me. A moment later Cotler made perhaps the most reckless and ill-advised decision he'd ever made up to that point. It was also perhaps the best he ever made.

"What makes you think I have some magical kingdom to take you to?" he asked with an annoyed tone. No matter. He was won over. And he already had a place in mind. Where or what I didn't know, nor did I care.

7

Outside of Leesburg, Cotler pulled off into a store parking lot. "How much does Steve know," he asked, "about all of this?"

"Everything. He knows everything." Cotler nodded. If it bothered him that Steve knew before he did, or that Steve had reacted more favorably, he didn't show it.

"Good. Because we need him now. I'll be right back." He was at the phone for maybe five minutes.

"Where are we going?" I asked, like a man in a dream. Cotler looked over, small bits of fear creeping back into his eyes. Less than before, but still present.

"A place I know. No one knows about it, no one. You'll be safe there and no one will bother you."

"My parents. Your dad. They'll kill you for doing this."

"I'll handle things back there. You just get the rest you need. Okay?" I nodded and felt warm. Drowsiness was beckoning and flooding through my veins like a very expensive drug.

Somewhere high in the Blue Ridge, Cotler stopped for groceries one more time. We drove silently over twisting, turning roads covered by lush tree canopies, surrounded by creeks, farms, and darkened houses. Then we were there, a small comfortable-looking timber-framed cabin overlooking some vast, open field. It was utterly dark except for the starlight, which was mesmerizing now that the clouds had moved east. In the west, the outline of a mountain range was barely visible. Cotler seemed not to notice the scenery as he helped me out of the truck. I felt like I weighed five hundred pounds. I was led to a room with a big four-poster bed, where I collapsed onto the mattress. He covered me with blankets and left to build a fire. I was comatose, instantly. The Sleep had begun.

8

The last thing Cotler had shown me before I passed out was the bathroom in the same room. I used it a couple of times, in the nights mostly. He set out a pitcher of water, and when I awoke thirsty from time to time, I partook of that, too. At one point I stripped to my underwear. Otherwise I slept, sometimes dreamless and sometimes restlessly, for more than a day and a half.

9

May 26. Late on Sunday morning, I opened my eyes and found I didn't want to close them again. I felt heavy, numb, and distrustful of being awake, but further sleep I did not need. I turned in bed and found that I was sore and that I was famished. I threw off the covers, felt the strangeness of the floor beneath my feet, and made for the kitchen.

Cotler had provided the things I would have wanted around me in this pleasant little place with the skill of a well-paid concierge. The fridge was filled with food, food he knew I liked, and I made a small feast. After that I took a long shower and noticed a few other things he had left; two short stacks of clothes and underwear, directions for the use of everything in the cabin, directions to a nearby store with a phone in case I needed anyone, and a promise that he'd return in a day or two. There was a man, he said, a retired friend of the family's who would stay during the night, and I could expect him around seven. I should get something ready to eat for him if possible, and the bottle of bourbon was for him. It was clear from my intense sleep, he wrote in so many words, that I would need more than the weekend here. Through his hideous handwriting I saw that he meant to talk to my parents on Sunday after church.

So they knew already. They knew I was gone, presumably safe, unwilling to come home. Only Cotler knew where I was and wasn't telling. *That should go over well,* I thought. I read the letter one more time and walked out onto the porch to greet the day.

The field was the first thing I noticed, beginning across the road just beyond the porch. It was an expanse of short, soft-looking yellow grass, and it sloped down, down, for miles it seemed to a creek and a tiny looking wire fence. Beyond that was a green yard with a barn and farmhouse. The scene appeared utterly two-dimensional: the house, the brightly colored red barn, the gentle slope of the hills, and the road moving westward toward the mountain range. Even the plain sight of tiny roosters and a goat moving slowly across the yard couldn't fully shake the illusion. I stood, struck by that scene for some minutes, then looked behind me and found a comfortable high-backed rocking chair where I sat in silence and contentment until the sun appeared overhead and began to make its slow descent over the mountains.

In the hours before sunset, I ate a little more and sifted through the books Cotler had brought for me. I found I didn't want to read or write anything and was content to sit and watch the sun go down, full in the belly and looking forward to sleep when nightfall came. When the sun did set, it sent an array of reds, oranges, and blues streaming through the field from behind the mountains. The colors coated every blade of grass like a billion paintbrushes, and before I knew it I was up and bounding out into it, over the fence and through the grass. I stood out there letting the grass brush my legs until near dark. I had thoughts, but they were scattered and pointless. Steve one minute, Lon the next. Then Cotler, then April, the girl from December, and then home, and my family. Images went flying through me and I felt them wash over me tenderly for now. It wasn't a numb sensation like before, but loose and bathing. I let things in, and even the terrible memories weren't stinging me up here. All that week when I did feel a coldness or a fear coming on, I went running back to the field and found the terror whisked away as if the grass and sky in unison had commanded it to leave. This was relaxation like I'd not known since before I developed memory.

At 7:00 a short, stocky, older black man named Wilson appeared at the door with a slight smile and a pleasant nod. He told me he lived in the cabin up the road and that the

Cotler boy had asked that he stay up here with me. He was the regular caretaker of the place when folks were away for long periods, so it was normal for him. Was that okay? I answered that it was and thanked him. He came in, ate a little, and made himself a drink. We spoke for a few minutes, and although a friendly guy, he had even less to say than Cotler. I offered him a cigarette and he took it. He didn't ask me a single question about why he'd been asked to watch me or what I was doing here; he was content to drink his bourbon, read, and rock in one of the lazy chairs. When bedtime came, he said that he normally slept in the side room and off he went. He was always gone when I awoke, much as if he'd never been there, and reappeared in the evening. The next five days went pretty much like that first one.

10

Friday, May 31. Cotler came in quietly and set down some groceries on the kitchen table. He seemed to examine the house for a moment, looked satisfied that everything was in order, and turned and saw me lounging on the couch in the front room. I was reading some passages from a copy of the New Testament Spencer had highlighted for me. Cotler smiled cautiously when he saw me and tossed me a carton of cigarettes from one of the bags. Perfect timing: I was almost out.

"Thanks," I said, smiling. He nodded and came over and sat down in the big chair opposite me. There was still something in my eyes he didn't like, I could tell. Something bland and soft and too tranquil that he was neither familiar nor comfortable with. I wasn't asking him questions about where I was; I know that bothered him. All of our lives I had tortured Cotler with questions: Where are we? How far is that over there? What's that called? How does that work? It was the natural flow in our friendship; he usually drove and almost always knew where we were going. He had names and some sense of usefulness for everything we saw: animal, vegetable, mineral, or machine. But now I asked nothing of my surroundings or my exact whereabouts. I really didn't care.

"I talked to your parents again today," he said. It was almost sheepish. "Your dad pressed a hundred dollars into my palm when I left. I tried like hell to give it back, but it looked like it'd be more painful for him if I refused, so I took it. Anyway, the goodies are all on him, from now on. You mind if I build a fire? It's a touch chilly out there and I mean to stay until morning, if that's okay."

"I'd like that," I said smiling. My calmness and unnatural reticence were not initially pleasing to Cotler, but eventually he relaxed and seemed to realize that I was, for a time anyway, becoming like him—holding my thoughts until I was ready to birth them slowly and carefully, letting silence and the low sounds of my environment fill in the spaces between words. In its own way, Cotler's quiet contentedness made him more a lover of life than me in my eternal desire to color it in. Romantics and writers must set impossibly high standards for their world and feel in it a tragic disappointment because they are never at a loss to conjure stories and scenarios to dress it up.

I said nothing about going home and Cotler didn't ask. But I knew I was getting ready. Things inside me were far from intact, but they were straightening, quieting. My mind was less of a cauldron, and even the worst of what might await me at home had normal, un-bloated proportions. Even the thought of Kelly running around somewhere, desperate and alive with the truth of him known to Cotler like an open sore, was wild and terrifying but somehow livable. I knew that Cotler was watching my home and family, and up here I felt infinitely secure. There were a couple of hours on some nights where sleep would not come for the thought of him out there somewhere, but even these thoughts came and went like nightmares, waning softly as I settled back listening to the wind outside and hearing Wilson clear his throat occasionally from his easy chair.

We could have talked about these things, I guess. An ocean of buried topics seemed to await us, but that's all they did. They did not beckon. Like the stars and the field outside, they were simply there if we wanted them, which for now we didn't. Cotler was gone the next morning when I awoke, and I was back in the field for the day, sitting and soaking up the sun and serenity.

I wish I could tell you that something dramatic and cataclysmic happened to me during the Sleep, or that something life-changing and profound took place deep in my soul, but I cannot. The truth is, I had a long way to go before and after I came to the cabin, and no measure of quiet, secure time was going to flush out the darkness that filled most of me. There was no magic, no thundering change. But I was able to release a valve or two, to allow myself to breathe, and to feel something other than constricting panic and crushing guilt. And somewhere in the days and nights, alone and unbothered, my thoughts swam back into some focus, and in their clarity I was no longer terrified and confused. Out here in the hills things were far from perfect, I knew, but somehow the field and the cabin and the pretty little farm reminded me that it was a big world, and that at least part of it was still sane and orderly. I sat in the field and felt the evil leak out of me. I sat and sat and sat.

Chapter Eleven: June

1

Sunday, June 2. I wasn't particularly surprised at the sound of the knock at the door. There had been other visitors besides Wilson from time to time during the Sleep. Neighbors, mostly, wanting to say hello and not seeming suspicious in the least. A few seemed like they were checking up on the place. Most just wanted to give greetings. So I wasn't surprised when I heard the knock. I was surprised when I opened the door and saw the image of Dan Cotler.

"Sheriff," I said, resigning myself at once to the fact that my vacation was over. How he'd found me I didn't know. I doubted that Cotler had caved in, but in any case it was academic. It was time to go.

"Hello, John. May I come in?" He wore faded jeans, a light red denim shirt and big, brown boots. The strain of the last few months was raw on his kind face. He glanced around and seemed to take in the front room with familiarity.

"Yes, sir," I said. "I guess I know why you're here. If

you'll just give me a minute to gather my things and clean up, I'll go quietly, I—"

"I'm not here to arrest you, son," he said, interrupting me gently.

"You're not?" He shook his head.

"I'm not even in my jurisdiction. I came to see if you're all right, that's all. Can we talk a minute? How 'bout on the porch. It's a pretty view, isn't it?"

"Yes, sir. It sure is."

"I begged him, Mr. Cotler," I said as we settled into the big rocking chairs on the porch. "Please understand that. I begged him to hide me. I couldn't go back home. A lot has happened and I needed to be alone, I needed—"

"I know, John. I know," he said, and he spoke low because his voice was cracking. He composed himself fast and cleared his throat. "I don't blame you or Francis. There's a lot of us who need to get away for a while, and you're probably first among them. Your friend did as you asked, and it looks like you've been fine here."

"It's more than fine, sir," I said, feeling a ripple of emotion come up in me like the wind that sent waves through the grass. "I'm better now. I . . . I can't say much about it because I really don't understand what's happened, but I'm better. I feel okay about things . . . and this place . . . it's helped. It's so peaceful here. I don't know how Cot . . . Francis knew about it, 'cause I've never been here or heard him talk about it, but it's beautiful. It's just beautiful and my only regret is that I spent the first couple of days mostly inside."

"I'm glad for that, son. I love it, too."

"But whose is it, the cabin and the land?"

"His name is Reyerson—Jack Reyerson—he's a banker

from Richmond. Makes commercial loans. Big ones. He grew up with Louise, loved her, I'm sure of it, from the time they were little kids. But Lou May fell in love with a trooper from so far north in the state he might as well have been from Maryland. Poor Jack." The sheriff smiled.

"He was in love with Mrs. Cotler and you married her, but she still came out here?"

"He lost her to me, but he didn't stop loving her. I thought it was odd, too, but I got used to it. They were family friends. Lou was coming up here from the time she was three or four. She brought me up here when Jack's parents still owned the place. Jack had a steady girl too, by that time, and we spent many a pretty week-end up here, sometimes with them, sometimes sneaking up by ourselves after we'd been hitched."

"It didn't bother this guy Jack? Her loving you and not him?"

"Not on the surface. Jack Reyerson's never been any-thing but a gentleman and a friend to me. He could have made a lot of noise about the job I had to Louise's folks, the hours, the risk, the God-awful money. But he didn't, not a word to them or me. He invited me up here, showed us where the key was, and met us out here on week-ends for years. I guess I've always known he did it because he worshipped, I mean *worshipped*, Louise. He was just one of those odd types who kept on worshipping, even after she'd gone down the aisle with another man. When she died, Jack did even more for us and took it worse than anyone outside the family."

"Is he married now?"

"No. Never been. He goes through about five or six women a year, I'd venture, but he never found one who measured up. He travels a good bit, spends much of his time in Europe. That's where he is now."

"Do you all take care of this place for him? Is that how Francis knew about it?"

"No. Francis and I have been up here a few times to help clear brush and trees after some big storms, but it's been years. A local man named Wilson maintains the place. Jack wouldn't take a key back from us, though, after Lou passed. It's still our hideaway, as far as he's concerned. That's why I figured Francis brought you here."

"But I've never heard about it," I said, missing completely the older man's careful steps around the subject. I was angry again, angry at uncovering yet another piece of Cotler unshared. "How could this place be so special to your family and he not say a word?"

"This field," Dan said, shifting in his chair, "was Lou May's favorite place in the world. Jack says she used to sit out there in the middle of it for hours at a time just picking flowers and showing them to the bees. This is known as Lou May's Field. He named it for her, years ago."

"Oh," I said, instantly relinquishing the field back to its rightful owner. I was beginning to understand.

"Francis was conceived out there," he said, a thin smile on his face. "Now, I don't think he knows that, but we were pretty sure of it. This field, this house, this view, it was his momma's, all of it. This place meant more to her than her father's farm."

"And he swore he'd never come back up here after she died, didn't he?"

"Once he was old enough, yes. Yes he did."

"But you knew he would."

"For you, John? Yes. For you, I knew he would."

I leaned back in the tall chair and let my eyes close. We let a minute or two pass. *You're at it again, Cotler,* I thought. *Outsmarting me. Out-planning me. Out-loving me.*

"It's not your fault, son," he said. "He did this for you willingly and would do it again."

"Thanks," I said, through a dim mist in my voice. "Listen, should I come back with you, Sheriff?" He shook his head and uncrossed his legs, leaning forward in his chair.

"I'm here to see if you're okay. That's all. Your father is my best friend, and I'm here for him. Your parents are frightened. They're confused. They don't understand the things that are plaguing you and it hurts that you can't tell them. Under normal circumstances they'd probably have begged me to roll you up in a blanket and carry you home. But these . . . these aren't normal circumstances."

"I'm feeling better now and it's just about time to come back. Tell them that for me, if you can. Tell them I'm sorry and I love them and all."

"They know," he said. He made no move to leave, and the sheriff was not a man to dawdle when there were things to do. I waited for a moment.

"There's something else?"

"Yeah. There's something else. I haven't seen my older son in four days. Do you know where he is?" He looked at me with a face that had been lied to professionally for twenty years, and for the moment I answered him truthfully.

"No sir, I don't. When he brought me here I was in a pretty bad way. A few things happened at once and I begged him to take me out of town, anywhere. He's been here to check on me once or twice and to bring food and such. He was here last on Saturday, I think. But we didn't talk much the times he was here and I don't know where he's gone. To be honest, there's a lot he doesn't tell me. Always has been, I guess." The sheriff smiled.

"His mother thought the same thing. Francis had his own little world out there someplace, she'd say. He'd bring back pieces from time to time, but he'd never take anyone there with him. Between you and me, Lou used to say she loved her son more than life itself, but hated his eyes, sometimes. 'He's got eyes like a flat lake on a cloudy day,' she'd say. 'You know it's deep, but you can't see a thing underneath.' She thought he was way too young for eyes like that." He chuckled and gazed out at the horizon, seeing something out there, coming up from behind the mountains.

"Jim Kelly's missing, too," he said, and I jumped in my skin. I hadn't mentioned Jim Kelly because he hadn't, and I had assumed correctly that Cotler hadn't mentioned Kelly or our incident to anyone. But what his disappearance meant I didn't know. Under my shock, I saw that the thing he was making out on the horizon was a bank of clouds, a coming storm. "His shop is closed and his trailer's bolted up. Jim's been known to go off for a few days at a time on a hard drink or a hunting trip, but I usually know about it when he does. And his cars are all there, too. I'd like to know where he is. I'd like that very much, and I don't like the idea that Francis is gone, too." He looked at me. "You okay? You look as pale as milk."

"Oh. No, I'm fine. Francis being gone scares me, too, I guess. Is Calvin okay?"

"Yeah, he's fine. Spends a lot of time at your momma's, but that's practically home to him anyway. It's no excuse for Francis to run off, though. I've got the whole county falling apart at the seams and now my own family is runnin' wild on me."

"He'll be back here. If he's true to his word he'll be back within thirty-six hours. When he comes I'll have him call you. I'll force him if I have to." He nodded and stood up to leave.

"I'd appreciate that. What about you? You okay here until he does come? Do you need anything now? That's why I'm here, it's no trouble."

"No sir, I'm fine, thank you. "I've got all I need here. Francis covered everything." He nodded, and studied me for a moment, kindly but with the cop's eyes that he could not help having. His eyes told him that Cotler's disappearance and mine were related. They told him that I was, or had been before, part of something interestingly large that was consuming me. But he said nothing of it.

"You're a fine young man. I've always thought so. Your daddy and I are proud of the sons we've raised. We all miss you and want you home whenever you're ready."

"Thanks, Sheriff. I'll be home this week, I'm sure. It's about that time. I still want to graduate this summer."

"You've got a birthday this week, don't you?" I nodded. It was the next day.

"Maybe I'll be home for that."

"Your folks'd like that," he said, smiling in a guarded but open and generous way. It was disarming, sometimes, the love I knew surrounded me. He climbed into his truck and backed out onto the road, waving once and getting on his way.

2

The storm that swept over the valley later that afternoon was lovely, dark, and sonorous, and it left a cool, breezy gray evening in its wake. Brisk wind tinkled the chimes on the porch and whistled lightly through the screens as the usual profound darkness enveloped the land. Wilson and I dined together and he turned in early. I read for a while, listened to the wind, and turned off my table light at 11:00, falling into a deep and peaceful sleep.

***

The dream was about Cotler. He was sitting beside me in the dark, his hands between his knees, watching me as I lay there. I stirred, kicking an extra blanket off of me. Someone had closed the window and it was warm in the house.

It was no dream. I was awake, facing the wall, and Cotler was beside me in that plain wooden chair from the other side of the room. I was about to acknowledge his presence when he began to speak.

"It's Francis," he whispered. "My momma once said that sleeping people could hear you, somewhere in their head. When she was in the coma after Calvin was born I sat beside her bed and told her all sorts of things. I hope she heard." A long pause. "It's over now, John. Maybe I can tell some other part of your brain, 'cause I can't tell you outright. I never could do a damn thing about what was really bothering you all these years. Sometimes I'm pretty sure that knowing me has been the worst thing that could've happened to you. Steve's better at being the kind of friend that suits a person like you. You're the smartest person I know. You're the best person I know. So I did for you all I knew how to do. It won't ever be enough, not after all that's happened, but it's all I could offer. Happy Birthday, Johnny. He's gone for good."

He got up, placed his hand lightly on my head, and left the room. I was paralyzed. *He's gone for good.* There are many things about that time I have yet to discuss with Cotler; some things I am simply unable to describe. Of the things I wish he could know, first among them is the wave of relief and gratitude, I cannot quantify it, that spilled over me as Cotler left my room as quietly as he'd come in. It started as a weeping, then a shaking cry, then uncontrollable sobbing. I buried my face in the pillows and cried as if I'd never cry again. When I suspected that all of it had left me, another wave would come from inside and flow out. At the end of it I lay panting in bed like a man wracked with disease. After a few minutes the laughter came—silent, heaving laughter that I let flow from me as I had let the tears flow. I might have passed out for a time from it, I can't remember. Then it was all over and I pulled my shirt off and dried my face with it. I rolled over and looked at the clock. It was 4:15 a.m, June 4, 1985. I had been eighteen for four hours and fifteen minutes.

Cotler had given the devil his due.

***

I awoke to the sound and smell of breakfast being made and Cotler scurrying around the kitchen cracking eggs and laying strips of bacon into a pan. The sun was up and climbing behind the house; already its brilliance was feeding the trees on the western mountains in my view. My arms and legs felt lighter, stronger as I rose to dress. I doused my face with cold water in the bathroom and looked into the mirror. The face there did not urge me to look elsewhere. The face there was heavy, and tired. But alive. My Sleep was over.

After breakfast we loaded my things into the truck and cleaned up after ourselves once more. Cotler asked me how I felt as he busied himself tying down things in the back of the truck. I hadn't said a word, either about his father's visit or his own last night, and I knew I probably never would. Without my prodding, Cotler mentioned that he'd spoken to his father the previous evening, telling him he thought I'd be coming back soon. He was happy I was going back with him.

"Better," I said. "A whole hell of a lot better. This is exactly what the crazy doctor ordered. Thank you for bringing me here."

"It's nothin'," he said, concentrating on placing the tie-downs. "I'm glad you feel better. Your folks are going to be glad to get you back today. The guys are, too."

"Cotler," I said, and waited until he looked up at me. "I won't forget this." He nodded, held a smile for an instant, and climbed into the truck. An odd emotion was plain on his face, but with a little thought it made sense. That emotion was relief. I climbed in after him, and the old thing started with a roar. I glanced back at the house that had been my passageway from the brink back into life, and to the field that had licked my wounds and made me better inside again by its sheer beauty and simplicity. It melted behind us as we headed down the hill. "It's mighty pretty up here," I said. Cotler gave the field rushing away beside us the slightest glance.

"It is," he said. "It is."

3

Monday, June 10. "You'll graduate," Coach Bonner said to us as he walked in and set his leather folder down on his desk. The warm sunlight streaming through the dingy school window blinds illuminated him like the god that we truly believed him to be. Vic and I, sitting like accused men awaiting a jury verdict in his empty classroom, both heaved a sigh of relief.

"Thankfuckingod," Vic breathed. The coach, working his fingers over his temples as if he had a terrific head-ache, looked over at him distastefully.

"It wasn't by much," he said. "For either of you. Frankly, if this school hadn't been turned upside down the way it has been this year, I wouldn't have had a chance." We nod-ded solemnly and listened as he described the hurdles we would have to jump to get our diplomas the following week. For Vic, the hurdles were even higher and the coach had al-ready arranged for Spencer to basically kidnap Vic between now and graduation to get it all done and pass the tests he needed to pass. Vic and I glanced at each other during each list of requirements as if to ask each other if we were really up to fulfilling them. But the look in Bonner's eyes when he finished removed all doubt. The look told me, anyway, that he had gone to bat for us at some cost to his reputation and balance of goodwill with the principal.

"Are there any questions?" he asked as he finished, the weight of his message still hanging in the heavy June air of the classroom like a powerful perfume. Slowly, we both shook our heads.

"I guess we'd better get to work," Vic said at low volume.

I nodded, and we got up to leave.

"Vic, Spencer's waiting for you in the library," Bonner said. "John, let me talk to you for a second, if you don't mind."

"Sure," I said. Vic stopped at the door and glanced back at the coach with a deep and silent display of gratitude and respect that was not Vic at all, but perhaps something Vic was being nudged toward being. He looked like he wanted to say something else, but turned and got going. In any event, the look was not lost on John Bonner. He smiled broadly after Vic and seemed to hear in his heart exactly what it was Vic wanted to say to him. Then he turned his gentle, twinkling eyes to me and seemed to relax.

"It's good to see you here," he said, and I was no surer then than I am now about how deep that statement went.

"It's good to be here," I said. He paused and seemed to search himself for a moment.

"How did you do it?" he asked, a little furtively.

"I don't think you want to know," I said. He smiled and let his eyes rest on mine.

"I wish I could tell you it doesn't get more complicated than what you've seen already, John."

"It's okay. I'm not going through it alone."

"That's obvious. I'm glad for that."

"We'll take care of Vic, Coach. I promise."

"I know."

"I can never thank you enough for this."

"Actually, you can," he said. "I only ask one thing of you now, son."

"Name it, Coach."

"Take the next step," he said, looking at me intently.

"I'm not sure I understand."

"You've survived some sort of nightmare that I don't

fully understand. That being said, I know enough to know that in doing so, you've borne a weight over the last year that few understand at three times your age. You've felt responsible for an entire town, including its most helpless citizens. It's time for you to think about *you* for a while, and your recovery. Will you do that for me?"

"I'm not sure I know how," I said, looking down. "Spencer's been reading some books. He wants me to read them."

"That's a good first step. You may want to take some others. I'll be here to help, if I can."

"I want this to be over," I said.

"I know. Does it feel over?" I thought about the dreams, the guilt, the still-lingering fear. I sagged and let out a breath.

"Not yet. Not totally, anyway." He stood up and put a hand on my shoulder.

"You're a survivor, Johnny. The other boys . . . well, it was their time. Surviving is wonderful, but like every other good thing it bears a price. I'm not trying to create more worries for you. I just want you to have the greatest life you can have. I want you to have the life you deserve, after all this." I looked up at him and understood in that moment how much of all of it he had put together. I hadn't expected one, but an overwhelming tide of emotion rushed over me.

"It feels really random, sometimes, to tell you the truth. I'm still here, and so many of them never had a chance. Marty, all the kids . . ." I broke off and swallowed hard to keep from choking up. Bonner folded his arms and looked at me with silent understanding.

"It's a long road to making sense of any of this," he said.

"Take your time, then take it one step at a time." I nodded and waited for myself to calm.

"Will I ever make sense of it?"

"I don't know."

"Does anyone?"

"A wiser man than me, John."

4

Friday, June 14.

I confess to Almighty God, and to you, my brothers and sisters, that I have sinned through my own fault, in my thoughts and in my words, in what I have done, and what I have failed to do . . .

"What time is it?" I asked Steve as the two of us stood before the grave of Marty Moreland. Around us the air was thick and hot. It was June in Virginia and summer had come early to sit like a wet, sweaty load on the shoulders of the atmosphere.

"Four forty-five. We don't line up 'til six. You've got time."

"He was the only innocent one," I said, kneeling and arranging the stones I'd set there.

"You were all innocent," he said. "Even Vinnie."

"I know what I am, Steve. I don't hate myself for it, not anymore. But I know what I did, and what I didn't do. It's not a bad thing, to face that." Steve frowned and looked around the grounds for a moment.

"Wanna know what I think?"

"Mmm?"

"I think if Marty is someplace where he can see you, he's happy about one thing and one thing only, that you're alive. Everything else is bullshit. You're either breathing or you're not. You are, so Marty's happy. Go forth and make the world less shitty, if you want to. I think maybe you owe the boys here that. But the victory is you standing here, John." Steve motioned for us to move away from Marty's grave. I started to ask why and then I heard them. Cotler, Vic, and Spencer were coming over the hill, their voices high with excitement and happiness on this, our graduation day. Steve didn't want us to be at Marty's stone when Vic approached. They came into view, silhouetted against the skyline, these friends of mine, and when they saw me they raised their arms and smiled.

"What are they doing here?" I asked, smiling and waving back.

"I told them you wanted to come out here with me before going to the school. I hope you don't mind. Spencer had the idea for us all to meet up. They're here for you. C'mon."

As we met halfway up the hill, Vic broke off and strode over to Marty's grave. He stood there for a moment, his head down, as if listening for something. It was an odd sight, Vic at Marty's grave, and no one had to say so. He stood for a moment and came sauntering back as if he'd just talked to the pretty girl we'd all been looking at on the beach.

"Marty sends his congratulations," he said grinning. "He says for us all to get laid tonight."

"Sure he did," Spencer said. But even he smiled. The five of us stood side by side and looked down the hill to where the cars were and to the sloping face of the town beyond. Sly smiles were on the faces of the boys, and I was at a loss to explain them. Cotler broke the silence.

"Spencer's got something to say. Go ahead, Spence." Spencer smiled at me, at all of us, and turned and stood facing our group. He paused. Birds sang around us in the hot, hazy air and flocked over the trees in the afternoon sun.

"We're here today to celebrate life. John's life, and ours, together. Of all the hands God could have dealt us, here we are. He's chosen to let us share this moment together, every one of us as friends. Every one of us as survivors. We're going to walk from here, John, and we're going to go over to where our lives begin. We're here for you. We're here to raise our voices in praise of the one who gave you back to us." Everyone bowed their heads, even Vic, and finally so did I. "Dear Lord, thank you. We'll be back to this place, to remember our dead. But when we come back, we'll be here as life forces, to remember and to mourn, but not to despair or doubt. Marty, we miss you, and we'll be back. We know that you're proud of us and we know that you understand us. We're not walking away from you. We're just walking to what is out there for us. Take care of the other boys here, Marty. Show them what they'll need to know in the next life. In Jesus name we pray, amen."

"Amen," we all said.

Spencer looked up, his eyes shining, into the tearing eyes of all of us. There was a long, contented pause with only the sound of the birds and the feel of the warm, lilting breeze.

Steve gave a yell. It was a barbaric, bellowing, gut yell from the bottom of his lungs and he threw his arm up as he gave it. Cotler joined him, and then Spencer, and then Vic and me. We stood on the hill, yelling for all of our might and clasping hands. Then we headed down to the cars below, hurrying to make the lineup and don our gowns for the ceremony. Tender grass splayed flat against red earth under our dress shoes and Vic's sneakers. Curious squirrels and startled, frightened rabbits spied us with black eyes as we ran out of the hot quietness of the cemetery and into the shimmering, blazing afternoon that was the light, the life, of everything before us.

5

James Rodman Kelly never stood trial in a Virginia court. Instead, the forum for determining his guilt and sentence was the very woods in which he had done his work on the soul of our town. The woods fed James Kelly. They hid and protected him, if innocently. They turned blind eyes and deaf ears upon the slayings and the beatings and the molestation, and in their depth and thickness they helped to swallow the screams and conceal the blood and gradually render unrecognizable even the clothes and the shoes. The woods had done their duty with mute passivity for James Kelly for a generation. They had served him well, and no one knew them better.

Except for one other.

After our run-in with him, Kelly had disappeared. Cotler had disappeared also, after bringing me to Sleep. But Cotler had not slept. Time had run out for Jim Kelly in Belle Ridge; his changing appetites had finally made it too hard for him to conceal his passions and their byproducts. It was time to move on, and if he was a sane man at all when he died, he knew the move he was making was to be final and would alter his life forever. He had his instincts, strength, and experience. By a path of back-acre farmland, undergrowth, and scrub trees, he could move by night beyond Winchester and into the mountains, where Virginia tends secrets much older than her English name. What he hoped for was one precious opportunity to get home, cover his tracks, grab what he could carry, and go. But Cotler was on to him now.

If Cotler's most reckless gamble was not taking me to a mental institution on the afternoon of the twenty-third of May, then his second largest wager was not telling anything to his father that weekend. Cotler waited, and Kelly waited. Thus began a dance between them that lasted the week I Slept. Kelly watched his trailer from afar, and Cotler watched Kelly. I don't know if Kelly was aware of this or not; in his hubris he probably did not care—Kelly had been hunted before. Jim must have interpreted Cotler's refusal to go to the authorities as a great move for him. Cotler was slick, but Kelly was slicker. Kelly could live in the soil and eat what he found there. He could outwait the young man and kill him, and he would.

Kelly's only problem was that he was, in some form or another, severely emotionally compromised. He had become an impulsive man, and an impulsive man is not a careful man. Cotler danced with Kelly most of the week. He watched his trailer, maybe even let himself be seen creeping around it at night, looking in windows. He waited with aching patience and kept Jim at bay. As the week wore on, Kelly moved slowly west and made camp in a couple of places outside of town. Cotler faded back. Given a few days of waiting, he hoped Kelly would move east again, for one final shot at visiting his place. For Jim, it was that or gathering provisions and clothes some other way, like burglary or shoplifting. What I believe is that Kelly was becoming convinced that his young protégé was being foolish enough to keep their conflict one on one. If that were the case, then Kelly needed only to kill Cotler, then find me. Cotler faded back and waited.

Then on June 3, Cotler laid his trap. It appeared, on the day before I turned eighteen, that a young boy had wandered into the woods. Perhaps he had a fight with his mother. Or maybe he was just adventurous and foolish as most young boys are. The route this imaginary boy took into the woods bisected the route Kelly would have to take to reach his home, and the boy had left a trail. It wound deeply, expertly in a haphazard curling pattern that looked altogether unplanned and aimless. It led toward a place where Kelly had spent time with other boys but veered appropriately at a thicket where a confusing detour was necessary and misdirection could easily follow. This carefully staged misdirection was followed by what looked like vertigo, circles, tangents, backtracking. A trail. A trail easily followed by Kelly, punctuated occasionally by a wrapper, spit, even blood. Very subtle.

This boy in Jim Kelly's imagination, I believe, left behind every trace of agonizing, pre-pubescent bumbling confusion. A trail. Kelly's attention was diverted. A prize had been dangled too close to his nose to ignore. He followed the trail easily. He followed it to its end and has never been seen or heard from since.

Dutifully, Cotler went to his father on the day after he'd returned with me from the cabin and told him what he knew. Yes, he admitted, he'd been watching Jim for a few days on a hunch. Something about Jim's behavior of late wasn't right, and Cotler decided he would observe him for a couple of days from the woods at his lean-to campsite. His hunch had really taken shape when Jim Kelly had woken him up at his campsite before dawn on the morning of June 3, Cotler told his father. Jim, according to Cotler, had looked unrested, disheveled, and plenty scared. He had shaken Cotler out of his sleep in a near panic and needed help. There were things he needed at his trailer. Clothing, weapons, gear. He couldn't risk going there himself. Some folks, crazy folks with wild ideas, were after him and he needed time to sort out the mess he was in. The town was in a frenzy and for some reason it was Jim they were after now. Could Cotler go in through the side window and gather these things, then meet Jim further back in the woods? Cotler claimed that his suspicions were growing, but he told Kelly he would go. Cotler did go, he told his dad, and found some things in Jim's trailer that he believed his dad and his investigatory contacts should see.

Cotler's story continued: He went into the woods toward the spot where he was supposed to meet Jim, in order to confront him about what he'd found back at the trailer. He never found Jim Kelly, he told his dad, but he did find a blood trail that he wasn't going to follow on his own. They should take a look. They did, starting at the trailer with a search warrant.

On June 6, it was announced that Jim Kelly was wanted for questioning in the murders of Terrance Hark, Jeremy Bingham, and Chris Forrester. His trailer and shop were searched, and clothing belonging to at least two of the boys was found there. The blood trail the men followed led nowhere but contained a very large amount of blood, matching Kelly's blood type according to his military records. A tooth believing to be his was also found, identified by a gold filling Kelly had bragged about from time to time, as were parts of his wallet. But where the blood ended there was no Jim. Dogs were unable to follow the trail much farther than that.

Within a week, arrest warrants were obtained in James Kelly's name for murder, abduction, sexual assault, and mayhem. He remains a missing fugitive and given the amount of blood that was found in the woods he is believed dead. At the top of the list of suspects in that crime and also missing himself is Lon Chambers, the young man who had lived with him and whom no one had seen since mid-March. In Kelly's trailer a personal ledger was found, with payments to Lon noted at regular intervals and sometimes in large amounts.

The information gleaned from the birth certificate Lon had obtained in the city of Sandusky, Ohio, did not check out. He had apparently created an intricate life for himself that was all but untraceable. The birth certificate was genuine, but the information provided to obtain it was obviously not. In time the authorities did find out his real name and a history on him, but it yielded few relevant answers. The young man who had called himself Lon was legally named Brandon Collier. He went by Buddy.

It was quite disturbing to the sheriff and the others who investigated his case in the months following: There simply wasn't anyone, including the aunt and uncle with whom he'd lived briefly, left in his life who cared about him enough to provide any useful personal information. His basic life story was known, but no one in Belle Ridge or the town he was from could claim him as a friend, son, brother, or even enemy. He was, in the truest sense of the word, an orphan. He remains vanished; a shameful, missing puzzle piece in a system capable of losing a child in the way a speeding car may lose a hubcap on a bumpy road.

Cotler, it seemed, had outsmarted his dad after all, but once again the story was accepted because it was so tempting. Cotler was sternly reprimanded for playing what his father and his contacts saw as a reckless game with a killer, but his story added up. This was because Cotler in his simple slyness had kept it uncomplicated. The bottom line was that it added up enough for the beleaguered investigation team, and when the search of Kelly's home brought out what it did there was plenty more to worry about.

6

By the end of June, the boys started coming forward. At least twelve of them, by my count, many younger but one or two older than we were. Their stories were all remarkably similar; their reasons for not coming forward were time honored and typical. What they said about Jim Kelly matched sites, M.O.s, and times. The town listened with wounded ears. I listened, but I did not come forward with them. I had done my confessing, some of it to boys who were themselves now dead. I kept quiet, and those around me understood.

Cotler's dad, in the end, did not suffer politically from what occurred during those months. He had remained steadfast regarding the whole business with Armand Lillington, who continued to live in Irmo, South Carolina as a mechanic's assistant. Along with the old, cantankerous Commonwealth's Attorney Stewart Delbridge, he was credited for keeping Tolland County, now in its 240th year, from being swept into the race-tinged and unjust prosecution of Armand. He remained in office for many years after, his hair thinner and grayer for the experience, and I doubt he ever looked at his life, his job, or his town the same. We were all pretty much in the same boat that way.

***

I wish I could tell you what exact fate met James Rodman Kelly at the end of that blood trail, but I cannot, for I do not know, and it is possible I will never be told. What I do know only became apparent to me after weeks of putting the clues together and then years of reflection on them. Things only I saw, and only I know about the trapper, have made what ultimately happened apparent to me. As careful as he was, Cotler did leave clues, although they have been useful only to me. They are nothing to anyone else.

I have imagined a thousand things in my mind; one clean shot, fired by an experienced hunter into Kelly's face as he stumbled into a clearing. I have imagined dozens of variations of some sort of confrontation, bitter words, a grim smile, perhaps a brief struggle and then a plunging blade. Less noisy, after all, than a hunting rifle out of season. But more dangerous. Maybe a bludgeon, maybe a pit. I don't know.

What I do know is that James Rodman Kelly has not left those woods, and it is doubtful that he ever will, unless some developer's dozing blade cuts into his body some cold spring morning as a preliminary roadway is being paved. Of course, there are parts of the woods that are unlikely candidates for development, parts that are particularly unsuited for such purposes, at least for another 20 years. And Cotler knows where they are.

***

During the month of July, Jim's trailer was searched, boarded up, and finally hauled off by the county under Sheriff Cotler's direction. Francis and I, mostly for beer money, assisted in breaking the concrete blocks away from the base of the trailer so it could be hooked up and pulled. We were joined in our efforts by three guests of the county. Two blacks and a redneck, all very amiable guys, in for a few months apiece on non-violent stuff. I watched my friend all that day for some sign of recognition. I watched him closely for some guilty air or twinge as we swung sledgehammers and pulled away broken concrete from the base of the trailer.

Sweaty strands of thin, sandy hair played across Cotler's forehead as he worked. A wide area of red deepened across his shoulder blades and the freckles there stood out like tiny dark lilies on a pond, rippling over his muscles as he swung, but his face showed nothing.

We broke for lunch at 1:30, and Cotler and I set up our lunches in the back of his truck. Cotler had a cooler of Michelob, so we decided to trek away a bit from the three inmates, all of them chatting pleasantly with a deputy, Ed Miles, as they ate their state-provided lunches. Cotler chuckled as he noted the menacing .870 shotgun over Ed's knee.

"Nothing but a prop," he said, shaking his head. "They ain't goin' anywhere, and he probably wouldn't use it anyway. Gotta have it, though. Those wrecker guys'll talk if he so much as lays it down, and then someone'll complain that Dan Cotler don't watch his jail labor close enough on a road job. Politics . . . geez."

I had been planning this day for some time. Here, in the blinding July sunshine, not the typical place for confessions, I would ask him, in as round about a way as I could. With butterflies in my stomach, I forced down a bit of my sandwich and tried to sound casual as I asked my friend what had been on my mind for weeks.

"So, where do you think he is?" I asked. Cotler continued to chew. If anything moved in his eyes it was gone in less time than I could recognize it. He looked over at me.

"In Hell," he said, over roast beef and turkey. It came out a muffled "hail." I nodded slowly, trying to shake and hide the resentment that was building inside. I wanted more, of course. For my varied eighteen-year-old reasons, I wanted in. I wanted the job to be shared by us. I wanted the pact to be sealed, and the resulting bond formed between two young men over a deed of rough justice that had presented itself when reason and logic had fled and left only brutality and hard choices to fill the void. And of course, to a certain extent I felt as if I deserved to be in. I had, after all, been a victim of Kelly's. For a brief time I was quite hurt that I wasn't invited to participate in whatever happened to him, as ugly as that sounds. But that's not Cotler. A more foolish young man, for the sake of bravado or immature camaraderie or plain stupidity might have entertained such a notion, but not him. This deed was not a game, Cotler knew. It was irreversible, and very dangerous. It was, in his opinion, not for me.

At the very least I wanted to know. I wanted Cotler to lean back on his big, red arms and ask me where I thought Kelly was. But he didn't. And in grudging, boyish embarrassment and frustration I realized he probably wasn't going to, no more than your father will share all of his heart's contents with you. No cutting of the thumbs. No last-scene confession that would tie us together for life with the words of an abysmally deep truth.

"He's gone, though, you think?" I asked finally. My lunch sat like a stone, but I kept my eyes on him. I wanted to punctuate the comment with a ghost of a smile, but I couldn't bring one to the surface. Cotler met my look and, unsmiling, popped the last corner of his sandwich into his mouth.

"Yeah. He's gone. And he ain't comin' back."

Kelly, of course, isn't the only one who didn't come out of the woods that week. Cotler didn't come out either, at least not as the person he was when he went in. For years, I have avoided a definition or even a solid recognition of the change in him for fear that I will simply manufacture it in my writer's mind. But it is there. The apparent difference, especially in a lifetime stoic like Cotler, is minuscule. He is, as Steve would say, a throwback, an odd, kind anachronism with a complex emotional framework but also with the ordered, halting ability simply to accept what is and walk quietly with it. The heavy plumbing of Cotler's emotions have valved shut any second-guessing or agonized reflection on what transpired between him and Kelly, at least to an extent where it would keep him up nights. He responded to a monster in the way his culture and instinct directed him, and that is that.

As for me, the older I grow the more clearly I see that Cotler's secrecy was simply another act of love, another unconscious and ever-present manifestation of his caretaking role over me. Self-preservation is not what keeps him silent on the subject. He knows this secret would be safe with me. He surely knows what I suspect, and he has never, to my knowledge, made any serious moves to distance himself from my suspicions.

We are silent on the subject, and there is an unspoken understanding between us that we will remain so for some unspecified amount of time. Maybe some long night in some lonely place, some many years down the road the story will be told to me. Or maybe not. For now, as far as he is concerned, all I need to know is that Kelly is history. Yes, Cotler changed, and perhaps this has put some distance between us. Small as it may be, I still mourn it as another casualty of that miserable year.

***

Decades have passed. Cotler's woods continue to serve him well. They tend his secrets as they tended James Kelly's. The greatest good and the blackest evil of my life, before, since, and probably forever, both came to these woods for silence. But in the end, Cotler gave the final order.

7

During *the summer we were eleven, I saw Cotler kill a copperhead that had wandered into our campsite on a warm Saturday morning in the woods. It wasn't approaching us or menacing us in any immediate way, and I asked Cotler why he had killed it.*

"We cain't co-exist with it," he said, flipping it into the

brush with the walking stick he had used to crush its bronze colored head. "Some things you can live beside. Some you cain't. That's just the way it is."

I think of that day, a small moment in our lives, more often than I should. I also think of Copperhead Road, the path through the madness of my childhood that had, by legend and the observation of boys, often hosted bathing snakes on sunny, cool days. Some things you can live beside. Some you cain't. I wonder how many more copperheads I will encounter on the wide, bare path of life through the mute woods. I wonder if I will have Cotler beside me to crush them, or if the ones I will encounter from here on out will wear different clothing and be vulnerable to different weapons than the ones we have.

Now, on a dry July day it is Cotler and I standing beside his truck on the edge of a field. It does not appear nearly as large as it did one spring day in 1972, but it is the same dusty, overgrown patch of grass, oddly undeveloped as the houses around it have gotten older. To the west though, the tree line defining the beginning of the woods is gone, encroached by several blocks of new homes. I invite him to walk out to the middle of the field and there I lay out a blanket.

"I thought we'd catch a little sun," I say. "It's a nice day."

"Nice and hot. Yeah, sure, I'll set a spell." Cotler nods toward a nearby home. "Isn't that where we had a babysitter, Shannon something?"

"You've got one hell of a memory," I say. "Our mothers picked us up here one afternoon and we went running into this field. Do you remember it?" Cotler ponders. If it is there, no matter how deep in the well of his memory, he will bring it forth. I smile because I know this, and sure enough after a long moment he looks out from where we are to the truck. In his eyes I see that he is seeing our mothers standing beside our station wagon and waving at us. He smiles, slow and broad.

"Your mom looked beautiful that day," I say. He nods slowly, going back there.

"She did. She did at that." He lies back on the blanket and begins to watch the clouds, high and billowy, sliding by as if on slow, silent rollers.

It is Friday, July 26, and tomorrow Steve and I depart for initial training in Volunteer Service-Corps, a group that may mark our actual entrance into the international relief circuit. Neither of us are ready for college, and although my parents are perplexed, they are happy to see that I am awake, alive, and whole again. Vic is already at Virginia Tech, enrolled in an intensive remedial summer program that, if he can pass, will allow for his entry into the school and a college running career. Spencer, in a move of unprecedented if not uncharacteristic generosity, will postpone entry into a prestigious flight school in Florida and instead will follow Vic to Virginia Tech to study engineering, keep flying, and keep Vic in school. Cotler will start community college this fall, a wicked irony between the two of us if there ever was one, with the goal of entering the police academy to become a sheriff's deputy in Tolland County as soon as he is of age.

This is our last afternoon together, and I have asked that we spend part of it in this field. Cotler probably thinks this strange, but he is used to such ideas from me, knowing they fulfill some flighty, creative need that, in his opinion, goes happily unmet in his simpler framework.

"What do you see in that one?" he asks, pointing to the cloudbank directly above us. I consider the cloud, cocking my head to get a different angle.

"The state of Vermont. What do you see?"

"An Indian arrowhead. You're a Yankee at heart, Johnny. Always have been."

"I'm a Virginian," I say with a shrug. "No Yankee blood left in me." Cotler looks my way.

"Say that like you're proud of it, John Ray." I look back at him and hold his gaze in mine.

"Damn proud, Francis. Damn proud." He smiles and turns back to the clouds, moving ethereally across the blue face of the sky like mansions in heaven.

About the Author

Roger Canaff is a widely known child protection and anti-violence against women advocate, legal expert, author and public speaker. He has devoted his legal career to the eradication of violence against women and children, first as a prosecutor in historic Alexandria, Virginia, then as a Special Victims ADA in the Bronx, and then as Deputy Chief of the New York State Attorney General's Office Sex

Offender Management Unit. Most recently, he was employed as a U.S. Army civilian, serving as a Highly Qualified Expert training and advising military prosecutors on sexual assault and other special victims cases. With over 20 years' experience, he has prosecuted and consulted on cases involving sexual and physical abuse of children and adolescents, sexual assault against adults, and crimes against the elderly and persons with disabilities. Mr. Canaff continues to provide training to other attorneys, medical experts, law enforcement officers, victim advocates and the general public on all issues related to the investigation and prosecution of child abuse and sexual assault. He teaches law, comments on special victims issues for major networks, and is the author of three novels. He lives and works in New York City.